"You are of bo___ ___ ___, Sidvareh said. "But you belong here."

"Who?" Merikan demanded in a hoarse whisper. "Who was she, Lady Angelica's mother? Who had that power?"

Sidvareh regarded him with deep deliberation.

"Who had the strength even with her last breath to grasp her courage and summon the power to save her child?" the Faery asked. "Who had magic enough to send a spirit across worlds, not just for a small time, but for all time if needed? And who could instill the need to continue her duty to protect the Royal House, and their charge, into a babe? I think you know the answer to that, Lord Protector Merikan."

Angie didn't think his face could grow any paler, but he proved her wrong. Merikan looked like a ghost, his eyes—dark pits staring out of the pastiness—filled with a combination of painful comprehension and awed disbelief, which seemed a neat if unsettling mix to Angie.

"Lady Sorceress Katerina," his voice fell half an octave with raw grief. He stared hard at Angie. "This is her child? She survived?"

Sidvareh spoke softly, her voice a gentle bell. "And she has no idea of who she is, nor of the power she wields."

OTHER BOOKS BY KELLY PEASGOOD

Druid's Daughter

Spirit of the Stone

IN DREAMS WE LIVE

***

Kelly Peasgood

A Kelly Peasgood Publication

For Susan Deefholts, who only ever heard this idea. We all miss your smile and inspiring insights.

A special thank you to Anne Clarke for loving everything I write, Jennifer MacKenzie for her continued excitement and support for what I do, and Evelyn Somer for being the first to read this book.

With loving appreciation to my parents, who continue to encourage me in all things.

And as always, I remain eternally grateful for the incredible love and support of Mike. Love you forever.

I couldn't do this without you all.

Chapter 1

A knife flashed in the half-light. The damp stain she knew would glare red in daylight spread about the blade where it met flesh, rivulets of crimson snaking down his side to the rich carpet below. *I can't let him die!*

But even as Angie wrapped trembling fingers around the blade's handle, as she clamped onto the weapon and pulled with all her might, she knew the futility of her actions. The King stared with sightless eyes at nothing.

Panic clawed up her throat and tore through her lips in a frustrated wail of anguish.

Angie sat bolt upright in her bed, breath heaving out of her lungs in painful gasps as she swallowed her terror. Darkness stabbed into her eyes, so much less welcoming than the half-light of Karundin.

She longed to go back, to change what had happened. To somehow keep the King alive. But her dreams didn't work that way.

She had always had them, for as long as she could remember, off and on since childhood, but more frequently in the last few years. Dreams of a far-off land with kings and queens, castles and dungeons, courts and countryside wild with intrigue. Magic. She knew them as the normal fantasies of a child, and later, the continuing products of an overactive and fertile imagination.

After the first few, she had even begun to write them down,

and now had half-a-dozen little notebooks full of her night-time adventures in the land of Karundin, where nobles and sorcerers fought to influence history. Her dreams, always vivid, flowed so easily onto the pages that she had thought, more than once, to make a story about them. But she never did, wanting to keep this fantastic world all to herself, all the while ignoring the feeling that to reveal her knowledge of such a land—no matter how fanciful—would bring undue danger her way. Just an added intrigue to her fantasy world.

For in Karundin, she did not bear the name Angie Wilson, restorer of antiquities; rather, she held the title of Lady Angelica, the mysterious observer and Protector of the Royal Family, able to influence the course of events to her liking.

"At least most of the time," she admitted to herself as her breathing slowed from her latest 'adventure' and she wiped tears from her cheeks. She flipped on the bedside light and reached to the nightstand for her notebook, cursing as it slipped from her still-trembling fingers.

"Bloody hell," she scowled down at the little book. Throwing off her sheets, Angie retrieved the book from the floor, glancing at the passage it had opened to.

The black robes and little goatee were a dead give-away. They screamed 'bad-guy' even louder than his dark, pitiless eyes, shadowed in his face. So I dismissed him from the dream and turned to comfort the terrified child, trying to still his high-pitched screams. That's when I saw the giant cobra, poised to strike. What the hell was I supposed to do with a snake that topped me by more than a head with a flared hood almost as wide as my outstretched arms? I closed my eyes and tried to think, knowing the snake would wait with me (stopping time in a dream simply by not looking is one of the cooler things I've discovered here). I needed help, so I summoned the nearest ally, whoever that may be. When I opened my eyes again, the black-robed man had returned and stood opposing the snake, sending daggers of magic into the beast, whereupon the coppery-green scales withered into ugly grey-green puffs of smoke. Shows what I know about appearances. I guess the old westerns have a thing or two to learn about the apparel of heroes.

Angie had to smile about that. Not only had that man proven a good guy, he was the Lord Protector of the Royal House. Which meant he acted as chief bodyguard to the King and his family—those she often dreamed about but had seldom seen.

But tonight's dream differed, and the smile fled from her lips. Not only had she finally seen the man she helped to protect from the shadows, she had watched him die. And couldn't prevent it. She rarely couldn't change some aspects of her dreams—whisper a warning, flick aside a blade, switch a drugged cup of wine—so when her dreams became nightmares where she had no control whatsoever, she always woke in a panic.

I've never woken with blood on my hands though, she thought in renewed fear, seeing the crimson smear on her palm. She remembered grabbing the hilt of the knife in the King's side, trying to wrench it free, to stop the blood, to save him. To change what her dream showed. Wet with his blood, the blade pungent with some form of poison, it had refused to budge. His life draining out on the red and gold carpet, the stain spreading, coating her hand.

Just a dream! she shrieked in her head, her heart pounding painfully against her ribs. So why did she have blood on her hand? She rubbed at it and felt the sharp sting where her fingernails had bitten into her flesh, and breathed a little easier. The nightmare must have spilled into reality enough that her fist had really tried to grab the imaginary knife, and instead had sent her own nails slicing half-moons into her palm.

She rose, went into the bathroom to wash and bandage her hand, then returned to bed and picked up her pen.

It was dark in the King's chambers, but as always, I could see everything.

***

A terrible scream ripped through the castle, tearing Gavin from a light sleep. Pausing only to snatch up a robe, the Prince flung open his door and sprinted past the startled servants who stumbled sleepily out of his way, his guards racing alongside him without a word. The cry had come from his father's chamber, though Gavin didn't know how he knew that.

Merikan reached the King's outer room at the same time as Gavin, the black robes of the Lord Protector flapping loosely without a belt to hold them secure. The door to the inner chambers stood ajar, still in motion from the hurried entrance of the hall guards. Merikan's outstretched arm prevented Gavin from throwing himself into the room after the soldiers. Whoever had uttered that ear-piercing wail—a woman's scream at that—had not done so in joy, but in terror. From his father's room, though the Queen had died several years ago and King Grayton had never taken another to his bed.

Gavin ignored Merikan's advice to remain in the hall and instead followed the Lord Protector in.

And beheld a sight that stole his breath and left him cold.

A spreading pool of blood stained his father's most favoured rug, a gift from the southern reaches of Sahkarae. He saw the hilt of a knife, and whose body it invaded.

Finally, he saw the tear-stained face of a woman as she tried to save the King even as she vanished into nothingness, oblivious to the levelled pikes of the guards.

Beside him, Merikan drew in a sharp breath.

"It's her," he whispered, drawing Gavin's attention and letting the Prince know he had not imagined the ghostly presence. "The Lady Angelica."

***

"Tell me what happened," the voice commanded. Rogan genuflected to the cowled form sitting on the throne of mist that had appeared before him. As always, Rogan's benefactor contacted him at his own leisure through his sorcerous arts, projecting his image into the solitude of the assassin's sparse chamber and ensuring no face-to-face confrontations.

"My Lord," Rogan greeted, knowing better than to even attempt to murmur the Sorcerer's name. The man had put safe-guards on all those in his employ, so that none could betray their allegiance, on pain of death. Rogan had seen the spell do its work, choking off the supply of air and asphyxiating the one who might have uttered their employer's name. It mattered not that others had Compelled that one to give up his master; the spell didn't care about motivations, only results. No one must know the depths of the Sorcerer's machinations.

"King Grayton lies dead," Rogan confirmed.

"And none saw the deed?" the voice asked.

Rogan hesitated.

"None saw the knife strike, My Lord. But as your spell transported me to safety, I thought I saw ..." Rogan paused, wondering if the dark had played tricks with his vision, if perhaps the coruscating effects of the Sorcerer's spell had put images in his mind that had not in truth existed. Yet he would not cast doubt on matters involving magic. If he had imagined it, the Lord Sorcerer would know.

"I saw a woman appear, My Lord," Rogan continued. "She came out of nowhere and rushed to the King's side."

"Did she see you?"

"No. She had eyes only for the King. Then your spell took me to safety."

"Yet you're sure the King is dead? This woman could do nothing to save him?"

"Nothing, My Lord. The poison on the blade hastened the damage of the steel. He lay dead before she appeared."

The Sorcerer said nothing, and Rogan had never felt a need to fill in silences.

"What did this woman look like?" the Sorcerer finally spoke into the quiet.

"The dark hid her features. I only saw long hair and a short gown, perhaps a night-shift. When she crouched over the King, she displayed a woman's physique. I saw no more."

"Did she touch him?"

Rogan considered the scene, replaying what he could of the incident he still wasn't sure had really happened.

"I remained mere breaths, My Lord. It could be that she reached for the knife's handle, but I cannot swear to it."

After another stretch of silence, the Sorcerer rose from his indistinct throne.

"You have done well, Rogan. Payment as usual. I will attend to the King, see if this woman left any trace." Rogan bowed his head before regaining his own feet. "And Rogan,"—though the assassin couldn't see the Sorcerer's eyes, he could feel the heavy heat of the gaze that pinned him from the deep folds of the cowl—"keep yourself available. If I find this woman, I will have another task for you."

Rogan bowed again, fist to his chest in a salute, as the

Sorcerer dispelled his image and faded from the assassin's apartments.

***

Angie hadn't managed much sleep after her nightmare. Just a few snippets of rest with jumbled dreams that had nothing to do with Karundin. She could always tell which dreams would lead to her fantasy land, and though she usually enjoyed her time there, she found herself just as happy not to return after such a horrible scene.

Although she would have enjoyed more sleep, she had a full docket today. Restoring the last of the McGuire's eighteenth century dining set would take most of the morning, even with Jerry's help. And after that, the museum had entrusted her with some old scrolls and a centuries-old painting that 'had some issues.' Angie didn't know exactly what that meant, and Irving, being overly fond of messing with her head, hadn't said anything more specific in his message. Just one more thing to see to before she could really enjoy her first cup of tea.

Angie liked her work, and was quite proud of how much she had accomplished since partnering with Irving Wallman in the antiquities business five years ago, but some days she almost regretted her diversity. Selling all the old stuff was one thing, and something Irving did extraordinarily well. But restoring it to near mint condition—something the museum appreciated more than the general public—was Angie's job. Thankfully, Jerry had turned out to be a big help. Though still in his last year of university and so not always available to work, he was a natural, nearly as good as Angie. Irving was thrilled. Having two professional restorers (though granted, one still in training) brought him no end of business. And Angie no end of work.

"Work not getting done if I stop to think about it all," she grumbled to no one in particular as she unlocked the office door and pushed her way in.

The kettle was first on her list, along with her favourite mug and a bag of tea. An old pair of overalls awaited her in the warehouse. She slipped into them as she waited for the water to boil.

By the time Irving made it in, Angie's second cup of tea sat at a safe distance from her work and she was well on her way to removing dozens of years of grime from an oak table with more carvings decorating it than some churches she had seen. And it was only eight-thirty in the morning.

"Hard at work, I see," Irving, ten years her senior, commented as he leaned against a work table, careful to keep his suit away from the chemicals Angie had mixed to help with revealing the true finish of the McGuire's furniture. Had to dress up to schmooze customers, but he knew better than to get too close to his workers on a mission. Today, though, he wore protective gloves and had gingerly placed a framed painting on the table behind him.

"That the piece from the museum?" Angie asked, using the tip of the paintbrush in her hand to point.

"Yup. Wanna have a look, Mermaid?"

Almost from the moment he met her, Irving had taken to calling her 'Mermaid,' referring to the unusual colouring of Angie's eyes—one blue and one green. It still made her smile. Angie straightened, shrugging her shoulders to stretch her back muscles into shape. A small crack rewarded her efforts and relieved a kink she hadn't even noticed until then. She pulled off her heavy-duty gloves, careful of the bandaged cuts on her right palm, and moved to where she could see better, knowing by the glint in Irving's eye that she would either love or hate what he had to show her. When she stood even with him, he shifted to give her room to peruse the painting, but he didn't move away entirely, waiting for her reaction. The print depicted a truly life-like representation of a castle and its grounds.

"Fourteen, fifteen hundreds," she mused, studying the detail and the shape of both frame and canvas. "Good condition." She shook her head and looked up at Irving. "Okay, I give. What does the museum want? This doesn't need restoring."

Irving's broad grin lit his rugged face. He indicated a small spot in one corner that he had managed to keep covered, a tiny imperfection that a first glance might overlook. Angie bent closer, then recognising the significance, pressed her face so near that she could feel her breath curling back up to heat her cheeks.

"Irving," she whispered. "Is that what I think it is?"

"If you're thinking it's writing beneath that castle, then it sure is."

She stared up at him, still folded nearly double.

"And the museum ...?"

7

"Wants you to see what's under there. They're thinking seventh century—"

He had to stop as Angie sprang up with a little squeal of child-like glee and crushed him in a bear hug. She pushed back, her gaze drawn to the castle again.

"Do you have any idea how important a find like this could be?" she asked in a soft voice. Irving, prudently, ignored the question. Of course he knew, just as he had known what Angie's reaction would be. Something like this could make a person's career. That the museum had chosen Angie and Irving's practice to do the work spoke volumes.

"They want you to start today, if you have the time, Mermaid." He raised an eyebrow. "Assuming you have any interest?"

"Irving," she slapped him on the back, hard, her own grin threatening to split her face in two. "How the hell did you get them to consider us?"

"It's your work, kid," he answered. "They've been so damned impressed with what we've done for them before that they figure you to be some kind of expert. Go figure."

She stuck her tongue out at him, the effect ruined by her beaming smile.

It was turning out to be one hell of a good day.

***

Jerry worked on the last of the McGuire's chairs as Angie carefully dabbed at the museum's artwork, slowly revealing the first oddly shaped letters beneath.

"Not our alphabet," she murmured.

Jerry didn't look up from his work across the room. "But it is writing?" he asked.

"Oh yes," she replied, uncovering another shape. "It's almost familiar ...." Her hand paused, eyes drawn to the tiny script before her, the strange letters seeming to shimmer and waver and coalesce into something she could almost read—

"Ange," Irving called from the door, his voice solemn. Angie blinked, seeing only a cramped script in an unknown alphabet on the canvas. She glanced up, noting with sudden dread the troubled expression on her boss's face. The gleam had definitely left his eyes. "There's a phone call for you, Angie. It's Eastport."

Angie frowned. Why would the hospital call her?

"They say why?" she asked, her tools already set aside as she took a hesitant step forward, peeling off her latex gloves.

"Just that it was an emergency."

Angie's heart leapt to her throat.

"My folks?" She rushed to the phone on the far wall. Irving shrugged. But who else could it be? Angie had no siblings, was in fact considered a miracle baby herself, and none of her extended family lived anywhere near the area.

"Hello?" she blurted anxiously into the receiver, trying to still her suddenly throbbing head enough to hear the person on the line.

"Angela Wilson?" a woman's voice asked.

"Yes, this is she."

"I'm afraid there's been a terrible accident ..."

***

Angie stared without seeing as she peeled herself out of her overalls.

"Ange, I'm so sorry," Irving said. He knew how close Angie was to her parents. He knew them himself, and tears threatened his own vision. "Please, let me or Jerry drive you. You're in no condition to get there yourself."

Angie nodded numbly.

"I'll take her," Jerry said quietly, already out of his own coveralls. "You need to stay and take care of the shop."

"Hell, it's almost closing time anyway," Irving murmured. "I'll follow behind."

"My car—" Angie began.

"We'll take care of everything, Mermaid, don't you worry."

"This is no way to say good-bye," Angie swallowed hard. "I don't want to see what several tons of truck can do to decent people."

Irving heartily agreed. They all knew the damage was too great. Angie would lose her parents before the night ended. But with luck, she would make it to the hospital before the Wilsons breathed their last.

***

Rogan wanted away from this miserable place. The Sorcerer

had allotted him three turns of the water-cup to accomplish the task, and Rogan knew his time had almost ended. Soon, he would escape from the heavy noise, the stifling air, the strange metal beasts that spewed forth foul-smelling fumes, that ate and then spit out the oddly-garbed people of this bizarre world. So many of these strange people wandered around that he feared finding the right one. But the Sorcerer had said he would take care of that. Somehow, the Sorcerer had managed to lure the woman to this place of glass and stone where Rogan waited in the cold shadows of a nearby massive building. How the Sorcerer had discovered this abnormal place whence the woman who had tried to tend the King had fled to, Rogan didn't know. But he knew he didn't like it here.

And that he wouldn't have to endure it for much longer, for there she stood, waiting as one of the metal beasts roared past in front of her. A glittering haze outlined her to Rogan's sight, a method of identification that the Sorcerer had employed before to ensure that the assassin killed the right target.

She hurried up to the front of the glass and stone building. Rogan pulled his longbow from the concealment of his cloak, drew a poison-tipped arrow, the fletching tickling his cheek, and sighted down the shaft. As he released his missile, Rogan knew a moment of panic, for the woman turned, as though sensing something, searching for something. For him.

But then the arrow hit its mark. The woman fell. Rogan allowed himself a smile as the air about him shimmered and the disturbing world faded from his vision, the Sorcerer's spell returning him to more hospitable—and familiar—surroundings.

***

Angie charged across the street, Jerry several paces behind and Irving still getting out of his car. She really appreciated them coming with her, but she felt an overwhelming sense of urgency and couldn't wait for them to catch up. So she stood alone as she reached the glass door to the hospital emergency entrance ... and sensed something new. Some sort of instinct that warned her of danger. She turned, not knowing where to look or even what she looked for. A shaft of lancing pain bit into her left shoulder, close to her chest. It spun her around, slamming her back against the door before she crumpled to the ground, not understanding what had happened. Her shoulder burned and her vision darkened, swallowed to a shining point. The last thing she saw was Jerry's startled face as he crouched over her, Irving running to her side, and a general confusion of sound as they shouted for help.

***

"My Lady Sorceress, can you hear me?"

Angie absently wondered to whom that tinkling voice spoke. She looked around for the speaker, but found she couldn't move, nor could she see beyond the utter blackness behind her eyelids. All she had was the sound.

"My Lady?" the tiny voice called.

Who are you talking to? Angie wanted to ask, but she had no voice, her mouth refusing to obey her mind.

"You can hear me," came the relieved answer. "Good. Then hope yet remains."

Angie blinked, only her eyes didn't move. She remembered a searing pain in her shoulder, the memory evoking the feeling to reality, and a scream ripped through the silence in her mind, even though it couldn't escape her lips.

"Please calm yourself, My Lady, or I cannot be of any assistance. I need your help."

If she could, Angie would have laughed at the absurdity of her having the ability to help anyone in her present circumstances.

"I need you to come home," the voice demanded.

What are you talking about? Angie cried. *Who are you?*

"I am Sidvareh of Faery, bound to you through your mother. And I am the only chance you have to survive, My Lady Sorceress. Without me, you will die. You must come home."

The voice sounded more distant and Angie had difficulty understanding it. It made little sense, but somehow she knew that her only hope lay in following that voice.

How can I go home? she whispered. *I don't have my car.*

"That is not your home," Sidvareh said. "Here is your home. You must come home."

Where is here?

"Karundin."

Angie held her breath—at least, she would have could she breathe. Of all the times to have a dream ...

11

But if she truly lay dying, as the voice suggested, why not have one more adventure? Perhaps then she would at least regain her senses. She didn't like her immobility, her loss of sight, her loss of everything but pain and this one voice in her dreams.

So she relaxed, and chose to follow the voice.

All right, she told the Faery. *I'm coming home.*

Chapter 2

Gavin's stallion pranced, as restless as the Prince, and eager for his rider to allow him the freedom of the reins. Gavin kept the horse in check, containing Praetorian's energy much as he held his own frustration and grief in a tight fist. His father's murder was far too raw, too sudden and immediate for Gavin's rage to have a focus. But he couldn't simply sit around the castle another moment, not knowing his enemy, not knowing if he, or worse, his son, might be next.

Gavin glanced behind to where the young Prince rode, ringed by soldiers, discreet enough that the boy saw them as compatriots at the ride rather than a circle of steel guarding him. Past events, such as that cobra attack last season, had shown that even the smallest of the Royals did not stand immune to danger. But no one had thought an assassin could penetrate right into the King's bedchamber with no one the wiser. Gavin did not plan to take any chances with his son. So when Gavin sought the freshness of the country air away from the sombre atmosphere in the castle following the death of the King, he took young Rayton with him.

And of course, the Dho'vani, or Heir-Apparent, could not go without proper escort—and protection—so Lord Protector Merikan rode at Gavin's side, his dark eyes scrutinising the landscape as though expecting the trees themselves to move to stop them. In truth, Gavin didn't mind the company. Though Merikan could not have foreseen last night's events, and could do nothing to change the outcome, his renewed vigilance somehow comforted Gavin. He didn't think anything would get past the Sorcerer today.

About a dozen furlongs out from the castle, Merikan called for a sudden and unexpected halt. Gavin glanced to the Lord Protector, but the Sorcerer's gaze had riveted on to something beyond the edge of the path. Merikan dismounted, Gavin following suit, motioning for the others to remain on the path where they sat their restless mounts. Commander Nervain, the head of Gavin's personal bodyguard, disregarded Gavin's wishes and followed his charge, performing his duties with even more diligence since the death of King Grayton; Gavin expected no less. The Dho'vani didn't need to tell the captain of the guards remaining with his son to keep Rayton safe, but his pointed stare reinforced those instructions. Gavin ignored Merikan's own pointed glare, letting the Sorcerer know that he had no intention of staying behind. Gavin had never been inclined to leave the danger to others.

Hand resting on the pommel of the sword at his waist, ready to pull the weapon at a moment's notice, Nervain a close presence at his back, Gavin trailed behind Merikan as the Sorcerer pushed his way into the crowd of trees near the path.

"Did you see, or sense?" Gavin asked the older man in a low whisper.

"Sense," Merikan replied.

Magic, then. Given recent events, Gavin didn't object to the protective shield Merikan erected around him. Every Royal had the ability to weave a shield of protection about his body, and some, like Gavin, had talent for other magic too. But the added safeguard Merikan provided couldn't hurt.

They crept ahead, passing from tree to tree like shadows, and just as quiet. At the edge of a small clearing, no more than a few paces wide, they halted. A crumpled form lay in the grass. The clothing looked strange, what Gavin could see. Especially on a woman, for long honey-dark hair fanned out across the ground, and her visible hand bore delicate fingers. Her other arm lay pinned beneath her body.

Nervain took up a guarding stance several paces back, facing the direction of the path, though his eyes travelled every inch of forest, trusting the Lord Protector with Gavin's person. Merikan scanned the area and finally, discerning no danger, crouched next to the woman. He took her shoulder and gently rolled her over. The shoulder bled, the broken shaft of an arrow protruding from the wound. Merikan leaned forward and inhaled swiftly.

"Pranik," he spat with disgust. Gavin heartily agreed. Pranik was a deadly poison that left a sour stink. Assassins highly favoured it for its speed and efficacy, if not for its exorbitant cost and rarity. It had also helped kill the King.

With a sudden frown, Merikan brushed the woman's hair from her pallid face with his strong fingers. He pulled back with an oath at what he found.

"The Lady Angelica," Gavin breathed in wonder and dread. "Spirits have mercy." The wound alone was not mortal if treated, but combined with pranik ... the mysterious Lady whom Gavin had seldom seen would die before they could learn how she had gotten into the King's chamber last night. How she always seemed on hand in moments of menace, to thwart the danger or alter events to the best advantage of the Royal House. And why she always disappeared afterwards.

"Gum leaves, now," Merikan snapped, his finger pointing to a nearby squat bush, grabbing Gavin's attention. Gavin didn't hesitate. He might not see a way to save her, but Merikan would try his best regardless.

The Lord Protector took the leaves, rolling them swiftly between his palms as he invoked his magic with soft words. A handful of dirt and a pinch of some substance he retrieved from an inner pocket of his black robes went into the concoction.

"I need to get to the wound," he said, glancing meaningfully at the odd blue tunic she wore. Gavin drew his belt knife and knelt next to the Lady. He didn't allow himself to think of any impropriety as he cut the fabric and tore a hole through the cloth, leaving a bare patch of surprisingly tanned skin, bloody and mottling with the spread of the pranik. Merikan took the sticky substance he had formed and pressed it around the wound, right up to the edge of the arrow's shaft. As he did so, a golden glow spread from his hands to her shoulder and upper chest.

An answering glow, this one suffused with streaks of golden-green and silver, rose from within the Lady Angelica. Merikan's eyes widened in bewilderment, and his hand might have faltered had Gavin not placed his own hands over the Lord Protector's, holding them in place. Gavin felt a tug on his spirit, from where he knew his own magic rested. He didn't resist. He loosened his control, watching without understanding as the Lady's magic and Merikan's drew in his own, adding a turquoise light that brightened and focussed on the wound.

15

The shaft quivered, startling the men yet again. By the look in Merikan's face, Gavin knew the Sorcerer was as much a tool in this spell as Gavin, lending strength without direction. Something else instructed the flow of magic, yet Gavin could tell he still had control of his power. He could take back what belonged to him at any time. The arrow shifted again, wriggling loose. Merikan snatched it in one hand and set it afire with a snarled word, tossing the ashes away. The other he kept lightly over the injury, Gavin's hands cupping it, both held just far enough from the flesh to watch as the bleeding slowed. A trickle of yellow-black mixed with the blood as it oozed from her shoulder, the poison being drawn from the wound. When both poison and blood stopped flowing, the skin drew closed, reknitting itself, the flesh made whole, if pink and tender. She would have a scar, but she would live.

The aura of magic subsided. Gavin drew back first, his mind in a daze of wonderment. He gazed at the Lady's face, more alive with colour now, though she remained unconscious. She had a gentle face in repose, the nose a little small and the cheeks more angular than most women's, the jaw more square and the lips less full. Perhaps a season or so younger than Gavin, she possessed a striking appearance. More handsome than beautiful, her mystery only added to her appeal. But that mystery might become problematical. Should she prove a threat to the kingdom—to Rayton—Gavin mustn't hesitate. Though they had somehow saved her life, both he and Merikan knew their duty.

Gavin wondered why the thought of harming her disturbed him so.

"We should get her back to the castle," Merikan said, leaning back on his heels. "She'll need time to recover, and we need some answers from her." He glanced around. "Unless I'm mistaken, there's nothing out here save the forest creatures and the path."

Gavin understood the frown. He had the same thought: no tracks marred the area, so where had the Lady Angelica come from, and how had she made it to this place? And did whoever shot her still hover nearby?

He scooped the Lady up, cradling her face against his chest, not knowing why but certain they must keep her identity a secret until they had more answers. Merikan's hands remained free in case of attack.

"Scout the area," Gavin ordered Nervain when the Commander turned at the motion. "The Lady's been shot. See if you can find any trace of the culprit. I'll send three men back to assist."

Nervain waited for Merikan's nod of understanding that the Lord Protector alone had charge of the Dho'vani until they reached the rest of the men, then turned his attention to Gavin's orders.

Gavin and Merikan hurried back to their horses and Gavin sent the promised men after Nervain.

With Merikan to steady him, Gavin mounted Praetorian and settled Lady Angelica before him, her hair acting as a mask. Waiting only long enough for the Sorcerer to climb on his own horse, Gavin turned back to the castle and headed off at a gallop.

***

Sleep left her slowly. Angie didn't remember partying hard last night, but she sure felt rough this morning. Or perhaps afternoon? She slit open an eye, seeing only a dim light. Good heavens, had she slept straight through 'til night? With a groan, she reached for her notebook, intending to write down what she remembered of Sidvareh—a character new to her Karundin flights of fancy.

The dull pain from just below her collarbone drew a sharp gasp and her eyes flew completely open.

This wasn't her room. Moreover, it wasn't even her apartment. A canopy spread overhead, lit by a single candle on a small bedside table. Angie sat up, trying to ignore the twinge in her shoulder that drew a hissed breath through her teeth. A strange sight greeted her vision.

The bed stretched nearly as large as hers yet held far less comfort. A dun coloured duvet with bold slashes of red and blue had covered her, its heavy warmth now puddling in her lap. What she could see of the walls in the candle's glow made her think of the stonework of England's castles; dark and slightly forbidding, and definitely in need of some colourful tapestries. Though the room stretched into shadows, she could only discern one other piece of furniture; an armchair that looked like a marvellous recreation of something out of the fifteenth century, but with more flair. It had carved wooden legs and velvet upholstery of a rich brown hue trimmed in gold.

It also bore the weight of a woman in her forties, wearing a long brown dress that would have camouflaged her against the chair's fabric had she not also worn a white apron, the whole belted with a black cord of some sort. The woman and Angie stared at each other a moment.

"Who are you?" Angie finally asked. The woman blinked, a small frown creasing her forehead. Angie glanced around, sweeping the room with her right hand. "Where am I?"

The woman flinched as Angie gestured, so she let her arm drop. The puzzled expression let Angie know the woman didn't understand her. Angie sighed, looking at her surroundings again, wondering where to find the door, and, if she could reach it past the woman, where it would lead. She threw off the rest of the covers, intending to find out. The white gown wrapping her body made Angie pause. She knew she didn't own sleepwear like this, that looked somehow both delicate and of an antique priggishness. She didn't know anyone who did, although the mystery lady with her tight bun and old-fashioned dress probably had a closet full of such outfits.

Angie shook her head, already annoyed with this game. She hauled her feet over the side of the bed. A wave of dizziness washed over her, and she clutched the mattress, eyes closed, trying to regain her senses. Hands gently gripped her shoulders, trying to push her back down. Angie stared at the wide-eyed woman from inches away.

"You mustn't try to rise yet, My Lady," the woman said in a soft voice.

"You do speak English," Angie accused, but the woman frowned her incomprehension again, shaking her head in frustration.

"The poison is gone and the wound healing, but your strength needs time to return. Please lie back, My Lady."

"What wound? What happened? Where am I?"

"He never said you spoke a different tongue," the woman said, her voice as soft and gentle as before, coaxing rather than perplexed, though her expression belied her tone. "But then, you never had the opportunity to speak, what with being unconscious and all."

18

"Different tongue?" Angie whispered. Then louder, "But I understand you. Why can't you understand me?"

"Now don't you fret, My Lady," the woman soothed as she made Angie lie back under the duvet. "Surely the Lord Protector will know what to do. He may understand your language."

"Lord Protector?" Angie sat up again, which seemed to distress the woman, but Angie barely noticed. "You mean the Lord Protector of the Royal House? This is Karundin?" The woman tilted her head to the side, perhaps recognising the name, or merely trying to figure Angie out. Angie stared off at nothing in particular, her mind whirling. She didn't stop the woman from urging her back to the pillow.

Am I dreaming? It didn't feel much like her dreams, but then she remembered her encounter with the Faery Sidvareh again. 'You must come home,' she had said, and Angie had agreed. Home to Karundin.

She had never intentionally dreamed of Karundin before. Maybe that's why this felt different. *Does that make sense?* she wondered. Maybe if she closed her eyes, told herself to wake up, everything would go back to normal.

Back to the hospital, where pain shot through her body, where her parents lay dying, where her life lay on the cusp of disaster. She couldn't bear the thought of her parents dead, all in some stupid accident, but reality seldom cared how you thought. It simply was, and you had to deal with the messy results.

She angrily wiped at her tears. Crying wouldn't change the past. She had to go see her parents.

But no matter how hard she tried, Angie couldn't make herself wake from this nightmare.

"My Lady?" a man's voice said. No one back home ever used such an appellation, so Angie knew she still dreamed. She squeezed her eyes tighter until little streaks of red lightning danced across the inside of her eyelids, but the man didn't go away. Instead, his gentle but insistent hand shook her right shoulder. She finally opened her eyes.

Black robes, goatee and dark eyes. Just like the first time she had seen him, except this time, the Lord Protector's expression held concern rather than just cold competence. He stood alone in the room with Angie, the matron gone.

"My Lady, can you understand me?" he asked.

"Of course I can understand you," Angie griped. "The question

19

is, can *you* understand *me*?"

His quizzical frown was answer enough.

"Well, what the hell is wrong with this dream anyway?" she grumbled.

"You must alter your magic's focus," said a tinkling voice. Sidvareh.

"Um ... what?" came Angie's less than intelligent reply.

"Your magic is attuned solely to your senses right now. You understand their words but they cannot make sense of yours."

"He's got magic," Angie said, noting the man's disquiet and wondering if he could hear Sidvareh too. When it came down to it, Angie wondered at her own ability to hear the voice when she saw no body to match. *Maybe this is what going crazy feels like. Hearing voices that aren't really there, visiting lands that don't exist.* Yeah, crazy about covered it. But she went on nevertheless. "Why doesn't he use *his* magic to understand me? And what do you mean, 'my magic' anyway?"

"He's using his magic for other things at the moment," Sidvareh said, ignoring Angie's second question. "Primarily as a precaution against you."

"What?"

"Concentrate on his eyes, his hands. What do you see?"

Angie looked into the man's eyes, really concentrated, and saw a spark of inner light glowing from his dark orbs. She glanced to his hands and they appeared ever so slightly out of focus, hazy, as though the air about them gave off waves of heat. And his lips moved furtively in words she could not hear.

"That light is his connection to his magic, the haze the evidence of a spell," Sidvareh explained. "Some magic depends on the use of certain words, strange languages. He does not use his magic to understand you because he fears you use your magic to cast a spell. He guards against it."

"Listen, Faery, I don't have any magic. This is all just some dumb dream that I'm working on waking up from—"

"This is not the dream, Lady Angelica. This is where you belong. Not in another plane where you are Angela Mira Wilson, restorer of antiquities. But here, where your mother sacrificed all that you might live and protect the Royal House."

Angie stared in utter shock, not knowing what to make of Sidvareh's words. What did her mother have to do with Karundin and Angie's dreams? But the Faery went on, snapping Angie's attention back to the man leaning over her, his eyes glinting with the hue of power.

"Now, I suggest you concentrate on making him understand your words before he does something you both will regret."

But I don't know anything about magic. Except for what she could do in her dreams. And this was just another dream, right? If she treated this like any other night-time adventure, perhaps things would work out. *As long as whatever I do works better than they did with the King.*

She focussed on the Lord Protector, bent her concentration and will to one single goal which she uttered in her mind like a mantra: *Understand my words. Understand me.* Then, with an effort to keep her voice calm and steady, she spoke, maintaining firm eye-contact despite the eerie gaze that stared back.

"If you would kindly refrain from trying to blow me to bits, maybe we can answer some of each others questions."

He jerked back as though struck and blinked at her. The haze left his hands, but he appeared just as dangerous as before.

"Can you understand me now?" Angie asked.

"Yes."

"And you're not going to try to hurt me?"

He tilted his head, a considering weight in his demeanour.

"That will depend entirely on your own actions, My Lady," he replied, retreating far enough to settle into the empty chair. If Angie hadn't known he protected the same people she did, his bearing might have frightened her more. As it was, the black robes and villainous goatee still gave her pause, but she could ignore his sinister appearance as merely an effective affectation.

"Well, right now, I plan on sitting up," said Angie. "If you try to wallop me with some spell for that, I'll be most disappointed."

That tugged a reluctant smile past his lips, which Angie took as a good sign. She sat up slowly anyway, just to be sure. Her left shoulder protested a bit and she scowled at it, but she had other concerns. Such as how it had gotten hurt in the first place.

"So I don't have to call you by title, 'Lord Protector,' mind telling me your name?" she asked.

Again, the smile twisted his mouth. He gave a half-bow from the chair.

"I am Lord Merikan, Lady Angelica."

"Hi Merikan. Call me Angie."

He looked briefly horrified.

"So what happened?" she asked. "Why does my shoulder hurt? And how did I get here, wherever here is?"

He pursed his lips, gaze lingering on her bandaged hand a moment, though Angie didn't know why her hand should fascinate him when her shoulder ached so.

"'Here' is the palace. Dho'vani and I found you in the forest a dozen furlongs out and brought you here. You had the broken shaft of an arrow laced with pranik embedded between your shoulder and your heart. No tracks led to or from the site save our own."

Angie blinked several times, trying to make sense of what he said.

"Okay, so who's Dho'vani, how far is a furlong again, and what is pranik?"

His eyes narrowed as he regarded her, but he didn't answer her questions. Instead, he asked one of his own.

"How did you hurt your hand?"

Angie looked down at the bandage across her palm, covering the marks made by her own fingernails. It seemed of little importance to her, but he had answered her first questions; it seemed only fair to return the favour.

"That happened last night when I tried to take the knife out of the King," she murmured without really thinking. "But for some reason, I couldn't help like I usually can."

She shook her head at the futility of some dreams.

"I guess I grabbed the hilt so hard that my fingernails cut my hand before I woke up." She looked back to the Lord Protector, thinking it odd to explain a dream to a character out of her imagination. Merikan stared back in wonder.

"So you *were* there," he whispered. He cleared his throat, his voice growing hard with resolution. "You tried to help the King?"

"Of course I did," Angie retorted with indignation. "Did you think I would try to harm him?"

"How did you get into his chambers?"

"It's just a dream!" she shouted. "I fell asleep and I came here, and his danger called to me, so I came to try to help. But I couldn't. It's all just a dream!"

"Enough of this!" Sidvareh's musical voice grated like a chorus sung off-key.

Both Angie and Merikan watched as a violet mist formed between them, resolving into a figure only as big as Angie's

22

outstretched hand. The Faery wore a diaphanous, short bark-brown dress that still managed to cover all the important areas on her shapely golden-green body. Iridescent double wings, like those of a dragonfly, whipped back and forth in annoyance, fanning her coppery-gold hair. She came to rest on a piece of air, somehow made firm enough for her tiny bare feet. Emerald eyes almost too big for the little face, slanted like crooked teardrops, bore down on Angie.

"My Lady, I have told you, this is not a dream. It is where you belong."

"It's not real," Angie insisted. "How could it be? I'm talking to a Faery, sitting in some medieval room with a sorcerer, all in a fantasy land that I've dreamed about for as long as I can remember—it's ridiculous!"

Merikan stared from Sidvareh to Angie and back again, before he rose and sketched an elaborate bow to the Faery.

"Forgive me, Noble One," he addressed the little creature, awe tingeing his words. "But what does she say? I've lost the thread of language."

"Yes, she doesn't know control in her anger and confusion," said Sidvareh. "She rails against her situation. She knows this land as no more than a dream." Sidvareh turned her large eyes to the Sorcerer. "I suggest you use your own methods for the nonce to follow her speech."

She turned back to Angie.

"If it's all a dream, My Lady, why can the Lord Protector not understand you?"

"He just wants to piss me off," Angie snapped. "It's just my mind trying to make it all real. Or maybe it's you trying to make me believe this crazy story."

"Do your dreams often try to convince you to believe black is white?" the Faery pressed. "Do they control your mind, your reason? Or do you control them?"

"I influence my dreams; I don't direct them, not really. Dreams are dreams. They have a life of their own, but that doesn't make them real."

"And you always know when you dream?"

"I know Karundin is a dream," Angie nodded, though a panicked part of her had begun to wonder. She pointed to Merikan. "I know he's a dream. And so are you," she turned her glare back to the Faery. "Faeries don't exist, magic isn't real, and Karundin is just a place I made up when I was little; a make-believe world to escape to at night."

"How can you be sure you made it up?" Merikan asked. "If you have never set foot in a place before, and then you visit, have you made it up simply because you had not seen it before? Or did it always exist and you merely hadn't visited yet?"

"It's not like the Grand Canyon or some mystical Mayan temple off in some other part of the planet," Angie scoffed. "This is a totally different world, with different rules and customs and—"

"And therefore not real," Sidvareh finished, her expression disapproving. "Is that it, Lady Angelica?"

"It's Angie. Lady Angelica is a persona I made up along with this world—"

"Lady Angelica is who you are," Sidvareh insisted. "If any persona is false, it is Angela Mira Wilson."

"A moment," Merikan raised a hand, drawing the attention of both women. "If I may ask a question for clarification." Sidvareh nodded magnanimously; Angie scowled, wishing she could just wake up; fearing she could not.

"If this is the Lady's dream world, what is her real world? And how can she bridge a gap between the two?"

"Because it's a dream," Angie snarled.

"Because her mind is of this world," Sidvareh said. "And her body is from her Earth. Her mother sent her child's spirit across the realms so that it might live."

Merikan drew back in contemplation, as though something in that sentence made sense to him. Angie stared in bafflement.

"Mom did what?" was all she could think to say.

"Enemies of the Crown hunted your mother. Before they could destroy her, and her progeny with her, your Lady Mother cast a final spell that would take your spirit across the worlds so you could survive and grow in safety. She designed the spell to find a vacuum and fill it with your life.

"That vacuum resided in the womb of Darlene Wilson of the Earth you know. Her child's spirit had died. Your mother's spell saw that yours took its place."

Angie knew the stories about her being a miracle baby; how the child Darlene carried had died and come back to life. It baffled doctors, how in the beginning stages of labour, the little heartbeat had stopped, and yet when the delivery occurred, life filled the tiny lungs and sorrow turned to joy. Mom had already suffered three miscarriages, and this was their final try at a baby. When the doctors announced the flat line, mom was too far-gone in labour; she had to deliver the dead infant, and it broke her heart. When Angie's first cries split the stunned silence in the delivery room, a nurse had proclaimed, 'It's a miracle!' Mom and dad had been so overjoyed that it became part of Angie's name. Their little angel, Angela Mira.

"You are of both worlds," Sidvareh said. "But you belong here."

"Who?" Merikan demanded in a hoarse whisper. They looked to his suddenly pale face. "Who was she, Lady Angelica's mother? Who had that power?"

Sidvareh regarded him with deep deliberation.

"Who had the strength even with her last breath to grasp her courage and summon the power to save her child?" the Faery asked. "Who had magic enough to send a spirit across worlds, not just for a small time, but for all time if needed? Who knew the secrets of Faery and could bind such a one in loyalty to herself and to her offspring? And who could instill the need to continue her duty to protect the Royal House, and their charge, into a babe?" She shook her head, a wistful smile tightening her mouth. "I think you know the answer to that, Lord Protector Merikan."

Angie didn't think his face could grow any paler, but he proved her wrong. Merikan looked like a ghost, his eyes—dark pits staring out of the pastiness—filled with a combination of painful comprehension and awed disbelief, which seemed a neat if unsettling mix to Angie.

"Lady Sorceress Katerina," his voice fell half an octave with raw grief. He stared hard at Angie. "This is her child? She survived?"

"This is also your child, Lord Protector," Sidvareh spoke softly, her voice a gentle bell. "And she has no idea of who she is, nor of the power she wields."

Chapter 3

"I'm sorry ... what?" Angie spoke into the thick silence.

Sidvareh's serene gaze took her in a moment, but the Faery's attention suddenly snapped to the door and the little creature vanished. Angie had a second to blink in surprise before the door flew open and a man swept into the room.

Angie could only stare. She had seen handsome men before, but this stranger took her breath away, made her want to say things like 'wow' and 'golly,' like some tongue-tied, love-sick schoolgirl. It was more than his outdated clothing—he looked like he'd just stepped off the set of some medieval or Tudor-age film, with his red and gold tights, red knee-length tunic cinched with a thick gold belt and a leather baldric hinting at a simple looking sword hilt resting comfortably at his hip. He bore himself with an air of absolute nobility—which Angie hadn't known she could identify until this minute—yet with a sense of arrogant-tinged pride. The anguish etched on his face made her stomach clench in sympathy even as her libido responded to his sheer masculinity. It was embarrassing. She had never reacted to anyone this way before, dream or no dream.

His stride purposeful, his dark wave of hair streaming gently past his shoulders in the breeze created by his quick pace, he barely noticed as Merikan rose to his feet to greet the newcomer with a small bow. His chiselled features grim, his brooding eyes never left Angie's face.

"How did you do it?" he demanded in what she might consider a very nice voice under different circumstances.

"Do what?" Angie asked, at the same time that Merikan spoke, a cross between a greeting and a warning: "Dho'vani."

The man waved Merikan aside, his gaze still intent on Angie.

"How did you get into Father's room?"

She stared at him, searched his features. She saw a definite resemblance to the man she had failed to save. This Dho'vani was the King's son.

And she didn't know how to answer him. She began to doubt she could ever escape this nightmare. The possibility that this represented some form of reality rather than her dream-world had her distrusting her senses. But even taking her active imagination into account, would she have come up with half the things Sidvareh had claimed as truth? Why would her mind try to make her believe Karundin was real to this extent, unless it *was* real? And yet, magic and Faeries and princes out of the middle ages ...?

Angie felt lost. She didn't know what to believe anymore.

"I dreamed myself there," she said finally, having no other answer to give.

"You ... dreamed," he stammered. "I don't understand."

"Neither do I," she whispered, staring down at her hands in her lap. The bandage on her palm caught her attention. Had she really stood there, in the King's chambers, after someone killed him? Had she really tried to remove the knife, not as part of a dream, but as a reflection of reality?

What the hell was real anyway?

"Lady Angelica is ... accustomed to a different way of life, Dho'vani," Merikan said. "Her powers stem from that other world, where her dreams give her access to her magic."

Angie glanced to the Sorcerer—her father in this world if Sidvareh spoke true—and considered his words. She could change things in her dreams, and that might be construed as using magic. At least it brought it down to a concept she could understand.

"Other world?" the Prince asked.

Merikan grimaced.

"You always did pick up on the slightest slip of the tongue. We are still trying to determine just what happened to the Lady, but as far as we can tell, she can claim ancestry from Lady Sorceress Katerina. Before her untimely death, the Sorceress sent her child's spirit to another plane. This is that child."

The Prince looked at Angie in a new light, one of renewed respect and a little awe. His voice dropped to a revered whisper.

"That's why you were in Father's rooms, why you were there to protect Rayton."

Angie shrugged, not understanding the man's words or reasoning.

"Who's Rayton, Dho'vani?" she asked.

"Gavin's son," Merikan murmured, drawing Angie's gaze from the intensity of the Prince's eyes. "Next in line to rule, should anything befall Gavin."

Angie looked from the Sorcerer's face to the Prince's. A frown tugged her brow down.

"I thought Dho'vani stood next in line."

The men stared at her with matched expressions of puzzlement.

"Dho'vani *is* next in line. He is Heir-Apparent. Hence Dho'vani."

Angie blinked a few times. Her dreams were never this confusing, which only frightened her more as her brain slowly let the truth sink in. *Not in Kansas anymore,* started running through her mind.

"I don't understand."

The Prince suddenly smiled, and Angie's breath caught in her throat. *Wow.* She swallowed.

"I think I can explain," he said. "I apologise for my rude entrance earlier. I should have introduced myself. I am Gavin, Dho'vani of Karundin. Dho'vani is my current title, roughly meaning 'Prince and Heir-Apparent.'"

"I see," said Angie. "So ... why does it suddenly make sense that I would try to save your father?"

"Lady Sorceress Katerina stood as Protector to the Royal House of Karundin," Merikan explained. "It was more than her position; the responsibility defined her, a role birthed into her very being. It seems you have that same conviction, that same duty instilled in you, even across worlds."

"Protector of the Royal House," Angie repeated numbly. "How am I supposed to protect what I didn't even know existed? I'm no sorceress. I'm just an antiques' restorer. I don't know magic."

"On the contrary," Merikan objected. "I'd say you know a very unique and potent form of magic, one not easily countered."

"What?"

"Your magic works through dreams. Or, more specifically, by utilising the rules of dreams. In a dream, most anything can happen. You are not bound by any preconceived notions about magic and therefore will likely have fewer inhibitions about what you can accomplish."

"Are you saying that my ability to influence things in my dreams can translate to the real world? To this world?" she hastily amended. "That, because I can control a lot of what goes on in my dreams, I can do magic?"

"I'm saying that that in itself *is* a form of magic. That because of your upbringing in a world where magic does not seem to exist, your inbred nature found an alternate outlet that your mind could accept, developing your power in the form of your dreams. And that," Merikan concluded, "makes you both powerful and unpredictable."

"And an exceptional, and honoured, protector," Gavin added. "The Royal House could have no one better to assist Lord Merikan in keeping us safe to guard our charge."

"Your charge?" Angie parroted.

The men shared a long look.

"Something to discuss at another time, I think," Merikan said. "You have enough to think about right now, and you must recover your strength."

The ache in Angie's shoulder again registered in her mind. She put a hand to it as she rolled and stretched the protesting muscle.

"You said something about an arrow?" Merikan nodded. "So what happened that got me shot?" Angie asked.

"You don't know?" Gavin asked.

"What's the last thing you remember?" the Sorcerer wanted to know.

Angie's hands fell to her lap, clutching at each other as though seeking support and solace.

"The hospital called, telling me of a terrible accident involving my parents. When I got there, before I could go in, I felt something painful hit my shoulder. Jerry and Irving came running, trying to help, but everything went black. And then I heard Sidvareh's voice for the first time, telling me to come home. Then I woke up here."

"This hospital," Merikan asked, "your assailant shot you from within the building?"

"No, he stood outside."

"So you had not yet reached the hospital?"

29

"I was about to go through the door."

Merikan's head tilted to one side, his expression contemplative.

"Then how did the arrow penetrate your shoulder? The shaft protruded from the front. If you faced the building, yet were not shot from within, how did the arrow not hit your back?"

"I—" Angie hesitated, forcing herself to remember every detail. "I felt something. Something warning me of danger. You know? Like when you feel someone watching you. Only this was stronger, an alarm in my head. I didn't know the source, though; only that something bad was coming. I turned around to see what it was."

"Did you see him?" Gavin's intense tone matched the furor in his gaze.

Angie closed her eyes in concentration, but finally had to shake her head and open them again.

"I didn't know what to look for. All I remember when I turned is the pain."

"What about last night?" Gavin asked. "Did you see the assassin? Did you see who killed my father?"

"I saw blood," Angie stated, knowing somehow that this man did not want to hear sympathy, but truth. "If another stood in the room, I didn't see them. Only the knife and the dead eyes of the King. And I couldn't stop it." Angie heard the frustration in her own words.

Merikan placed a gentle yet restraining hand on Gavin's shoulder, guiding the Dho'vani to the chair. His dark eyes turned back to Angie.

"Is the use of poison on arrows common in your world?" he asked.

"Not that I've ever noticed," Angie said.

"But they do exist?" Angie nodded and the Sorcerer continued. "Is it possible someone would think to use them on you? To confuse the situation?"

"I don't see why anyone there would want to hurt me, but ... I suppose someone might think it amusing, given my work."

"Your work?" Gavin asked.

"I restore antiques. Using a weapon from the middle ages might seem fitting for someone with a bizarre sense of humour."

"But the chances of that are slim, yes?" Merikan pressed.

"Well, yeah. If someone wanted me dead, they'd have

probably used a gun."

The Sorcerer looked to the Dho'vani, his demeanour worried.

"The two incidents may very well be linked, Dho'vani. Your father's death and the attempt on Lady Angelica's life."

"But who?" Gavin demanded. "And how do they know about the Lady?"

"How did they get to her world?" Merikan added.

And does that mean I can get back? Angie wondered.

"There is magic against us," Gavin said. "That much seems clear. But who and why? Why now?"

"Did they attack me for me, or because I saw what befell the King?" Angie was very surprised to hear herself ask. Then she heard Sidvareh's tiny voice in her mind.

'I apologise, My Lady Sorceress, but I needed to ask the question, and I have already risked much by exposing myself to Lord Merikan.'

Uh, sure, Angie thought. *But maybe you could warn me next time, before you take over my voice?*

A musical tinkling laugh answered her as the men pondered her—or rather, Sidvareh's—question.

"Either is a disturbing possibility," Merikan admitted.

"But it's likely they will no longer view you as a threat," Gavin mused. "Pranik is a dangerous and fast-working poison. Had we not found you when we did, had Merikan not known what to do ... you would have died. We must hope your enemy believes you dead."

Oh, that's comforting, Angie thought, biting her tongue to keep the sarcastic remark silent. She had never had anyone mad enough at her to try to kill her. That she now had some unknown enemy, and one probably from what she had always thought of as a dream, was downright scary.

"Still, we will take precautions," Merikan said. "Only you and I know her identity and only we and Tabitha thus far have seen her features. Unless someone sees her up close, people will not recognise her as a sorceress, but she is a stranger to our land. Any enemy will grow suspicious of a newcomer, no matter what story we concoct."

"Excuse me," Angie interjected. "But what do you mean, someone will know I'm a sorceress if they see me up close?"

"Your eyes," exclaimed Gavin, startling her as he leaned forward intently. "Their colouring marks you as one born to magic."

Angie stared at him. She had always considered her unusual eyes merely something to talk about at parties, not anything portentous. Her left eye shone blue, her right, green. Like light on the ocean. *Or the eyes of a mermaid.* Some days the contrast was quite noticeable, and others, you really had to look close to note the difference.

"Merikan's eyes aren't like mine," Angie protested. "He has magic."

"Only the rarest of sorceresses reflect their profession in their eyes," Merikan said. "The Sorceress Star, half blue and half green to signify unity with the forces of spirit and nature, is often emblazoned on a sorceress's robes. But those with great power, such as your mother, and apparently yourself, have no need for such a symbol. Your strength shines for those who know what to look for."

"Wonderful," she huffed. "So I'll be a target, and I won't even know who's after me."

"As I said," spoke Merikan. "We will take precautions. You'll be shielded at all times and under my protection until you learn your own defence."

"That doesn't seem wise," Angie interrupted, drawing surprised looks. "If you're supposed to be Lord Protector of the Royal House, then you can't expend any effort keeping me safe when you should be looking after them."

"They need *you* to protect them," Merikan disagreed. "It is my duty to guard the Sorceress who stands as Protector, not the Royals. That is your task. I guard you, you guard them."

"So what happened to leave my m-mother without any defences?"

"My guess would be either the arrows riddling my body at the time, or the knife wounds draining my blood."

Angie bit her lip. She was sorry she'd asked.

"Which is why you must learn your own defences as quickly as possible," he went on, not sounding at all angry at her outburst.

Gavin rose.

"I'll see to your accommodations, My Lady," he said with a small bow. "If you need anything, Tabitha will help. I'll send her in later."

He turned then and strode from the room, his movements graceful and proud. Angie admired the view.

"You must also learn our language," Merikan said when they found themselves alone again.

"But I thought ..."

"I helped him understand you, and you him, but without that spell hovering around you constantly—and I assure you, the wrong elements could pick up on such a continued drain of power—you will remain ignorant of our words. Unless you learn them. I doubt your Faery friend will want to provide constant translations for you."

'He's got that right,' Sidvareh mumbled in Angie's mind.

"So I learn your language," Angie agreed. "When do I start?"

That pulled a lop-sided grin from Merikan.

"As soon as I find someone I trust to do the teaching."

Chapter 4

The castle was impressive, the Sorcerer had to admit, the lands it guarded rich and fertile, abundant in food and resources. Once a part of the southern kingdom of Sahkarae until a long ago war had divided the two realms, Karundin lived up to its reputation as a wealthy land, but that wasn't why he coveted it. Or at least, not the whole reason. No, what he wanted lay in the keeping of the Royal Family. A secret it had taken him many double-seasons to uncover, and then, only in part. He knew they guarded the spell book he had devoted his life to finding. Six spells only it contained, but perhaps the six most powerful weapons in the world. Here in Karundin, so close, yet beyond his reach. Despite all his research, he had yet to learn its exact location. Karundin was not an insignificant kingdom, and the Royals kept their secrets well.

It didn't help matters that he had to work with such delicacy. Though messy and not always reliable, torture may have yielded some results by now, but failure in achieving an answer would alert the Royals to the real threat. Right now, they feared assassins. Kidnapping and torture could give away his true intentions, and their guard over the spell book would only increase. Of course, that might give him a clue as to its location, but with added protections, the information would prove too little too late.

Magic would provide little aid in a true search, given the nature of the book and its guardians. Though not sorcerers like himself, the Royals did have access to magic, and, it seemed, could discern any efforts to locate the spells through the use of such arcane powers.

Long before he arrived, back when he had had the first glimmering of evidence that the book lay in Karundin rather than in Sahkarae, he had thought the Sorceress Katerina held the keys. She had eluded him and very nearly escaped before he learned she merely guarded those who had the true power, the knowledge he needed. It was a costly, though ultimately fruitful matter to dispatch her and her unborn offspring, leaving the way open for him to step into the vacuum and gain the trust of the Royals. But others beat him to it, and he once again had to find another way to his goal. A way that involved no overt magic in his search, no interrogations to warn of the threat he posed.

It had taken nearly twenty double-seasons before he found a way into their court, a means of ingratiating himself into life in Karundin without any suspicion falling on him. Another eight double-seasons before people stopped looking at him and his ward as foreigners and thought of them instead as trusted advisors and members of the Royal House. And yet another season before he had made his first forays into testing the fortifications around the Royals. No doubt the serpent had frightened young Rayton and his father, but it was the King's reaction the Sorcerer had watched. Fear for his family, understandable measures taken against this new threat, but no identifiable precautions to guard against the possibility that someone wanted the spell book. Members of the court were, of course, scrutinised carefully, yet no fingers pointed his way. All saw him as additional protection around the Royals, not as the one working to bring them down if that proved necessary to win the book and regain the land.

An altogether successful experiment. As was his most recent foray. With the King dead, perhaps he could glean how the location of the spell book transferred to Gavin. And if that failed, how it would pass on to Rayton—for surely the young Prince, a mere seven double-seasons old, did not yet know of the charge his family guarded. To ask a child so young to keep such a secret would seem foolish, unless it became of the utmost importance. Such as the death of his father, the soon-to-be-King, and his own ascension to the throne, should such a course become practical.

Yes, the possibilities had finally begun to open for him, after so many seasons of effort. And with the only potential witness to Rogan's work dead—and it had taken him most of the night and a good portion of the day to discover *her* hiding place—no one could possibly trace the assassination to him, even should they happen to find Rogan and the man talked; a remote possibility in itself.

So he could continue to wait and watch. His opportunity would come soon enough. Gavin's coronation took place in mere days, and he intended to stand in the forefront, watching for any signs that would lead him to the spell book and all its potential. Waiting for his chance to seize what he had worked his whole life to attain: unopposed power for his people in the land that should have been their birthright.

***

Angie stared out the window. Her new room overlooked a secluded courtyard, well-kept, but rarely used from what she could tell. The trees and pathways edged by bushes and flower beds might have come from any park back home. But marble benches instead of wrought-iron or wood, combined with marble or stone statues flanked by elaborately trimmed greenery, reminded Angie that she stood amid unaccustomed opulence, a castle from another time.

The room Gavin had provided held more warmth than the room she had woken up in yesterday. For one thing, it had more furniture—a huge bed, a beautifully carved armoire, a delicate vanity and oval mirror beside a small table bearing a porcelain bowl and ewer of water, and a velvet-covered armchair. And that just described the main bedroom. A receiving room through the tall gilded door held two more chairs and a sofa, a low table in front of the couch, a roll-top desk complete with writing implements, ink and stationery, and three smaller tables dotted about. Both rooms had large fireplaces, as well as fancy tapestries and thick carpets, mostly done in bold colours. Although Angie had never done any restoration that involved fabrics, she knew the value of such things, and how difficult some of the colours were to obtain; at least on Medieval Earth. Though many features of the castle reminded her of late fourteenth and fifteenth century European art and architecture, various aspects also spoke to other eras and locations, a confusion of inconsistent styles that made Angie's head swim. Yet even with the contradictions, everything Angie could see appeared priceless; at least to her twenty-first century estimation.

Someone tapped gently on the outer door. Angie turned from the window, but before she could respond, she heard the maid Tabitha's call of alarm.

"No, you can't go in there!"

Running footsteps alerted Angie to an intrusion, followed by a young boy. He stopped when he reached her room, looking up. She gazed back. He had the same grey eyes and dark hair as Gavin, but the face still bore too much of a child to discern if he would take after his father's breathless handsomeness. Tabitha rushed in on his heels, looking much as she had when Angie had first woken in Karundin, though her dress today was a paler brown.

"My pardon, My Lady," Tabitha said, trying to grab the child's arm.

Angie smiled and waved her away.

"That's OK, Tabitha. I don't think young Rayton here means any harm."

The boy blinked.

"You speak just fine," he said in a high child's voice. "Lord Merikan said you didn't know our language." He frowned. "How do you know my name?"

"Your father told me about you—" Angie began.

"I remember you!" Rayton's eyes widened. "You made the Lord Protector make the snake go away."

"Yes, I did," Angie looked up at the distraught maid. "Tabitha, could we possibly have some tea?"

Tabitha stopped trying to drag Rayton away and glanced at Angie.

"Of course, My Lady," she said with a bob of her head, but her gaze returned to the young Prince.

"Would you like to join me for tea, Rayton?" Angie asked. He grinned.

"With honey?" he asked hopefully.

Angie laughed.

"Anything you'd like." She raised her eyes to Tabitha, and the maid finally curtsied and left to fetch the tea. Angie had been quite happy to learn that Karundin not only brewed her favourite drink, but that it actually tasted how she expected. Some people didn't truly start their day without a cup of coffee; for Angie, it was tea.

"Come on," she said to Rayton. "Let's go sit in the other room where it's more comfortable."

Rayton glanced around, only now realising that he stood in Angie's bedchamber. He blushed bright red and hastily retreated to one of the big chairs in the sitting room. Angie followed him out, but paused when she saw a young woman waiting for her.

"I apologise for his manners," she said. "My nephew does tend to forget propriety when he's excited."

Long auburn hair complemented a pert, beautiful face in its mid-teens. She wore an azure gown, its full skirts dusting the carpets and its sleeves made longer by trailing cloth that dangled nearly to the floor from each tightly-cinched wrist. Although most of her hair hung loose down her back and over her nearly exposed shoulders, an elaborate net of pearls and gold wire pinned it subtly out of her dark eyes; eyes similar to Rayton's. Angie had never seen an ensemble quite like it before. Almost Medieval European, but like the décor, somehow blending other cultures and eras too.

The young woman dipped in a small curtsey, her gaze taking in Angie's own attire. Angie had managed to find her jeans, clean but hidden deep in the armoire as though someone had feared to throw them out, yet hoped Angie would not find them. Her shirt had died a sad and miserable death, what with blood and pranik and having to be cut from her shoulder—though it had taken some persuasion for Merikan to admit even that. So she had to settle for a tunic and belt, the only kind of top she felt comfortable enough getting into herself. She had ignored the few dresses gracing the armoire, which did not leave her many options. Though truthfully, the tunic felt quite comfortable, if not the proper style for a Lady.

"Greetings, Lady Angelica," the young woman said as she rose from her curtsey. "My name is Kaeley. The Lord Protector has asked young Rayton and I to instruct you on the use of our language." Angie heard just enough inflection in the words to let her know that Kaeley questioned the need for the lessons, likely having heard her exchange with Rayton, but would not contradict whatever Merikan had said.

"I'm Angie, and thank you. I've sent for tea. Perhaps we can start once it arrives."

"Whatever you'd like."

Angie gave a half-smile and swept the room with her arm.

"Why don't we sit?"

Kaeley nodded but waited until Angie had plopped down on the couch before she gracefully took the empty chair for herself.

The two women stared at each other a moment, at a loss for words. That didn't bother Rayton though, and he soon put forth his own questions.

"Papa says you're a sorceress, but not like Lord Merikan. Is that 'cause you're a girl?"

"Rayton, your manners," Kaeley admonished. Angie just grinned.

"That's OK," she said and turned to face Rayton.

"I'm from a different place," Angie went on. "Where magic is ..." *Make-believe,* she wanted to say. *A fairy tale, something that doesn't exist.* But that clearly didn't apply here. "Magic has a different sense there. Given that, my magic has different properties than Lord Merikan's does. And," she finished. "I'm sure there are differences between boys and girls when it comes to magic." Actually, she had no idea, but somehow it seemed right. Rayton nodded as though it made perfect sense to him.

Angie looked at the other woman.

"So, Rayton's your nephew?" she asked.

"Yes," Kaeley replied. "I am Tre'embra, youngest child of King Grayton and sister to Dho'vani."

Angie frowned, trying to figure out the title.

"Gavin said Dho'vani means Prince and Heir-Apparent. What does Tre'embra mean?"

Kaeley pursed her lips, but whether in amusement or disapproval, Angie didn't know.

"Princess of the Royal Blood of Karundin." She tilted her head to the side, a few strands of auburn hair draping over her shoulder. "You can see why we shorten such a mouthful into a single title," she grinned, her smokey eyes sparkling. Angie smiled back, deciding she liked this young woman.

"And what about you?" Angie asked Rayton. "Do you have a special title?"

"Right now, I'm Prince," he said, youthful face earnest. "But when Papa is King, I become Dho'vani."

Tabitha chose that moment to enter with the tea and a platter full of small cakes and biscuits. Angie's mouth watered at the sight, and Rayton nearly squealed with delight.

Once they had settled into their snacks, tea or cake in hand,

and as Tabitha left with a small smile on her face, Angie heard Sidvareh's voice in her head.

'You might want to let them know that you won't be able to communicate shortly.'

Angie felt a moment of panic. What if something happened where she *had* to understand these two virtual strangers with her?

'Don't worry,' the Faery said, and Angie would have bet the little woman had a grin smeared across her face, given the tone. 'I won't leave you at the moment. I'm simply letting your mind work out the language itself, rather than helping you translate it through your magic. If something needs your immediate understanding, I won't leave you in the dark.'

Angie nodded to herself with a sigh of relief. Then she looked at Kaeley again.

"I'm going to drop the magic in a moment, so I won't be able to understand your language, or speak it. Do you understand?"

Kaeley's eyes widened slightly, but she nodded.

"Really?" Rayton piped. "You're using magic to hear us now?"

Angie shrugged a shoulder. *Apparently,* she thought, though she hadn't known the ability was partially hers and not all Sidvareh.

"Wow," the boy's eyes shone with excitement, then clouded with concern. "So, you won't be able to hear us soon."

"I won't be able to understand you," Angie corrected. "But then, that's why Lord Merikan sent you, isn't it? To teach me."

Rayton's smile lit his whole face. *He can't be more than six or seven,* Angie noted, smiling herself at his renewed enthusiasm.

"OK," he leaned forward, studying Angie with surprising intensity. "I'm ready."

'And so are you,' Sidvareh whispered. And dropped her aid.

"Kia ti balandor dy?" Kaeley asked. Angie stared and shook her head.

"No idea what you just said."

"Coit!" Rayton exclaimed. "Don raboy dushin mikaela abott faeloae?"

Kaeley laid a hand on her chest.

"Ta ni Kaeley," she said and Angie nodded, pointed to herself and replied, "Ta ni Angie."

Kaeley smiled. Rayton, his expression serious, lifted the cake in his little hand.

"Rikae," he said. Angie repeated it, picking up a cake of her own. Rayton grinned and stuffed the pastry in his mouth.

And so they passed the remainder of the morning.

Chapter 5

The Karundin language echoed through Angie's sleeping mind, along with the murmured reminders of Sidvareh, a subtle reinforcement and enhancement of Angie's learning. Then the dream took her, and she nearly lost herself.

Though daylight streamed through the church windows, Angie recognised the subtle shadings and quality of light that reminded her of Karundin—the Karundin of her dreams. *Strange,* she thought. *I've never seen a church in Karundin before.*

But then, to her shock, she found she didn't stand in Karundin, but at her church back home. *So why does it feel like Karundin?*

She moved to the front of the church, to the two draped caskets waiting there. Her heart thundered painfully and her throat constricted. She feared to see who lay in those coffins, yet knew without having to look; she attended her parents' funeral. As though to emphasize that reality, the coverings disappeared and the lids stood raised enough to show Angie the still, dead faces of those she loved.

Before the cry of grief could escape her mouth, a line of people appeared between her and the coffins, speaking in subdued voices, dabbing at wet eyes. And then a priest stood, his words lost to Angie as she sat near the back. A heavy sigh from the man beside her ripped her attention from the front. She turned, and stared at Irving.

"Irving?" she called softly, but he did not hear her.

"It's such a shame," a woman said to her companion in front of them. "They always wanted children, were even talking of adopting after all these years. Now they'll never get the chance. They've no family left."

"But they had a lot of friends," her companion replied, and their whispered words grew too quiet for Angie.

"But they had family," she cried. "They had me."

Beside her, Irving stirred. He glanced to Angie, a frown tugging his brow low as his eyes tried to focus on her and yet gazed beyond.

"Irving?" she tried again. Then, knowing no one would hear her in the dream, she screamed his name, her voice holding tight to her grief and frustration. "Irving!"

"Mermaid?" His choked whisper spoke to his confusion.

Angie's breath caught. But then she stood before the coffins again, where she could see the mourners rise to watch her parents wheeled from the church. She couldn't move, couldn't speak. And all she could hear reinforced the fact that everyone believed that Darlene and Greg Wilson had died childless. She looked around wildly for Irving, but he had slipped out.

Had he really seen her? Why else would he use her nickname like that? And if he had seen her, surely he knew who she was. At that moment, it seemed very important that someone know Darlene and Greg had not died alone. *Only they had,* she heard herself say. *I wasn't fast enough. I didn't get there in time, and then I left them.*

"I left them to die while I saved myself in Karundin." The words came out bitter, the despair nearly overwhelming. "They may as well have died childless and alone, for all the good I did them."

"Lady Angie?" she heard the distant voice calling to her. Her vision narrowed to the church aisle and the two coffins wheeling further and further from her.

"No!" she cried out, trying to reach after them, to follow, to go with her parents. But she couldn't. The aisle grew longer and darker, her past receding with greater speed the harder she tried to hold onto it.

"Lady Angie!" the little voice grew more insistent. The light from the church snapped out, leaving her in darkness.

"Angie!" Rayton's shrill voice called, his hands shaking her shoulder.

The dream broke and Angie bolted up in bed, her arms clutching her knees to her chest as she shook. She stared at the young boy, distantly noting as relief replaced fear in his eyes, reflected by the flickering candle placed by her bedside.

A small tap at the door announced Tabitha. The maid slipped

in, a second candle held in her hand.

"My Lady?" she called softly. "I thought I heard ..." She bit off a gasp. "Rayton! What are you doing in here?" She sounded scandalized.

"I—" he hesitated. "Lady Angie had a nightmare."

"And you knew this how?" Tabitha demanded, her one hand angrily on her hip. "You heard her from several rooms down when I heard nothing from just beyond her door?"

Rayton cast his gaze down. He glanced briefly at Angie, then stared at his bare feet. "I just knew," he mumbled, too quiet for Tabitha to hear.

Without knowing quite why, Angie reached to his chin, lifting his eyes to meet hers.

"You knew I was dreaming?" she asked gently. He shrugged one shoulder, his stance nervous.

"Lady Angelica—" Tabitha began, but Angie shushed her, her attention focussed on Rayton.

"You slipped in, past Tabitha, to wake me from a dream?"

"You—I thought you were in danger. I don't know why, but ..." Tears suddenly sparkled in his eyes and his lower lip trembled. "I had to help," he whispered.

"Biantae," Angie said, the warmth in her voice stilling the boy's fears. "Thank you," she repeated.

Rayton stared at her a moment, as though wondering if she mocked him. But Angie made sure to show him that she spoke with sincerity. Going home to a life without her parents would be hard; but going back to a world that somehow didn't know she existed would terrify her. And that was the earth she had dreamed. Rayton finally nodded, his expression serious, and a fussing Tabitha led him from Angie's room.

The maid popped in again a moment later, moving toward the bed, ready to tuck Angie in.

"I apologise, My Lady. I would never have allowed such an intrusion to your slumber. The Prince is young and impetuous, but his manners don't usually fall so far from propriety—"

"Tabitha," Angie interrupted, her gaze fixed on the candle. "Rayton did not intend any impetuousness or rudeness." She looked up at the maid, her expression forbidding the woman from fluffing pillows or rearranging the duvet. "He in fact may have just saved me from a horrendous fate. So please don't apologise for him."

44

By the look on her face, Tabitha clearly didn't understand, and likely did not really believe Angie's defence of the boy's actions. But she would hardly disagree with a sorceress.

"Of course, My Lady," she said, reaching again for the bed covers. Angie shook her head.

"Leave it, Tabitha. I'd like to sit up for a while." Tabitha didn't seem convinced, but she left Angie in peace, retreating from the room.

It was *all just a dream, right?*

"Just like Karundin," Angie whispered. A dream that was not a dream. She stared at the candle a moment longer, then threw the covers off and, grabbing the little light, went to the outer room. To the desk. She sat, retrieving a sheet of parchment, a quill and the ink. Angie hesitated, then began to write.

The light quality spoke of Karundin, but I knew I was back home ...

***

"Tabitha!" Angie called, rummaging through the armoire. The maid hurried in and, with a disapproving gasp, practically flew to Angie's side.

"My Lady, let me help," the older woman said, deftly pushing Angie out of the way. "What do you seek? A dressing gown? A dinner dress? A day dress?"

"A pair of pants," Angie replied. Tabitha paused and gazed at her with a blank expression.

"'Pants' Lady? What are 'pants'?"

Angie suppressed the desire to roll her eyes.

"Pants," she said, pointing to her discarded jeans on the bed. "Trousers, slacks, leggings. Something without a skirt or bodice."

Tabitha actually paled a shade.

"But, My Lady ... you ... that is ... it would be unseemly for a Lady of your stature to appear in men's clothing."

"First of all," Angie replied, trying to keep her temper in check, "no one is supposed to know I am a Lady of any stature. Second, I'm not supposed to appear to anyone who hasn't already seen me in my jeans. And third, I refuse to wear a dress everyday, especially when there is no special occasion that demands I dress up."

"But we ... My Lady, there's nothing like that designed for a woman," Tabitha's voice had shrunk to a whisper and flickers of fear danced in her eyes. *Damn,* thought Angie. *If I'm supposed to be a great Sorceress, losing my temper and scaring the staff won't help.*

She took a breath and spoke in a gentle voice.

"Is there anyone who could design and make such clothes, Tabitha?"

The maid eyed the denim on the bed dubiously.

"I have never seen such material before."

Angie smiled.

"I don't care about the material, Tabitha. If it's comfortable and I can move freely in it, then I'm happy. But I want pants, not dresses. Can you do that?"

"We will need that for measurements," Tabitha nodded toward the offensive piece of clothing. *Which means I can't wear the jeans either, if she takes them away.*

"How long will it take?"

Tabitha looked at Angie, as though to gauge her reaction. *If it's more than a day ....* Tabitha sighed, picking up the jeans. "I'll get on it right away. I'm sure the seamstresses will have some appropriate fabric. You can have these back shortly, and some 'pants' by tomorrow." She gazed at Angie a second, then asked with a hint of trepidation, "What does one wear with 'pants'?"

Angie frowned, glancing in the armoire. Obviously T-shirts were out. The tunic she had found yesterday wasn't half-bad but ... then she had a brainstorm.

"Tabitha, can your seamstresses design something new?"

The maid's shoulders drooped as she undoubtedly awaited whatever new horror Angie would demand.

"Yes, My Lady. But they would appreciate some direction."

"Could they make something like a tunic, a bit shy of my knees, with long flowing sleeves similar to what Kaeley wore yesterday? Tied at the waist with a belt. With a V-neck, or perhaps a scooped neckline. Something like that?" Angie gestured with her hands as she spoke, the maid following her every movement.

Tabitha's face brightened a little.

"Yes, Lady Angelica. I'm sure we can design something suitable. I'll get right on it." She bobbed a curtsey. "Is there anything else?"

"Not right now, thank you. You go ahead, Tabitha."

The woman nodded and left the room, a light bounce to her step. Angie grinned, reminded of her mother when Mom had a new task to tackle. But the smile quickly faded as Angie's dream returned to her.

'They've no family left,' the woman had said. As though Angie had never existed.

She glared down at herself. At the nightdress she wore. Clothing that didn't even belong to her. Her only physical proof of Earth and the life she knew before had gone out the door with Tabitha.

"As though it never existed," Angie growled to herself. She stared hard at the armoire and its offending offering of medieval clothing. The clothes themselves were exquisite—that wasn't the problem. To give up her last vestige of her former self grated.

"A pair of jeans," she griped. Something to remind her that she was still Angie Wilson of Earth, not just Lady Angelica of Karundin. "All I want is a simple pair of jeans."

She turned to the bed, ready to throw herself on the plush comforter in a pique of self-pity as the suggestion of a headache threatened her temples. But what she saw stopped her. A comfortably worn pair of jeans rested slightly askew on the pillow, as though just tossed there. She stared dumbfounded, knowing they had not existed a moment ago. Then she felt the blood drain from her face as she tried to figure out how they had appeared, fearing she knew the answer.

A few seconds passed before she heard the outer door slam open, followed by a man's quick steps.

"My Lady?" Merikan called as he reached the bedroom door, breathing hard as though he had run to her room. "I thought I felt ..." He hesitated, glancing around. "Do you require assistance?"

Angie pointed wordlessly at the jeans. The Lord Protector stepped into the room, looking without comprehension at the newly arrived piece of clothing.

"They just appeared," Angie whispered. She gazed up into Merikan's dark eyes, glowing faintly with unleashed magic, her own dual stare bordering on hysteria. "I dreamed of home, of my parents' funeral, only no one remembered me. And I woke up and just wanted something normal, something my own, but

47

Tabitha took my jeans to use as a pattern and I ... I don't know. I felt kind of helpless and lost and ... I just wanted something normal."

"So you wished them into existence?" Merikan asked gently, recognising Angie's fears.

"I don't know," Angie's voice shook. "I guess I ..." She took hold of herself and went over what he had first said in her mind. "What did you feel? You said you thought you felt something, and that brought you here. What did you feel?"

He regarded her steadily.

"I felt magic," he said, and looked around the room. "Nothing else seems out of place?" he asked.

Angie passed her gaze over her surroundings and shook her head.

"Just the jeans."

"Can you make something else appear?"

Her eyes locked on his.

"Like what?" she asked, losing some of her trepidation with this new challenge.

"Anything. See if you can reproduce the effect."

Angie considered a moment, then nodded. She thought about a T-shirt, figuring that if she brought something else onto the scene, it might as well be something useful. But nothing happened. Her brow furrowed as she narrowed her eyes, her nose crinkling in an unconscious manner so reminiscent of Lady Sorceress Katerina that Merikan's heart caught in his throat. No amount of concentration helped, though, and Angie shook her head with a frustrated sigh.

"Nothing. I don't know what I did, but wishing doesn't seem to work."

"We will have to set aside some time after Dho'vani's coronation to explore how your magic works. I would caution you against using it again, but ..."

Angie harrumphed.

"But seeing as I don't know what I did, I won't know how not to do so again."

'I will help you understand what I can,' Sidvareh offered for Angie's ears alone.

"When is the coronation?" she asked.

"Two days hence," Merikan replied, a frown of concern on his face. "As the Protector of the Royal family, you must attend, but we must also keep you hidden. In the meantime—"

"In the meantime, Sidvareh will help me avoid such mistakes again, and I need to learn as much of your language as possible," Angie said, her authoritative mien and renewed control helping to reassure the Lord Protector.

Merikan nodded, admiring Angie's quickly regained composure and her ability to focus on things of importance. Only then did he notice that the Lady wore nothing but her nightdress. He reddened and bowed to her, turning his gaze aside.

"Then I will return to my duties, My Lady." He coughed. "The young Prince and Princess will arrive shortly for your language instruction. I will leave you to dress." He hurried from the room.

Angie turned and reached a tentative hand to the jeans.

"If I didn't wish them here, what did I do?" she whispered to Sidvareh.

'In a sense, you *did* wish them here, My Lady.'

A violet mist formed, as it had before when the Faery first appeared to Angie, and from that mist stepped Sidvareh's golden-green figure. Large emerald eyes peered at Angie from the tiny face.

"You have used magic through instinct, often made stronger by emotions. In this case, you had anger and despair to fuel your power. In a dream, you may not have thought anything of the sudden appearance of clothing."

Angie had to agree with that.

"But your dream ability manifested in this reality, without your conscious direction, and that both pleases and troubles me." Her wings fanned gently in the air, though she stood as though on solid ground, and Angie wondered if Sidvareh used her wings for support or if their movement signified the Faery's agitation. "It signifies that you can touch your gifts and direct them, but until we discover how you may control when desire becomes reality, you must try to restrain your excesses of emotion. And that, I fear, will sorely test you."

Chapter 6

Rayton bounded into Angie's sitting room, followed by a more sedate, though obviously amused, Kaeley. Tabitha had already arranged for tea and cakes, and the maid had left in search of Angie's new clothing, promised today by the seamstresses. Angie sat with a steaming mug of tea in her hands, watching the young Prince and his aunt.

"Ba dae, cholen adestae, Angie? Rikae!" Rayton greeted; 'Good morning, how are you, Angie? Cake!' He plopped himself down with the gleeful abandon of a child and plucked up a pastry.

"Rayton, your manners," Kaeley admonished before settling into a chair.

Angie admired the girl's grace, how she could glide into the room and arrange herself and her lovely lilac gown so smoothly upon the cushion without falling on her face or ripping the fine fabric and yet still look picture-perfect. Angie had found the simplest dress in her armoire, a pale blue sleeveless affair cinched at the waist with a silver belt, and sat with it tucked beneath her knees, her legs curled on the couch. She felt, not under dressed, but rather like the poor cousin. But then, she wasn't a Princess and didn't feel confined by the fashions of Karundin.

They exchanged pleasantries, then Angie explained what she felt she needed to know, slowly and with a little help from Sidvareh as she struggled with the Karundin language.

"Tell me about the coronation. Who will attend, what I should expect. Tell me of the Royal Family and those who look out for them."

Kaeley nodded, laying a hand on her chest.

"I am Tre'embra, which, as I mentioned before, means Princess of the Royal Blood of Karundin, but it also means 'youngest'. Dho'vani, Gavin, is eldest. We have a brother, Alvin, born between us. He bears the title Tre'vani, Prince of the Royal Blood of Karundin. The title also indicates that he does not stand in direct line to the throne, though he does stand next in line to young Rayton here, who becomes Dho'vani upon Gavin's coronation. Do you understand thus far?"

Angie pieced together the meaning, surprising herself on how much she *did* understand through the language-barrier.

"Please continue," she said, and Kaeley smiled her encouragement. But Rayton picked up the lesson.

"My mother, Hydae, was Dho'embra, wife to the Heir-Apparent. Had she lived, she would become Queen beside Papa."

Angie searched his young face for any sign of grief, and it seemed Rayton understood her intent.

"Mama died just after my second name day, so I don't remember her. I've seen portraits though, and you can see them when Papa is crowned, 'cause they're lining the Great Hall. That's where Chief Priest Romtani will perform the coronation."

He sipped at his tea and Angie refilled their cups.

"Now let's see," Rayton frowned in concentration. "There's Aunt Maraenda. She's Uncle Alvin's wife. I like her; she lets me sneak candied meats from her solarium when her ladies aren't watching." He grinned, picking up a small cake and placing it deliberately on his plate. Angie grinned back and noticed Kaeley hiding her own smile behind a delicate hand. The Princess took up the family history then.

"Maraenda holds the title Cardae, meaning Princess of Karundin, not of the Royal Blood. Her father is King of Sahkarae, the kingdom to our south. When you can, you should speak with her, for she also had to learn our titles, names she deems elaborate yet useful. Sahkarae uses simple titles that do not detail where in the Royal House one stands; Prince or Princess, rather than Dho'vani, Tre'embra, or Cardae. She finds our titles clarifying, yet complex."

"There are a lot to keep track of," Angie agreed. Kaeley tilted her head in acknowledgement before she continued.

"Just as Karundin's royal line has the Lord Protector—that's Merikan—and the Protector of the Royal House—you, Lady

Sorceress—Sahkarae's royal line has sorcerous guardians. Maraenda's Sorcerer is named Shanor. These all will attend the coronation.

"Gavin and Merikan will stand upon the podium with Chief Priest Romtani, Rayton one step down. Alvin, Maraenda, their young daughter Maraedeth, and myself stand in attendance upon the second step. Shanor kneels next to Maraenda, to signify his connection to her and the Royal House, yet his lower station among the Royals. The nobles gather around the dais as befits their rank. Any others who wish to witness the coronation may do so, from the floor of the Great Hall behind the nobles and from the balconies ringing it. Gavin will have Karundin's soldiers placed as he sees best, both as guards and as witnesses."

"And after that, there's a big feast planned," Rayton chimed in. "A few, actually. There's the one Papa has to attend, and then a bunch of others all around the city so that everyone can have some food, from the highest nobles right down to the lowest peasants. No one goes hungry when Karundin crowns a king." Although the words sounded arrogant—and like something parroted by a seven-year-old trying to sound like an adult—Angie found the idea of providing for all a noble one, even if it only happened once in a great while.

Or so she hoped, remembering the bloody knife that prompted the need for a coronation. Someone *had* killed the King, and now a new one stood to take his place, not knowing the culprit or if his own life stood in danger. Staring into Rayton's innocent face, Angie prayed fervently that Gavin did not meet his father's fate, leaving this child bereft of a parent to imitate.

"Had you come to us under normal circumstances, Lady Sorceress," Kaeley said, smiling fondly at her nephew, though her eyes held worry, "you also would stand upon the podium. In fact, as Protector of the Royal House, you would stand above Lord Protector Merikan at Gavin's right hand."

Something in the tone of the Tre'embra's voice alerted Angie.

"Will the absence of such a Protector of the Royal House harm Gavin's position?"

"But you aren't absent," Rayton protested. "People just won't know you're there."

"Exactly," Angie replied, holding Kaeley's gaze.

The Princess nodded.

"Some few might see the visible absence as an ill omen, but

you must remember that Karundin has been without the Lady Sorceress for nearly thirty double-seasons. The absence is not unexpected. And rumours of your ... spirit ... keeping watch over our family without your physical presence have persisted, maintaining a level of hope and strength in the land. Do not fear, Lady Angelica; this deception will cease soon enough, leaving you able to fulfill your duty unrestricted."

"My duty," Angie murmured. "To protect the Royal House so that they can protect their charge."

Kaeley nodded.

"What is your charge?" Angie asked. "What do you protect?"

Kaeley's eyes clouded, losing focus.

"I—" she frowned, shook her head as though to clear it. "We guard—" Again, Kaeley paused, her lips forming words that refused to translate into sound. Angie stared hard at the girl, noting the smallest hint of golden light dancing in her eyes.

"Aunt Kaeley?" Rayton asked, leaning forward.

The girl paled, her lips pressed firmly together as a fine tremor shook her body.

"Kaeley?" Angie shot out of her chair and grabbed the Princess's arms, forcing her to look Angie in the eye. She recognised that eerie light as a form of magic, like what Sidvareh had shown her in Merikan. "Rayton, does Kaeley have magic?"

"Just the protective kind, like all the Royals."

Kaeley gasped and shook harder, her skin growing cooler beneath Angie's anxious grasp.

"What's wrong with her?" Angie asked, meaning the question for Sidvareh, though Rayton answered first, the edges of panic squeaking his voice.

"I don't know!"

'A spell to prevent her from answering your query, I think,' the Faery intoned.

"Rayton, find Lord Merikan. Tell him magic affects Kaeley; a spell. I will do what I can until he arrives."

The boy stared at her with wide eyes, and Angie tried to calm him.

"She'll be fine, but I need Merikan to make sure this doesn't happen again. Don't worry," she forced a smile. "I'll take care of her."

It helped. Rayton nodded and dashed out of the room. Angie turned back to the girl.

"Kaeley, listen to me. I retract the question. Do not try to answer me. Just forget I asked."

Kaeley blinked, her eyes still not quite in focus. Angie concentrated, dearly wishing she could take back the last few minutes, return Kaeley to normal.

"Kaeley!" She squeezed the girl's arms. "Please, Kaeley, stop. I'm sorry." Angie blinked away the heat of tears ... and felt the faintest tingle run up her arms and into Kaeley.

Kaeley sighed and grew limp, then blinked suddenly clear eyes at Angie.

"My Lady?" she asked, her colour returning, her skin gaining its proper temperature. "Are you well?" She covered Angie's hands on her arms with her own.

Angie's breath came out in a gasp and she hugged the Princess hard.

"Thank God," she murmured, then drew back, studying Kaeley's face.

"Are you okay?"

"I'm fine Lady Angelica, but ... why do you kneel before me?"

Angie frowned.

"You—" Her head tilted to the side as she thought about her answer, about what—exactly—she'd said to the Tre'embra. "You don't remember, do you? What I asked, what happened."

Kaeley slowly shook her head from side to side.

"What do you remember?"

"We spoke of the coronation, of any repercussions your apparent absence might cause. Of your duty to protect the Royal House." She paused, glancing to the vacant seat beside her. "Rayton?" Her smokey eyes widened, a thread of fear igniting in them. "Did something happen to Rayton?"

"No," Angie soothed, pulling back so that she crouched before the girl rather than clung to her. "I sent him for Lord Merikan when I couldn't get you to answer me." She held up a hand to halt Kaeley's next question.

"I don't know exactly what happened, but it seemed like some magic affected you."

"But it affects me no longer?"

Angie shook her head.

"It appears to have left."

"Was I attacked?" Kaeley asked calmly. "Do you stand in danger, Lady Angelica?"

Angie shook her head.

"It wasn't an attack. More like a trigger to a question I asked."

Kaeley considered that, her head canting to one side.

"It seems unwise to ask 'What question', yet I find myself curious," the Princess confessed. "What kind of question would trigger an attack?"

"The kind you cannot answer," said a voice from the door. Angie and Kaeley turned as Merikan strode in, a pale Rayton trailing close behind. "It is a question no Royal may answer save by leave of the King or his Queen."

Angie rose to face the Sorcerer.

"Then you cannot answer either?" she demanded.

"After the coronation."

Angie snorted in disgust, which made Kaeley start and Rayton giggle.

"So if I simply refrain from asking about this mysterious charge, she'll be fine?"

"I believe so," Merikan replied.

"Are there any other topics I need to keep away from? Anything else I should be free of?"

Merikan frowned his incomprehension. Rayton hurried forward and tugged at her sleeve. Angie knelt down beside the boy as he whispered urgently in her ear.

"I think you mean *tsutae*, not *datsuae*. *Datsuae*, freedom; *tsutae*, steer clear."

Angie felt her lips quirk at his solemn correction, then raised her eyebrows in surprise as she realised that she had spoken the Karundin language unaided for the entire conversation.

"Thank you, Rayton," she said, then looked back up at Merikan.

"Are there any questions I should refrain from asking? To steer clear of?" she said with a wink to the young Prince, but keeping her attention on the Lord Protector.

"Do not ask about their charge. Without a king in place, they cannot answer. The magic that protects them forbids it."

"So," Angie spoke slowly as she thought. "Do I not need to know what they guard to protect them?"

"My Lady," Merikan hedged. "Many things will become apparent after Dho'vani's coronation. Until then," he shrugged apologetically. "You must have patience." He stepped closer, lowering his voice. "What they guard is critical to the survival of peace in our land, but the magic that protects them does not yet recognise you."

He stepped back and spoke so that Kaeley and Rayton could also hear his words.

"The coronation would normally involve a ceremony to acknowledge the Lady Sorceress and the Lord Protector as guardians of the Royal house. As we cannot yet reveal Lady Angelica's presence, Dho'vani and I have arranged a more private ceremony with only the Royal Family in attendance. At that time, you will meet Tre'vani Alvin and Cardae Maraenda, along with Maraenda's Sorcerer. Shortly after that, if all goes well, we can introduce you to the people of Karundin."

"If all goes well?" Angie enquired.

"The more you can learn of our language, customs, and of your own magic, My Lady, the better for all," Merikan replied cryptically before he turned and walked away.

***

Later in the afternoon, before Tabitha arrived with the evening meal, Angie sat alone in the courtyard. The distant sound of a funeral procession earlier had wafted over the walls, but now she sat in silence.

"Is it safe to talk, Sidvareh?" she asked the Faery.

In reply, the familiar violet mist formed and the small woman appeared in front of Angie.

"It is, My Lady. What do you wish to discuss?"

Angie frowned in concentration, organising her thoughts and trying to put into words what bothered her—well, what bothered her most right at that moment.

"I'm speaking Karundin right now, right?"

Sidvareh nodded.

"And everything Kaeley explained this morning, that wasn't easy stuff to understand, at least not by someone who's just learning the language."

Again, the Faery nodded, her head tilted to the side as she waited for Angie to continue.

Angie looked at the Faery, her blue-and-green gaze meeting the other's large emerald orbs.

"Did you allow me such understanding?"

"That was your own doing, Lady Angelica."

"But how is that possible?" Angie demanded. "I have but a few days of learning, yet I now speak and understand as though schooled for years."

"I have helped hasten the learning process, yet even that would not account for your present ease. I do not know the answer definitively, but I do have a hypothesis, if you do not mind supposition."

"Any explanation would help."

"Your desire, even need, to learn the language has caused your magic to make it happen. You do not use your magic to learn, rather your magic has altered the way you think, making it possible to grasp the language as your own. I also believe that your Lady Mother laid the groundwork for this learning."

"What do you mean? How?"

"Tell me, Lady Angelica, when you dreamed of Karundin, did you understand the language?"

Angie thought back to all her dreams growing up. She always knew what people said on those occasions when anyone spoke. It had never seemed odd, but then, she had thought them mere dreams; of course she would understand the language in her own mind.

"You instinctively knew the language of your mother, the words she would have spoken when you lay in her womb. She kept you connected to this world and, perhaps, kept a link open in your mind so that when the time came, you would learn Karundin as though one remembering something merely forgotten. These lessons with the Royal children have served to remind you of what you already know."

Angie nodded, wrapping her mind about these concepts. She *had* felt as though Rayton's and Kaeley's instruction refreshed a lesson long thought forgotten. Sidvareh's supposition made sense in a way that told Angie the Faery was right.

What a frightening thought.

Chapter 7

"My Lady?" Tabitha's gentle hand on her shoulder woke Angie from a dreamless slumber. The woman carried a candle to light her way, but the room lay in darkness beyond that small halo.

"Tabitha?" Angie said, blinking sleep from her eyes and sitting up. "What's wrong?"

"Nothing, My Lady," she reassured. "But Tre'embra Kaeley waits in the next room."

Angie frowned.

"What time is it?"

"A little more than two water-cups past deep night, Lady Angelica," the maid replied unhelpfully. Angie didn't know the time measurements of Karundin yet. She chose to interpret a water-cup as about an hour, and assumed deep night meant midnight, though it could as easily refer to moonset, which Angie didn't know anything about either. She decided that the time didn't really matter beyond the fact that night still ruled the land.

"Did Kaeley say what she wanted?" Angie asked as Tabitha helped her push off the covers and get to her feet.

"She merely requested your presence, My Lady. Here," Tabitha handed her a robe to cover her nightgown. "The night has a bit of a chill to it."

"Thanks," Angie thrust her arms through the sleeves as she stumbled after Tabitha to the door. In the sitting room beyond, Kaeley waited with her own lantern. She wore a simple ebony gown that made her grey eyes seem darker, and her auburn hair hung loose and unadorned down her back.

"Lady Angelica, I apologise for disturbing your sleep," the Princess began.

"That's OK. Is something wrong, Kaeley?"

Kaeley turned to Tabitha.

"Thank you, Tabitha. You may retire now. I shall have your mistress back shortly."

The maid curtseyed and retreated to the adjoining room where she slept.

Kaeley turned back to Angie. Angie stepped closer to the young woman and noticed her red-rimmed eyes and drawn features.

"Kaeley, what's wrong?" she asked, putting her hand on the other's arm. Kaeley smiled gently.

"We sit vigil this night for our father," she began. "Although we walked his funeral procession earlier, it is tradition that the Royal Family fare-well the old monarch on the eve of the new monarch's reign. We each take a turn, starting with the youngest. Alvin sits with father's memory now, but Gavin will take his turn shortly. He has asked me to bring you to him."

"Of course," Angie said, then looked down at herself. "I should change."

"Here," Kaeley turned to the chair, picking up a bundle of clothes. She handed Angie a dress similar to the one the Princess wore, and a long hooded cloak. "These are mine. They should fit you well enough." At Angie's raised eyebrows, Kaeley gave a mischievous grin. "It wouldn't do for a strange woman to disturb Dho'vani, but his little sister will engender few questions, should any see her enter the tabernacle."

***

Shanor waited in the dark recesses for his charge just outside the tabernacle. Maraenda had gone to meet her husband as Alvin finished his vigil and the two shared a quiet moment near the entrance. Merikan and Gavin remained within the stone confines, which suited Shanor well. He did not feel up to talk tonight, not with so much to prepare for tomorrow's coronation.

While he didn't have nearly the details to oversee as the Lord Protector, Shanor had enough on his mind that he looked forward to returning to the comforts of his room. As Sorcerer and Protector to Maraenda, Shanor had made himself invaluable to Karundin's Royal house, in service to his own King as much as to Maraenda. In said service, both Shanor and Maraenda stood as representatives for Sahkarae in the coming Royal festivities as well as members of Karundin's extended Royal family.

The coronation of a new King required much planning and details, especially given the nature of the old King's death. Gavin's security had increased since his father's assassination, as evidenced by the discreet presence of so many soldiers in Karundin's livery stationed around the tabernacle and roaming the streets that led to the palace proper where Gavin would process on the morrow.

So when the cloaked figure slipped past Maraenda and Alvin as the duo approached Shanor, the Sorcerer paid her a good deal of attention. Until he recognised Tre'embra Kaeley's garb and the grace of a noble-born. He grimaced. The girl should know better than to wander the area unsupervised. Especially given the renewed caution of those who guarded Dho'vani.

But the girl's disregard to prudence did cause Shanor to note how the younger Royals seemed to come and go as they chose, without reprimand or reproach. His grimace turned into a brief sneer as he considered how someone with few scruples might use such information to their advantage.

Then Maraenda and Alvin gained his side, and he escorted the royal pair back to their chambers.

***

"Just act like you belong, like you know where you're going and have every right to go there, and most of all, as though no one has the right to stop you or question your actions."

Kaeley's instructions rang in Angie's mind as she gently closed the giant oak door to the chapel behind her. So far, such a demeanour had worked. A proud and purposeful bearing had led her down the silent avenue connecting the palace to the chapel, bypassing a host of private dwellings and shops. Lanterns on tall poles lit the way, aided by a cloudless, star-filled night and a waning moon—after a brief glance at the foreign constellations overhead, Angie had kept her gaze riveted on the course before her, pushing her uneasiness at yet another bit of proof that she no longer walked Earth to the back of her mind. She had encountered no one at this late hour, and only glimpsed a couple of armed guards in the distance.

Until she turned from the oak door to face the inner sanctuary of the chapel, where she found herself face to chest with a burly man in dark blue livery, a golden tree with outspread branches emblazoned across the polished armour of his breastplate. He held a gleaming pike casually in his right hand.

"What are you doing back here, little imp?" he whispered, a grin implicit in his deep voice. His amused tolerance vanished when he saw his mistake.

Angie saw the guard stiffen the instant he understood a stranger stood before him rather than the Princess whose cloak she wore, and she had a moment to regret coming here in disguise as the pike shifted in his grip and she suddenly found herself staring at the burnished point of a very dangerous weapon.

"Ah, Kaeley—" Angie began, pausing to clear her throat and collect her thoughts. She kept her hands in sight to show herself unarmed.

Act as though no one has the right to stop you or question your actions, Kaeley had said, and Angie wondered whether the Princess had envisioned this or had just assumed no one would stop her. Either way, Angie found the words somehow heartening. She drew herself up, pried her eyes from the weapon menacing her, and looked up at the guard.

"That is," she continued, her voice steadier. "Tre'embra Kaeley informed me that Dho'vani wished to speak with me."

"Not gonna happen, lady. No one approaches the Dho'vani that I don't know, and I don't know you."

"It's all right, Nervain," a familiar voice said softly from the shadows, soon followed by the Lord Protector himself as Merikan stepped into the light—which Angie saw came from two torches, one to either side of the door. *Funny the things you don't immediately take note of with sharp, pointy things jabbed in your face,* she thought. "Dho'vani is expecting her."

"Your pardon, Lord Protector," the guard Nervain replied. "But like I said, I don't know her, and I take no chances with my liege's life."

"And I applaud your dedication and diligence, Commander." Merikan gave a small bow to Nervain. "As to not knowing the Lady, take a closer look."

Merikan held up his palm and a globe of golden-white light appeared above his hand. He sent this little ball of magic to hover near Angie's face. Nervain followed the progress, his eyes narrowed in concentration as he studied Angie. When his gaze reached her eyes, his own opened in surprise, then in awe.

"My Lady Sorceress, forgive me!" The pike snapped away and Nervain dropped to one knee, head bowed. Angie stared at him, then at Merikan, a baffled and pleading light in her eyes. Merikan's lips twitched as he held back a smile, but he said nothing to aid her, merely doused his conjured light.

"Please don't do that." Angie gestured for the man to rise, and he did so, albeit with reluctance.

"Lady Angelica has grown accustomed to working unseen," Merikan said. "She finds such displays of honour unfamiliar."

Commander Nervain nodded his acceptance of this explanation, and with great daring, met Angie's gaze, somehow looking down at her without making her feel his height.

"My Lady Angelica, please forgive my impertinence, but I did not expect you. Indeed, no one will."

"My mother felt it behooved her to keep me hidden until such time that Karundin needed to see her Lady Sorceress again."

Merikan's calm facade almost broke at that, and Angie kept her own grin hidden. The words had seemed appropriate, and after all, she had not spent so many nights dreaming of this land not to know how and when to use flowery speech to sooth the fears and misgivings of others. She just hadn't thought it would become so real. *Or feel so right.* She pushed that thought to the back of her mind to examine later.

"My Lady Angelica," Nervain clapped a fist to his chest, above his heart, in salute to her. "You are most welcomed back. I look forward to working with you to preserve the Royal line."

Angie inclined her head in what she hoped looked like acceptance.

"Please call me Angie, Commander, and I thank you for your greeting."

Nervain nodded back, then stepped aside so that Angie and Merikan could pass further into the chapel.

Once they had gone out of Nervain's hearing range, Angie turned to the Lord Protector.

"Is it the eyes?" she asked.

"Your eyes do mark you, yes."

"But couldn't someone counterfeit that?" Merikan looked blank at the thought. "Use coloured lenses or some form of magic to make their eyes multi-coloured like mine?" Angie pressed.

"I would detect the presence of magic, especially around the eyes. Such alterations are difficult to maintain and often leave a trace." He thought for a second. "How would someone use coloured lenses? What are they?"

Angie felt her own expression turn blank at that, but then realised that Karundin probably didn't have such things as contact lenses.

"You know what glasses are, right? Eye spectacles?"

"Of course."

"Well, in my world, you can get lenses that do the same job, only they go right on the eye, and you can get them in pretty much any colour you want."

Merikan paused as he thought this concept through, drawing Angie to a stand-still also.

"You put glass in your eyes?"

Angie briefly considered trying to explain the difference between hard and soft lenses, and discarded the idea as beyond her, especially given the lateness of the hour.

"Basically, yes," she replied instead. "Specially made glass. But the point is, in my world, someone could disguise their eye-colour. So assuring everyone I'm the Lady Sorceress solely based on my eyes is probably not the wisest course of action."

Merikan presented a grim smile at that.

"It is not based merely on the Sorceress Star, Angelica, but also on you. Many have seen you through the years in your ... dealings with Karundin, and your visage is known to some. Nervain is one such, as am I." He nodded at her shocked expression.

"I guess that makes sense," she said after a moment. "After all, I knew you and Rayton, and I've seen my own share of people in my dreams. It's only fair that they've seen me, too, even if we didn't know that we were all real at the time."

Merikan chuckled at that, then resumed walking.

Silver-streaked black marble pillars with fine etchings lined the sides of the chapel, and niches with statuary and carved wooden reliefs dotted the walls at regular intervals. Two rows of padded stone benches, like and yet unlike pews, ran the length of the building, leaving a wide, clear aisle down the centre where Angie and Merikan walked. At the far end—their destination—stood something resembling an altar; a raised dais made of a solid block of gold-veined white marble. This platform supported a bier upon which rested an effigy of the late King, surrounded by a veritable garden of picked flowers—the good-will offerings of a nation to their fallen leader. If Angie understood correctly from Kaeley's explanation as she dressed in the Tre'embra's clothing, the King's body already lay below in the Royal crypts, the kingdom having bid him his final farewell in the ceremony Angie had noted earlier. The one that she had only heard from afar, given her continued need for concealment, and therefore her inability to attend. This effigy would join the mortal remains of King Grayton as Karundin crowned a new king in the morning.

Gavin sat quietly to the side on a bench slightly more elaborate than the rest; special seating for the Royals. He wore a simple tunic and leggings, and nothing else, and he still managed to look scrumptious.

"He will remain thus until dawn." Merikan explained in a subdued voice, as though expecting Angie to question the Dho'vani's appearance. "Then he will emerge with the sun and walk the streets to the palace. The people will line the avenue to watch for his approach." Gavin had turned his head to watch, but made no other move. "At certain intervals, someone will step forward and offer him the regalia of King. He will shed the simple tunic for one made of silk, the finest doe-skin boots will adorn his feet, and an ermine-lined cloak with the Royal colours will grace his shoulders. A golden belt and polished sword, each specially commissioned for this day, will be presented by the master smiths who crafted them. He will gain a Sceptre, the Royal Seal, the Scrying Key and the Rings of Intervention, each given to hold in trust."

Angie didn't know what all that meant or entailed, but she kept her silence. They stood next to Gavin now, and he indicated with a small nod that they should sit, apparently content to let Merikan continue his lesson.

"A black stallion will await him at the gates to the palace, along with silver bridle and saddle, which he will ride as far as the inner courtyard. By the time Dho'vani reaches the Great Hall within the palace proper, he will have acquired all the trappings of his new station, save the crown itself. That, Chief Priest Romtani will present at the end of the coronation, and Dho'vani shall become King."

Angie nodded, waiting, wondering why he told her all this, but Merikan now fell silent. She gently sucked in her bottom lip, then raised her brows in question, yet still he said no more. She turned to look at Gavin, who returned her stare. Finally, she had to ask.

"And Merikan? Does he proceed with you to watch for magical assault?"

"I must wait closer to the gate," the Sorcerer replied.

"So Dho'vani does all this without you to guard him?"

"Yes," Merikan answered.

"He goes without guards?" she blurted, swinging her attention back to the Lord Protector. "With an assassin on the loose, you're going to let him wander the streets alone?"

"I won't be alone," said Gavin quietly, drawing her gaze, a smile tugging his lips. "My guards will follow my progress."

"Great, but what about protection against magic?" Angie briefly marvelled at her own quick acceptance of the possibilities magic provided, wondering if she drew on her knowledge from genre books and movies, or if her certainty came from somewhere deeper. "Whoever killed your father probably used magic to get in unseen, which means assassins are as likely to use magic as physical weapons. So how will you guard yourself against that if Merikan can't go with you?"

"That is why you will walk with me."

Angie stared bewildered at Gavin. His left lip pulled up in a half-smile.

"I will?" she asked stupidly. Then she shook her head. "I thought you wanted my presence kept quiet."

"We will disguise you as one of my guards."

"And I'm supposed to do what?"

"One guard walks with me to deliver tokens of thanks to those who provide the accessories of kingship. You will be that guard. I have other women among my soldiers; you will not stand out."

Angie shook her head.

"That's not what I mean." She sucked in a deep breath. "How can I guard you? I don't know how to use my magic."

"I have faith in you," he replied with a grin. The smile stopped Angie's breath for a moment, but his misplaced trust disturbed her. "You have always known how to help in your dreams, haven't you?"

"Well," she glanced to King Grayton's effigy, "not always."

Gavin grimaced, but kept his attention on Angie.

"For the most part, then?"

Reluctantly, Angie nodded.

"Then if anything should happen, just act as though we walk through your dreams."

Angie blinked at him, wondering if it could be so simple, fearing it could not.

Chapter 8

Dawn brushed lightly against the horizon, as yet a thought waiting to explode into being, but the presence of this new day loomed with promise. People lined the streets, their voices hushed yet expectant. The bakers, awake for hours, shared out loaves of bread and pastries, their generosity encouraged and supplemented by the palace. For today, a new King took the throne, a young man many had watched grow to adulthood, knowing the strength of his heart, the compassion and fair dealings taught to him by his father. And though the people of Karundin still mourned for the loss of that man, they rejoiced in the hope that his son would lead them to a future as prosperous as they had come to expect. No one knew how long peace could last, nor who stood as enemy—for had not someone murdered the old King?—but everyone lining the streets from the tabernacle to the palace held high hopes for Gavin's reign.

Gavin waited until Commander Nervain and most of his guards had exited the tabernacle before stepping out to greet the day, his timing matched to the sun cresting the horizon. Half the guard would go first to make sure the path remained clear and the other half would follow, but Dho'vani would walk without their shields. Merikan had placed a small protective spell around Gavin, a spell augmented by Gavin's own natural protection as a Royal, yet strangely, with Lady Angelica at his side, garbed in the blue and gold of the Royal Guard, Gavin felt safe even without Lord Merikan's precautions.

While the Lady wore a light coat of mail beneath the Royal colours and a helmet that shielded her eyes and helped mask her identity, Gavin went clad only in his linen tunic and leggings.

No covering adorned his head, nor boots his feet. He walked among his subjects with head bowed, a humble supplicant, as tradition demanded. Only through his people's permission and acclaim would Dho'vani rise to become King. Though he expected no opposition, the mere fact that, should one of those chosen to provide the accessories for the coronation refuse to part with his or her gift, Gavin's right to the throne could stand in jeopardy. It left him feeling vulnerable and humble indeed.

Gavin strode down the two steps of the tabernacle not to the sound of applause, but to an expectant silence. Again, protocol suggested the approval or disapproval of his people would only find voice at the entrance to the castle. If Gavin truly had the support of Karundin, then he would hear it at the moment he mounted the stallion and not before.

The Lady Angelica matched his stride, though two paces back. She carried a gold-lined wooden box, its lid bedecked with lapis jewels and sapphires in the likeness of a horse. The box contained thank tokens; specially crafted gold coins, each designed with the doner's occupation in mind. Merikan had explained each one for her, confident in her ability to remember which token went to which artisan.

Five paces from the tabernacle, a man and a woman stepped forward, a blue silk tunic cradled in the woman's arms. Gavin and Lady Angelica stopped and Dho'vani bowed respectfully to the pair. The man stepped forward, taking Gavin's old tunic from his shoulders. Next, the woman offered the new silken garment. When Gavin had pulled the soft shirt over his head, he saw that the woman already held the token picturing the tailor shears in her hand. She smiled and she and the man, folding Dho'vani's old tunic with care, returned to the waiting masses. The tunic, still in excellent shape, belonged to them now.

Gavin resumed his walk. After another ten paces, a man strode from the crowd, an elegant pair of doe-skin boots held reverently in his calloused hands. Gavin stopped again, offering his bow. The man knelt and proffered each boot in turn, sliding them onto Gavin's feet. Even without stockings, the boots fit perfectly and most comfortably. This time, he saw the Lady Angelica extend the thank token, the image of a thick needle embossed on the face of the coin. The man also smiled, then clapped a hand to his chest in salute as he retreated to stand with his fellows.

The walk continued. With each new addition to Gavin's regalia, he could feel the mounting excitement of the people. Every artisan received Dho'vani's bow and the appropriate thank token. Smiles blossomed on every face Gavin could see. By the time he reached the palace gates, seeing the great black stallion for the first time, Gavin finally allowed a touch of that elation to mark his own countenance. He grinned his appreciation as the saddler hefted an intricate saddle etched in silver plate for Gavin's appraisal. Gavin handed the Sceptre and the Royal Seal he had already received to the Lady Angelica, who tucked them in the crook of her arm as per Merikan's instructions, balancing the near-empty box of tokens in her left hand. The Scrying Key and Rings of Intervention each hung from a separate leather thong around Gavin's neck and would not interfere in saddling the horse.

Gavin extended a hand to the stallion, making his scent known to the beast, before he took the saddle and placed it on the animal's back. The bridle he received from the silversmith who had gilded the tack. Gavin did not rush through outfitting the horse, knowing that to hurry now would not endear him to his kingly mount.

When all stood ready and both saddler and silversmith had received their tokens and had faded back into the crowd, Gavin turned to the Lady. He noticed her pinched lips and guarded expression, recognising her tension. He did not know whether she had sensed any outside magical influence—certainly Gavin had not—but he could understand her concern. Though she claimed not to know how to use her magic, he had no doubts about her ability. He did not understand why he so implicitly trusted her, yet he could not shake that trust. And so he offered her a smile of reassurance now. She gave him a small smile in response, then dropped to one knee, setting aside the empty token box. She made a brace of her hands and assisted Gavin to mount the stallion.

The crowd burst into uproarious applause.

Lady Angelica handed up the Sceptre and the Royal Seal and Gavin settled himself atop the stallion. The beast shivered his excitement, longing to race, yet his training kept him obedient to Gavin's will. He pranced in place, a triumphant little dance that Gavin allowed before placating the animal with a gentle hand. As Lady Angelica passed the gold-lined wooden box with its adorned lid to the man who had bred and trained the stallion as the final thank token, Gavin bowed to him from atop the magnificent animal. The crowd cheered again.

Keeping his mount to a sedate walk so that Lady Angelica and the soldiers following would not have to run, Gavin made his way to the inner courtyard of the palace. Here, he dismounted, handing the reigns to a waiting stable boy. Those soldiers trailing Gavin fanned out, placing themselves in their appointed spaces around the courtyard. Merikan stepped forward from the palace proper, bowing low. Gavin returned the bow and followed the Lord Protector up the stairs to the entrance of the Great Hall where the Royal Family waited. Gavin could not help his smile at Rayton's proud demeanour yet serious little face, Kaeley's mischievous wink before she schooled her own visage into the appropriate semblance of cool competence, and Alvin's calm air of support marred only by the twitching of his lips as he tried to hold back his own grin. In the Great Hall itself, Gavin knew he'd find the nobles and other visitors of state, and Chief Priest Romtani waiting before them all, ready to crown a new king.

Gavin took a steadying breath at the enormity of that, then gave the signal for his guards to precede the Royal Family into the hall. Merikan would go next, and Gavin himself would enter last, this time allowing Lady Angelica to lead him. Though most would see the loyal guard advancing before her liege, Gavin knew he followed the Lady Sorceress Angelica, Protector of the King and Royal Family, and that knowledge gave him great comfort.

***

Angie followed Merikan up the aisle, her tension mounting. She had found the coronation walk daunting, pressed close on every side by so many people, each a possible threat that she had no idea how to guard against. She might have found the experience more enjoyable if she knew how to use this magic that supposedly protected the Royal Family—*and why does that thought actually make sense*, she wondered—but instead, every muscle taut, she continued to worry as her imagination concocted numerous ways in which this whole morning could screw up. At least she had managed to hand out each token to the right artisan.

Gavin's smile as she had boosted him up to the saddle out at the gate had given her a little thrill of pleasure, a small measure of reassurance in this unnerving journey. She had wondered at his ease, so gracefully making it to the back of the horse without that great cloak getting in the way, or the new sword and scabbard fitted at his belt entangling in his legs. She had no idea how anyone could manoeuvre around such cumbersome obstacles, but Gavin made it look so easy. She wanted to turn and watch him now as he brought up the rear of this momentous procession, but she almost itched with the need to look everywhere at once, to keep her senses open in case ... something happened, something she could fight if necessary. Assuming she could work her dream power at all. Her shoulders bunched a little tighter as her tension raised another notch, just by her thinking.

Be calm, she thought to herself. *Be easy. You're no good to anyone if you're too worked up to notice there's a problem.* Besides, Merikan stood right there, able to work up any magical defence if trouble arose. The thought helped ease her a bit, and she moved to stand with Commander Nervain at the foot of the raised area in the centre of the Great Hall where the Chief Priest and the rest of the Royal Family now waited.

As Kaeley had explained, she and three others, along with a little girl, occupied the second of three steps, and Rayton stood by himself a step higher. The younger of the two men with Kaeley looked enough like Gavin and the dead King that Angie had no trouble identifying him as Alvin, the middle sibling. The golden woman at his side could only be his wife Maraenda, holding the hand of their young daughter Maraedeth, and the older gentleman kneeling next to Maraenda and farthest from the centre must be her Sorcerer, Shanor. Angie peered at him intently, but could get no sense of magic. She shook her head. *As though I know what another's magic would feel or look like.*

The Lord Protector stood at the top of the podium beside an austere-looking man in royal blue robes. Behind them sat a golden throne, a cushion cradling a magnificent crown resting on its seat.

Gavin waited at the foot of the steps until Chief Priest Romtani had spoken some words and invited the Dho'vani to take the stair with his son. Angie didn't pay attention to the words; she watched the people. As Gavin ascended, all the nobles knelt.

71

She glanced briefly at Nervain, but at the subtle shake of his head, she remained standing, along with all the other guards placed unobtrusively around the room. Kaeley and those with her took a knee as Gavin strode the tread they stood upon, but Rayton kept his feet, gazing solemnly up at his father as they came even. Romtani said something else, and together, father and son sank to their knees facing the podium.

The Chief Priest laid his hands first on Gavin's head, then on Rayton's. Angie glanced at Merikan, but this seemed part of the ceremony, for the Lord Protector watched with a satisfied air, not as one worried about this action. Angie paid attention to the next words as Romtani now held a hand over the head of each Royal before him, the Prince and the soon-to-be-King.

"From you, Gavin of Karundin, I take the title of Dho'vani. To you, Rayton of Karundin, I bestow the title of Dho'vani. Rise, Heir-Apparent to the Throne."

Little Rayton stood, his bearing proud yet humble. *Just like his father,* Angie thought, watching the two together. She realised that this was the first time she had seen them together. Their hair and eyes certainly matched, and she found herself wondering what Rayton had inherited from his mother. Remembering the boy's words about the portraits in the Great Hall, Angie let her eyes roam the walls. Many portraits lined the Hall, but she could only make out a few. The raised dais stood roughly three quarters of the way along the room; a room which spanned a fair distance, so most of the pictures seemed like distant blurs. What she could see gave the impression of a journey through the ages. Angie longed for a closer look, if only to see the beauty of masterpieces from various times in Karundin's history. Not unlike some of her restorative work for the museum back home. She shook her head, pulling herself away from thoughts of Earth and back to Karundin. She did not know which portrait depicted the late Dho'embra Hydae, Rayton's mother.

An affirmative shout rose from the gathered nobles, startling Angie. She looked towards Gavin and the Chief Priest, but Gavin still knelt on the top step, and Romtani had yet to pick up the crown.

Why does my mind keep wandering? Angie had thought this whole ceremony would enthrall her, give her a chance to observe those destiny had chosen her to protect, a chance to heighten her language skills, even a chance to watch the handsome Gavin unfettered. Instead, she kept missing parts of the coronation.

'It is often the way of dreams, is it not,' Sidvareh's voice whispered in her mind. 'To dwell on certain details, trusting everything else to work out right?'

Angie shrugged uncertainly.

'Your magic seeks out interference,' the Faery reassured her. 'By allowing your mind to wander, you in fact allow your magic to do its job.'

So my magic will make me scatter-brained? Angie thought. The Faery chuckled in response.

'To follow all of the ceremony would require a great deal of concentration, concentration that you can best utilize by letting your magic flow instead. However, if you consciously try to direct your magic, the King's enemies might locate you. The Lord Protector guards against visible attack; you guard against the unforeseen, the unknowable. Believe it or not, Lady, this unconscious use of your magic, the instinct rather than the will, will help you understand its uses later. Allow it to follow its course, and let your mind keep picking up the small details instead of watching the whole picture.'

Sidvareh's voice faded as Gavin stood, taking the last step up to join Chief Priest Romtani atop the podium. Angie watched, her gaze drawn to the crown the priest now turned to heft. He raised it high for all to see, the light glinting off its jewels looking almost as though the headdress itself emitted a sparkling radiance. Angie found she couldn't take her eyes away from this symbol of kingship as Romtani slowly lowered it to Gavin's dark locks. She watched the Chief Priest's lips move, but did not hear the words. If any spectator shifted or coughed or made any motion at all, she did not know. No sound reached her, nothing beyond that instant when the crown rested on the new King's brow.

The shimmering radiance of light beaming off the coronet exploded into shafts of power shooting out over the crowd. Angie had time only to note that six thin streaks of golden brilliance speared from the crown in six different directions, passing through objects as though they didn't exist, before a seventh cord of braided silver arced from the circlet directly toward Angie herself.

She dropped to her knees as light flashed in her head.

Angie looked up to see the workroom of Irving's shop, looking lost and forlorn with only emergency lights to provide any illumination. A painting stood on an easel in the corner, covered with a protective cloth. As she ghosted toward the tripod, the cloth fell away to reveal the painting of a castle from the fourteenth or fifteenth century; the painting which hid writing that the museum had wanted her to explore. The castle, Angie distantly noted, where a new King had just received his crown.

As she watched, the same silver light that had brought her here, the luminescence still swirling in her mind, flashed between her and the painting, and the castle morphed, becoming the words beneath, words she could almost understand. She studied them, committing what she could to memory. Just as she thought maybe she grasped the smallest hint of the meaning of this hidden document, something tugged at her, pulling her away. She tried to fight it.

'Now is not the time, My Lady,' Sidvareh called gently. 'When you need the spell, you will find it again.'

Angie blinked, seeing grey-streaked white marble beneath her hands where she knelt. She jerked her head up as Chief Priest Romtani pulled his hands back from the crown atop Gavin's head. It seemed no time had passed, but something had changed. No one had noticed her collapse, the movement looking like a loyal guard paying her obeisance to the new King, a commoner kneeling to royalty. Then she met Merikan's gaze.

The Lord Protector had not moved from his spot next to the Chief Priest, but his eyes had locked on Angie. She blinked and swallowed hard, then gave the tiniest of nods. Merikan took that as reassurance and she actually felt his regard shift away from her and back to his surroundings. She desperately hoped he could help explain what had just happened, because when she tried to ask Sidvareh, the little Faery remained strangely silent.

***

The time had finally come. Shanor knelt next to his royal charge studying the coronation proceedings very carefully. As Romtani conferred the title of Dho'vani from Gavin to Rayton, the Sorcerer kept all his senses attuned, physical and magical, but he saw nothing strange in the ethereal realm. As Gavin took to the top of the podium and the Chief Priest reached for the crown,

Shanor felt the first stirrings of power. He stared greedily at the soon-to-be-King, knowing none would think anything of his avid attention, as every noble in the Great Hall stared exactly where Shanor did, if for different reasons. A glance at the Lord Protector assured him that the subtly building power did not emanate from the other Sorcerer, but from the crown itself as it descended onto Gavin's head.

Had Shanor not prepared himself for this moment for so many seasons, had he not known to lock his concentration on each minutiae of the ceremony and commit to memory every little detail, the sudden radiance erupting from the crown might have blinded him enough to miss the significance of this sign only visible to those who could wield magic. That six points of light emerged rather than just one startled him, but the number did force him to hide a small smile as he attempted to follow each shaft.

But the pointers to power did not last nearly long enough and he struggled to contain his frustration. He had only discerned where one led, and could grasp a general direction for perhaps two more. Three out of six spells, though only one assured.

Shanor flicked his eyes briefly to Merikan again to gauge whether the Lord Protector had noted his interest, but the other Sorcerer had glanced at something behind Shanor. A surreptitious peek revealed a kneeling guard, a shimmer of silver reflecting off her helmet, but nothing that concerned Shanor.

Well and good then. The Sorcerer of Sahkarae returned his focus to the remains of the proceedings, though his attention turned inward. The book of spells did exist and the Royal Family guarded it, tied somehow to King and crown. Somewhere in time, it appeared that someone had divided up the spells, hiding them in different locations rather than keeping them together in one book. That would make Shanor's task more difficult, for he did not know which spells hid where, nor what additional precautions might exist to safeguard them. But he had a starting point. He would retrieve the one spell he knew of for certain and work from there. After all, he had waited so long already to achieve his goal and had perfected the art of patience. Soon enough, he would gather all six spells.

At that point, it would be up to Gavin and the Royals of Karundin whether they ceded their land and its riches back to Sahkarae willingly and returned themselves to the rule of true

Royalty, or whether Shanor would get to employ one or more of the ultimate spells to force them to his bidding. He thought he'd enjoy the latter a great deal more.

Chapter 9

"You couldn't have suggested this before I stood around for three hours in the heat of that helmet?" Angie complained, staring at the gown Merikan proffered now. The Lord Protector chuckled, then left the gown in the capable hands of Tabitha as the maid shuffled Angie off into a nearby room to change.

After the coronation, Gavin had held an open audience with nobles and commoners alike who wished to petition the King on some small matter, or simply to extend their congratulations. A sort of meet-and-greet to which Angie, still in her soldier's garb, had stood in attendance. Angie still wasn't clear on whether these petitioners had been previously assigned or had approached the King spontaneously. None had offered anything but pleasant attitudes and best wishes, and Angie soon found the slight weight of the coat of mail burdensome and the confining helmet felt like a sauna.

When Gavin finally dismissed the audience, Angie only wanted to yank the helmet off her head and shuck off the armour pressing down on her shoulders. She hadn't expected a whole change of wardrobe.

"The Royal Family will gather together for a time before the King progresses through the city, visiting several of the feasts," Merikan had explained. Angie had managed to remove the helmet and wipe her sweaty brow as he spoke and she nodded to show she heard. "In that brief respite, we will present you to the Royals and complete the ceremony that will reaffirm our connection as Protectors of the Royal House. You remember I mentioned it before?"

Angie had stared at him.

"I remember you said something about you and Dho'vani having arranged a private ceremony. That's all you said." He had regarded her with quiet consideration, but did not elaborate. Angie sighed. Apparently the men of Karundin did not always feel a need to explain things unless directly queried. "So what do I need to do?" she asked.

As though summoned by the question, Tabitha had hurried around the corner and, with a curtsey, handed a wrapped bundle to Merikan. The Lord Protector undid the silk ties of the bundle and pulled aside pale cloth to reveal a gown of finest silk in shades of blue and green.

"A gown suitable to the Lady Sorceress Angelica, Protector to the Royal Family. Tabitha will help make you presentable and bring you to the receiving room King Gavin has arranged. There we will have a simple ceremony where you merely must act as yourself, and then you will walk next to the King in your rightful place for all to see unfettered by any disguise."

"Wait! I thought you said I had to keep hidden. Do you think it safe to reveal my presence now?"

"King Gavin has deemed it appropriate, yes," Merikan had replied.

Angie had narrowed her eyes. "That's not a yes on your part."

Merikan only smiled enigmatically.

"I suggest you hurry, My Lady. I'm sure the gown will prove more comfortable than chain mail and helmets."

The room Angie now found herself in boasted a basin with steaming water. Not a full bath—she suspected she did not have time for that—but at least she could clean up a bit after sweating in the soldier's regalia for so long.

In little time at all, Angie found herself staring at her own image in a full-length mirror Tabitha had directed her to off to the side of the room. Someone had obviously made the dress to her measurements. The bodice swept down at front and back, and to a lesser extent on the sides, half sapphire and half emerald. It had a scooped neck trimmed in a subtle display of diamonds and opals. Sleeves of an iridescent blue-green material far paler than the bodice billowed from the shoulders to cinch at the wrist without a seam between the two, leaving the undersides of her arms bare. The sleeves flowed to delicate points part-way down the matching skirt, full enough to allow freedom of movement yet not so full as to prove cumbersome. Soft-soled slippers, one topped with a sapphire and one with an emerald, felt remarkably comfortable and somehow did not look garish or gaudy as Angie had first feared.

Tabitha had arranged Angie's honey-dark hair into an intricate collection of gentle curls, some pulled back into a kind of tail and others draping artistically about her neck and back. The maid had threaded diamonds and emeralds into the coiffure. A sapphire and opal necklace graced Angie's neck, and similar jewels dangled from her ears. She could only stare at the woman gaping back from the mirror, each eye accentuated and enhanced by the dual hues of the ensemble. She looked like a Princess.

"Tabitha," Angie breathed in awe. "Look what you've done. It's incredible. But I can't go anywhere looking like this. I look like ... well, like a Royal."

Tabitha's image appeared beside Angie's in the mirror.

"I've only brought out your nature for all to see, My Lady," the maid replied with a gentle smile. "You do shimmer as bright as those jewels. You keep King Gavin and the Royal Family safe, and you'll be more than a Royal to us. You're the symbol of hope."

"Tabitha," Angie turned to her, a quivering fear in her gut at the woman's words. "I am not more important than the King. I'm just me. I don't know anything about ... that is, I don't know how—"

Tabitha's hand on her arm stopped Angie, and her serious tone had Angie paying real attention to the maid's words.

"My Lady, I know you have had a difficult time of things, that your situation is a tad confusing and discomfiting. Know though that the appearance of the Lady Sorceress, especially on the day of the King's coronation, *will* bring hope to the people. With the tragic and mysterious death of the old King, to know that King Gavin has you at his side will bring comfort and a certain piece of mind. Whoever has struck at the Royal Family will surely think twice before attempting to do so again with you guarding the King. The King shelters us and leads us, but you make that possible by sheltering him."

"But I don't know how," Angie whispered.

Tabitha smiled and patted her arm.

"Just keep on as you have, My Lady. Even if you have to pretend for now, if you keep an outer calm and semblance of competence, the people won't know your doubts. You'll figure it out soon enough, and our confidence in you will be rewarded."

Angie stared at the woman, glimpsing whole new levels of complexity and pragmatism from her. Impulsively, she hugged her.

"Thank you Tabitha," she said.

"My Lady!" Tabitha tried to disentangle herself from Angie's grip, her face flushed with embarrassment and amusement. Angie laughed.

"I guess it's time to meet the rest of the Family," Angie said and followed Tabitha to the door.

***

Gavin had assembled his family in the Lesser Hall, explaining only that one thing remained of the coronation before they could advance to the Feasts around the city. Kaeley wore a slight knowing smile and Rayton bounced on his toes, a frown of speculation on his face. Maraedeth sat playing at her parents' feet as Alvin and Maraenda stood chatting amicably of inconsequential matters with Gavin. Alvin knew he could not pry a secret from his brother if Gavin didn't want him to know something, so he kept the subject light. Maraenda had tried to win a hint of Gavin's intentions with a couple of charming smiles and suggestions, but she also knew her attempts would fail, as always. She did so more out of habit than expectation.

"One day, I'll win past your guard, Your Majesty," she said with a smile, though in jest. "If I can ever ferret out one of your secrets from your very lips, surely I will have the luck of the gods."

"And what need of luck for one of your charm and beauty, Cardae?"

Alvin smiled at his brother's reply. Although his marriage to Maraenda had begun for political reasons, the two deeply loved each other, and Alvin knew he need never fear Gavin's interference.

Maraenda's Sorcerer Shanor stood slightly apart from the Royal Family, yet Gavin made sure to make the man welcome. Gavin's father had believed in keeping relations with Sahkarae strong and Gavin saw no need to alter that stance. Maraenda had become family through her marriage to Alvin; Shanor, as her sorcerer, had in a sense also joined the family, and his council and protection added to Merikan's. While Merikan stood as Lord Protector, Shanor assumed a similar position to his own charge, for although Maraenda had become a Princess of Karundin, she did not have the same kind of protection that those of Karundin blood shared. With Shanor able to concentrate on ensuring the safety and well-being of Maraenda and Maraedeth, Merikan need not stretch his own abilities beyond the Royal Family.

Or rather, that *had* detailed Merikan's position, until the arrival of Lady Sorceress Angelica. Now his duties would revert to their original intention; to protect the Lady Sorceress while she watched over the Royals. Once this last ceremony became official.

As if in answer to his thoughts, the Lord Protector swept into the room. He carried the helmet that the Lady Angelica had worn as she followed Gavin on his procession. With a low bow to Gavin, Merikan presented the helmet to the King, then took up a position facing the entrance. Gavin moved to stand nearest the door, the head gear tucked under his arm. The rest of the family took up their assigned places with varying degrees of speculation on each face, forming two small rows. Rayton stood across from Gavin; Kaeley moved to Rayton's side, mirroring Alvin; and Shanor took up the next spot, facing Maraenda, her daughter in her arms, while Merikan stood nearly between those two not of Karundin blood, so that the eight members of the group formed a slender U-shape.

Merikan spoke in a strong voice.

"Your Majesty, King Gavin of Karundin, and the Royal Family here gathered, I present to you the Lady Sorceress Angelica." The Lady glided into the Hall with the announcement.

Gavin clenched his jaw to keep his mouth from dropping open when he saw her. Already a handsome woman, the ministrations to her hair and clothing had transformed her into a rare beauty, easily as striking as any queen. The sun streaming through the windows caught the gems in her bodice and hair, causing sparkles like fire to dance about her and give her an added air of mystery and otherworldliness.

The indrawn gasps from those who did not know of Lady Angelica's presence and their recognition of the connection between the helmet and the Lady brought Gavin's attention back to his duties.

He gave her a regal nod, which she returned with a small

curtsey.

"My Lady Sorceress, I bid you welcome to the House and kingdom of Karundin," he said. "If it please My Lady, I beg that she consider renewing our contract. As I guard my land and my people, I ask that you extend your protection to myself and my Royal Family that we may fulfill our duties and safeguard our Royal charge."

Lady Angelica regarded him solemnly with those jewel-like eyes before drawing in a breath that only trembled slightly.

"I will continue to protect you to the best of my ability, my liege," she replied, her voice clear of any trepidation. "To you and the Royal Family of Karundin, I pledge my support and assure your refuge under my care."

She extended her right hand and Gavin took her fingers in his. His bow and her curtsey mirrored each other and Gavin felt a spark flare between them. By the Lady's slightly widened eyes, he knew she had also perceived this bonding, proof of the ceremony's success, but she made no other reaction. With a hint of reluctance, Gavin released her grip.

"My Lord," Merikan intoned, contributing his final touch to the ceremony. "I humbly request that you accept my continued service to Karundin and to Lady Sorceress Angelica." Gavin gave a small nod. "My Lady Sorceress," Merikan turned to his daughter. "As Lord Protector, it is my duty to guard you with my life. It would honour me if you would consent to my continued guidance and support while you discharge your duties to the Royal House. Will you accept my meagre assistance?"

"I will, Lord Protector Merikan, and I thank you for it."

And thus did the Lord Protector resume his original purpose; to protect the Lady Sorceress, that she might devote herself to the care and well-being of the Royal House who guarded the spellbook of the Sorcerer Borun, so that his six most powerful and dreadful Spells of Supremacy might not fall into covetous hands.

***

Shanor hadn't known what to expect when Gavin had the Royals gather in the Lesser Hall before they made their way through the city to some of the commoner's feasts, but he certainly had not anticipated the appearance of a sorceress, let alone *the* Lady Sorceress to the Royal House of Karundin. The helmet Merikan had presented to the King had clearly identified her as the supposed soldier who had walked at Gavin's side during the procession through the city, an indication of her protection even when no one knew of her presence.

Or rather, that few knew of this woman. From the reactions of those around him, Shanor suspected that only Alvin, Maraenda and little Maraedeth had remained as ignorant as himself about the existence of this woman. Obviously Gavin and Merikan had known her, and Kaeley's pleased smile strongly hinted at a previous acquaintance. Rayton's reaction, however, caught Shanor completely off guard.

The child had waited solemnly while the small ceremony took place, but as soon as the ritual ended, the little boy broke into a wide grin and flung himself at the woman.

"I'm so happy you can meet everyone now, Angie," he had said.

The implication of why she had remained in hiding nearly vanished in Shanor's surprise at the familiarity between the two. How long had this Lady Angelica graced Karundin with her presence? Had the death of King Grayton brought her out of hiding? And from where? Surely had she concealed herself anywhere close to the castle, she would have appeared right after that murder, or even found a way to prevent it, yet he only learned of her now.

Then a more troubling thought: how did Karundin come to have a Lady Sorceress at all? The last had died along with her unborn child, so where did this Angelica fit in? An imposter would not fool Merikan, so she had to have legitimate claim. Unless the Lord Protector hoped to draw out the previous King's murderer by introducing an unknown element? Her eyes marked her as a true sorceress, but did she truly have claim to the title Lady Sorceress of Karundin?

Shanor suddenly had a memory of Merikan's gaze drawn by the guard at the coronation, the reflection off her helmet, at the moment that magic had revealed the location of the six spells. What if Merikan *had* in fact noted Shanor's interest and had looked to the Sorceress to gauge her reaction? Or if the Sorceress had seen something that Shanor missed?

Without knowing more, he could not guess the extent of her powers or what these Protectors knew. He might have to accelerate his plans, begin his search immediately, before this Sorceress could discern his intentions or find a way to block his actions. He must work quickly to achieve his desired goal, and yet maintain a certain degree of caution, even more necessary with another of the power keeping a watch on affairs.

Or must he instead tread far more carefully, use an even greater degree of caution where he would rather hasten his search?

His mind worked furiously, conceiving and abandoning plans, though his face and manner revealed nothing. Even while he greeted this mysterious woman face to face with the utmost propriety and respect, none could guess that he planned to conquer or else destroy those she sought to protect. Gazing into her bi-coloured eyes, he wondered what powers she held, and how long he had before she knew to oppose him.

What excuse could he make to escape the rest of the coronation pageantry and begin his real search without raising the suspicions of royalty and sorcerers alike? Could he escape the Royal Feast that evening, or perhaps even the procession through the city before that? Who would miss the Cardae's Protector, especially with a new Sorceress to gape at?

How long before he must test his strength against this stranger, a strength aligned with the might of the Lord Protector? He desperately hoped that the first spell he found proved one of the more powerful ones. Although among the highest sorcerers Sahkarae had produced in generations, Shanor would feel far more secure with a powerful spell in hand once Merikan and Angelica learned his true intentions. The more time he had before that, the better for Shanor and his own King.

Surely no one would notice if he slipped away once they left the Lesser Hall.

Chapter 10

Angie woke to the grey light of predawn with gritty eyes and a fierce desire to just roll over and go back to sleep. But she couldn't. Gavin had informed her of a breakfast meeting that she must not miss despite the late night they had all shared.

After touring through the city with the new King and his family, visiting numerous feasts in the streets with wildly cheerful people—all the more joyous when they learned of Angie's presence and that she had stood with the King through the entire coronation ceremony, thanks to that helmet that Gavin had insisted she carry with them for recognition—the Royal Family had moved on to their own great feast with Karundin's nobles in a huge Hall that took quite some time to walk through. After many flowery speeches, far too much food and more than a little wine, servants had cleared a space for dancing, and the carousing of nobles had lasted far into the night. As Protector to the Royal Family, Angie could not leave until Gavin did, and as the newly crowned monarch, he could not—or at least had chosen not to—leave until the last noble had stumbled from the Hall. Having already lost most of the previous night preparations for the coronation, Angie had clung to wakefulness by a hair.

And now, with perhaps two or three hours of sleep, she felt pretty miserable, her only consolation that she had drunk very little so at least she didn't suffer from a hangover. Someone had watered the wine, and though she touched the cup to her mouth after each toast, she had done no more than wet her lips for the most part.

Still, she might manage another few minutes of rest ....

"I am afraid not, My Lady," Sidvareh said, the small Faery appearing in a violet mist in front of Angie and standing on a platform of air. "The King will explain his charge today, so that you will understand what you protect. That is the purpose of this early meeting."

"That doesn't explain why I can't sleep just a bit longer," Angie complained, her jaw cracking in a huge yawn as she tried to snuggle under her warm blanket again.

"I cannot attend that meeting." Something in the small woman's whisper, so solemn yet firm, drew Angie erect, blinking furiously as she tried to explain her sudden unease.

"Will you be safe waiting here?" Angie asked. "Do we need to hide you somewhere?"

A tiny smile tugged at the Faery's mouth, but her eyes looked almost sad.

"I cannot accompany you any longer, My Lady Sorceress. I must return home."

Angie stared at her, not wanting to comprehend yet already feeling the loss.

"But ... why?"

"It is not a Faery's place to dwell overlong in the mind of a human."

"Oh, Sidvareh, I haven't hurt you, have I? I didn't realise that you being with me would cause pain."

"No, My Lady," Sidvareh's smile blossomed across her face. "It does not hurt, but neither is it natural. I have simply accomplished the task to which your Lady Mother bound me. I helped you find your way home and guided you in remembering the duty to which you were born. It is not for me to learn the secrets that must remain yours."

"That duty, Sidvareh, to protect the Royal House; how can I do that when I don't even know the first thing about this magic I have? I can't define it, control it, influence it; how can I use it? Who will teach me if not you?"

Sidvareh laughed, a tinkling of chimes.

"Oh, Angelica, I could not teach you even if I knew how your powers worked. I am a creature of magic; to explain how to work magic would be akin to trying to describe how to breathe. I *am* magic; I cannot wield it. And yours is a very special kind of power. I do not know any who could teach you the full might of your abilities."

Angie stared at her in growing horror. This little woman had brought her here to this strange land to perform miracles, then told her no one could help her.

"Do not fear so, Lady Angelica," she soothed. "You do not stand alone. Others will assist where they may."

"But you just said—"

"I said none could teach you the full might of your magic, not that you stood alone. Lord Merikan will lend you great support, and the King too. All will help you learn what you must, but they do not understand what you can do any more than the rest of us. You are unique, My Lady, and you must feel out what you are capable of doing. But do not fear that learning. Experiment, let your instincts guide you. When you dreamed of Karundin, did you ever have to stop to think 'What will I do next? What action can I take?', or did you simply do what needed doing?"

Angie thought about that, tried to remember events from her dream-world. And realised Sidvareh spoke true.

"I just did what I had to," she conceded. "Without having to wonder if I could or whether it made sense. But I always knew that I dreamed, and that most of the time, things would work out well in the end."

"And that is the instinct that you must learn to trust and follow here and now."

Sidvareh walked forward on her invisible road of air and reached out a small hand to touch Angie's cheek, the sadness in her large green teardrop eyes once more.

"I have brought you as far as I can, my dear child," she said softly. "But this is as far as Lady Sorceress Katerina bound me. I must leave before you learn of the charge given unto House Karundin, and thus complete my own charge."

"So this is goodbye," Angie whispered, her voice hoarse and her eyes burning with more than sleeplessness. "Will I ever see you again?"

Sidvareh's smile threatened to spill Angie's unshed tears down her cheeks as the Faery floated backwards on iridescent dragonfly wings.

"If you have need of me, you have but to call."

Angie bit her lower lip as she nodded her understanding.

A gentle violet mist enveloped Sidvareh.

"Goodbye Angie," she whispered, and the Faery faded, taking Angie's last link to Earth with her.

"Goodbye Sidvareh," and the dam burst as Angie cried.

***

When Commander Nervain opened the door to the King's solar and announced the arrival of the Lady Sorceress, both Gavin and Merikan rose to greet her. She wore an emerald green tunic that fell to just above her knees with long tapered sleeves and a curved neckline over something akin to tights, only worn looser about the leg. It reminded Gavin somewhat of the clothing he and Merikan had first found her in, though the cloth appeared new. On another woman, the strange combination of a man's garb tailored with a female form in mind would seem disturbing, yet somehow, on Lady Angelica, Gavin thought it just looked right.

The sheen in her slightly red-rimmed eyes, however, did not look right, though she tried to cover it with a smile. Gavin thought at first the excessive drink from last night might account for her condition. Servants had kept the glasses full, every noble felt he or she had to offer a toast, and of course, the King and his entourage had to drink along with every good wish. Luckily, Gavin had had the foresight to make sure the head table only received well-watered wine. Still, after so many toasts, even taking the smallest sips, he knew he, at least, had consumed more than enough, and the Lady Angelica at his side had matched him. But her expression now hinted at sadness rather than discomfort.

As he tried to form the words to enquire about her distress, Merikan simply moved forward and took her arm, guiding her to a cushioned chair by the fire.

"My Lady," he queried, "are you well?"

Gavin knew an unexpected instant of resentment that the Lord Protector had stepped in to offer comfort before he himself could, but quashed that unfair thought quickly. The Lord Protector watched over the Lady Sorceress, his own daughter; the King should have no feelings beyond approval for that, yet Gavin wished his own hands guided her. He shook his head at such foolishness and pushed past any examination of these ill-advised sentiments.

"Can I get you something, My Lady?" Gavin asked instead. "Rayton tells me you have a fondness for tea."

"Tea would be wonderful, Your Majesty," she replied.

"Please call me Gavin in private, My Lady," he said as he moved to fetch the tea from the table his man Jamison had prepared earlier.

"Then you must call me Angie," she stated.

He kept the cup in his hand from rattling as he savoured that simple sentence; not Angelica, but Angie, the shortened name made so familiar somehow seeming that much more intimate. Again, he thrust aside the absurdity of his pleasure, knowing she asked all those she liked to use the foreshortened term of endearment.

For goodness sake, he chided himself as he passed her the steaming cup and basked in her appreciative smile, *you barely know her. Stop acting the addlepated suitor.*

"Tell me what's troubled you this morning, child," Merikan said, sitting across from her. Gavin took the third chair set near the fire.

"Just ... a little overwhelmed, I guess," she answered. "The thought that I was alone in a strange place now, abandoned by whatever force brought me here." A shadow in Merikan's eye suggested the Lord Protector understood her angst. Angie gave a small, wry smile. "But I'm not alone, am I?" she said, reaching for Merikan's hand. She turned her face to Gavin and her expression near took his breath away. "I have you all to help guide me."

She inhaled deeply, released Merikan's hand and perched forward on the chair, tea cup in hand.

"Now," she said, her tone turning to the matter at hand, "if I am to guard you, I must understand what you protect. Is that correct?"

"It is," Gavin confirmed. Merikan rose and moved to the side table where Jamison had also arranged the morning repast.

"Some charge passed down through the generations," Angie said. "Something no outsider might discover through questioning the Royal Family. Which, given poor Kaeley's reaction, seems to have a rather potent side-effect."

"As to that," Merikan said, handing Angie a plate with bread, fruit, cheese, and a boiled egg, "I'm afraid it was your nature that caused so strong a reaction. Because of your magic, and your desire to learn, I believe the protections around Kaeley triggered at a critical level. Yet you also knew enough to reverse the spell, instinctively. Kaeley came to no harm."

"That's hardly the point," Angie frowned as Merikan retreated back to the food. "*She's fine now so no harm done?* That's the best you can do? What if I'd intended her harm? What if I hadn't retracted the question and wished so hard that those few moments hadn't happened? The Royal Family has enemies; do you tell me now that to incapacitate one of them, you simply ask after their charge then wait for them to choke to death?"

"Of course not!" Merikan turned to stare at her, a half-filled plate held tightly in mottled fingers. "The spell reacted to *you*, to your desire to understand. Your own magic tried to overcome that spell, and Kaeley's magic tried to protect her. I didn't think any had power enough to trigger such a reaction. Any other sorcerer of strength would simply have found Kaeley mute to such questions, or hearing nonsense that he thought as truth until later reflection proved the blatant falsehood."

The Lady Sorceress paled, her bi-coloured eyes wide in shock.

"You mean," she whispered, "I nearly killed her because of my ignorance in magic."

"No," Gavin shot Merikan an angry glare. He wanted to hold her, give her some comfort in the face of her misery, then decided he could at least go to her, show his support. He rose, then knelt beside her chair, laying a gentle hand on her tense arm. "She might have fainted, 'tis true," he reassured her in a soft voice, "but she would not have suffered lasting damage. You, of all people, cannot cause such damage to a Royal in ignorance. You do need to master your powers, to learn what you can accomplish, but you must also understand that without provocation, your very nature will not allow you to harm us. Once you saw the problem, you found a way to fix it."

Merikan moved to stand on Angie's other side, the food plate forgotten behind him on the table.

"What happened to Kaeley cannot happen again, My Lady," he said, his expression pensive as he watched Gavin rise and retreat to his seat. "You found a unique flaw in the spell, one I believe only someone of your stature could exploit. You asked the question when no monarch sat the throne, so the spell tried to find another way to safeguard the girl. Had you asked yesterday after the coronation but before the Royals recognised you, the spell would inform Gavin of Kaeley's distress and even your formidable powers would have to contend with the protections of the spellbook through the King. Now, with the ceremony of Recognition between Protectors and Royals in place, you could ask Kaeley the same question and she would refer you to the King."

Gavin watched as Angie tried to process all that. He sympathised with her confusion and nearly smiled when she turned her perplexed regard to him.

"All this mystery because of a spellbook?" she asked with incredulity, surprising a laugh from him.

"Indeed," he said. "A powerful and terrible spellbook." He nodded his thanks as Merikan retrieved a plate of breakfast for him, his demeanour reverting to solemnity. "It once belonged to a Sorcerer named Borun, around the time when Karundin became independent of Sahkarae." Gavin, of course, knew this history well, having learned it from an early age, yet he found relating it to Angie invigorating, almost like reliving his favourite lessons as a child. Without meaning to, he dropped into the cadence of his old tutor as he told the story.

"Long ago, Sahkarae and Karundin stood as one land, though even then, the monarchs made the distinction between the northern and the southern portions of the kingdom. The Royals would divide the rule between siblings, so that the same Family oversaw the administration of the whole kingdom, yet each could look after the trials of his or her portion without sacrificing the needs of the whole land. Each child looked to the guidance of the Over King or Queen, for supreme authority rested with the eldest Royal, regardless of gender, but the everyday rule belonged to the siblings.

"The southern kingdom, now Sahkarae, bordered the sea and derived much trade and resources from its port towns, including the pearl-beds off the shore from the capital. It also had access to a wealth of iron and silver from mines in the western foothills.

"The northern kingdom, now Karundin, had fertile land that grew a plethora of crops to trade and keep the people in abundance even in lean times. We also had forests of silkworms, mines of gemstones, and rivers of gold. Each resource necessitated oversight, yet with the divided rule, each Royal could devote a suitable amount of time and energy into utilizing these riches in the best way possible, to the greatest benefit of the people. And as the rule of the land resided in one Family with many parts, the entire land benefited from each part.

"It became a centre of wealth and learning, a draw to all manner of people. As with any large centre of commerce, the bad came with the good; those hoping to benefit from the hard work of others, thieves and criminals, yet mostly the land flourished. The learned came to teach and pass on their knowledge, building schools, universities, libraries. The skilled came to offer their labour and prowess, giving us master stonemasons, carpenters, gold- and silversmiths, artists. And the powerful came to spread their understanding of the nature of magic, sorcerers and sorceresses looking for apprentices, searching for new spells, seeking to share their skill by giving aid to those in need.

"One such Sorcerer was Borun, a man with a great gift for magic, a keen intelligence and ingenuity."

Here Gavin paused, sipping at his tea to regain moisture for his drying tongue. Merikan took up the tale while the King took a bite of cheese, reminding Angie that she, too, held breakfast in her lap. Her gaze turned toward the Lord Protector as she nibbled some fruit, her attention rapt on the unfolding history.

"Borun had a high facility to adapt old spells or create new ones," Merikan said. "While the ability itself is not necessarily rare, Borun's aptitude bordered on genius, even revolutionary. Masters sought him out to discuss and test their theories, apprentices vied for his guidance and attention, and the nobles courted him for his advice and to add to their own prestige. Borun loved nothing better than to overcome a challenge, to accomplish the impossible, as it were. He was basically a good man, prone to the trials and temptations we all face, and susceptible to flattery and folly alike. I think it important to remember that. Even though what he created could wreak incredible harm, Borun did not intend his work to cause strife. He wanted to accomplish what others could not, and so he did. His pride led to the downfall of many, yet his scruples and skill also saved countless others. His is a cautionary tale on many fronts, not the least of which is that you cannot control how others might try to use your work, regardless of your original intentions or goals."

"As Borun sought to make a name for himself," Gavin took up the tale, "the Royals fell into dissension. Over King Markalan had chosen a child of his second marriage over the middle son of his first Queen to rule in Karundin after a hunting accident killed the previous Royal. It was not unheard of for half-siblings to rule, but Amaekar, the passed-over son, felt slighted. He had a terrible temper and an over-inflated opinion of his own worth—just two of several unsavoury drawbacks to his character—that King Markalan recognised as unsuitable for a leader. He assigned other tasks for Amaekar and had thought the lad settled, but Amaekar merely bided his time, building his fury and ambitions to a fever pitch. He found others dissatisfied with their lot and began, in secret, to foment rebellion and war.

"Into this fragile situation came Borun, perhaps ignorant of Amaekar's true intentions, but likely thrilled with his Royal patronage. Amaekar charged Borun with creating hypothetical spells that could win kingdoms with little damage done to the populous. In that manner, Amaekar hoped to appease Borun's morals, for if one could fight a war with little bloodshed, then few would suffer the caprices of tyrants overlong. Or so Amaekar implied and Borun believed."

Gavin saw Angie shiver as she finished her tea and set the cup aside, no doubt envisioning the manipulations of cruel men from long ago. He left Merikan to explain the spells Borun devised for the spurned Royal.

"Borun developed six spells to fulfill Amaekar's desires, six brilliant and terrifying incantations that changed the world.

"Transformation may not seem like much, but imagine having the ability to walk in on your enemy in the guise of a friend, or being able to fly across an otherwise impassable chasm, charge over many furlongs in the fleet form of a stallion or wildcat, or spy upon any you wished as a favoured pet. Any shape so long as the mass closely resembled your own.

"Normal spells of healing take time and energy, but imagine Instantaneous Healing, a sort of continuous infusion of health and the ability to heal all but the most mortal wounds, and even that, I'm not certain Borun's spell couldn't counter.

"Mind Control could wreak much havoc, turning even the most loyal of comrades into bitter foes.

"One spell he called Adoration, which would force people into willing slavery, eager to do anything for the one they Adored, unable to think for themselves or do anything save the will of the spell caster. Their own needs and desires paled in their effort to please their master."

Gavin could hear the disgust in the Lord Protector's description and found himself restless rehashing this troubling history. He rose to stand in front of the fire, conscious of Angie's gaze as she listened to her father.

"One spell can create an army out of clay, birthing soldiers immune to pain, mud people to fight against flesh and blood, thus sparing your own troops much of the battle.

"And finally, perhaps the most frightening spell of all; Immeasurable Power. By siphoning the life-force of others, the sorcerer could endlessly augment his strength and use of magic. Every spell has a cost, draining strength and vitality, the stronger the spell, the more exhausted the spell-caster. But imagine having no limit, being able to cast spell after spell with no consequences to yourself. And imagine having Borun's other five spells in your arsenal and no limit to your ability to wield them. Truly a horrifying premise if one lacks the conscience to stay such magic."

Angie gaped at them.

"Someone such as Amaekar?" she whispered. "Did he use those spells?"

"He did," Merikan confirmed, a solemn weight in his expression.

"The war was terrible," Gavin said. "It ripped the kingdom apart. There is a swath of dead land between Sahkarae and Karundin now where it is said fields of clay soldiers sprang up, then died in untold numbers, taking several thousands of humans with them. Magic from those trying to oppose what Borun had created and Amaekar took for his own flew day and night until finally, one sorceress found a way to counter the worst of Amaekar's vanity. With the help of Borun himself, who had seen what his genius had wrought yet had been unable to wrest his spells from Amaekar unaided, the evil Prince was defeated. But Sahkarae and Karundin were left rent in two, both geographically and culturally, for countrymen had fought each other, and the immediacy of the perceived betrayals lay heavy on every mind. It did not matter that magic had turned neighbours into slaves with no minds of their own; it only mattered that people remembered their feelings of helplessness and loss of trust, and such feelings of betrayal do not heal quickly.

"The Over King had perished along with most of his children as they sought to aid their people, and many nobles had died with them. The kingdoms agreed to remain separate, under their own rule as they strove to find some normalcy of life, and to seek time to recover.

"Borun took up his spellbook and placed it in the hands of the surviving Royal chosen to govern Karundin, garnering his pledge to guard the book. The Sorceress swore to protect the Royal, and Borun promised to protect the Sorceress.

"And thus came about the Lord Protector and Lady Sorceress who would guard the Royals of Karundin while they ensured the safety of Borun's Spells of Supremacy. That spellbook, My Lady Sorceress, Angie, is what lies in my charge."

Angie shook her head slowly, her eyes wide. Her hands gripped the arms of the chair as though seeking some sort of lifeline away from the chaos she had just heard.

"But why?" she asked softly. "Why guard something so vile? Why didn't Borun or the Sorceress, or the Royal even, just destroy the book?"

"That, I'm afraid, is part of the pride of Borun," Merikan answered, kneeling before Angie and prying her right hand from the chair so he could hold it, perhaps to instill his own strength and calm to her, or maybe seeking his own share of comfort. "He believed his creation a mark of the highest striving of human achievement, something others could look at and see that war could only lead to folly, as the use of such spells would ultimately prove. He hoped, in his naivete, that seeing this absolute display of the capabilities of magic in warfare would inspire people to abandon dreams of conquest at the cost of so damning one's soul, which, if all men shared his morals, might seem all the more noble, yet proved in fact selfish and far too simplistic. But at the time of inventing these spells, Borun truly believed his genius would save the world, and so he made his spellbook indestructible so that it would endure throughout history. By the time he realised his folly, he had no way to erase what he had done. So he did the next best thing, in his mind, and created a link between the Royals of Karundin and his spells."

"And what's to stop a Royal from misusing that charge?" Angie asked, looking directly up into Gavin's eyes as he stood beside her by the fire. "If another Amaekar should rise from the ranks of the Royals, what's to stop him from taking his charge and turning it against those he's supposed to lead?"

Gavin smiled grimly. He remembered asking his father the very same question.

"Magic, Angie. Borun linked us to his book in such a way that we cannot misuse his spells. Our protective magic stems from the book, though some of us have powers beyond that. Should we seek to misuse the book, that protection turns deadly. To my knowledge, no Royal of Karundin has ever felt the temptation to employ Borun's spells. In fact, one of my ancestors hoped to make the possibility of finding the book even more challenging by separating the spells and securing each page in a different location, each with its own separate safeguards."

"Which explains the six points of light," Angie murmured, staring into the fire.

"You saw them, then?" Gavin asked. He had noted the strange brilliance as Karundin's crown descended upon his head, remembered how time seemed to slow as the knowledge of each spell's location and safeguards settled into the back of his mind. If he concentrated hard, he knew he could discern the status of each page, though he didn't know if he would understand which spell lay where, and he certainly had no desire to find out.

Angie nodded. "It looked like the light caught the reflections off the crown and sent glitters of gold through the room, but I definitely saw six points of radiant power." She brought her gaze back to his. "If *I* could see that," she wanted to know, her voice turning anxious, "then couldn't others? What if the person who ... who killed your father could see that too? Is it possible an enemy waited for just that possibility? To find Borun's spellbook?"

Gavin frowned at the thought.

"Only those connected to the Royal House and the direct line of protection would see anything unusual," he said. "The Monarch and the Protectors. Not even Rayton, as next in line, would see where the power led. Who else would even know to look for anything out of the ordinary?"

"Katerina would do that," Merikan said, his tone highlighting a new worry and drawing Gavin's attention. "She'd jump to conclusions no one else saw that later proved true. I believe she saved Angie that way." The Lord Protector regarded Angie's worried visage. "I don't know if Lady Angelica shares that talent, but now that she has voiced this concern, I don't think we can dismiss it." He rose to stand beside Gavin, his hand still in Angie's, and looked at the King. "I hope it just a fear brought on by hearing of Borun's folly, but we should not disregard the

96

notion."

Angie stood to join them, pulling her hand away from Merikan's to wrap her arms about herself as though chilled.

"You can tell if the spells are safe?" she asked Gavin. He nodded. "Then it is time I started doing my duty to Karundin." She smiled sardonically. "And to do that, I must learn about magic; my own, and the capabilities of other sorcerers. I know Merikan can teach me much, but if I recall correctly, you also have a library that will help fill in the appalling gaps in my knowledge of Karundin and her surrounding lands." She paused, gritting her teeth in frustration. "But I also must stand beside the King as he administers his new duties. How am I supposed to protect you and learn everything I need to and still manage a bit of sleep?"

Gavin snorted his amusement then quickly schooled his features into a careful blankness at Angie's glare.

"We'll work something out," he promised, then winced as he recalled the rest of his duties for the day. "Until then, I'm afraid I do have the afternoon full of audiences and petitions, which the nobles will expect you to attend."

"Will I offend them if I bring a book, in case they prattle on like some of them did yesterday?" she asked in a cross between hope and dismay.

Gavin grinned.

"My dear Lady, I very much look forward to seeing their expressions when you so callously dismiss their concerns."

"I know just the book," Merikan added, having sat though innumerable unfruitful audiences in his time as Lord Protector. Gavin knew that if something requiring the attention of either sorcerer should occur, they would not hesitate to show their support. He just wished that he could get away with a book too, just to winnow out empty flattery versus something of import that the King must attend to. Sadly, he knew that option did not lie before him, and he envied Angie the possibility even as he understood just how very much she had yet to learn.

Chapter 11

Angie had never gone on a Royal Progress before, had never even considered such a thing, Royal or otherwise, until three days ago when Gavin had announced he would begin one and Angie would accompany him. As the newly crowned monarch, one of Gavin's duties entailed that he see the kingdom and its citizens for himself, or at least parts of it. They would journey through the country, stopping at various nobles' manors and castles, as well as visiting with the common folk, as Gavin connected with his people and they with him.

While such a Progress often took place in late spring or early summer in order to take advantage of the most favourable weather conditions, Gavin had decided to go now, in mid-autumn, in part to give Angie a chance to study the history and current customs first hand. It afforded her the perfect opportunity to learn the land and her peoples while travelling it, and it gave Merikan the chance to teach her about magic away from the prying eyes of the court. For protection and escort, Gavin brought Commander Nervain and fifty elite soldiers to watch over himself and Kaeley, leaving Angie and Merikan to deal with magic.

"I'm going to miss you, Angie," Rayton said as he gazed up at her from large, moist grey eyes. "Who's going to eat cake with me?"

Angie smiled and crouched to put herself on an even level with the young Dho'vani.

"You'll just have to see if you can sneak a few past Maraenda, now won't you?" she said with a wink and a twinkle in her own eyes so that Rayton wouldn't tear up. "And maybe, if you talk really sweet, your Uncle Alvin will have a bit on hand to tide you through all those meetings."

Behind Rayton, Tre'vani Alvin smiled, Gavin's younger brother a shorter, paler version of the King. Gavin had left Alvin in charge of Rayton and the day-to-day governing of the city. Though governing officially fell under Rayton's duties as Dho'vani in the absence of the King, the boy had only seen seven years, and few expected him to sit unsupervised through lengthy audiences. Rayton would accompany Alvin to the majority of meetings and court sessions to familiarise himself with the processes and peoples, but Alvin, together with Karundin's ministers and steward, would take care of any administrating that could not wait for Gavin's return. Shanor would act as magic defence for the Princes, and Gavin's guard, save those travelling with the King, would keep the Royals safe from physical harm.

"We could probably have a piece of cake or two hidden away for emergencies," Alvin quipped, his voice a soft tenor. Alvin and Maraenda had a daughter, Maraedeth, three years younger than Rayton, and the fond look Alvin bestowed on his nephew spoke volumes about the man's familiarity with children. Over near the castle wall, Maraenda held the squirming Maraedeth's hand to keep the inquisitive girl out from underfoot.

"Besides," Angie said to Rayton, "you'll be too busy with studying and swordwork and horse riding and playing with Maraedeth and the other children to worry about cake. You'll tell me all about your adventures when we get back, won't you?"

"Of course!" The little boy grinned then threw his arms around Angie's neck in a tight embrace.

"You'll take good care of Papa, right?" he whispered, his tone turning serious.

Angie hugged him back and whispered, just as solemn, "Best care ever."

He pulled away and studied her eyes a moment, as though searching for the truth in her vision. Angie reminded herself that this child had already lost a mother and a grandfather, and though he put on a brave front, he knew the dangers that lurked in the absence of the discovery of the assassin, and those dangers frightened him. She put all the confidence she could into her expression, enough anyway to reassure this small Prince. His tenuous smile brightened and his eyes swallowed their worry. Then he turned and flung himself across the courtyard toward Gavin. The King bent and scooped up his son in a practiced fashion, not even pausing in his last-minute instructions to the steward.

Angie rose to her feet, a fond smile following the pair.

"My Lady Angelica," Alvin said, drawing Angie's attention. "I want to thank you."

"For what?"

"Rayton is a good boy, but often given to melancholy, even petulance. He seems lonely at times, as many tend to see his station before they see him as a person, and he has not yet reached an age where he can overcome such unintended discrimination. I have seldom seen him so ebullient as he is with you. He has bonded to you so quickly, and it gladdens my heart to see his joy, to see him act as any boy of seven might rather than a child burdened with too much responsibility."

Angie didn't know what to say to that, so she simply offered a firm nod.

Kaeley emerged from the castle in the wake of Tabitha and her own maid Dorthaea, the two servants hefting the last of the Tre'embra's luggage onto the carriage. Although Angie had very little acquaintance with horseback riding, the thought of bouncing around in a carriage where she couldn't see out the front did not thrill her. She had always suffered a mild case of motion-sickness, especially when she didn't have a good view of what approached. While driving hadn't bothered her, being a passenger sometimes had an adverse effect on her stomach, and sitting in the back of a vehicle worsened the nausea. Now she would travel with Kaeley and their maids in an elaborate carriage pulled by four horses, and she hoped the novelty of this different mode of transportation—different for her—would keep her motion-sickness to a minimum. Still, she almost wished she had a horse to ride instead, even knowing the unfamiliarity would cause huge muscle pain and bruises. Having to fight nausea or having to deal with an inability to walk properly ... neither option sounded fun.

Kaeley glided over to Angie and Alvin, her trim gown the colour of mushroom caps. She kissed Alvin chastely on the cheek and smiled at Angie.

"Good morning, Brother," she said. "My Lady Angelica."

"Good morning, Kaeley," Alvin said. "Do you have everything you need?"

"And lots more besides, I'm certain," Kaeley laughed. "We're only gone for a month, yet I'm sure Dorthaea has packed enough for a full double-season. And the cooks have spoiled us something awful. You'd think we travelled on campaign and needed to provide all our own meals rather than share the occasional feast with Karundin's noble Houses, there's so much food."

"You know Gavin likes to prepare for anything," Alvin said, his eyes crinkling merrily.

"So long as he remembers that the nobles will take offence if he refuses their hospitality." Kaeley turned to Angie. "Our dear brother would prefer not to burden any of his people with this Progress, but to even suggest that they do not need to cater to the King will throw many of those people into an uproar," she explained. "They would see it as a slight against their own capabilities, even those who really cannot afford to house our little expedition. So Gavin will accept what hospitality he must, yet put as little strain on our hosts as possible."

"Tre'embra, Lady Sorceress," Commander Nervain marched up to them, a respectful nod also greeting Alvin. "We are ready to depart, if you would take your seats."

A brief flurry of activity ensued, the cacophony of horses snorting and whuffling, stamping their iron-shod hooves on the cobbled road, soldiers calling to each other, the rustle and jingle of cloth and armour, the slap of boots against the ground as folks scurried and settled. Men and women expertly lifted themselves into saddles and found their place in line, servants hurried to make sure that lashings still secured each chest of luggage onto the carriage and pack horses had all the supplies needed, and Tabitha and Dorthaea ushered their mistresses in to the plush confines of the carriage.

Angie slid in first, staring out the far window, open enough to let in a breath of air but not enough to actually stick her head out, and waited for Kaeley to bid farewell to Alvin. A weight shifted at the front of the vehicle, marking the driver taking his seat as he waited for the order to move out.

As the Princess joined the Sorceress, the King mounted his great stallion and smiled encouragement and love to his son as the steward led the child to the edge of the courtyard where Maraenda and Alvin waited with their daughter and Sorcerer Shanor. Merikan sat his horse to one side of Gavin, Commander

101

Nervain on the other, awaiting the King's pleasure.

When everyone had found their place, Gavin gave the command to set out, returning Rayton's enthusiastic wave as the King's horse passed him. Angie and Kaeley did the same as the carriage rolled before the Dho'vani. The procession clattered through the courtyard, under the portcullis, across the drawbridge, and into the streets of the city. People lined those streets, bakers, seamstresses and smiths rubbing elbows with merchants, priests and bankers, their smiling faces and cheers following the parade. Even the urchins and ne'er-do-wells traipsing through the crowd, the less honest perhaps relieving those more fortunate of a valuable or two, and the city watch doing its best to curtail such activities while keeping order, paused in their endeavours to show support for the King as he and his entourage wound its way through the throng and toward the east gate.

When they finally emerged onto the open road with fields and farms lining the way, Angie sat back and tried to ignore the swaying of the carriage, glad of her pants as she kicked off her shoes and curled up on the seat, head leaning against the window. Kaeley smiled in sympathy.

"It won't be long until you find your travelling stomach, My Lady," she said. "In a couple of days, the scenery will captivate you and take your mind off any lingering queasiness."

Angie tried to smile in response, though she rather feared it came across as more of a grimace. A couple of days indeed. She hoped she made it through the next few minutes without hurling. She had about a month of this Progress to endure, and here, so close to the city, engineers kept the roads in good repair. What would the more outlying portions of their journey entail, out where, as Merikan had mentioned, the roadways saw less maintenance? Maybe she could learn to ride a horse by then.

***

Shanor stood quietly near the castle gate with Tre'vani Alvin and Dho'vani Rayton. He watched as the Progress made its way out of the courtyard and passed from sight. He kept an outward air of patience and contentment with just a hint of boredom as he waited for either Prince's pleasure, but inwardly he grinned widely. He couldn't believe his luck. For days he had bided his time, seeking out the Spells of Borun that he knew about, yet never able to approach their actual locations for fear of discovery. He had made and discarded many plans to out-think and outmanoeuvre Merikan and that damned Angelica, as well as Gavin, but nothing would work flawlessly so long as those three could come across him at any inopportune moment in his hunt.

But now they left the city, travelling far enough away that, when Shanor made his move, they would have no way to stop him in time. By week's end, these so-called guardians would suffer their first defeat in a war they had yet to realise had begun. Shanor would uncover the first spell, learn and counter its safeguards, and take it into his possession without fear of reprisal. By the time Gavin could turn his host around, Shanor would surely have the second spell also, and no one the wiser. No doubt Gavin or Merikan—or that strange Sorceress—would initiate a search, likely enlisting Shanor's aid in the process, and they would hunt for the culprit. Even could they prove the Sahkarae Sorcerer guilty, Shanor would hold two of the most powerful spells in his hand, possibly even three should fate smile on him, spells he would not lightly relinquish.

Plus, Gavin had left him a very potent shield. Not only had he entrusted Shanor with the safety of his regent Alvin, the King's own beloved brother, he had also unknowingly given his nemesis a hostage in the form of the Dho'vani. What wouldn't Gavin do for Rayton?

Shanor grinned down into the trusting eyes of the boy as Rayton looked up at him. Rayton returned the smile, then turned and led the members of the court and the Royal House back into Karundin Castle. Shanor managed to contain his laughter, but the anticipatory gleam in his eyes followed those who would soon find themselves crushed beneath the boots of their true King, he who would rule with the backing of Shanor's might.

He had but to wait a few more days.

Chapter 12

Angie slept in the carriage most mornings while the Progress moved from village to village, castle to keep to manor. It helped to keep the nausea of travel to a minimum, but mostly, she just needed the rest. Each evening, the Royal party would attend a banquet prepared by whichever host provided their accommodations, and often these feasts would last well into the night. Angie could not leave before Gavin, and Gavin made sure none of his hosts felt slighted by retiring early himself. Merikan always sat next to Angie, imparting what instruction he could, but under the watchful eye of so many, Angie learned little of magic at those times, and much of how a travelling Court worked. Which left after the feasts as their most prosperous time for Angie's lessons in the use of magic.

Merikan explained the history of many sorcerers and sorceresses and what they had accomplished and recorded. He demonstrated some of the spells they used, detailed what potions worked for which ailments, theorised about the flow of power in different regions and peoples. But both quickly acknowledged that Angie's unique form of dream magic followed none of the rules Merikan could describe. It didn't stop him from teaching what he could, and Angie from doing her best to learn the capabilities of others, for how best to understand how to counter something than to know the likely thought-processes and abilities of rival magic-users?

This extrapolation most often led to late nights that stretched into the early morning hours before Angie could find a bed. She compensated by sleeping in the carriage until the Progress stopped for a break at lunch. She had no idea how Merikan managed to haul himself into the saddle and ride awake and alert beside the King every morning when they travelled without falling off his horse in exhaustion. He never even looked tired, while Angie struggled not to yawn in Tabitha's face as her maid helped Angie prepare for the day.

After the lunch break, Kaeley would instruct Angie in the history of Karundin, concentrating on each section of land as they travelled through it. The Princess described the noble they would visit that evening, from physical attributes to political standing, temperament, familial connections; everything the Lady Sorceress might need to know—and a lot Angie hoped she need never recall as Kaeley's knowledge of every detail near overwhelmed her.

By the time the Progress arrived at each destination, Angie prayed her head wouldn't explode from the influx of information flung her way, and that she wouldn't misidentify some noble or his or her exploits in her exhaustion.

Not every day passed thus, for the Progress did stay in some areas longer than others, usually based on the size of the holding or the standing of the noble. Angie slowly came to understand how Karundin politics played out in this manner, but mostly, when they stayed for more than one night, she just looked forward to sleeping in without interruption. She fervently hoped she could do so tomorrow morning, as this morning's adventure had started with the rising sun so that they could travel all day to reach Baron Hestian's keep by nightfall, where they would stay for two nights. If all went according to plan and they kept their mid-day meal brief. One more day past the Baron's keep would mark the half-way point in the Progress, according to Kaeley.

Angie had managed a light doze for the first two hours (or water-cups, as Kaeley would call them) of this morning's trip when she suddenly found herself wide awake, staring intently out the window. She barely noted the trees sliding past as the carriage bounced along the road, didn't even acknowledge the sway and shift of the vehicle or how it normally affected her stomach, even given the strong gusts of wind beginning to buffet the sides of the conveyance. She didn't see her surroundings at all, overlooked the leaden sky darkening the day, the lashing branches, the heavy, close sensation of a looming autumn storm. The weather didn't really register, but she felt ... something.

"Kaeley, where are we?"

Kaeley, used to Angie's delicate constitution in the confines of the carriage, kept herself from flinching at this change, noting a shimmer of silver in Angie's eyes that she had never seen before. The maids didn't dare move, startled by the Lady Sorceress's sudden intensity, afraid to disrupt her magic, for what else could attract such attention from she who protected the Royal Family? They waited for an attack that only the Sorceress could deflect.

"We've passed the outer farms that fuel Lady Fairlae's domain," Kaeley said quietly. "These lands belong to a handful of minor lords who work together to—"

"What lies in that direction?" Angie interrupted, her hand pressed against the window on the left of the carriage, her attention riveted by nothing the Princess could see.

"Farms, fields, some villages," Kaeley spoke slowly. "Much lies in that direction, My Lady."

"A half-glass away or so," Angie whispered.

Kaeley considered briefly.

"I believe that's Chasta Village. A mid-sized holding bordering the Incae River. They have a decent trade in wool and some metalworks."

"Stop the carriage," Angie ordered.

"I—of course," Kaeley signalled to her maid, and Dorthaea instantly popped her head out the window, her dark hair threatening to escape the confines of its thick braid as the wind slammed against her. She grabbed the attention of the driver and relayed the instruction before pulling herself back in to the protection afforded by the wooden enclosure.

Shouted commands, the whinny of horses, the jingle of harness and weapons loosened as guards formed up around the slowing carriage. The uncertainty as men looked for danger, an ordered presence even as they sought the unknown. Kaeley watched Angie closely, but the other woman paid the Princess no attention.

When the carriage came to a halt, Angie didn't wait. She pushed open the door and jumped down. She took three steps, then stopped, pointing toward what her inner sense told her led to danger—not their own, but of the King's people. To the guards who instantly formed up around her, it looked as though she pointed to a stand of trees.

Galloping hooves announced another arrival.

"What is it?" Merikan demanded, following the direction Angie indicated, though he saw nothing out of the ordinary.

"Pain," Angie whispered, her arm dropping to her side. "Heat, smoke, danger."

Merikan looked at Angie, saw the same silver shimmer in her eyes that Kaeley had seen, and marvelled at this display of magic that they had worked hard to discover only to fail again and again. Magic brought about by instinct rather than training.

"Does it affect the King?" Commander Nervain wanted to know, swinging his own horse in beside Merikan's.

"Not yet," Angie said. She blinked, the silver fading as she turned to regard her father. "I see a village engulfed in flame, a collapsed building, panicked villagers, some trapped, others unable to help. I see a disaster unless we can help them."

"Is this village on our route?" Nervain wanted to know.

Gavin, having followed Merikan and Nervain, though ringed in protective steel, dismounted and stood in front of Angie. The wind blew his hair across his face but made no other impression on his stance. Angie focussed on the King.

"Sire, this village lies out of our way, but we must help them."

"Why?" Nervain asked. Angie did not look away from Gavin.

"They are your people, Your Majesty. You must see to those you protect."

Gavin regarded her in silence a moment, then, turning his head without taking his gaze from hers, he ordered a detour.

He glanced to his man Jamison, who drove the carriage, and those surrounding the carriage where Kaeley stood. "Follow at a distance with the Tre'embra; prepare for anything." Turning back to Angie, Gavin announced, "You will ride with me. Show us the way."

With that, Commander Nervain turned his mount and reorganised the Progression. Gavin boosted Angie up onto his stallion and she did her best not to panic atop the large animal. Gavin mounted behind her, Merikan sticking to their side like glue.

"What did you see?" the Lord Protector asked, voice low. Angie looked at him, then stifled a gasp as Gavin's horse, Praetorian, moved forward at the King's silent command. She grabbed the pommel, her body tense.

"Relax," Gavin murmured from behind as his arms came

around her for support, reins held expertly. "I won't let you fall."

Angie found that sentiment, and Gavin's reassurance, vastly comforting. She eased herself as much as she could, trusting the man she protected, though her hands still clutched the pommel tightly.

Merikan waited for her to gain her equilibrium, then, "My Lady?" he prompted. Her eyes flew to his. "You said this disaster did not affect the King *yet*. If this village does not lie in our path ..."

"You want to know why we must turn aside."

"No Angelica," he surprised her. "I want to know why the *King* must turn aside. Why could he not send his soldiers to deal with the threat rather than ride into danger himself?"

"I—" Angie blinked in confusion. "I said we had to help."

"Actually," Gavin interjected, "You looked right at me and said 'You must see to those you protect.' Me specifically."

"But I meant ..." Angie paused, studied the last few minutes in her mind, tried to remember exactly what she had felt, what she had seen, what she had *known*. "Yes," she said, keeping her voice private as the two men had, almost lost in the trance of what she had foreseen. "You must see to this, Gavin. *You*. If we ride by, if you don't stop to help, the village will die. The survivors turn to banditry, they see aid going to other villages and wonder why they had to suffer. When the war comes, they act against you, knowing you could have helped but did not even try. But with your compassion, with you willing to see to the good of your people yourself, not leaving it to others, they respect you, honour you, are willing to fight for you as you will fight for them. The influence of the common folk of this region will spread, their tale of the new King who helps rather than ignores or dismisses the plight of the commoner will inspire others who might otherwise try to stand aside when the dark army brings terror to the kingdom."

The stamp of advancing horses, of tree limbs and tall grasses bowing to the strengthening gusts, the squawk of birds and forest animals startled by the presence of so many men and mounts rushing past in the gathering storm, the wind slapping at Angie's face as they rode, but momentary silence from her companions. Finally, Merikan spoke.

"What war?"

"What?" Angie blinked over at him, sure she had misheard

over the drumbeats of Praetorian's flashing hooves.

Gavin, his arms to either side of her hard as rock with his tension, clarified.

"Your words, Angie. *When the war comes, when the dark army brings terror.* Do you remember?"

"I ... don't know what it means," she whispered. "I just ... it's a feeling. I don't understand; I don't even know how I know about the village. I just do."

Angie felt Gavin nod behind her, even though he sat taller than she.

"We'll figure that all out later," he said, Merikan nodding agreement. "For now, let us hope we reach the village in time."

Angie nodded her own agreement, grip almost painful on the pommel, hair whipping in the wind where not trapped by Gavin's body, tears stinging her eyes, and not all due to the wind of their passage. Was this her magic sending a warning? Did they truly ride toward pain and destruction and fire, or had she in fact merely dreamed? How could she send this company off on a wild chase without really knowing what she did? And why did they follow so blithely?

Angie would have feared such folly if her instincts didn't scream of the veracity of this mad dash. However she knew about the plight of the unknown village, the danger remained. Gavin had to help those people or risk greater loss in what she somehow knew was a dark future. Angie shuddered at what this strange new magic implied. What war indeed?

***

Gavin tried to focus as Praetorian led three dozen elite guardsmen along the road to Chasta Village, racing the storm, but the feel of the woman nestled against his front, her hands clinging to the pommel before her despite the protection of Gavin's arms, distracted him. He gritted his teeth as her honey-dark hair wreathed them, not because the soft strands acted as whips in the wind, but because of its alluring sensation against his face. He tried to bring his mind to bear on their upcoming situation—what problems did Chasta face and how had the Lady known? What war and terror did she sense looming, and how far in the future did that trouble exist? Did it have something to do with his father's murder?

But his thoughts kept returning to the warmth of Lady Angelica—Angie, he reminded himself with a smile he quickly hid—and how she pressed harder against him whenever Praetorian altered his gait. Longings he had not felt since Hydae's death five years ago rose in a cresting tide at the sound of Angie's voice, the sight of her smile, her obvious joy at interacting with Rayton and Kaeley, and now, to have her snuggled in his embrace as he helped her maintain her balance atop his galloping stallion .... Ridiculous to have any such feelings for a woman he barely knew.

Again, Gavin forced his thoughts beyond this absurd obsession, knowing a King must look to political stability and advantages in a union over any feelings he might harbour. That he and Hydae had found joy in each other came as an unexpected blessing. Hydae's family stood close in power to that of Karundin's Royal Family, and so his father, King Grayton, had arranged the marriage between her and his eldest son to solidify that house's support when the two remained but children. With the birth of Maraenda of Sahkarae, Grayton saw the advantages of uniting the two kingdoms through a marriage between her and his second son, and Sahkarae's King agreed to such a joining, even permitting his daughter to live as a ward of Karundin for three double-seasons prior to the official match when she turned nineteen. Hydae had died two months after Alvin's wedding, else the two reigning monarchs might have arranged for Gavin to take Maraenda's hand instead of Alvin. But all such powerful unions occurred for some advantage where affection or love did not figure in. For Gavin to even imagine he could woo and win Angie's affections, she would have to bring some unifying stability or political advantage to the rule of Karundin, and she did not come from any noble house.

Or did she? he found himself wondering as he chanced to glance at Merikan riding at his side, expression grim as the Sorcerer contemplated what awaited them ahead. For in truth, after the Royal House, who held greater power or esteem in Karundin than the Lady Sorceress and the Lord Protector? Gavin shook his head violently, trying to quell such thoughts. The motion brought Angie's questioning gaze as she twisted to bring him into her view. He dredged up a grim smile and hoped she would mistake any disquiet she saw in his eyes as anxiety for what lay at the end of this road rather than the turmoil that lay in his heart.

She pried one hand from her tight grip of the pommel and patted his arm in reassurance, nearly undoing Gavin entirely.

Then he found his attention wrenched to the present as the acrid tang of burning wood intruded, blown away almost immediately by the swirling wind, and he found he could concentrate on something else after all.

Billows of smoke first obscured then revealed Chasta Village, giving the illusion that the buildings disappeared and reappeared as through a fog. The sound of terrified screams and the shouts of men trying to find some order in the chaos of disorder, all distorted by the angry howl of the storm, drew the King's party toward the centre of the village. Hurrying shadows revealed people running to and from burning shelters, mostly centred around one large building.

Gavin signalled a halt far enough back that the horses would not add to the confusion and swung out of Praetorian's saddle, quickly reaching up to help Angie dismount. Commander Nervain, at his side in an instant, already issued orders to his men in the silent motions of hand-talk, splitting the troops so that some took charge of the mounts while the others formed up around their leader. Gavin only waited long enough for Merikan to join them before striding up to the nearest villager, a matronly woman with a soot stained apron favouring her right foot.

"Pardon, madam, but what has happened and how might we assist?" he asked.

The woman blinked pale eyes at him, took in their fine, unmarred clothing and alert stances, and tried to sink into a curtsey. Gavin caught her arm before her injured leg could betray her, Angie steadying her from the other side.

"My Lord," the villager began, but Gavin shook his head.

"No time for curtsies, gentle woman. Where is water? Buckets? We need to stop the fire from spreading."

She gestured vaguely toward the flames and Gavin could see the beginnings of a ragged line forming.

"There," he pointed out to Nervain. "I think it's a bucket line. Let's go."

"The children," the woman whispered, and Gavin froze. She held up a shaking hand to the large building at the centre of the conflagration. "Took shelter from the storm in the inn. All the little 'uns. Sparks from the wedding fire caught in the thatch of

111

the mill, spread. Didn't notice in time. Roof collapsed. The children—"

Angie took the woman in her arms and stared intently at Gavin.

"Go," she whispered. "Save them."

Gavin didn't hesitate. He ran for the inn, Nervain, Merikan and the rest of the men at his heels.

He could hear their screams now, children trapped, frantic parents trying to get closer as the heat of the blazing inferno kept them at bay, the angry wind fanning the flames. The villagers not lost to blind panic tried to organise a bucket brigade, but too many stared in numbed shock as smoke and fire licked from the mill to the inn to the wood and thatch houses nearby.

"Commander, form the men, help the bucket line, there," he pointed out the nearby river now visible as they found the mill. Nervain was already moving. "Merikan, we need to get those trapped out. How?"

The Sorcerer studied the greedy flames, the mighty blasts of the wind fouling any attempt to quench the fires as it spread the inferno and breathed continuous life into its heated maw. He stared up at the boiling, seething mass of blackness contained in the clouds above.

"If I can coax the rain to break, I might help douse the flames, Sire, but I cannot do anything about the structural stability of the building."

"Do what you can," Gavin ordered, leaving Merikan to work his magic as the King himself moved to the desperate parents. He took one red-faced tearful man by the shoulder and turned him so that he could see the line of villagers and soldiers now passing buckets of water from the river to the conflagration. Gavin had to shout to be heard over the roar of the wind and fire.

"We can't get to the children until we clear a path through the fire. Help us."

The man blinked angrily at Gavin, seeing only a stranger, but then something penetrated his fear. He followed Gavin to the line, drawing most of the unfocussed villagers in his wake. In moments, everyone had joined the lines, sending bucket after bucket of river water into the flames. The first fat raindrop hit Gavin's face seconds later, yet even the roar of the downpour could not drown out the cries of the children and the sudden crack of timber as another section of the inn collapsed.

A hand grabbed Gavin and pulled him out of line. He stared at Angie's face as she stared at the inn, a silver glow gleaming in her Sorceress's eyes.

"Pain, Sire," she whispered. "Hurry; come with me."

Gavin didn't question; he just followed as Angie led him toward the burning building.

"Sire, no!" he heard Nervain call out and glanced back to see Merikan restraining the larger man. He also saw the red-faced villager he had urged into line right behind, following Gavin. He opened his mouth to protest, but Angie took the man's arm in her free hand, drawing both forward.

"The fire will not touch you," Angie said, a strange resonance in her voice. "As long as you keep moving, it will not harm you."

Then the three of them plunged into the heat and destruction of the blaze.

Gavin choked on the heavy bite of smoke, coughing to clear his lungs. He heard the others do the same, then many coughs, moans, screams. He followed them to their source, sound being the only thing he could use to locate those trapped as sight became unreliable.

His skin dried and itched in the intense heat, but the fire did not reach him. In fact, it almost seemed to bend around and away from them. More than his own protective magic sheltered him now. Gavin did not question how Angie turned away the searing flames, attuning his concentration instead to the small bodies huddled under the stairs.

Parts of the walls and ceiling had collapsed atop the stairs, forming a small hollow free of fire and debris, but flames already licked at the edges. Without having to discuss anything, he and the man began wrenching the timbers and rubble they could move out of the way. Angie squirmed her way through the gaps they created, reaching for the children and pulling them free. She pointed wordlessly to a path etched on the floor, a silver ribbon of light leading to the door. The freed children did not hesitate, just ran with hopeful sobs for the exit. Two of the older children could not run, their legs crushed when the ceiling had fallen in, having used their own bodies to protect the younger ones. Angie pried up the beam trapping them with incredible strength. The villager picked up one child, and Gavin the other. Angie let the wood fall from her grip with a moan. Her gaze met Gavin's.

"Run," she wheezed. A crack from overhead, loud enough to overcome the snap and hiss of flames, the drumming of the torrent of rain, the howl of the wind. Gavin cradled the child to his chest and ran.

He stumbled out on the heels of the villager just as the inn gave a huge shudder and caved in. He found himself flung to the ground in the backlash of the building's collapse, his body somehow curled protectively around the injured boy he carried. A weight fell on his legs, then rolled off as Angie crawled up beside him, heaving great gulps of sodden air. Gavin found himself echoing her, along with the villager and their two charges.

Dozens of legs surrounded them, several hands came to offer assistance, and a grateful cry ripped from the throat of a woman as she took the hand of the boy in Gavin's arms, hugging both child and man in her relief as she thanked him over and over. Gavin released the boy to his mother's arms then pushed himself to his feet. He turned to face the stony stare of the head of his guards. Nervain said nothing for a moment, his heated glare shared between Gavin and Angie. When finally he spoke, his tone remained devoid of the fury and fear that sparked in his eyes.

"We've stopped the spread of the fire, Your Majesty. The inn is lost, but all villagers are safe."

"Thank you, Commander," Gavin replied, voice rasping as he coughed out a lungful of smoke.

"Your Majesty?" the red-faced villager said, staring with wide, reddened eyes at Gavin. "You're ... you're the ..."

"The King," Nervain scowled at Gavin. "Yes, he is."

"But ..." the man stammered. "But you ran into the fire."

"So did you," Gavin said.

"My girl—" he gestured weakly, then stared hard at Gavin, not sure whether to meet the gaze of the King or not. "You could of got killed!" he protested.

"So could you," Gavin replied.

"But I ain't the King! I'm just the miller."

"No less important for that," Gavin insisted. "Without the miller, how would we grind the flour? How would we make bread? How would we eat? A King is nothing without his people."

The man stood a little straighter with Gavin's words.

"We owe you a great debt, Your Majesty," he said with a crude bow, somehow made more noble by the rain drenching his hair and the soot smearing his clothing, the cloth frayed and burned at the edges. "You have saved our village, our future. Chasta Village stands eternally grateful, Sire." The miller dropped to his knees in the mud, the entire village following suit. Gavin placed a gentle hand on the man's shoulder, then pulled him to his feet, gesturing the others to stand also.

"I require no thanks, good sir," Gavin murmured. "See to your girl."

The villagers found rooms for Gavin and his people, insisting the King, Angie and Merikan take the mayor's home for their use while they dried off and regrouped. When Kaeley and rest of the Progress arrived, the villagers welcomed them warmly. Gavin made sure to share out some of their own supplies, knowing that the inn and mill—the latter partially saved from the fire, but quite damaged—would have housed a good portion of the village's food stuffs, especially given the festive preparations the inn had housed earlier in the day.

The wedding the villagers had planned, whose flame the storm had stolen to cause such havoc, took place that evening, the flustered bride and groom shy yet honoured to know that the King himself stood in attendance for their special day, and sharing of his own table to make this near tragedy into the celebration they had dreamed. Gavin danced with the bride, and Kaeley with the groom, making the event even more special for the couple.

Gavin asked Angie to dance, but the Sorceress declined, stating that she did not know the steps. Gavin quite forgot at times that Angie had not grown up in Karundin. Already she seemed like such a part of their lives that he sometimes found it difficult to remember a time without her presence. He wondered just how displaced she must feel when constantly faced with situations unfamiliar to her yet common-place to the rest of them, even something as simple as a dance. He marvelled at how she always seemed to display a high level of comfort and competence despite the fear shadowing her eyes, and found himself admiring her and her bravery even more.

***

Fear battered at Angie's self-control. Not the heart pounding terror of mortal danger, but a more subtle eroding of her calm facade as she waited for Merikan and Nervain to chew her out for her reckless endangerment of the King earlier.

Tending to the children rescued from the fire, and then the preparations for the wedding festivities, had put off the confrontation she expected, but now that she had escaped the celebrations and retreated to the temporary refuge of the mayor's house, she found herself waiting anxiously for the arrival of either the Lord Protector or the Commander of Gavin's personal guard, both of whom had made note of Angie's flight. She knew they wouldn't both confront her at once, if only because at least one had to remain with the King to ensure his safety, although Angie *knew* he faced nothing save the best of intentions from this village now. *How* she knew with such absolute conviction she preferred not to examine too closely at the moment.

Angie had time for a couple of deep breaths to steady herself before the door opened behind her and she heard the heavy tread of sturdy boots. She turned to see Commander Nervain gently close the door. He regarded her silently for a moment, his expression inscrutable. Before he could deliver a no-doubt much-deserved lecture on placing the King in such danger, Angie spoke.

"I'm sorry, Commander, but I had to," she said, hating that her voice squeaked at the end, like that of a frightened child. "I don't know if I can explain exactly why, but I know the King had to go into that fire." She gathered her hands into fists to keep them from shaking.

Nervain blinked at her, his brows forming a little valley as he frowned in consternation.

"My Lady, are you ... did you ... you don't have to explain."

"You mean, you aren't mad at me?" came Angie's surprised reply.

"Well, I can't say I was any too happy about you dragging the King into that building," Nervain chuckled. "But I know you could never hurt him. I might not understand what you do or why you do it, but protecting the Royals is at the heart of everything you are," he said with utter conviction. "Mind you, a little warning next time might go a long way." He grinned at Angie's dumbfounded expression.

Angie let out a sigh of relief in a rush of breath, then shook her head in bewilderment, leaning back against the dining table and staring at the floor.

"Commander, sometimes I just don't understand this world. Here I am, all worried about you yelling at me, and instead, you find it in you to laugh, and then you place such conviction in my actions that it scares me."

"My Lady," he stepped forward so quickly that Angie jerked back in surprise, looking up at his earnest face. "You are the Lady Sorceress; why would I not trust you?"

Angie remembered then that Nervain did not know her past. He thought she had stayed hidden somewhere in the kingdom, protecting from the shadows, but knowing everything that one Karundin-born and trained in magic should. She wondered whether Gavin and Merikan had a reason for keeping the man in the dark or if they had simply not thought to share the truth. As the person in charge of the King's personal safety, Angie believed that Nervain deserved to know who and what he truly worked with.

"Commander, please sit with me," Angie said, pulling out a chair from the table and sitting, waiting for Nervain to join her. "I feel you must know something few others do. Then maybe you will understand my own concerns."

As Angie proceeded to relate some of her past—how she knew a different world, had thought of Karundin as a dream, how little she really understood her magic or how it seemed to work on instinct rather than knowledge—she watched Nervain's face for any reaction, but he maintained a stoic expression throughout.

"Today, I don't know how I knew to come here, only that we had to, or we would risk Gavin's reign," she concluded. "Though truthfully, Commander, I didn't even know for certain until we smelled the fire whether I was crazy for sending us all out on this unexpected quest, if I had just somehow made it up or dreamed and couldn't tell the difference between dream and reality. And that scared the hell out of me, that all of you followed so blithely.

"And again, when I took Gavin to the burning inn, I *knew* the fire wouldn't touch him and that, if we acted quickly, we could save those children, but I don't know *how* I knew; didn't even stop to wonder at the time. He followed without a thought, trusting that I knew what I was doing. What the hell kind of place is this that you all follow me so blindly?"

Angie heard the confused bitterness in the question, though

she had not intended to put words to those fears. To her surprise, Nervain's huge hand covered both her shaking fists on the top of the table, not as an attack, but as a show of comfort. Angie felt a lump of emotion form in her throat as she met the sudden compassion in his eyes.

"Angie," he said, startling her by using the name she preferred, though it gave her some measure of normalcy. She suspected he knew as much. "You are the Lady Sorceress. We trust you because you can do naught *but* the best for Karundin. That is the nature of the Lady Sorceress. You may not know Karundin or her peoples like a native, but we all understand your role. I will not pretend to understand magic of any sort, let alone your apparently unique form of it, but I can tell you the Lady Sorceress will *always* find a way to protect the Royals, unto her last breath, because that is how her magic works. Just trust your instincts. From what I've seen, so long as you do not doubt yourself when it matters, you will do what is right to protect the King. Trust that, as we trust you."

"That's an awful lot of trust for someone who's stumbling along in the dark," Angie whispered.

Nervain winked and pulled his hand back.

"We all stumble sometimes. Just believe you'll find your way when you have to, and know that others will help you if you fall." He pushed back from the table and stood, looking down at her.

"Thank you for trusting me with this, My Lady."

"Nervain," she said before he could turn to leave. "Why did you come in, if not to yell at me for earlier?"

The left side of his mouth quirked up in a half-smile.

"Truth to tell, Angie, I did come to express my displeasure at you hauling off the King instead of someone more expendable. And honestly, even knowing you'll likely have reason for such future actions, know that I will yell at you when you do so again. But also know it's my frustration at failing to find another way to protect the King. It won't save you from a tongue-lashing, I warrant, but at least you'll know it's nothing personal."

With a lighter step, the Commander left the house, accompanied by Angie's laughter.

Chapter 13

Shanor stole down the dark hallway, his slippered feet making no sound as they padded along the stone floor. Not that anyone yet remained awake in this part of the castle, so late at night. Or early in the morning, rather. Two cups past the middle of the night saw only guards making their rounds, and Shanor had watched and waited this past week until he knew the schedule and habits of every soldier likely to tromp through these halls. None would dare question him at any rate, but best to avoid possible confrontations that might lead to unpleasantness before he had finished what he had come down here to accomplish. For in one of these lower storage rooms lay the first of Borun's spells, and he intended to claim it as his own before the morning dawned.

Although he carried a lantern, Shanor kept it hooded, relying on a pair of ensorcelled spectacles he had created years ago instead. The vision-enhancers, rather than improving sight in the usual manner, provided illumination in the dark, visible only to the wearer. Anyone else wandering these lower halls would need light that Shanor would see long before the discovery of his own presence, while the glasses could not betray him, as only he could see what they revealed. He still moved quietly, but he need not exert himself in furtive motions.

He paused at a junction and faced a seldom-used corridor. Extending his awareness to ensure that no one roamed nearby, Shanor murmured a simple spell and swept his right hand forward, guiding a breath of wind that cleared the dust from the hallway. No need to leave an obvious trail of footprints after all, or to gather unexplained grime on the hem of his robe.

Path cleared, Shanor walked up to the fourth door on the left and halted. He closed his eyes, imagined himself back in the Great Hall for the coronation, and pictured that streak of golden light extending from the crown to these rooms. Yes, this room before him. Opening his eyes, he tried the handle and found it locked, which did not surprise him. A quick spell overcame that minor obstacle, and Shanor glided into the room, shutting the door behind him. The chamber smelled of disuse and neglect, a swirl of dust settling in the wake of the door's closure tickling his nose.

He removed the spectacles and slid them into an inner pocket, then unveiled the lantern, letting the warm glow of the trapped flame pick out his surroundings. The glasses could show him outlines and obstacles, but the lantern revealed details, and this room had many to discover amid the dust of ages.

Scrolls and books littered a table near the door, and banners and pennants from past victories hung from the ceiling, interspersed amid a myriad of cobwebs. Shields and surcoats that bore unfamiliar coats of arms lay stacked against walls lined with tapestries; daunting weaponry, including massive broadswords, double-edged axes, and wicked pikes, rested in weapon racks—all obviously spoils of war, tokens of respect and conquest—and everything of value lay draped with Preservation Spells, leaving the empty spaces to gather dust and webs. An apt room, thought Shanor, for spells dedicated to warfare in a land currently at peace.

He moved to the table as a logical starting point to his search, yet did not hold out high hopes that the spell would rest in so obvious a place. Disturbing the parchment dispersed the dust enough to send Shanor into a brief spat of sneezing. To sweep away the dust would send the pages flying; he could suffer through a few sneezes. So he disregarded the discomfort as he perused the contents of the table.

Most of the scrolls depicted old maps, some from before Sahkarae had split from Karundin. He could read battle tactics outlined in some, see land disputes resolved in others, watch as cartographers birthed current-day Karundin. A few scrolls even detailed treaties or policies instead of maps, though all lay bundled together.

The books held a fascinating mix of history and personal journals spanning centuries, but nothing of Borun's spells.

Shanor had spent two turns of the water glass inspecting the contents of the table with nothing to show for his efforts save an irritated nose and dry hands from parchment and inks that leeched the moisture from his skin, each sheaf so well-preserved that someone might have penned them yesterday had their styles and intent not so obviously reflected an earlier age.

He took in the rest of the room with a contemplative gaze, determining where to continue his search. Magic overlay everything here, confusing senses attuned to such intricacies. Did he dare a spell to reveal what he wanted, assuming such a spell would work? Gavin and the Sorceress had left nearly two weeks prior; if Shanor did use magic now to find the spell, the King could do nothing about it. Shanor did not have an abundance of time, not if he wanted to locate the other two spells he might discover as well, yet he hesitated to give up any hope of surprise just yet.

A more mundane search, he decided, and if he found nothing, he would return the next night and cast his spell then.

Another glass passed before Shanor ceded defeat. Any longer and he ran the risk of encountering someone on the way back to his chambers, a chambermaid or cook's assistant or one of the guards changing shift. He snarled and turned from the far bank of weapons he had just carefully rifled through. With impatient steps, he headed for the door. The hem of his robe caught on the edge of a blade and he wrenched it free, stumbling as he careened away, managing to upset a stack of shields against the near wall. He watched with a disgusted curse as the shields tumbled across his path, sending up a plume of dust, and almost kicked them out of his way. Instead, he curbed his irritation, found his calm, and knelt to replace these ancient symbols of a defeated enemy, waving the dust particles away from his face as he fought the urge to sneeze yet again.

When he reached the third shield back, a triangular ornament depicting a grey tower on a brilliant sapphire background, Shanor almost missed the subtle difference of the magic coating the device. A Spell of Protection, yes, but also something more. He paused, staring at the piece of armour, willing his perception to see what truly lay beneath his hands. The shield stubbornly remained a shield.

Undeterred, Shanor took up his prize, certain that he had found the first of Borun's spells. Now he had but to unlock the secret to its disguise, overcome any other safeguards configured into its protection, and he would stand one step closer to forcing Karundin back to its rightful place under Sahkaraean power.

He rearranged the rest of the fallen shields with a whisper of power and a flick of his wrist, blew out his lantern, and took out his illumination spectacles once more, settling them on the bridge of his nose. A quick wave of his hand over his robe loosened whatever dust may have swarmed over it, leaving him free of any incriminating tells. Then he left the store room, re-locked the door, and made his way quickly back to his own abode. He only had to avert the attention of two servants on the way, a small use of his magic.

In his chambers, Shanor settled the ensorcelled shield against the wall near the hearth in the sitting room and dropped with weary satisfaction into a chair, contemplating his success.

"Now I just have to figure you out," the Sorcerer said, a smile stretching his lips wide.

When his serving man arrived a glass later, he found his master sitting in a chair facing the unlit fire with a strange smile on his face. He saw nothing of the shield, hidden beneath Shanor's own spell of concealment, and wisely kept his thoughts to himself.

Chapter 14

The people of Chasta Village had extended an invitation for King and company to remain another day, but Gavin did not wish to burden them further. He did leave six men behind, volunteers all, to help the villagers rebuild what they could, equipping them with their own provisions. The soldiers had instructions to return to the capital in two weeks, or sooner if the village no longer required their aid. Meanwhile, Gavin and the rest of his Royal Progress proceeded on to Baron Hestian's keep.

The Baron promised to send his own work crew to aid Chasta village, along with a cart full of foodstuffs to help the villagers until they could repair the mill and produce their own flour again. Gavin appreciated the gesture, especially given that Chasta did not rest in Hestian's domain. The Baron assured the King that the coalition of minor lords who did oversee the area around Chasta, at least in name, would not find fault in Hestian's actions and would, in fact, applaud the Baron's generosity as it would leave their own coffers and stores untouched.

"They scrape by well enough," Hestian explained. "But they do not have an overabundance of extra resources. They will look with favour on anything that helps those they oversee yet does not impinge on their own well-being. Besides, by the time the lords sorted out who should send what aid, Chasta would no longer require it."

Gavin wondered if he ought to visit the lords in question and remind them of their duty.

But not tonight. The Progress had spent most of the day journeying from Chasta to Hestian's keep along roads made muddy by the storm, and the Baron had arranged a welcoming feast, yet another affair meant to honour the King. Even though he understood the belief for the need of largess on the part of the nobles he visited, Gavin preferred something more simplistic. He knew better than to insult his host, though, so he had retreated to the rooms set aside for him to freshen up and allowed Jamison to help dress him in a fresh set of clothing for supper.

A knock sounded on the outer door as Jamison tugged the last bit of finery into place, and the manservant hurried to answer it. Gavin followed in time to see Jamison admit Merikan. Nervain stood with another guard just outside the door and Gavin nodded to the Commander as he peered within for anything amiss before the door closed again.

Gavin dismissed Jamison and invited Merikan to sit, having asked the Lord Protector to arrive early for a reason. Gavin hadn't deemed they had enough privacy to discuss this matter on the way to Hestian's Keep so he had mulled over his questions and concerns on the road in anticipation of this meeting. He wasted no time getting to the point.

"The Lady Angelica's premonitions; did Lady Sorceress Katerina share any such ability?"

"Not as such, Sire. Katerina had many gifts and great powers, and at times it almost seemed she would intuit the course of the future, but I never heard her speak with such certainty as Angelica did yesterday."

"What could she do?" Gavin asked, leaning forward in his chair. "She died not long after my birth, so I have only ever heard stories and read the histories."

"Most of those are accurate. She held a wealth of power, knew potent and dangerous spells, could commune with and often command many of the Hidden Peoples; Faeries, Elementals, Centaurs. She could scry to far-off places, cast glamours and protections, even influence some with weak minds, though she always held such coercion and darker secrets with distaste. Yet if some dark magic stood as the only measure to protect the Royal Family, she would not hesitate, shouldering the cost of such spells without question or complaint. Hers was the magic of the Sorceress, strong, sometimes frightening, yet understandable to those of us who know that world. Angelica's magic, though borne of Katerina's, defies any rules I know. That is, I do not understand its mechanism beyond having a basis in instinct, though I can clearly see the results."

"Perhaps it comes from Angie's world," Gavin mused, shaking his head. He regarded the Sorcerer. "And Lady Katerina's ability to send a spirit to another world? I realise I know little of the greater magics, yet that seems an extraordinary achievement."

"It is, Sire, but it is not unique," Merikan said. "With some kind of bridge, or physical connection, a powerful sorcerer or sorceress might span worlds, though I admit I know of none other with such long reaching attributes as what Katerina achieved with Angelica. Most could only span the planes for a short time; Katerina created a bridge to span untold seasons."

"How did she do it?" Gavin wondered. "Send her unborn child entirely into another plane? What kind of connection did Lady Katerina have to Angie's world?"

"Not so much a connection as a bridge. Kat bonded a Faery to watch over our child, a being of magic who could slip between worlds enough to keep a small portal open between them. Or at least, that's what I've managed to discern. I honestly don't know how she did it, either in terms of magic or under the dire circumstances which compelled her to attempt such a feat."

"So for someone else to perform a similar process, to bring someone from another world, or hide them there, would require strong magic?"

"Definitely. To say nothing of great knowledge and access to that world in some form."

"Yet could such a person be used to assassinate a king?" Gavin wanted to know. "How did the assassin get into and out of Father's room, Merikan? Could a sorcerer have pulled him from another world, then sent him back, leaving no trace? Is it possible that we must look farther than our own lands, our own world even, to learn the truth?"

"A very distant possibility, Gavin, but one I do not think likely," Merikan replied solemnly. "I believe someone mastered a teleport spell, not the ability to traverse different planes."

"But you do believe someone used magic to kill my father."

Merikan sighed heavily, then nodded.

"I do. And strong magic, to overcome both the castle's and your father's own defences without sending up any alarm."

"Save the alarm that drew Angie from her world to the King's side," Gavin murmured. "Would that she could have come sooner."

"Indeed, Sire," said a voice from the door. The two men

lurched to their feet, startled, and turned to see Angie as she closed the door behind her. "If I could turn back time and dream myself to your father's side earlier, I would do so."

She strode over to stand between Gavin and Merikan, dressed in a sapphire gown and looking quite refreshed after the long day's journey. She gazed up into Gavin's eyes and the King felt his heart lurch.

"I have wondered, Gavin, about the search for the assassin," she said into the silence. "Do you realise that this is the first I have heard you speculate on his origin? I have heard general sentiment about the assassination, yet I have seen no evidence of any search for his identity, until now. If I might enquire, how far has your investigation gotten?"

"We are exploring several avenues," Gavin stated stiffly, suddenly resenting her implication of his complacency. How dare she suggest he had not done everything to find the person responsible for killing his father! Of course he had ... hadn't he? He tried to recall all they'd done in the wake of the murder, but her voice distracted him.

"I mean no offence, Your Majesty, and I do not mean to pry, but I feel I must ask. Though of necessity I have not been privy to much before your coronation and could easily have missed all the efforts that must have gone into the search for the assassin in the days following King Grayton's death, I have seen no results, and I am forced to wonder why. Please," she held up a hand to still Gavin's spluttered reply before it could leave his lips. "I do not question your resolve or your need to find the truth. I question why it has taken until now for you to voice your suspicions." She turned to look at Merikan.

"Surely, Lord Protector, you have noticed this same lapse. Or," she narrowed her eyes as she took in Merikan's dark expression. "No, perhaps not. Let me ask this then. You believe someone used magic as an aid in the death of the King; is it possible that magic has clouded the search for the assassin?"

Gavin frowned and exchanged a glance with Merikan. Perhaps the Lady had not recovered from the rigours of the journey after all.

Angie puffed out an irritated breath, then reached out her arms.

"Take my hands, both of you," she commanded. When neither Gavin nor Merikan made a move, Angie snarled and snatched up their hands anyway. Gavin tried to jerk back from her firm grip, noted the Sorcerer do the same, and hesitated long enough to wonder why. That brief moment of indecision gave Angie the time she needed.

"Look at this situation through my eyes," Angie said. "What do you see?"

And suddenly Gavin understood.

He saw his father's body, the knife in his chest, blood dribbling from the wound as Angie faded from view, but his mind only went to wondering where she went. He knew the grief of his father's death, but the question of who did the deed kept slipping from his thoughts. When he rode out with Rayton on the day they found Angie, he thought only to keep his son safe, never quite jumping even to speculation on who he kept him safe from beyond the obvious danger. He questioned how Angie had found her way into King Grayton's chambers, knowing it had something to do with the King's death, but had not looked beyond to who else had stood in that room. Everything leading up to the coronation and during the walk itself had focussed on security, making sure no assassin could repeat his triumph, yet little effort had gone into truly learning that assassin's identity. Even the Royal Progress to meet his people, though given every security measure, had not addressed the actual event that preceded Gavin's ascension. Indeed, such a Progress, in light of an unknown assassin left uncaught, seemed utterly ridiculous. It only served to leave the castle and the Heir unprotected while the King ...

Gavin wrenched his hand free and stared at Angie in horror.

"Rayton," he croaked, fear for his son nearly overpowering.

"Is not King, Sire," she said with compassion. "He does not stand in as much danger as you do."

"How did you know?" Merikan asked, face pale and expression hard. "How did you know someone affected our thinking regarding the assassin?"

"I didn't," Angie replied. "But it struck me that something didn't feel right about how we've all avoided the topic until now."

"Yet you knew what to show us."

"No," Angie shook her head. "I don't know what you saw; I only made it possible for you to see it."

"How could someone block our memories like that?" Gavin demanded, anger and fear warring in his gut. "How could someone make us think we're doing all we can when we've done

127

nothing?"

"It's like Merikan said. Someone with great magic arranged the assassination. It would seem he continues to influence events."

"You saw through it," Gavin insisted.

"Not until now," she disagreed. "Perhaps his influence could only last so long."

"Or so far," Merikan mused. "The more distance between us and the person responsible, the weaker his magic's hold on us, giving our minds time to assimilate what we should have searched for long since."

"Who has that kind of power?" Gavin demanded, his mind only coming up with one name.

"Shanor might," Merikan admitted, confirming the cold knot of dread gripping Gavin's heart.

Silence as they contemplated the horrible implications of the Sahkarae Sorcerer arranging the death of King Grayton. Yet it made no sense to Gavin.

"Why would Shanor perpetrate such an act?" he asked. "What would he have to gain?"

"What would anyone have to gain?" Angie asked. "What did they hope to achieve by killing the King? Who benefited from his death?"

"It couldn't be to cause destabilization, or why make it so that no one looked for the assassin?" Merikan pondered. "If someone wanted to sow discord or chaos, they would want us chasing every lead, fearing every shadow, not ignoring the very deed."

"Why kill Father?" Gavin reiterated. "If Sahkarae was behind it, it would bring about a war they could not hope to win. If Shanor instigated the assassination, why? He would never hold power. Even if he also managed to eliminate myself and Rayton, and brought Alvin to the throne, putting Maraenda as Queen ... the people of Karundin will only follow those of Karundin Royal blood. Shanor couldn't hope for any true power even with his charge wearing a crown. So why would he start down this road?"

"Then someone in the shadows," Merikan said. "Someone we don't even know about. The thought of a sorcerer or sorceress hidden from us, holding magic strong enough to dull our curiosity and assassinate one of the Royals despite all protections, hardly bears thinking about. Yet think about it we must."

Gavin frowned heavily as he tried to recall what had prompted his line of questioning, see when this potential magic had lost its hold on him, but he couldn't place his finger on it. Hadn't even intended to bring up the murder. He regarded Angie.

"Did you work some kind of magic to erase his spell?"

"No. I had just come to let you know the Baron has laid out the feast and awaits your arrival."

Gavin turned to Merikan.

"I had intended to ask about Angie's premonition of war. So what prompted questions of the assassin instead?"

"Perhaps, Sire, those were the questions we really needed to ask," replied Merikan. "Angelica may not have worked a magic to wake our minds from such an avoidance spell, but she has allowed us to free them from the last vestiges of its grasp." He sighed heavily.

"We cannot keep Hestian and his guests waiting much longer I'm afraid," he said. "As we want to avoid inviting speculation and panic, however, we obviously cannot let our fears of what this new information portends show in our actions tonight. I suggest we use the time provided by the Baron's feast to sort out what other questions we have avoided asking and decide on the morrow how best to proceed."

Gavin agreed, his thoughts already leaping to all that he should have done in the wake of his father's assassination, the questions he should have asked, the actions he should have taken.

Someone had orchestrated King Grayton's death and hidden the consequences behind a wall of magic; what else had this Sorcerer planned? The one thought Gavin kept circling back to drove a spear of anguished dread through him; Shanor currently stood as Rayton's and Alvin's only real magical protections. If the man had had anything to do with the murder of a king, what would he do with a Prince and the Dho'vani? And if he stood innocent, and thus ignorant of this invisible plot, what could he do against a sorcerer with equal or greater strength than him?

Outwardly, Gavin maintained a pleasant facade as they made their way through Baron Hestian's feast, but inside he roiled with uncertainty and fear. His son, his kingdom, stood in unknown peril, and right now, he couldn't do anything about it.

***

Something woke Gavin from a troubled sleep. At first, he ascribed his pounding heart and sweat-soaked nightclothes to a nightmare, yet a feeling of disquiet continued to pervade his waking mind. He sat up and focussed on the feel of his surroundings. A comfortable chamber in Baron Hestian's keep with only the faint glow of embers from the banked fire to provide a hint of outline to the room's furnishings. Nothing out of the ordinary; certainly nothing to indicate danger.

Gavin tossed aside the sheets and slipped out of bed. He stood in quiet contemplation for a moment, following his sense of unease until he found himself facing a bare wall. Far beyond, he knew, he faced the direction of the castle. Something there had tugged at his awareness, warned him of danger.

And suddenly, he knew.

He threw himself across the room, finding the door to the outer chamber by instinct rather than sight, and charged out into the hall. He nearly ran into Angie, Merikan on her heels.

"Sire," she cried out, retrieving her candle before it could fall to the floor. "I felt your agitation."

"What is it?" Merikan asked, dark eyes urgently searching Gavin's face. "What's happened?"

"Someone is searching for Borun's spells," Gavin whispered, heart in his throat. "And I think they've found the first one."

Merikan swore.

"It's begun," Angie said.

Gavin stared blankly at her for a heartbeat, then turned and found Tera and Davok, the two soldiers Nervain had left to guard the King's chambers, standing at attention, weapons ready, senses fully alert, and awaiting his command.

"Wake Commander Nervain," he ordered them. "Have him make preparations. We ride for the castle at dawn with all haste. The Tre'embra and the servants will remain here, along with the baggage and the pack horses and a suitable guard. When it is safe to do so, they will return home also. The Lady Sorceress and the Lord Protector ride with me. We travel as lightly as possible. Go."

They saluted and Davok took off running, Tera falling back to resume his post, watching over the King at a discreet distance.

Gavin turned back to Angie and Merikan.

130

"I don't know what spell they've discovered, nor how. I can only hope that its mask will foil any attempt to read it, but we cannot depend on that."

"If they've found one—" Merikan began.

"I know," Gavin interrupted. "They'll search out the others. I cannot believe it is coincidence to stumble on one, so this is deliberate. It might help explain Father's death, but it changes nothing. I must return and gather up the other spells, move them, hide them, keep them out of enemy hands."

"And find out what spell is missing," Merikan said.

"Heaven help us if any of them are used," Gavin shook his head heavily. "We have a long, hard journey ahead of us."

"You're not alone, Gavin," Angie said, laying a hand on his arm. She hurried off to her own room to get ready for the trip. Gavin stared at his arm where her fingers had touched for a long moment before retreating back to his own chambers and calling for Jamison. They had much to do and very little time.

Chapter 15

Angie curled up in the small tent Nervain had retrieved from the pack horses before they had left Baron Hestian's lands. The Commander had acquired six such tents from their supplies, easy to set up and light to carry, designed for soldiers on campaign and often on the move. Angie remembered Alvin's words to Kaeley before they left: *You know Gavin likes to prepare for anything.* She wondered if the King had envisioned such a race home when he had ordered the tents packed.

They had ridden hard for four days now, one soldier sent ahead each morning as a scout, Commander Nervain, Gavin, Merikan and Angie following, flanked by four more guards, and a fifth man riding as rear-guard. They rode from dawn til dusk, pausing only briefly to pace and water the horses and take meals. Each horse, plus two extra mares they had brought to carry additional fodder and spell off the riders, carried provisions so that they need not stop in towns or villages, and they set up camp each night away from the road, somewhere the scout found agreeable. Angie certainly didn't know Karundin enough to discern their route, but she did recognise that it differed from the one they had travelled before, going around populated areas as much as possible. She didn't know whether this made the trip faster or slower, but she understood Gavin's desire to avoid any questions and the very real possibility of panic that seeing their party pass in all haste would raise.

Angie found a spot she could almost call comfortable and tried very hard not to move. Far from an expert horsewoman, she found the gruelling pace even more difficult for her unfamiliarity with staying in the saddle. For the first day, she had clung to the pommel with an aching grip, bouncing hard in the saddle until she finally found something close to the horse's rhythm. Her legs and arms and back—pretty much all her muscles—screamed their protest at the abuse, bruises formed on bruises, and blisters formed and broke and worked on repeating the process. She knew Gavin's frustration at any delay and attempted to keep her agony to herself, but she had definitely needed assistance in dismounting whenever they had stopped.

When they had halted that first night, Merikan had taken most of her weight and led her very slowly to the fire where Angie hesitated to sit for fear of never rising again, yet didn't trust her legs to keep her upright either. She had brushed angrily at her helpless tears and lowered herself gently to stretch out with her back to a fallen tree. She nearly wept when Gavin draped a soft blanket over her legs and handed her a container with a salve Merikan had provided, explaining how it would help with any saddle sores and bruising. With great difficulty, she had waited until she crawled whimpering into the tent Nervain set up later to apply the salve. The balm smelled of pine and mint, and the cool cream had an immediate effect on her agony, so much so that she fell asleep with the relief it provided.

When she woke around dawn to the sound of the men stirring in the camp, her whole body felt stiff and battered and she seriously contemplated just staying where she lay, but nature called and she groaningly obeyed.

Mounting that second morning took far too much concentration and she gritted her teeth behind firmly pressed lips and determined not to cry. The men looked at her with sympathy, no doubt remembering their first days as children learning to ride, but they set out at a quick pace regardless of her discomfort.

The second night mostly repeated the first, save that they ate roast rabbit rather than pheasant, snared by the scout, and Angie soon had the cooling balm of the salve spread over her hurts and slept deeply, only to awake even more stiff than the previous morning. She recalled how a new exercising regime always seemed to hurt more after the second day, and so it seemed with horseback riding also. But she persevered, refusing to allow her pain to slow their progress.

Now, after their fourth day of hard riding, Angie had mastered the aches enough that she could pretend to ignore them, at least enough to move slowly on her own without dissolving into tears, and she used less salve. Still, she hoped not to move in the night once she settled herself for sleep, expecting oblivious slumber again.

Instead, she dreamed.

She saw the village of Chasta engulfed in flames, the people staring blankly, all hope fled from their faces as they watched their world burn. Their dull despair morphed into joy as Gavin stepped from the fire, children in his arms, on his back, floating around him, unharmed, and the inferno fell away wherever he swept his gaze until the flames disappeared. The villagers roared his approval and lifted him up, holding him just above a darkness that crept along the ground. The black carpet devoured the villagers as it reached out for the King, yet it couldn't touch him so long as the people held him aloft. It ate away at the people and they cried out in pain, but none abandoned Gavin, each face fierce as they defended the man who saved them, though they died for their defiance.

Angie moaned in her sleep and the nightmare changed.

A bright star shone, facing the white glow of the moon. The star remained constant while the moon waned, the great orb growing dimmer until only a sliver of light remained at its outer edges, huge arms of darkness oppressing the light. Then the darkness obscuring the slivered moon surged forward, trying to swallow the star in its heavy embrace. The shadows of the moon hid the star, leaving only a reflection of its bright warmth as it struggled against the night.

In a flash, the scene changed again.

A great line of tall, strong trees, vibrant green and rich earthy brown, stood in a razor-straight row, looking out at a wide barren land, grey and lifeless. From the dust rose clay figures, human in form yet lacking any features or personality. Hundreds, then thousands, adding up to uncounted hordes of deathless soldiers, each aimed unerringly at the trees. They reached the demarcation between vitality and enervation and pressed against an invisible wall. The shield held for a time, but numbers told, and the wall bent inward, then fell. The golems swept into the trees, felling many with their very presence. The trees fought to keep the unnatural beings from their land, but too many of the creatures swarmed forward, their numbers overwhelming.

Behind the clay soldiers followed ranks of villagers masked

with vacant expressions, but Angie could see past their veils to the silent screaming terror of enslaved people beneath. Struggle as they might, they could not escape the influence of a power greater than themselves, forcing them into a war they did not want but had to fight. And beside them marched others eager to please the hand that held them captive, though they could not see the strings moving them.

These too fell upon the trees, tearing them limb from limb, ripping apart a peaceful world, following the whims of a shadowy puppet-master who worked to change the land into one more pleasing to him, where he dictated the rules and smothered those who stood against him.

Angie despaired, writhing in her sleep, wanting to help the trees even before they grew into the likeness of those she knew, though she knew not how. She watched as the people of Karundin emerged from the trees like butterflies pulled from cocoons, only to encounter the uncaring hands of the dark army set before them.

"Stop!" Angie cried out, and time obeyed, her voice the only sound intruding in the silent horror of her vision.

Everything froze as Angie's magic took hold. She could feel pressure building as something sought to overcome her power and resume the carnage, but she held firm, looking for anything that would help her.

The light altered, reminding her of when she dreamed of Karundin, and she grasped at the change, pulling it to her. She stepped forward ...

And stood in the office at work, looking into the workroom where she did most of her restoration. A painting stood on an easel in the centre of the huge room, light surrounding it from above and shading everything around it into obscurity. She walked toward the painting, recognising it as Karundin Castle, only now, someone had removed a corner of the paint to reveal the words beneath, words she could almost understand. She flashed on a brief memory of Gavin's coronation, when she had glimpsed the whole of the parchment hidden by the castle, and again, she felt a strange connection.

A slight scuff brought her around to face a man she had not thought to see again.

"Mermaid?" Irving gaped incredulously. "Is it really you?"

Angie stared at him, not knowing if he was real or just a

dream.

"Irving," she sobbed and threw herself at the man, clutching him in a crushing embrace. Irving hugged her back just as fiercely.

"I thought I had made you up," she heard him mumble, his face pressed into the top of her shoulder. "No one else remembers you, and I thought ..."

Angie pushed him out to arms' length and studied his haggard face.

"It's a dream, Irving," she whispered, not sure whether she assured herself or this mentor from her past.

"But it wasn't always," he said, squeezing her shoulders once before dropping his arms to his side and gazing into the distance. "Some days, I just go along with everyone else, follow the past they recall." He brought his attention back to Angie. "But sometimes, if I try to remember, I know a different past. One with you in it, Ange. Only, no one else remembers."

"What do you mean?"

"People know we do good work here, but if pressed, they point to Jerry as the expert. No one seems to mind that he's too young to have started out with me five years ago; they just shrug and assume I did the work back then, or someone who's moved on that they no longer remember as important. Even I have to really concentrate to know you're the reason I'm still here. And only since the funeral, when I imagined I saw you, though no one else did. Angie, what the hell's going on?"

Angie looked at the painting of her new home, then back to the man from her old life.

"Do you remember that day at the hospital?" she asked. "My parents' accident?"

Irving frowned in concentration.

"Ye-es," he said slowly. "There was a phone call, and ... I followed you and Jerry there."

"Do you remember someone shooting me with an arrow?"

"An arrow!?" Irving shook his head vigorously, then paused, a far-away look in his eyes. "You fell." Even his voice grew distant. "I ran to your side, and then ..." His gaze sharpened and he stared hard at her. "You disappeared. A moment of confusion, then Jerry and I went into the hospital, and completely forgot about you."

Angie nodded.

"That's when I went there," she pointed at the castle in the painting. "Karundin. A land I've visited all my life in my dreams. Only I went there in truth this time, and it's where I live now. Helping those who need me."

Irving stared at the picture for a long moment as though he had never seen it. The castle appeared so life-like that Angie imagined she could see a breeze caress the flags on the parapets, guards walking the battlements, perhaps even young Rayton watching out a window, waiting for his father's return.

Eventually, Irving spoke without looking away from the scene.

"Are you happy there?"

"I've spent the last four days on a horse racing across the country, and I hurt like hell."

Irving snorted out a laugh and regarded her.

"It's a different world," she went on, "but I've grown rather fond of the people there. Bad times are coming, and they need me, Irving."

"Then what are you doing here?" he asked.

"I think I saw the future," Angie said. "And it was horrible. I asked for help, and then I appeared here, with that picture. I think I need what's under the paint, the words hidden beneath."

"Is that why it's here, somewhere you recognise?"

Angie narrowed her eyes.

"It's here because the museum wanted us to work on it, uncover the writing."

But Irving shook his head.

"I've never seen this painting before, Mermaid. If you remember it being here, it's only because the museum would have wanted *you* to work on it. Only, you don't exist here anymore, so we never got the painting."

Angie blinked a few times, trying to process that. The painting wavered, starting to fade.

"No!" Angie cried, concentrating on keeping the picture in place. It stop flickering, but now had a sort of transparency.

"Irving, can you get that painting from the museum? Bring it here for real?"

"Here in the workroom, or here in your dream?"

"My dream?" she echoed.

"Well, I didn't bring us here, Mermaid. I can honestly say I've never dreamed this vividly before, and I can't affect things like you just did. So it must be your dream, and I'm just a visitor."

So is this real, or isn't it? she wondered.

"Don't doubt me, Mermaid," Irving said suddenly, reading her troubled expression. "Just tell me what you need."

"That painting," she answered immediately, clinging to a sliver of hope. "And any information you can get on it. Provenance, where it came from, who painted it and when, how long the museum's had it. I need to know what that writing says."

"I'll do what I can, Ange. Will you ..." he swallowed heavily. "When will you come back?"

"I don't know how, Irving," she said, holding back the tears that suddenly trembled at the rims of her eyes through sheer effort of will. "I don't even know how I came this far, or how long I can stay. I don't know how I'm doing most of what I do now."

He nodded once, firmly.

"Then when I do get the picture, I'll put it right there, where it sits now, so you can find it. In case I'm not here."

"Irving—" But the light faded, taking Irving and the workroom with it.

Angie found herself standing again on the cusp between the armies of living trees and the hordes of darkness, with every eye now trained upon her, their paralysis broken. Sound rushed out at her, as frightening in its volume as the silence that had preceded it. The trees cried out in protest as the golems turned to swarm toward her, blank faces stretched in unnatural hunger and feet drumming in terrible unison as they ran. Angie screamed.

And woke with hands shaking her roughly.

"Come on, Angie, wake up!" a familiar voice called urgently.

She sat up quickly and wrapped her arms around him, holding him close like a life-line while she shook and sobbed. Gavin held her gently, rocking slowly back and forth and murmuring comforting words.

When Angie could breath normally again, she sat back, scrubbing the tears from her face with her palms. Gavin let her go reluctantly. Angie turned to regard the other man crouched at her side, his concerned face illuminated by a golden ball of magic that showed how crowded her small tent had become.

"What happened?" Merikan asked.

"The future, and maybe a way to stop it from happening like that."

She told them everything she remembered of the nightmare,

138

speaking as though writing down the details in one of her dream journals. It helped her keep things straight, pretending the dream just another tale from her imagination, even though she knew better now.

Yet she couldn't help but wonder if she truly had spoken to Irving. It seemed impossible that he would just accept what she said, that she had stood on Earth again, however briefly, that any of it had actually happened. But if she had made that part up, why had it felt the most real? She had to believe she dreamed true, or any hope of saving them all from a bleak future lay in ruins. She needed that painting, the spells beneath, or the dark armies would overrun them all. And Irving could help her retrieve it.

Irving, the only person on Earth who remembered her.

She stifled a gasp as despair threatened to overwhelm her. Gavin reached for her hand and squeezed it softly, offering comfort. Angie gazed into his steadying grey eyes and found a small smile for him. She belonged in Karundin now and the people here needed her. Gavin needed her. She would see him safe, no matter what it took.

Chapter 16

Shanor stood in the western wing of the library, fists on his hips as he peered up into the vast arches of the great room. So many days and nights he had spent here during his first years at court in pursuit of Borun's spellbook, searching out clues, history, obscure and forgotten facts. He had even briefly flirted with the notion that he would come across the book itself, forlorn and forgotten in some dusty nook, but of course, such fantasy had ever come to naught.

He shook his head now, slowly, his gaze taking in the hundreds of thousands of books stored in the castle's library. At least one dedicated wing held the knowledge of ancient days, preserved from a golden age when Karundin and Sahkarae had stood as one, and no doubt, various tomes of like vintage lay scattered throughout the giant repository, according to topic. The other three wings contained books from every nation and time, right up to the most recent offerings by the mediocre storytellers and poets of the day. Volumes bound in specially treated animal skins lined the shelves right alongside cloth-bound editions, pages sandwiched between wooden slabs, even some books held together by shells, the cunningly devised covers created by the sea peoples in the east.

One special centrally located section with guards on the door held grimoires of the sorcerers of the past, each with its own unique protection. Shanor had seen all those books, and not one interested him at the present. No, what he wanted must lie somewhere in this great depository of words, yet nowhere so obvious as a guarded room.

He had stood in the Great Hall once more after gaining the first spell, mind purposefully blank of outside distractions as he sought to recall exactly where the other two beams of light he'd glimpsed at the coronation had led. He had then plotted every destination within the castle that lay along the shaft of those guiding lights. After exhausting the other possible locations, Shanor now found himself in the great library, staring at uncounted volumes, books he had passed untold times with no inkling that his great desire lay within his grasp, yet so ingeniously disguised that he had never truly thought to find it here. Yet here it must reside; but how to find it?

No one had confronted him about the disappearance of the previous spell he had recovered four days earlier, although it still lay frustratingly concealed in that infernal shield now secured in his chambers. He rather suspected that, with Gavin absent, no one would know of that spell's recovery until the King returned. Which suggested to Shanor that in fact no one but the King truly had a connection to the spells; at least no one present, for possibly Merikan or Angelica might discern the disturbance of something so potentially powerful. But neither Alvin nor Rayton, as the remaining Royals in the castle, seemed to sense anything amiss. Surely, then, Shanor could risk using his magic to probe for the location of the second spell. For if Gavin had felt any warning at such a distance, he would undoubtedly return home with all haste, limiting Shanor's window of opportunity to take what he most wanted. And already, the Sorcerer had wasted too long in narrowing down the location of the other spells.

He started simply, muttering a spell to outline everything with a magical defence or disguise, illuminating each object in his Sight. The entire library flared brightly in his enhanced vision as spells of protection surrounding the whole vast structure revealed their presence. Squinting against the glare, Shanor eliminated the magic designed to discourage fire, the backup enchantments that would draw air from the room to douse stubborn flames that did manage to start, and the additional precaution of tossing water on any fire that survived the first two deterrents from his Sight. The brilliant glare faded, leaving bright spots of more individual protections dotted throughout the library.

The entire section containing the grimoires remained well-illuminated, and Shanor phased it out of his search. If he failed to locate the spell elsewhere, he would look there, but having seen those books, he did not believe any part of Borun's masterpiece lay hidden among those lesser tomes.

He also eliminated the other three wings of the library. From what he had calculated, the spell lay somewhere in the west wing, so he would concentrate his efforts here.

Shanor gazed about at what yet glowed in his Sight. A remarkable selection of books and lesser artifacts drew his enhanced attention. He thought about the shield concealing the first spell, considered how unlike a page from a spellbook that disguise had proven, and for the moment, altered his own spell to discard showing him anything book-like.

The amount of illuminated items lessened, yet an astounding number of spelled objects hovered in his Sight. Who knew the library held so much non-written knowledge to protect? Still, he had narrowed his search from hundreds of thousands of elements to merely hundreds.

He studied his altered search spell, each layer more complex as he refined its parameters, so that he could recreate these specific conditions rather than start from the beginning next time he needed to cast it, then dropped the Sight, allowing his eyes to readjust to the normal conditions of the library. He had a place to start now, and strode deeper into the west wing to continue his search.

Whenever he came to a protected item, Shanor ran his hand lightly over it, keeping in mind how the disguised shield had seemed no different from its neighbours until he had physically touched it. He hoped such a phenomenon would recur to announce the presence of the hidden spell, but he also made a mental map of each trinket in case such proved not the case and he had to return and make a more thorough search of the ensorcelled treasures.

Some of the protections made sense to Shanor, but others befuddled him. He understood why someone might want to protect a historic artifact such as the plaque acknowledging the donation of a large number of tomes from the Fairlae Library nearly a hundred years ago, or the official seals of ancient Karundin and Sahkarae, set in a protective case in one niche, or even the quill used by the famed historian Dardanak II of Taerdan far to the north some two centuries past. But why would anyone place a spell over the slate used by some forgotten minor nobleman showing off his first pathetic attempt at letters in his fifth year, let alone maintain its stasis? Or the frayed ball of the gardener's favourite hound thirty double-seasons ago? Why would anyone want to keep that, let alone house it in the library under a magical shield? Shanor wiped his hand absently against his robes after brushing against that, imagining he could feel the slime of the mutt's saliva preserved along with the ball, and moved on with a disgusted shudder.

Just short of a water glass later, Shanor had made a cursory pass at most of the objects under Protection with no success, when a young voice spoke from behind him, snapping his attention to the child standing a few paces away.

"What are you looking for, Sorcerer Shanor?" Rayton's voice held genuine curiosity, but no suspicion. Shanor inclined his head in a small bow and considered the Heir a moment.

"What makes you think I'm looking for anything, Dho'vani?"

Rayton gestured vaguely off to the side to a table with an open notebook. A scholar had just finished tidying up his lessons and moved away, while a couple of royal guards lounged nearby, keeping an eye on the Prince.

"My tutor and I made it through a whole lesson in history while you moved up and down the aisles," replied Rayton, "but you didn't look at any books that I could see. And I saw magic glittering in your eyes when you moved past last time, so I thought maybe you were looking for something special. Can I help?"

Shanor stared at him, wondering how he had missed the presence of the Heir in the library as he hunted. No one had sat in this section of the library when he had begun his search; Shanor had swept the area with a spell to make sure of his solitude and had thought he had the wing to himself. Granted, once he had begun, Shanor had paid scant attention to his surroundings, but he had felt certain no one would interrupt him.

"My apologies, Dho'vani, I did not mean to intrude on your studies. I did not realise you took your lessons here."

"I don't normally," Rayton confided. "But I couldn't sit still in the classroom. I thought I'd do better in the library, though we don't usually come here. It's big," he paused, looking around at all the shelves. "How do you find anything in here? I'd use magic too, if I could. It would make getting the right book easier." He grinned up at the Sorcerer.

Shanor, however, suppressed a sudden chill. Could the child know somehow? Could he sense another's magic searching for

143

Borun's spell? Did this Royal, along with his father, have a subtle connection to the pages of the book after all? But if so, wouldn't he have known when Shanor had retrieved the first spell? Yet he hadn't confronted Shanor over that, so perhaps the Sorcerer overreacted now. However, if the child did have some connection to the spells, Shanor would do well to cultivate a relationship with him, just in case.

He forced a smile to his lips.

"Sometimes magic can help find things," he said to Rayton. "But I did not come looking for a book, young Rayton. I came to make sure the library had all its defences still in place. I will check the entire castle to make sure no one can sneak in, like they did with your grandfather." He watched the boy's face fall as he glanced quickly to his guard and back. "With the Lord Protector and the Lady Sorceress gone, we must be even more vigilant in regards to the security of the castle and Karundin's Heir. I intend to keep a close eye on you, Dho'vani, make sure nothing happens."

"Angie will be back soon," Rayton whispered, gaze unfocussed over Shanor's shoulder. "She'll bring Papa and then we'll all be safe again." He blinked, solemn face tilted back to look up at Shanor once more, voice full of confidence. "But until then, I'm glad you're here to watch over us, Sorcerer Shanor."

He turned and gathered up notebook and guard, then left the library.

Shanor watched with narrowed eyes, wondering whether the boy spoke of the Sorceress's return in hope or as premonition. Contemplating the possibilities, Shanor murmured a quick spell to ensure that no one else had entered this section of the library, then returned to his search.

When he reactivated his Sight spell, his eyes fell on a candelabra. He had almost dismissed it before speaking with the Dho'vani, but now, something about it piqued Shanor's attention. He studied it a moment, then spun to stare at the empty place where Rayton had stood. Crouching to put himself at the same height as the child, Shanor looked back at the candelabra. It stood exactly where Rayton could see it over Shanor's shoulder when the boy had lost his focus.

Shanor rose with a grimace as his knees protested, and approached the candle holder. It stood as high as Shanor, polished bronze curlicues sweeping up from an oaken base to form five fingers, one for each unlit blue candle. A delicate ivory etching of geometric shapes dyed red, blue, and green, capped in gold, sheathed the joint where the base met the bronze. Similar candelabra dotted the library, each preserved from tarnish and wear, and this one looked no different. Yet when Shanor reached out a hand, he almost felt as though the holder drew back from his touch, as though something didn't want him near it. Fancy, perhaps, or maybe part of a spell intended to keep prying hands from finding what they should not.

He wrapped his fingers around the base and felt the hint of a different kind of magic. Not quite the same as the shield, but unlike anything else he had discerned in any Preservation Spell.

Had the boy seen it, somehow recognised it? Or had he simply stared off at nothing, as children sometimes did (how many times had Maraenda's little Maraedeth stared wide-eyed at things Shanor could not see)? And if Rayton could sense the spell, could he unlock the means to read it too?

Shanor gazed at the candelabra, wondering how to remove such a large and awkward item without notice. Though he stood as the highest Sorcerer in the castle at present, by no means did he stand alone as sole magic user. One could always find lesser sorcerers in the castle, either citizens of Karundin or visiting scholars. At this time of day though, any of them might wander the halls of the castle, and while they would never dare to question someone of Shanor's standing on his use of magic, carrying around a candelabra concealed in a veil would require enough power to elicit talk should any observe him. Getting the shield back to his chambers undiscovered in the small hours of the morning had posed no problems, but striding openly through the halls in the middle of the afternoon might draw attention.

As he considered, he ran his hand up over the ivory etching, then down to the oak shaft, and paused. He felt the smallest difference in the spell. Closing his eyes, Shanor allowed a trickle of magic to trail down his fingers, searching for that difference. Three whispered spells of discernment and revelation later and a smile stretched across his lips. He opened his eyes to see his hand wrapped entirely around the etching, the ivory warm to the touch. He needn't take the entire candelabra after all; just this small part.

With a swift casting of magic, he severed the ivory from the oak and brass, slipping the etching into a pocket inside his robe.

He hid the broken sconce and shaft in a seldom-used corner, placing a spell of concealment over them, and with unhurried strides, left the library with his prize tucked safely away.

***

Rayton didn't know why he had felt compelled to ask his tutor to take his lessons in the library yesterday afternoon, but the same feeling made the boy seek out Sorcerer Shanor now, before he had to attend the morning audiences. Why, he couldn't say, just that he had to see the man. Rayton wished he could talk to Angie about this strange feeling instead, or even Lord Merikan or his father. He supposed he could ask Uncle Alvin or Aunt Maraenda, but he had almost reached Shanor's quarters, so he might as well just keep going. As always, Remy and Oniak trailed him, guarding the Dho'vani. Remy often made Rayton smile with his easy-going manner, and Oni sometimes snuck him snacks from the kitchen with a wink, but the child had no doubts that Remy and Oni would do everything they could to keep him safe. Though Rayton couldn't see what harm Sorcerer Shanor would cause.

He hesitated before the oaken entrance to Shanor's rooms, little fist raised, then shrugged and rapped on the door. A servant answered, peered with widened eyes down at the little Prince, then bowed.

"I want to see Sorcerer Shanor," Rayton stated.

"Of course, Dho'vani," the servant bowed again. "Please come in and I will inform the Sorcerer of your arrival."

Rayton nodded graciously and ignored the discomfiture of the servant. Leaving Remy and Oni to guard the door to the hall, Rayton strode in. He had never visited Shanor's quarters before, and the appearance of the Heir-Apparent had no doubt flustered the servant, but the man carried out his task with quiet efficiency, gesturing to a seat before the fire for Rayton before retreating deeper into the chambers to gather up the Sorcerer.

Rayton scrambled up into the deep-cushioned chair and settled himself. The child looked around the room, feet kicking idly while he waited. For some reason, his attention kept coming back to the hearth. Not the fire flickering lazily in the blackened stone fireplace, nor the few odds and ends dotting the mantle above, but rather to the blank spot beside the opening. Why this empty space fascinated him, he couldn't say, but again, just like the feeling that brought him here, Rayton knew he had to investigate.

He leaned forward and squinted at the wall, then covered one eye with his hand, and next tried staring with his eyes opened as wide as they would go. The wall space remained empty. He remembered his nurse once saying that one could see something from other realms if one caught it unawares out of the corner of the eye, so he peered at it sideways. Just when he thought he might have seen the area shimmer, Shanor walked in and Rayton blinked at him owlishly before remembering his station. He sat back regally in the chair and nodded politely to the Sorcerer.

Shanor bowed slightly and stared at him a moment, thoughts unreadable on an impassive face, though Rayton could tell the Sorcerer had something on his mind. That didn't concern the Dho'vani; he had come here for his own reasons, even if he didn't understand them.

"I had not thought to see the Dho'vani in my chambers," Shanor said. "How may I assist you, Highness?"

"I needed to ask you something," Rayton replied, "'Cause I didn't know who else to ask."

When the Prince didn't go on, Shanor settled himself into a nearby chair and turned to give Rayton his full attention.

"You may ask what you will, Dho'vani; I will endeavour to answer to the best of my abilities."

Rayton squirmed in his seat, not sure how to go on now that he had Shanor's attention. How did one ask *why did I feel I had to come here*?

"Something made me want to go to the library yesterday," he finally said, peering up through his lashes at the brooding man. "The same thing brought me here today. Why is that, Sorcerer Shanor? Did you want me to come here?"

Shanor sat back as far as his chair would allow, a frown creasing his forehead as he studied Rayton. The boy fidgeted under his scrutiny. As Rayton sought refuge anywhere else, his eyes drifted back to the blank space on the wall and he stared at it rather than meet Shanor's inquisitive gaze. After a few seconds, he forgot about Shanor at all as he again saw the space shimmer, then resolve into a triangular shield leaning against the wall. Rayton's eyes widened and his mouth dropped into a surprised little 'o' as he took in the sigil of the grey tower on the blue background of the shield.

"Where did you find that?" he asked, jumping off his chair and crouching before the shield, his previous question forgotten in his excitement. "I only ever heard of the Tenatric Crest, and that only in a story Nurse told me once."

Rayton didn't notice Shanor's stillness or his rigid grip on the arms of his chair, and only noted the silence when he turned to look at the pale-faced man.

"Tenatric Crest?" Shanor finally asked quietly.

"Oh, yes," the boy replied eagerly. "A great tale of ancient knights and fallen sorcerers and all sorts of adventures, and always there to put things right was the Knight of the Tenatric Crest, a mysterious noble who only appeared when things got desperate. Nurse only told it the once, but I never forgot."

Rayton turned back to the shield, then frowned slightly.

"But I think the tower's the wrong colour," he murmured, and without pausing to consider his actions, ran his hand over the image. The edge of the tower began to peel.

"Oh!" the boy cried out, yanking his hand away. He turned to Shanor with wide, pleading eyes. "I'm sorry Sorcerer Shanor. I didn't mean to ruin it."

But Shanor's own expression did not show rebuke or anger; rather his eyes glowed with sudden fervour and a strange smile curled around his lips.

"Not at all, Dho'vani," he said to the Prince, his gaze never leaving the shield. "Indeed, I had wondered what seemed off. Please, continue. Show me what you've found."

An uneasy feeling began to grow in the pit of Rayton's stomach, so much so that he nearly fled, taking the shield with him. But the Sorcerer had asked so calmly despite the intensity of his regard, and Rayton didn't want to upset the man.

With a quivering hand and a heavy weight in his chest, Rayton reached for the crest of the tower again. His fingers tingled when they brushed the defect. He tried to hide his shudder as he grasped the peeling edge of the tower and pried it off the shield. The grey tower pulled away, leaving an off-white tower on the shield, just like Rayton remembered from the story. The grey tower in his hand had writing on the back, but he couldn't read it. He turned to Shanor and slowly, with a strange sense of dread, extended the page toward the Sorcerer's waiting hand.

Shanor took the offering almost reverently, but when he turned the tower over to see the writing, his brow creased in puzzlement. He muttered something under his breath, and Rayton could see the golden glow of sorcery glitter in his eyes. His frown eased, but did not entirely disappear. Shanor glanced down at Rayton.

"An interesting find, Dho'vani, though the language, tantalizingly familiar, remains somewhat of a mystery. I wonder ..." Shanor paused, lips pursed as he regarded the young Prince. "I have something else I would like you to take a look at for me, young Rayton." And so saying, he pulled an ivory cylinder from a hidden pocket in his robes, about as wide as Rayton's palm. An etching, actually, with all sorts of colours and shapes. Rayton started to shake his head as Shanor leaned forward to pass the object into his hands, but stopped when the Sorcerer spoke.

"Please, Dho'vani, I believe this is what drew you to me this morning. Why you felt you had to speak with me."

Rayton considered that, staring into the Sorcerer's sincere eyes, then he shrugged and thrust out his hand for the etching.

He looked down at the piece, feeling its weight, admiring the colours and details, but it just seemed like some knick-knack. He rolled it around in his hands, watching the interplay of light on the gold top, then glanced up at Shanor, feeling a little foolish.

"What is it?" he asked.

"Oh, just something I picked up," Shanor replied. "A token of bygone days."

Rayton nodded skeptically, then looked back at the etching in surprise as it warmed to his touch. His fingers began to unravel a thread at the top edge, the gold filigree beginning to unwind. Rayton looked at Shanor again with wide eyes, but at the Sorcerer's encouraging nod, the boy continued to draw the gold wire out. It reached the strip of ivory, then kept unwinding, dragging the etching along until it resembled a long, hand-wide sheaf of stiff parchment. Words formed hazily on the back of the etching but, like those on the tower of the shield, they meant nothing to Rayton.

He turned again to Shanor. The man, nearly quivering in place with impatience, nevertheless waited until Rayton extended the strange item for his perusal. He looked over the words eagerly, though once more, he seemed as unable to read them as the

Dho'vani. It didn't deter him though.

He met Rayton's gaze.

"Dho'vani, I must thank you for this. You have done me a great service." If his tone held a hint of mockery, Rayton did not hear it in his confusion.

"What is it?" he asked again. "What are either of them? And why were they so hidden?" He thought a moment, then added, "And how come you couldn't find them?"

Shanor's left eye twitched.

"I had not thought to look with the curiosity of a child," he answered evenly, expression solemn. "I must bow to your wisdom and ingenuity, Highness."

Rayton grinned at the compliment, feeling a sense of pride under the Sorcerer's approval, and he did not notice the light in Shanor's eyes or hear the softly murmured words as they passed through the man's lips.

"Now, is there anything else I can do for you this morning Dho'vani?" Shanor asked. "I know you will have a busy schedule with your Uncle, and I do not wish to keep you."

Rayton thought for a second, couldn't think of any reason to stay, and finally shook his head.

"Then let me see you to the door," Shanor rose, bowed, and gestured gracefully toward the exit. Rayton nodded with great aplomb and accepted the dismissal.

Remy and Oni stood to attention just beyond the door.

"Did you find what you wanted, Dho'vani?" Remy enquired politely.

Rayton frowned, tried to remember why he had sought out Sahkarae's Sorcerer in the first place, then shrugged.

"Guess so," he answered as he strode down the hall. "I helped Sorcerer Shanor find something he wanted."

If Remy thought that strange, he kept it to himself.

Chapter 17

A lone rider appeared at the closed eastern gate of Karundin's capital in the small water glasses of the night. He exchanged brief words with the sleepy soldier who emerged from the guard house to peer out the grill of the sally port. That guard roused his companion. The second man hurried into the city, heading for the castle, while the first opened the sally port for the dismounted rider, who brought his heaving horse through.

They waited in silence, the rider taking time to water his weary mount and then himself from a flask at his saddle. A handful of moments later, eight more cloaked riders emerged from the dark, dismounted, and led their horses tiredly through the sally port. The guard bowed as the group moved past into the city. He peered around the abandoned streets to make sure no one lurked in the darkness, then glanced back out into the night and the now empty road beyond the gate, before finally closing and locking the sally port again.

When his companion returned from informing the appropriate parties up at the castle of the unexpected arrival, both men looked quietly at one another, exchanged a solemn nod, then went back to their duties with renewed vigilance. The King returning unannounced in such secrecy and haste, accompanied only by a small entourage, spoke of a certain gravity that the soldiers took to heart. They wondered what had transpired and how bad things would get in the coming days, but they never wavered in their resolve. They stood watch over Karundin, come what may.

***

Gavin paced as he waited, his exhaustion from the gruelling week-long trek home superseded by his anxiety over the welfare of his family. Angie sat in a cushioned chair by the fireplace, the hearth only recently rekindled, and Merikan stood by the mantle, brooding into the crackling flames.   They both understood Gavin's urgency for this late-night meeting and why he had felt the need to push through the darkness, leaving their spent horses at the last transfer station with a guard while they procured fresh mounts, but neither had felt what Gavin felt that morning.   Neither could truly know the gut-churning terror that had clawed at the King's chest when Gavin recognised the unveiling of two of Borun's spells, an unveiling only the hand of a Royal could accomplish. He did not know whether Alvin's hand or Rayton's had triggered the warning, and he feared for both.

A knock sounded lightly at the door to the private library Gavin had chosen. He stopped his pacing and turned as Nervain entered, followed by Commander Eniok. A burly man in full leathers whom Gavin, like his father before him, had charged with the castle's defences, Eniok's eyes swept the room and took note of the weary state of its inhabitants in an instant. Behind the two Commanders came Tre'vani Alvin and Sorcerer Shanor, the former still blinking sleep from his eyes, the latter alert though slightly dishevelled from a hasty dressing.

Gavin breathed a silent sigh of relief at the sight of his brother. A subtle nod from Nervain indicated that Rayton slept peacefully under the watchful eye of his guard, and Gavin finally felt some of his tension leak away, and with it, the adrenaline that had kept him on his feet and fully alert. He sank gratefully into the chair next to Angie and called this small council forward to join him.

Alvin took in the grim countenance of his brother and his unexpected early return with worried eyes.

"Kaeley?" he asked in a low tone.

"She's fine," Gavin quickly reassured him. "Hestian's hosting the Progress. I only brought enough for protection in our haste."

"Which brings us to why you're here, Sire, so late and in such secrecy," Eniok said.

"We've had a breach," Gavin said. "Someone has found what they should not, and I had feared some ill had befallen Alvin or Rayton. I am greatly relieved that both seem unscathed. But it now leaves us with some difficult questions."

"What manner of breach, Sire?" Eniok asked. "And what has been found?"

"In time, Commander," Gavin replied before swinging his gaze to Shanor.

"Sorcerer Shanor, have you discerned any unusual expenditures of magic in our absence?"

"Unusual expenditures, Your Majesty? No, nothing out of the ordinary," he answered, gaze turning inward as he pondered. "A couple of visiting scholars tested some theories on kiln heating versus magic-induced open-fire thresholds for pottery that caused a very minor fire, quickly contained; an entertainer called up some fireworks about two weeks ago to distract the children; the normal magics employed to maintain the aqueducts and farmers' fields, including a possible new innovation by the head of agriculture for pest control, but nothing I would call unusual." His gazed refocussed. "What kind of magics do you suspect?"

Gavin shook his head slightly to dismiss the question. He did not want to go into specifics until he had some idea of what had actually happened. Instead he turned to Eniok.

"Anything or anyone try to breach the defences, Commander? Any unexplained activity or unexpected occurrences?"

"None, Sire. A couple of petty thefts, some drunken brawls, a few minor disagreements, all within the city and all dealt with appropriately. I have detailed reports if necessary. Nothing reported amiss in the castle."

Gavin nodded.

"Commander Eniok, I want you and Sorcerer Shanor to go over everything from the past two weeks with Commander Nervain and Lord Protector Merikan, no matter how small or seemingly insignificant. The every day routines and anything that deviated, whether you think it in innocence or not. I want different eyes and ears to see and hear what someone might have missed." He held up a hand to forestall Eniok before the man could do more than open his mouth to question. "Until we can determine how and when the original breach occurred, I feel it best not to influence your recollections. We need *every* detail, not just what you might deem pertinent based on what our perpetrator took."

"Gentlemen," Nervain gestured off to the side, drawing the two to the far corner. Merikan followed behind.

"And me?" Alvin asked quietly, studying Gavin's troubled

expression. "What do you need?"

"Sit, Brother," Gavin replied. Once Alvin had done so, Gavin leaned forward, elbows on his knees and hands clutched loosely between his legs. "I need to know what's been going on."

"You feared for Rayton and myself, and you mentioned a theft. Can I take from that that you don't fear assassins so much as that someone has uncovered something of our charge?"

Gavin snorted softly. Alvin had the mind of a brilliant tactician and a keen intellect to go with it. If it did truly come to war as Angie's premonitions indicated, Alvin would lead Karundin's army. Gavin just didn't know against whom.

"Someone has found two of the spells." Only a slight pursing of his lips showed Alvin's reaction. "But more troubling, they found a way to unmask them this morning."

This brought a greater response. Alvin leaned forward quickly, just inches away from Gavin now, his eyes wide and his own hands clutched tightly together.

"But that means—"

"Tell me everything you remember since you woke up this morning," Gavin ordered.

Alvin nodded and proceeded to do just that, leaving nothing out. No indication that he had encountered or triggered the unmasking of one of Borun's spells, though.

"And if not me, unless the magic would recognise Maraedeth, only one other here could reveal those spells."

"I know," Gavin sighed heavily. "And I intend to see to Rayton soon." He ran a weary hand over his face. "Although another possibility exists."

"Another Royal?" Alvin asked incredulously.

"Magic," Gavin countered. "More specifically, magic to alter perception."

He went on to impart what they had learned on the night of Baron Hestian's feast, when Angie had pointed out that no real effort had gone into finding the assassin.

"To cloud so many minds so effectively would seem more difficult than to cloud just one mind," Gavin concluded. "So, although you don't remember anything that would lead back to uncovering a spell, we have to take into consideration the possibility that whoever holds those spells could have made you forget that you uncovered them."

Alvin nodded slowly, concentration etched on his face as he

thought it through.

"We'd have to corroborate my actions with others. Every move I made, everyone I spoke with, we'd have to check to see if it all really happened when and as I believed it to have happened."

"Which will likely bring up questions you do not wish to answer just yet," Angie said softly. Gavin had thought she had fallen asleep while he and Alvin spoke, but when he looked at her, he saw the alertness in her bi-coloured eyes.

"I need to speak with Rayton first," Gavin said, running a worried hand through his hair. "And his guards. If my son's day also bears nothing out of the ordinary, then we need to figure out how to question those with you earlier, Alvin, and those with Rayton, without raising suspicion or anxiety."

"You are positive none but a Royal could uncover the spells?" asked Angie.

Gavin nodded.

"It's one of the safeguards that all the spells share. A Royal hand can unmask the spell's disguise, though the words beneath will not be easily read. We still have time to retrieve the spells before the thief can use them, but we must know the thief's identity first. I can no longer sense the two missing pages, and that worries me greatly. I just hope Rayton can shed some light on this. Because if he can't ..."

"We will deal with that when we must, Sire," Angie said, laying a gentle hand on his arm. Gavin felt a calming tingle flow through him from that contact, and wondered if she had just instilled some magic in him, or if he merely reacted to her touch as a man to a woman. Didn't know what to think of that so simply accepted the comfort she provided and moved on.

"I must speak to my son," he said quietly.

"It's the middle of the night," Alvin murmured.

"I know," Gavin sighed heavily. "And I would prefer to wait until the morning, but every minute we let pass gives our enemy that much more time to truly uncover Borun's folly."

"I'll come with you," Angie said, rising from the chair to stand at his side.

The others across the room turned to look at the movement. Gavin waved them back before they moved to follow him.

"Gentlemen, when you're finished, get some sleep. We will reconvene in the morning. I wish to see my son before I find my rest."

So saying, Gavin strode from the room, Angie and Alvin trailing him. Two guards waiting at the doors flanked Gavin, and two more moved to cover Alvin.

Gavin paused and turned to his brother with a fond smile.

"Go back to your chambers, Alvin. Maraenda will no doubt be missing you."

They clasped hands and a sardonic little smile tickled at Alvin's mouth.

"Welcome home, Gavin," he said, shaking his head slightly. "Until the morning, then."

Gavin waited until Alvin passed out of sight beyond a corner, then sighed deeply, his shoulders slumping as exhaustion threatened. He wanted nothing more than to gather his son in his arms, reassure himself of Rayton's safety, then curl up and fall asleep next to the boy. Instead, he must wake Rayton up and ask if he had helped an enemy retrieve two deadly spells.

He took a deep breath, squared his shoulders, and faced the hall that would lead to his son's room.

He looked at Angie and offered his arm. When she took it without hesitation, he nodded and set off again, grim purpose in his stride.

***

Gavin leaned against the door frame, gazing silently at his son as the boy slumbered. The banked embers of the fire provided a whispered remembrance of warmth, and the candle in Gavin's hand sought to push back the darkness.

Angie stood behind him, silent, not wanting to disturb the King from his contemplation. She thought she understood his anxiety, his insistence to speak with Rayton immediately, but right now, as she watched the man watch his child, she wished he could just let matters lie for a few more hours. Gavin had driven them all hard to reach the castle quickly, himself not the least, and his exhaustion lay heavily upon him now that he no longer had to maintain the facade of strength. That he allowed her to see his vulnerability humbled her, and Angie hoped she could live up to such trust.

"He looks so peaceful," Gavin whispered without moving. "Would that I could join him."

They had left Gavin's guard with Rayton's out in the hall and

156

had dismissed Rayton's servant, leaving just the two of them to look in on the boy. For a moment, Angie felt like part of a family unit rather than a guardian.

Gavin heaved a great sigh before he pushed himself from the door frame and silently approached the bed. Angie hung back to give them some privacy.

The King placed his candle on the bedside table next to Rayton's unlit one and sat gently on the edge of the bed beside the young Prince. Rayton stirred at Gavin's hand on his shoulder, then sat up quickly and flung himself at his father.

They sat enfolded in each others arms for a few moments before Rayton searched the darkness near the door over his father's shoulder. When he found Angie's shadow, he sat back.

"Thank you for bringing Papa back safe, Angie, and for taking care of him," he said with great solemnity.

Angie kept her expression equally solemn, though her heart melted a little and she blinked back the hint of tears that tickled her eyes.

"Best care ever," she replied, just as she had promised him when they had left three weeks previously.

Rayton grinned, then sobered, looking back into Gavin's face.

"What's wrong, Papa? It's still night time."

Angie could see Gavin choose his words.

"Tell me of your morning, Rayton. What did you do today?"

Although Gavin had kept his tone light, Rayton chewed at his lip with a frown, and Angie thought he had picked up some of his father's worry.

"Well," the boy began, "I got all dressed up for morning audiences, 'cause Uncle Alvin says it's important to look all official-like to put the nobles at ease. So I put on a clean tunic and everything." Angie smiled at his earnest description.

"Then I ate porridge and bread and eggs with sauce and had some tea with honey, but only a bit 'cause it's better with cake, and cake's better with Angie, and there wasn't any cake anyway, so I just had a small cup of tea." Ah, how she had missed the little tyke.

"Then I went to see Sorcerer Shanor, 'cause I thought I ought to, though I usually don't. But he'd been checking on the castle's protections yesterday when tutor and I went to the library, and I guess I wanted to make sure the castle was still secure and all. Then I went to the audience chamber and sat with Uncle Alvin to

157

listen to what everyone else had to say. And we had some lunch. I worked numbers with tutor later. Did you know that you can add up cakes just like you can add soldiers into units and troops, only the cakes don't get swords, and you shouldn't have enough to make up a unit anyway? But the numbers work the same. And then I went to the lists and Remy showed me a new way to defend with the sword. But I can't show off weapons training with Maraedeth 'cause she's too little, so we just played chase instead.

"I wanted to play chess after supper, but no one else did, so we just listened to stories instead. Do you play chess, Angie? I think you'd do okay."

Angie, still trying to slow his barrage of words into coherence in her mind, smiled at that last.

"Maybe we could play tomorrow, Rayton," she said. "Although you might have to remind me of the rules."

He nodded happily, then glanced back at Gavin.

"Could we do that, Papa? Could we all just sit down and play for a bit?"

Gavin gave the boy a fond smile.

"I would like that," he said.

"And what about you, Papa? What did you do today?"

"We rode a lot," Gavin replied simply.

Rayton studied his father by the light of the candle. He looked over at Angie, then back to Gavin.

"Why?" Though a simple question, Rayton asked it with such seriousness that Angie knew the lad sensed trouble.

Gavin sighed and ruffled Rayton's hair.

"Maybe I just wanted to get home to see my son."

Rayton didn't respond to Gavin's small smile. Indeed, his face clouded with anxiety.

"What's wrong, Papa? What's happened?"

Gavin's eyes closed and he pulled his child close. Rayton peered around Gavin's shoulder, staring at Angie with wide eyes. Without conscious thought, she found herself drawn forward until she sat across the bed from Gavin, her hand on Rayton's back. She had hoped to soothe the boy, but feared she had merely added to his unease.

Gavin set him back, hands on his shoulders. Rayton reached back to take one of Angie's hands in his, though he kept his gaze riveted on his dad.

"Do you remember me telling you of Borun's spellbook?" Gavin finally asked.

Rayton glanced at Angie, then back to Gavin. The King smiled briefly.

"It's all right, Rayton, Angie knows of it."

Rayton nodded.

"And do you remember how Queen Teraenda hid each spell separately?"

Again Rayton nodded.

"It seems, now, that someone has uncovered two of those spells."

The grip on Angie's hand tightened.

"But how?" came the incredulous response.

"I don't know," Gavin admitted. "But it's worse than that, for I believe that, not only has someone found those spells, but they have unmasked them also."

Rayton gasped.

"But that's not possible, Papa! Not unless a Royal touched them."

Gavin remained silent. After a moment, Angie felt Rayton begin to tremble.

"That's why you came home," Rayton whispered, a quiver in his voice. "You wanted to know if I'd done it."

"Oh, Rayton, no," Gavin said, and Angie could see his expression shatter as he wrapped his son in strong arms. As Rayton refused to release Angie's hand, she found herself drawn very close to both King and Prince, certainly close enough to see the heartache in Gavin's eyes. With his cheek resting on Rayton's hair, Gavin tried to reassure the boy. "I needed to see you safe, Rayton. While the spells are of vital importance, I couldn't stand it if anything bad happened to you."

After a while, Rayton nodded and Gavin pulled back enough to see his son's face. Rayton ran the back of his free hand over his eyes then reached for Gavin's hand and held on tightly.

"We think it's possible that, whoever has the spells, also has the ability to cloud the mind, to make people forget things," explained Gavin. "This person made us all forget something very important, and only when Angie asked why did any of us start to question. That includes me and Lord Merikan. We fear that person may have made you or Alvin forget too. That's why I need to know what you did today, to see if there's any part of the

159

day missing, or that you forgot." Gavin cupped Rayton's chin gently and raised his son's gaze to meet his own. "If either you or Alvin revealed the spells, I *know* you did not do so intentionally or with malice. Do you understand, son?"

Rayton swallowed audibly before nodding.

"Yes, Papa."

"Ah Rayton, you know I love you."

Rayton finally let go of Angie's hand so that he could throw both arms around Gavin.

"I love you too, Papa."

Angie started to ease off the bed to leave them to their comfort, but suddenly found both hands captured, one by Rayton again, but the other by Gavin. She read gratitude in Gavin's eyes and comfort in Rayton's as they both turned to regard her. She froze under their combined scrutiny, then squeezed each hand in turn.

"I don't remember not remembering anything," Rayton said, looking back at his father. "But then, I guess I wouldn't. Maybe, if I think on it hard enough, I'll remember something different."

"I think if we all had a bit of sleep, we might puzzle something out," Gavin said, his exhaustion finally finding its way into his voice.

"Will you stay tonight, Papa?" Rayton asked in a small voice. "I'm ... I don't want to sleep alone."

"I will."

Rayton lay himself down on the bed and Gavin stretched out behind him after kicking off his shoes. Rayton drew his father's arm tightly across his chest like a safety blanket, then looked up at Angie with wide, pleading eyes.

Angie smiled and pulled her hand from his so that she could settle the blanket over the two. But when she stood to leave them in peace, Rayton called out.

"Angie!"

Both of his arms reached for her. She leaned over to kiss him on the forehead.

"Will you stay too?" he asked, voice breaking on the last word.

She wanted to say him nay, but somehow couldn't deny the mix of terror and hope that shone on his face. She sighed heavily, then sat and bent to remove her boots. He certainly had enough room on his bed, so she shimmied under the sheet and lay on her side facing them. Rayton took her hand in both of his and smiled, then closed his eyes on a contented sigh. Angie shook her head, then met Gavin's gaze. She couldn't read his expression and she didn't know what to show in return. So she edged up on her elbow and leaned over enough to blow out the candle. Then she settled herself again next to the King and his son and wondered just how she had gotten herself into this situation. Before she knew it, weariness swept over her and sleep claimed her for its own.

Chapter 18

Although the King examined both Alvin's and Rayton's movements on the morning in question, checking with everyone who interacted with the pair, he could find no discrepancies. So either someone had indeed used magic to cloud memories, or someone lied to cover their own involvement. Or possibly both. Gavin did not know which answer to fear more.

He also set in motion a definite search for his father's assassin, although with so much time past, the trail had grown cold.

And finally, he had sought out each of Borun's spells, keeping his movements clandestine, with only Angie and Merikan knowing the full extent of his search. What he discovered left a cold knot in the pit of his stomach. He had suspected the absence of the first spell when he found the passageway to the storage rooms beneath the castle swept clear of dust. The obvious signs of a search in the storage room itself further confirmed what he knew he'd find—or not find—even before he checked the stack of shields near the corner, and he hadn't bothered to suppress a shudder, discovering that he could in fact determine which spells had lain where.

His unknown enemy held the spell to create armies of clay.

The second spell had resided in the library. Merikan had somehow found the remains of the candelabra hidden behind a spell of concealment several stacks away from where the ornament had once stood, reconfirming that their nemesis wielded magic. Again, Gavin grimaced, praying that their quarry would remain ignorant of what the spells actually entailed, yet dreading that one clever enough to find and take said spells in the first place would eventually find a way to read them too.

And with one who used magic to alter memories already, what would he do with Borun's spell of Mind Control in his possession?

As for the remaining four spells, thankfully unmolested, Gavin did not know whether to gather them together and seek a new safe haven for them, or if he should leave them in their present locations with extra safeguards. Both presented problems.

If he collected them together, his enemy might find a way to gain the prize in one concerted effort. Yet two no longer rested behind their disguises, proving that somehow, someone had known where to look and that leaving them unsupervised could prove equally as dangerous.

Angie's question when she learned of Borun's spells had burned in his mind at that: *What if the person who killed your father could see the link to the spells too?* Gavin could no longer avoid that possibility, and now that they had returned to the castle, he found he did not shy away from the thought as he had before. Obviously, whatever had prevented him from looking deeper into his father's murder no longer confined him.

But it did not help him reach a decision on how best to keep Borun's remaining spells out of enemy hands, nor how to discern the identity of that enemy. Nor did it help to answer the question of how Alvin or Rayton had inadvertently helped that enemy reveal what he held.

Gavin hoped Merikan or Angie could find answers he had not.

***

Rogan had anticipated the Sorcerer contacting him after the unexpected return of the King, but he had not thought to see that cowled form appear in the privy, even if only as an image. He debated the prudence of performing his usual genuflection in the less than pristine location, then instead finished tying his trews and gave the image atop its misty throne a deep bow.

"You kept the King in your sights today?" the Sorcerer demanded in his usual curt manner, not bothering with greetings or formalities, or even to acknowledge where he found and now kept Rogan.

"I followed where I could," Rogan hedged. "But Commander Nervain has everyone under strict watch, and the King did not allow me to follow everywhere he went. Gavin took the Lord Protector and the Lady Sorceress only to watch over him and left the rest of us awaiting their return in corridors or side rooms, even the Commander."

A sound very much like a growl came from the Sorcerer, but Rogan refused to flinch. To show weakness, even to a projected image of the man, would only draw attention where Rogan did not want it.

"So no one save Merikan and that damned woman knows where Gavin went?"

"I can tell you our route," Rogan countered. "As well as where we waited. We might determine from that where the King then turned his search. That would narrow down where you would need to look for whatever you seek. But if you mean the exact location visited, or what they gazed upon once there, then yes, none save the King himself and his Sorcerous Protectors know where they went."

Rogan waited for the Sorcerer to digest that. He did not worry overmuch about his less-than-reverent tone, for he had long since established just how far he might push the Sorcerer, but he also made sure to keep his words diffident and reasonable. Rogan didn't know why the King had returned in such haste and secrecy, but he did know it had something to do with the Sorcerer's plans and actions, and that those actions had suffered before the Sorcerer could complete his task. Anything to aid the man in achieving his desired goal without having him question Rogan's usefulness could only help Rogan in return, even if his only reward entailed his continued ability to breathe.

"Take me through his every step," the Sorcerer finally ordered.

Rogan did so, keeping his report concise, though as detailed as possible. He had no doubt the Sorcerer would decipher what he needed, now that he recognised the soundness of Rogan's reasoning. Once he finished, Rogan waited in silence, keeping his breathing shallow in his odiferous confines, as the Sorcerer considered his words.

"I can use this," the cowled form finally said. "Continue with your duties until I contact you. Keep your eyes open and your wits about you. You will find a small payment on your bunk when you return to your quarters."

Rogan bowed with fist to chest, and when he raised his gaze once more, found himself alone in the privy. He quickly retreated to the hall where he could finally take a full breath, then returned without haste to his duties.

***

"A word, Sire, if I might?" Alvin requested, drawing Gavin aside as they finished the meeting. Gavin nodded to Merikan and Angie, dismissing the two to their investigations. Commander Nervain pulled back enough to allow privacy, but neither he nor the other guards left the audience hall. The steward, Commander Eniok and Shanor, each now armed with the knowledge that someone had employed foul magic to alter perceptions and obtain dangerous weapons, if not the full nature of said weapons, set off now to do their part in discovering how that person had managed the feat. This morning's information and strategy session just concluded, Gavin waited for Alvin to speak.

Alvin leaned against the table of the Lesser Hall, arms crossed loosely, his posture making him seem even shorter, so Gavin moved to join him, trying not to loom as his brother collected his thoughts.

"I had thought to wait until spring," Alvin began, turning so that his hip supported him against the table, but meeting Gavin's gaze now. "Take our usual trip to Sahkarae for Maraenda to visit her parents. We must find those spells and the person behind Father's assassination, and winter would afford us time to plan against the unthinkable."

Gavin nodded.

"But?" he prompted when Alvin just pursed his lips, countenance deep in thought.

"Maraenda's pregnant."

Gavin blinked, then clapped his brother on the shoulder with a grin.

"Congratulations!"

"Thanks," Alvin flashed a brief smile, but it faded into a grimace. "But the timing would put her too close to delivery to travel in spring, especially given her difficulties last time." He paused as both men remembered the Cardae's miscarriage two double-seasons prior. Then Alvin continued.

"With this pregnancy now in mind, I had hoped to take her and Maraedeth to Sahkarae when you returned from Progress,

165

winter-over there so as to have her mother in attendance at the birth like with Maraedeth. Yet now, with this new information ... I'm of two minds. Taking my wife and daughter to her father's court might afford them some measure of protection should the assassin strike again, yet why should they receive any special treatment when it seems unlikely either would stand as a target? Without the pregnancy, I don't know if I would even consider such a selfish act, but now—"

"It's natural to want to protect them," Gavin interrupted. "We can't know the real agenda of our enemy, though war does not seem unlikely. Getting the innocents to safety is not selfish. If I didn't fear Rayton already had a target on him, I might consider the same. That I can't guarantee his safety even under my care terrifies me, yet I still feel I can't send him away. That you have somewhere to shelter your family is a benefit. Maraenda's condition will raise no questions about timing and won't raise undue panic."

Gavin shook his head, a growl of frustration purring in his throat.

"The uncertainty is grating. We have hidden enemies with two terrifying spells, likely searching even now for the others, potentially in preparation for war, yet we don't know where to look for them, how to counteract an attack from an unknown direction. How can I justify a build-up of arms if I can't even point to a foe? Do I keep the populous ignorant of this possible threat or invite fear and chaos by delivering a warning that may not come to fruition? No, getting your family away from this hotbed, and in a manner that won't invite undue speculation or dangerous questions, is a good idea. I'm just saddened that we need to mask this joyful moment in subterfuge."

"Not subterfuge," Alvin disagreed. "Just not revealing all the details."

"To anyone." Gavin held his brother's gaze. "Not Maraenda, not King Dorn, not Shanor. If we don't know who to trust, we don't know who might listen in. Keeping our tongues might make all the difference."

Alvin nodded his understanding.

"I will take them to Sahkarae, see them safe, then return." Before Gavin could offer any objection, Alvin uncrossed his arms and stood to his full height. Though admittedly shorter than Gavin, Alvin had a presence that lent authority to his stance. "If it comes to war, you'll need me. I will leave Maraenda and Maraedeth under Shanor's care in her father's castle, and I will come home to help defend Karundin. Against whatever atrocities this upstart Sorcerer seeks to throw our way."

Gavin also straightened, then offered his hand.

"Fair journey, Brother. Keep me appraised of your progress, and of anything you need for your voyage."

Alvin grasped the proffered arm in a firm shake, then left to make his preparations.

With a heavy sigh, Gavin also strode from the room, Nervain his ever-present shadow. He had much yet to see to, and that started with learning if his Royal Protectors had discovered anything new. Alvin would need every piece of information that could point to the identity of their enemy and might help keep his family safe. Gavin wished he could as easily find a safe haven for the rest of his kin.

Chapter 19

Angie stared at the bare spot on the floor. Without the red and gold rug to provide comfort, the grey stone looked cold, almost forlorn in its nakedness. Yet she clearly remembered the scene two months previously when a King lay dead on the carpet that no longer covered this floor, his blood mingling with the scarlet hues that the maids could not entirely wash away.

"What do you remember?" Merikan asked softly behind her.

"Blood, the knife, the King's dead eyes," Angie took a breath. "The smell of poison on the blade as I tried to pull it free."

The two had come to the late King Grayton's chambers to try to glean some new information about the assassination. Now that the spell of avoidance no longer hampered their efforts to learn the identity of the assassin, they wanted to reexamine the scene. Unfortunately, with so much time passed and the servants having cleaned the room to the best of their ability before shutting the chambers away, little remained for the Sorcerers to examine.

Leaving Angie's dream of the event as the only place untouched by outside influences. Merikan hoped that bringing Angie back to the scene of the crime might spark her memory. Angie didn't hold out much hope, but she would do her best to accurately recount what she could.

"What about the rest of the room?" Merikan pressed. "Try to remember details besides the King for the moment. You saw him on the floor, but what about his bed? Did the assassin pull him from his sheets? Did you see any light, any movement in the shadows, anything out of place? Do you see anything now that does not fit what you saw then? Something added, something missing?"

Angie shook her head, trying to remember, but she only saw the empty stare of the King, his unseeing eyes somehow condemning her for her failure to stop someone from taking his life. She pushed that thought from her mind, closing her eyes, straining to see something different, to remember anything other than that moment.

She groaned her frustration, snarling at her inability to see beyond the King's death.

"I don't think I looked further than the King," she finally had to admit. "His danger called to me, not his surroundings. I remember his ripped shirt, that the knife met bare flesh. The blood ran down his side to drip on the carpet, unimpeded by any cloth. His blood mingled with the crimson of the carpet so that I couldn't distinguish the blood from the pattern beneath. I remember a pungent smell that spoke of poison. I heard no sound, nor felt any breath of air pass through the room." She turned to look Merikan in the face. "If I saw anything else, I didn't make note of it."

Merikan sighed heavily with a slight nod.

"It was a slim hope," he admitted, gazing at the bare patch of stone floor. "I had hoped standing here where it happened might trigger an unconscious memory. But alas. We cannot trigger what you did not see."

With a grimace, he turned away, striding to the far window to pull open the drapes he had closed to more closely simulate that fateful night. Sunlight streamed in, basking the area in a warmth Angie did not feel.

She frowned, staring back at the bare floor. Something in Merikan's words spoke to her and she attempted to discern what.

"Trigger an unconscious memory," she murmured, testing out the phrase. "Trigger." She closed her eyes, chasing down the thought.

A brief memory of a night out with friends at a vaudeville show niggled. Watching a stranger go up on stage, the performer mentioning the word trigger. The stranger doing a dance.

With a snort of laughter, Angie opened her eyes.

"Angelica?" Merikan hurried back to her side.

"I can't believe I'm even considering this," she muttered, then turned to regard her father. "Could you hypnotise me?"

Merikan blinked at her.

"*Hypnotise*?" he pronounced the word carefully, an unfamiliar term on his lips. "I do not know this word. It is from your world?"

Angie realised she *had* used the English word, and that no equivalent existed in the Karundin language. She wondered absently how many other English words crept into her vocabulary without her noticing, then dismissed the thought as irrelevant right now. At the moment, she had to figure out how to describe hypnosis when she didn't understand the mechanics behind it anyway, or know whether she really believed it worked in the first place. She almost dismissed the notion, even had her hand up to wave the topic away, but she had no other ideas.

If her magic worked on instinct, perhaps it spoke to her now, trying to show a way for them to learn something new.

Or maybe she just wanted to find answers so badly that she would let her imagination run away with her on a useless tangent.

"Some people say hypnosis is a parlour trick, fakery. Others claim it really works, that it can change your behaviour, or bring to light repressed memories. It's supposed to work on the subconscious.

"You put someone in a trance and you can make them do stuff, or remember things, by communicating with them on a subconscious level. You can implant some kind of trigger so that, when they're awake and aware again, you can trigger them with a word or phrase." Angie shook her head in frustration, not liking her own explanation. "Sometimes, in a comedy show or something, the performer would hypnotise a member of the audience, and when he woke them from the trance, they'd act normal until he said the trigger. Then the person would cluck like a chicken, or dance a jig, or whatever he had implanted in their subconscious. Which all sounds ridiculous, but seems to work on some people. But I've also heard of it helping to retrieve buried memories. That's the one I'm hoping you can do."

Merikan stared at her, eyebrows raised in incredulity.

"You wish me to help you remember by making you cluck like a chicken?"

"No!" Angie almost wished she hadn't brought it up. "Forget the chicken. We're not going for that kind of hypnosis." She huffed an irritated breath. "Can you put me into a trance, something that will take me back to that night, but that might see the details I missed? Bring out my subconscious to note what

170

my eyes did not see because they focussed too much on the King?"

Suddenly Merikan's confusion vanished as he grasped her request. His visage took on a pensive quality as he considered.

"Perhaps we can take it a step farther," he spoke slowly as he worked out the possibilities. "If we can combine this speaking with your subconscious with your own powers, recreate your dream and examine it from the outside, then we might, as you say, see what your eyes did not."

"But how do we make my powers work?" Angie demanded. "We've tried to bring them out before and they only seem to work on instinct. How can we combine them with your trance spell?"

"By providing a trigger," Merikan replied.

Angie stared at him a moment, then conceded with a small nod.

"So long as you don't make me cluck like a chicken," she said, and had to grin as he raised an eyebrow in speculation.

***

Gavin closed the door quietly behind him, then paused and looked on in confusion at the sight that greeted him. Merikan and Angie sat on the floor before the unlit hearth of his father's fire facing one another. Angie had her eyes closed and Merikan's hands cupped the sides of her face, not quite touching, a golden glow of magic suffusing his palms. The Lord Protector glanced briefly at Gavin, noting his presence, then went back to his daughter. Gavin leaned unmoving against the wall, not disturbing the pair.

"Relax your mind," Merikan spoke softly to Angie. "Find a calm centre. Good." He lowered his hands to his lap, the golden glow about Angie's temples slowly fading to a hazy nimbus, barely discernible in the sunlight streaming in from the windows. She took slow, deep breaths, but did not move otherwise. Gavin almost thought her asleep.

"Now, when I tell you, take us back," Merikan intoned. "Show us that night; everything about that night. You won't feel the panic, the urgency, the pain. You will watch from a safe distance, and we will see *all* your dream showed. Are you ready?"

"Yes," came Angie's gentle, almost peaceful whisper.

Merikan flicked his gaze to Gavin for an instant, warning the

King in that moment what they hoped to accomplish, then returned his full regard to the Sorceress seated in front of him. He passed a hand across her face, murmuring something Gavin did not hear. A shaft of iridescent light flickered between the pair, and then the room went dark.

No, not completely dark, Gavin realised, but a simulation of night. An odd half-light limned the scene and suddenly Gavin saw his father frozen in the last moment of his life. Gavin pressed himself more firmly against the stone wall though he longed to lunge forward and somehow change what he knew would happen next, but he also sharpened his focus, trying to see everything, knowing Merikan did the same. Here, at last, they might learn something about their enemy.

The drapes, drawn for the evening, did not move, for no breath of air caressed them; the assassin had not gained entry through the window. Nor did the door show any signs of tampering, for it remained firmly closed. No other means of entrance presented itself either, yet two shadows occupied the room.

Grayton had previously flung aside his rumpled bed sheets, either when pulled from his bed, or as he rose to meet his attacker, alerted somehow to the intruder's presence. The latter seemed more likely, else the grisly deed may not have left the bed.

Yet now, King Grayton lay on his treasured Sahkaraean rug on the floor, his nightshirt ripped open as evidence of a struggle. A second figure crouched over him, pulling a hand back from one last action, gloved fingers slowly unwinding from the handle of a blade twisted cruelly in the King's naked side. Grayton growled, reaching for his murderer even as the poison took hold, weakening his motions, his blood trickling from his wound to pool below. The assassin rose and stepped back, features lost in the shadows of a dark cloak, watching the final struggles of Gavin's father, all taking place in the span of a couple of heartbeats to Gavin. Without a word, the killer stared into the dying eyes of the King, then touched left fist to heart.

Even as the assassin completed the motion, another figure suddenly stood in the room. Angie, dressed in a strange short shift, her long hair tumbling carelessly over her shoulders, rushed forward, reaching for the King. The assassin vanished without a trace as Angie dropped to Grayton's side. Gavin glanced to the calm face of the Sorceress sitting across from

Merikan, then back to the alluring dream-image of the woman whose visage bore only fear.

"No," dream-Angie whispered, taking hold of the knife handle and pulling to no avail. "This can't happen. You can't die." Yet already Grayton's life had fled. With a shriek of anguish that Gavin well remembered pulling him from his own slumber, dream-Angie shifted her stance, one hand grasping the blade, the other splayed on the King's chest as a brace as she again tried to free the knife from the prison of Grayton's flesh. The chamber's entry slammed open in the dream, making Gavin flinch as the image of the door flew through where he currently stood. Grayton's guards, reacting to Angie's cry, rushed in, took in the sight of their liege and pushed forward, pikes levelled at Angie, who remained oblivious to their presence.

"Damn it!" she screamed, tears streaming down her face. And then Gavin watched himself and Merikan appear, even as Angie disappeared.

"It's her," Merikan-in-the-dream whispered reverently, as Merikan now said, "Stop."

The scene halted.

"Can you take us back?" he asked Angie. "Back to just before the assassin disappeared."

For a moment, nothing happened. Gavin pushed himself silently off the wall and moved toward the two, his eyes meeting the dead stare of his father. But then the image wavered. Gavin almost made a sound of protest before he realised that he again looked at the hidden form of the man who had murdered Grayton, frozen with his fist nearly to his chest just as Angie appeared.

"There," Merikan said quietly. "Hold it there for a moment."

He rose to his feet and moved to stand before the image, motioning for Gavin to join him. The two studied the cloaked figure.

"There's no face," Gavin noted. "And the gloves obscure the hands."

"There's the height," Merikan said. "Perhaps a hand shorter than you. And the breadth of shoulder suggests a man of average build or a woman with a bit of heft. Posture slightly hunched, so someone closer to my age than yours, or a person in an occupation that rolls the shoulders maybe."

"No hesitation in the knife thrust," Gavin saw. "Enough

strength to deal one blow with a twist to the handle. And a magic user."

"Not necessarily," disagreed Merikan. "See the position of the hand. I believe it's like a trigger." He glanced to Angie, still sitting, eyes closed, where he had left her. With pursed lips, the Sorcerer turned his attention back to the mystery person. "Using the left fist over the heart like this does not look natural, and see the angle of the wrist?"

Closer now, Gavin saw how the wrist actually curved down at an awkward angle.

"I think this motion acted as a trigger to a previous spell, a position you would not accidentally invoke." He raised his voice. "Angelica, can you still hear me?"

"I can."

"Can you start the dream from here?"

In reply, the assassin's hand completed its journey. As the wrist touched the chest, a subtle spark of violet enveloped the hand. As dream-Angie took her first step, the violet briefly shimmered to cover the cloaked figure, only noticeable to the two watching from their close proximity. Again, their quarry disappeared.

"Stop!" Merikan called, excitement tinging his tone. "The haze, did you see it?"

"A spell?" Gavin asked.

"I believe so. Someone teleported this person in, and then the assassin triggered the reversal with that gesture and teleported out, past any notice of the guards. But how did they get past Grayton's own defence? Why did his magic fail to protect him or raise an alarm?"

The assassin appeared again and both men jerked back, startled. Gavin had his sword half drawn before he noted the unnatural stillness of the figure and discerned it as merely the reappearance of the dream image. He met Merikan's surprised gaze, then turned as Angie rose from her position near the hearth and approached. She had her eyes open, though her face still bore a relaxed, trance-like quality. Whatever Merikan had done to achieve the recreation of this dream still held sway.

"Here," she reached out a languid hand, cupping it beneath the assassin's gloved fist. "This pushed through the King's shield."

Gavin frowned, not understanding.

"His glove?" Merikan's question held his own confusion.

174

"More than a glove," she intoned, voice somewhat dreamy.

Merikan and Gavin leaned closer, inspecting the covered hand, yet Gavin could see nothing to indicate the glove did aught but cover the fingers. He glanced up to Merikan's face, but the Lord Protector could only offer a slight shake of his head.

"I see nothing strange," Merikan admitted quietly.

Angie took hold of the dream-assassin's hand and bent his arm forward, drawing the fist away from the chest. Merikan gasped.

"How did you—" He bit his lip, not daring to distract her further from this ability to affect her own dream.

With her other hand, Angie lifted the second arm, then peeled back the clenched fingers until she revealed the killer's palms. A tiny emblem of a tree with outspread branches lay in stark relief in the centre of each hand, Gavin's family crest outlined in gold against the black background of the gloves, as though darker impressions of the true sigil.

"A negative impression," Angie murmured. "The same yet opposite, designed to slip past the Royal protections."

"No," Gavin couldn't believe something this simple would penetrate every layer of defence on his family, that this basic design could place Rayton in such danger.

Merikan passed a hand over the palms with a quiet phrase. The design flared a bright scarlet. He let out a heavy whistle.

"Someone has imbued this sign with an intricate spell. I cannot read it fully, yet it has the penetration of the Royal protections at its heart." He met Gavin's stare. "Your enemy has studied your family at great length to design something so complex."

As he spoke, Angie wriggled the glove off the stranger's hand. Once free, Gavin could see the outline of a hand at the assassin's wrist, but nothing of flesh and bone. He cringed at the sight.

"I do not know the texture or flesh-tone of our killer," she said distractedly as she struggled to turn the glove inside-out, "so I will not fill in false details." With the glove now reversed, Gavin could see that the inverse crest went completely through the fabric. She looked up into his eyes, and Gavin noted the silver sheen of magic dancing across her vision.

"Flesh to flesh," the Sorceress explained. "The sigil touched your father and his killer at the same time." She paused, narrowed her eyes, then looked at the King's body, studying it with a frown. She knelt next to it. After a moment, Merikan and Gavin joined her.

"What do you seek?" whispered Merikan.

"Flesh to flesh," she said again, holding out the glove. Merikan reached to take it, but once it left Angie's fingers, it faded away. She did not notice, her gaze intent on the King.

Then Gavin watched with a nauseous fascination as Angie's dream played slowly in reverse until the assassin crouched beside the dying King, hand again wrapped around the knife's hilt. The image grew transparent, showing the first instant Gavin had seen Angie bring to life.

"There," she pointed as the image, barely visible, halted. The assassin's hand pulled away from Grayton's chest, but where she indicated, Gavin could just make out a fading red outline; an inverse tree laid against the King's heart. "That's why he ripped the shirt." She peered abstractedly into Gavin's face. "Flesh to flesh, hand to heart. He attacked the King's greatest strength." And then she laid her own hand on Gavin's chest. "His heart," she whispered, staring into his eyes. Gavin had to swallow hard at the contact, but before he could react further, she pulled away and the dream shattered.

Golden sunlight again streamed through the windows and the trio found themselves kneeling on a patch of bare stone floor, staring at the empty space in front of them. After a long minute of silence, Merikan found his voice.

"You said 'he', My Lady." Angie turned to regard him. "At the end, when you referred to the assassin. Did you mean in general, or did you see something we did not?"

"I did not see a face, but," she hesitated, then nodded firmly. "I meant he. I don't know how I know, but we look for a man."

"Then this *hypnosis* trick of yours seems to have worked," Merikan stated. "We now know more than we did. Let us hope it brings us closer to discovering the truth, and quickly. I would rather avoid finding out how other of your instincts might come to pass." He left unsaid her prophesy of war, but the knowledge hung in the air between them nonetheless.

"I need to move the remaining spells," Gavin dropped into the silence. "We must prevent our enemy or his accomplices from inflicting any more damage to Karundin. And if he can penetrate our defences so readily, then we need to find new ways to protect us all."

The two Protectors of the Royal House agreed heartily, though none knew quite how to accomplish the task yet. How did one protect against an unknown enemy who knew them all so well?

Chapter 20

"You wish to go now, Highness?" Shanor struggled to keep his tone mild, an advisor merely confirming travel details. Inwardly, his gut churned with a mix of panic, fury, and a touch of desperation.

With Rogan's observations fresh in his mind, Shanor knew he could discern the location of a third spell given but a day or two, yet now Alvin revealed his desire to set out for Sahkarae before week's end, leaving Shanor with the burden of seeing to many of the details. So close to his goal, the Sorcerer feared this premature departure to his homeland would only serve to thwart his dreams rather than help realise them. He could almost laugh at the irony that his own actions had prompted this reaction from the Tre'vani. That they would return to Sahkarae did not displease Shanor, for he had planned to stand before his own King, spellbook in hand, ready to lead the way back to a unified land. Yet he had expected the winter to fulfill his desires, and now he watched as that possibility slipped through his fingers.

"Yes, Lord Sorcerer," Alvin replied. "I fear waiting too long to begin the journey, lest Maraenda's condition grows too uncomfortable." Shanor wisely kept his curse for the woman's timing to himself. Of all the times for his Princess to finally conceive again ....

"And given the uncertainty of the dangers here at the castle," Alvin continued, drawing Shanor's attention back, "as well as the disturbing nature of our adversary's magical prowess, removing my family to the safety of Maraenda's father's court seems a prudent precaution. You will, of course, continue to fulfill your role as guardian to my wife and daughter, see that no harm comes to them from unknown quarters."

"Of course," Shanor placated the man, knowing he could follow that demand without qualm. After all, he knew very well from which direction any danger might come; at least, such danger as Alvin alluded to, and Shanor had no intention of said harm touching Sahkarae's royal line.

"We will travel light so as to make the best time," Alvin informed him. "Two of Maraenda's ladies and Maraedeth's nurse, my valet and a carriage driver. An escort of twenty guards and the provisions to outfit the party and their mounts." The Karundin Prince shook his head briefly. "Any fewer might elicit unfounded speculation about our desire for haste and raise questions about the Cardae's health, but many more would slow our progress, and I do not wish to find ourselves hampered by early snows."

Shanor nodded his understanding, working out the necessary supplies in his head, figuring in the time required for such preparations and how he might eek out the time he needed to search out another spell, let alone work on deciphering the spells he already held.

"Two days may seem overly hasty for such preparations," Alvin continued, oblivious to Shanor's thoughts, "but we've made these trips often enough that I don't foresee any difficulties getting ready in time. Nevertheless, I have also informed the steward of our timeline and numbers. He will work with you to see that all stands in readiness for our departure."

A quick clasp of Shanor's shoulder to show his appreciation, and Alvin strode away to other business. Shanor only noticed the man's absence peripherally as he considered a way this voyage might work to his advantage. He repressed a savage grin by force of will alone as he went in search of the steward to make his arrangements.

If Shanor could discern the location of that third spell before their departure, he need not take it up immediately. Rather, he would have Rogan remove it *after* Shanor had left the city and teleport it to himself in the Prince's train, thereby providing Shanor with a perfect alibi, and leaving Rogan empty-handed when the King tried to discover who had taken his precious treasure. With the steward's aid in finalising the travel arrangements, Shanor would have the time he needed to explore Rogan's observations of the King's movements from earlier in the day and discover what disguised the next of Borun's spells without arousing suspicion.

He had two days. He could always sleep on the way to Sahkarae.

***

Rayton stared at the door in front of him, the oak grain inches from his nose. He raised a hand to knock, hesitated, rested his fist on the door without a sound, then dropped his hand again. He shook his head, struggling in his mind with whether to stay and go through with this, or just leave now. Beside him, Remy stood surveilling the hallway, stance calm yet watchful. Oniak stood opposite, watching where Remy could not.

Ever aware of his young charge, Remy gave the Dho'vani space to reach his own conclusion, trying not to influence the boy's course with the thoughts of a guard. Although his gaze swept the halls, he never took his attention away from Rayton. While Remy might not always approve of Rayton's methods, he would never abandon the child, here least of all.

Rayton had thought long and hard about Papa's words, about how someone had uncovered part of that horrible spellbook, and that the same someone had the ability to change memories. So Rayton had gone over his actions on those days Papa had asked about, trying to find anything strange.

And he thought he had.

He remembered a kind of compulsion, such a need to study in the library, then to seek out Sorcerer Shanor, that he had simply agreed with it and done so. He didn't think he had ever felt anything like that before. So he had gone to find Papa and tell him about it. But on the way, he had gotten hungry and decided a quick stop by the kitchens to see if Cook had any little snacks lying about wouldn't take too much time, and he didn't want his tummy growling when he spoke to Papa.

While he sat licking the last bit of honey off his fingers from the little cake Cook's Assistant Nella had snuck him, Rayton had looked up and seen Sorcerer Shanor sweep down the far stairs to the pantry.

Rayton had thought maybe the Sorcerer could help explain that weird feeling so that Rayton could then explain it to Papa, so he had gotten up and followed the man down the stairs. When he reached the bottom, though, he stopped, a thought tickling in his head.

Hadn't he gone to ask Shanor about that feeling before? What had he said? What had Shanor replied?

And Rayton thought and thought, his back pressed against the wall beside the arch leading from the stairs to the pantry, visible to anyone coming down from the kitchens, but hidden from anyone in the rooms beyond. Remy, his ever-present shadow, had stood mirroring the young Prince on the other side of the arch, two statues guarding the entrance to the pantry, while Oni guarded silently from above.

Rayton remembered asking about the strange feeling, and Shanor had said .... *What had he said?* Something about a puzzle? Something he found that Rayton helped him with? Though he chased the memory, the details remained oddly fuzzy. *Why can't I remember?* he thought, and peered cautiously around the corner, his mind churning.

At first, he didn't see the Sorcerer, but then a satisfied grunt drew his attention to a high shelf about two-thirds along the second row, and he could just make out the back of Shanor's head as the man climbed down from a ladder placed there. He wondered what the Sorcerer had found that had so pleased him.

Rayton knew Uncle Alvin and Aunt Maraenda had decided to go visit Aunt Maraenda's parents and that Maraenda would have another baby soon, and that Shanor would help get them all ready for the trip. Maybe Shanor had found some of those odd little biscuits that Aunt Maraenda had so liked when she waited for Maraedeth to arrive. Rayton remembered that he hadn't liked them very much himself when Maraenda had shared some. Certainly by the age of three, Rayton knew very well what snacks he liked and which he didn't, and he hadn't enjoyed those biscuits, and knew Papa hadn't liked them either, leaving them all for Maraenda. So maybe Shanor had found some hidden away on a shelf to take on their journey. Or he'd discovered some other provision he'd need in a couple of days.

Whatever the case, Rayton could hear the Sorcerer moving along the rows back to the entrance, and the Prince pulled back out of sight. What would he say if Shanor saw him lurking here? That Rayton had followed him to ask a question about a fuzzy memory?

Suddenly Rayton jerked as realisation struck and a horrible

suspicion began to grow in his mind. He held himself very still, saw Remy do the same, as Sorcerer Shanor strode through the entrance and back up the stairs without a glance in either direction. Rayton waited only a moment before he set out after the man, his motions cautious. He hurried through the kitchen as he saw the tail end of Shanor's robes disappear into the hall beyond, then slipped along quietly in the Sorcerer's wake, Remy and Oni at his back.

Rayton paused at the end of the hall when he saw motion ahead, then hid in the shadows as he watched Sorcerer Shanor exchange greetings with a group of people before moving away again.

Papa and Angie and Lord Merikan passed Rayton's hiding spot without noticing him, though Commander Nervain made a motion toward his guards that Remy acknowledge with a brief wave of his hand before they all disappeared toward the kitchens.

Rayton stood in indecision a moment longer. He should go to see Papa and Angie, share his worries and his questions. After all, he had set out to find Papa in the first place. But he hesitated, looking between the kitchens and the hall down which Shanor had gone.

What do I do? he asked himself.

His mind kept coming back to that horrible thought down near the pantry. *What if my memory of what me 'n Shanor talked about in his rooms is fuzzy because* Shanor *made me forget? What if Shanor stole the spells and I helped him uncover them, and he made me forget?* That thought held him immobile as he stared unseeing down the hall. *Papa came home early to see if I helped someone find what they shouldn't find,* Rayton thought bitterly, *and he was right to do so.*

With an angry swipe at the tears leaking from his eyes, Rayton made a decision and turned to follow the Sorcerer, his tight-lipped guards at his side.

So now he stood staring at Sorcerer Shanor's door, as he had for the last five minutes, fists clenched at his sides as he tried to make himself follow through with his decision. But he was scared. *If I'm right, what can I do about it on my own?*

He glanced at Remy, and with the Prince's attention on him, Remy turned to regard his charge.

Rayton blinked, then, with a frown framing his lips, he gestured the guard closer. Remy crouched next to him.

"When I came out of here before," Rayton whispered, "Did I tell you what me and Sorcerer Shanor talked about?"

Remy kept his gaze steady, his own thoughts in line with Rayton's.

"You said you helped Sorcerer Shanor find something he wanted, Dho'vani. You did not say what that something was."

"Oh, Remy," Rayton's whisper quivered. "What have I done?"

Before either could speak again, the door opened. Remy shot to his feet, hand on his sword but not drawing the weapon. Oni had moved to flank Rayton, also unarmed but clearly ready for action. Shanor's surprised valet stared with wide eyes at the guards, then down to Rayton, a bundle of cloth in his arms clutched tightly to his chest.

"Dho'vani?" the man asked with a bow, regaining his composure. "How may I assist? Did you wish to speak with my master?"

Rayton, his own eyes wide and his heart pounding, swallowed his fear, set his shoulders in unconscious imitation of his father and nodded.

"If he's available, yes."

The valet glanced back at the door, then down at Rayton.

"He's in his chambers. I shall announce you presently."

As the man retreated within, leaving the door open, Rayton stared up at Remy and Oni, who now looked quite fierce.

"Remy?" he said softly, drawing the man's gaze.

"I'm not leaving your side, Dho'vani."

The calm determination in that statement helped Rayton gather his own courage.

"We can't let him know what we think." Rayton barely breathed the words, but Remy nodded his agreement and understanding, then, with a signal to Oni to guard from without, Remy followed the boy when the valet returned to usher them inside.

Chapter 21

Angie didn't know what prompted her to watch the steward this morning, but she didn't ignore the feeling. The instinct, Sidvareh might have called it.

For two days now, Gavin had shown his court a composed, efficient, congenial face to keep unwanted speculation and panic at bay. Thus far, those who knew the real reason behind Gavin's hasty return from the Royal Progress had managed to spin the event in the King's favour.

To this end, Alvin had made Maraenda's condition known, and that he had requested permission for their journey quickly so that they did not have to risk winter travel should the weather turn sooner than expected. The departure of the Tre'vani would have left Dho'vani Rayton alone to care for Karundin. Obviously too young to carry such a burden on his own yet, Alvin had sent word to the King, asking his opinion.

Gavin, having received the news from afar, had returned to extend his Royal blessing and best wishes, urging Alvin to leave as soon as possible to ensure the Cardae's continued health and safety. Gavin designated Kaeley as his representative to complete the Progress in his absence with the prerogative to invite any nobles who might feel slighted to the castle as guests of the Crown, their expenses paid, as they helped to celebrate the joyous news.

Angie wondered if Merikan and Shanor had come up with some sort of magical reinforcement to that story, as no one seemed to question it. But then, few knew just how fast the King had travelled, or why, and none of those would speak to correct the assumption that the King had only returned as Alvin made his preparations to depart. However they managed to keep a lid on it, so far popular thought ran along the lines that Gavin had returned to wish his brother and his family well, arriving just in time for the leave-taking, and not days earlier.

Those few who had seen Gavin as he instigated the investigations into the assassination, as he searched out and then relocated three of the remaining spells—the fourth did not reside in the castle, though Gavin had somehow ascertained its security—as he made his way to and from closed-door meetings, did not report those sightings to others. Again, Angie suspected Merikan's influence in maintaining the illusion.

Now, two days after Alvin and Maraenda had left with Maraedeth and Shanor and a host of servants and guards, and gifts for the King of Sahkarae, Gavin had allowed affairs of state to slip into a semblance of normalcy. He had heard petitions and granted audiences to noble and commoner alike, and Angie had sat nearby through it all to watch over Karundin's King. The steward, ever vigilant, announced those who spoke, made sure the clerk recorded each request and decision, and arranged for refreshments as necessary. Yet something about him today kept drawing Angie's attention.

By mid-afternoon, Gavin called a halt to the proceedings and slowly, the audience chamber emptied. Angie knew the King would want to check in on Rayton, but rather than head out in Gavin's wake, she found herself trailing along behind the steward. The man's slightly stooped posture may have pointed to his more than sixty summers, but his pace evinced a younger man.

A slight shimmer flashed across Angie's vision and she froze.

"A spell to hide your actions," Merikan murmured suddenly at her side, the sheen of magic dancing in his eyes. Angie took in his serious expression, noticed Gavin and two of his guards right behind the Lord Protector, equally sombre, also encompassed in the faint shimmer, then turned and stared after the steward.

"I don't know what it is," she began.

"Something calls to you," Merikan interrupted. "Listen to it. None will see us."

Angie nodded, then hurried forward, following her quarry.

The steward swept through the halls, a sheaf of papers which he occasionally consulted in his hands. Nothing about the man seemed out of the ordinary to Angie, yet a low-level buzzing droned in her head when she looked at him, more felt than heard, and that had never happened before. Something about his normal actions and purposeful stride just didn't match his intentions. Angie paused at the thought. *How can I possibly know his intentions?* she wondered.

A pair of servants passed between Angie's hidden group and the steward, oblivious to either as they went about their tasks. The smallest jerk of the steward's head toward the pair shouted out to Angie, and she realised that, although the man's attention had seemed focussed on the papers in his hand, he in fact just used them as a ruse. He had a very firm destination and goal in mind, and the documents he held had nothing to do with it. Just a diversion, a reason to avoid the attention of others even as his own attention took in everything around him. Angie found herself very grateful for Merikan's precaution of invisibility.

Once the servants had disappeared into a nearby chamber, Angie set off after the retreating back of the steward, keeping him just in sight, but even more careful now that he not hear their following footsteps.

As they progressed, Angie's trepidation grew as the man's route became clear. Not by chance did the steward make his way into the residential section of the palace, heading toward a currently unoccupied suite of rooms. Angie almost ran to intercept him as he stopped just long enough to glance around, make sure no one saw him, then wrapped a hand around the door handle and give it a twist.

A firm hand on her arm stopped her. She turned incredulous eyes to the King.

"Wait," Gavin said, fury barely suppressed in that whispered word as he watched across the hall. "We have to be certain."

Angie nodded, but crept slowly closer as the steward took a key from his pocket and inserted it into the lock. The man slipped inside and gently closed the door and threw the inner bolt, but not before Angie watched his dark eyes sweep the hallway again.

Gavin made them wait another few seconds before he signalled to Merikan. The Lord Protector murmured a word and swiped his palm across the door. Angie heard the snick of the bolt being drawn back, then threw herself into the room on her father's heels. She could feel the warmth of Gavin right behind her.

They charged into Kaeley's bedchamber, Merikan's invisibility spell vanishing as they crossed the threshold. The steward's head whipped up from where he crouched beside a chest with its lid thrown open. His eyes widened and a slight growl of surprise escaped his throat. Angie saw his eyes narrow then, his arm move fast as a viper as he grabbed something buried deep in the chest. Merikan threw out an arm, an iridescent wave of power flung from his outstretched fingers to catch the man in the torso as he tried to fling himself backwards. The spell kept the steward from fleeing, but what Angie saw in his fist dried her mouth in fear. And anger.

He held what looked like a plate—in truth, one of Borun's spells—in a hand encased in a black glove. She couldn't see the mark on the palm, but knew that an inverse emblem of Karundin's Royal tree signet rested on that ebony fabric, a foul magic created to overcome the protections of Gavin and his family. Moreover, she saw the cunning in the man's face as he suddenly grinned and twisted his wrist.

"Stop him!" Angie screamed, already leaping forward, but too late. The faintest of violet shimmers briefly encompassed the hand and the plate, and then the steward held nothing as his accomplice teleported Borun's folly away.

Angie took little delight in the startled countenance of the steward as only the spell and not the man disappeared before she smashed into him and the two tumbled to the ground. The man had a few decades on Angie, but he had a surprising amount of muscle hidden beneath his court robes, and he obviously knew how to fight. After all, this man had killed a king.

Angie tasted blood as his elbow jarred her jaw, and she saw stars through darkening vision when her head slammed into the ground. But she had only one concern as she grappled with the man, trying frantically to get a grip on his gloved hands.

Those gloves could harm Gavin, penetrate through his Royal defences and destroy the King. And already she could see how close Gavin stood, though Merikan tried to hold him back so that Gavin's guards could do their duty. It would only take this man touching the King with one enspelled hand while the other wielded the flash of metal she could see him reaching for in his belt, and Karundin would lose another king.

As her vision greyed, she reached for those hands, managed to intertwine her left hand in his. With a snarl, he pushed his other hand against her throat. She grabbed as much of it as she could, then concentrated.

Distantly, she could hear Merikan calling to Gavin's guards that they needed the man alive, Gavin bellowing to get the man off Angie, and the meaty sound of fists on flesh as the two guards punched at the steward, who in turn hung on tenaciously to Angie's neck. But none of that mattered. Even as he began to crush her hand and throat, Angie envisioned the man with bare hands, her only concern removing the danger to her charge. A flash of sapphire popped in her narrowing sight, pulsating with the overwhelming throb of her frantic pulse as blood pounded in her ears, then nothing.

Oblivion claimed her.

***

They had another two or three days of travel before they reached the border with Sahkarae. Shanor wondered if he dared wait that long.

He had sensed his teleport spell trigger earlier as they rode and had resisted the impulse to search his saddlebag, to look in the satchel where he had linked the teleport, so that he might hold his newest prize. Having found and marked the hidden spell in the pantry nearly a week ago, Shanor knew what he would find now, but he longed to take it up in triumph nonetheless. He would do so soon enough when the rest of the party slept, but not yet.

They had only just arrived at the inn in Tarnaekin, Alvin's valet and guard having gone within to confirm the arrangements Shanor had made earlier in the preparations for this journey. The rest of the party saw to horses and the carriage, meals, and unpacking what they might need for the night. As Shanor waited with Maraenda as the Princess corralled her daughter toward the entrance to the inn, he made calculations on how much time he still had before any word from the castle reached Alvin, assuming any such communications took place.

Alvin might want people to believe that he took his wife and daughter to her ancestral home in preparation for a birth, but Shanor knew his hidden reason for this trip. While the Royals had tried to mask their anxiety for the turmoil in the capital, Shanor, obviously knowing the cause of such strife, did not for a moment believe that Alvin planned on remaining in Sahkarae with his family for the winter. Gavin would need his chief tactician available in his misguided attempt to safeguard Karundin from whatever mischief Borun's spells might elicit.

Too bad for Gavin that Shanor did not plan on allowing Alvin to return before the Sorcerer finished with his own schemes.

Shanor bit off a small laugh, his eyes tracking little Maraedeth's antics. He laughed, not at the child, but at his own jubilation as years of effort finally neared fruition. He would have liked access to all six of Borun's spells, but the three he now possessed would do quite nicely. He had unravelled the secrets of two—the first just after his return from marking the third, and the second late in the evening right before their departure—and eagerly wanted to know what the third contained. For that, he would need Alvin's hand to unmask the first protection. Given his successful experiment with the first spell on the Dho'vani and his guard, Shanor had no doubt Alvin would do as Shanor required. He just had to time it right, before Gavin sent word of the disappearance of the third spell.

But not tonight. Tonight, Shanor would secure his latest prize.

Tomorrow would take them that much further from Karundin's capital, bring them a day closer to Sahkarae and safety, and to the reunification of the two lands, with Shanor's people taking their rightful place. Tomorrow evening, when they stopped at the next well-furnished inn, Shanor would take Alvin aside, utter the brilliant words and gestures of a long-dead wizard over the Karundin Prince, and claim the loyalty and expertise of Gavin's tactician. Together, they would reveal the nature of the third spell and make plans to incorporate all the weapons now in Shanor's arsenal.

What, Shanor wondered, did he hold to complement Mind Control and the ability to create armies out of clay? No wonder the Sorcerer laughed with such delight.

***

Angie woke with fiery tendrils of pain burning her neck, a throbbing drumbeat in her jaw, and the taste of copper in her mouth. She tried to speak, but the vise of torment squeezed her abused throat, sending her into a fit of coughing that added whole new levels of agony exploding through her skull. A hand encircled her upper arm, then an arm snaked around her shoulders and back, helping her sit.

"Easy," a voice cautioned beneath her hoarse hacking. Panic grabbed her when another hand, long fingers splayed wide, touched her neck. Reflex and blind terror had her own fingers clawing at that hand—revealing in that motion that someone had also jabbed red-hot pokers into her left hand—before she focussed on the speaker.

"Rest easy, My Lady," Merikan said, clearly suppressing a wince as her fingernails scored across the back of his hand. "I can't heal you if you don't calm down."

Angie blinked away tears as her mind caught up to her situation and she stopped fighting her father.

Gavin knelt beside her, propping her up and supporting her weight while Merikan gazed at her throat as the spark of magic illuminated his eyes. A flash of uncomfortable warmth flared between his palm and her neck, not quite painful, but certainly not enjoyable.

She tried to distract herself by studying the room. Beside her rose a large canopied bed, and an open chest rested not far from that. Still in Kaeley's room, then.

One of Gavin's guards had stationed himself near the door, hand resting on the hilt of his sword though the weapon remained sheathed at his side. The other guard loomed over the battered and insensible form of the steward, the dishevelled traitor lying face-down on the floor with slow streams of blood from a broken nose and several gashes on his face adding unwanted colour to a blue and gold rug. They had lashed the steward's arms sharply behind his back at an angle that Angie suspected would cause great pain when he woke. She couldn't summon up any sympathy for the brute.

Without warning, a sharp lance of sheer agony enveloped Angie. It shot from her neck to her face to her hand, making her injuries pale by comparison. The horrible sensation of floating in a blinding haze of torment lasted an instant that felt like eternity before it faded into a dull throb, taking most of her wounds with it.

She blinked tears from her eyes and realised she lay in Gavin's lap, his hand combing hair off her sweat-soaked forehead in comfort, as Merikan pulled back, magic fleeing his gaze.

"How do you feel?" asked the Lord Protector.

Angie considered that a moment as Gavin helped her upright again.

"Like I just survived a train wreck."

Gavin snorted amusement.

"You will have to teach me this secret language of yours," he said with a small smile.

Angie frowned.

"Secret language?"

"Words like *train wreck*, *shit, son of a bitch*."

Angie felt her mouth drop open and her face heat with embarrassment.

"When did I say that?" she asked, aghast.

"When the magic took the worst of your injuries and knitted you back together," Merikan replied. "You were quite voluble in your opinion of the process and shared some words from your own world." The twinkle in his eyes made Angie wonder if he knew what she had, apparently, said.

"If I had to guess," Gavin mused, "I would suspect some of those words included choice curses. Based on my experience with hastened healing."

"Um," she bit her lip and searched for something to distract them. They both laughed gently, and Angie understood in that slightly forced sound that they, in fact, had sought to distract her. She gazed searchingly at Merikan.

"How bad did he hurt me?"

He sobered.

"Broken bones in your hand, and a nearly crushed larynx. Potentially crippling, but not necessarily fatal if left untreated."

Angie shivered and Gavin squeezed her shoulder before helping her to her feet.

"You will need sustenance soon," Merikan advised. "That kind of healing takes much of your own strength."

Angie nodded her understanding, then glanced at the occupants of the room again, finally noting who did not stand within.

"Where's Commander Nervain?" she asked, trying to recall if she had ever seen Gavin without the man, save at their first meeting.

"When you started after the steward with such an intent expression, I suspected some kind of foul play," said Gavin. "Not knowing the full extent, I sent Nervain to find Rayton and fetch him to safety as a precaution." The King frowned at the prone captive, then glanced toward the guard at the door.

"Tera," he called. The guard gave Gavin his full attention. "Find Commander Eniok and have him arrange an escort for our traitor there." He thrust his chin in the steward's direction.

"Yes, Sire," Tera saluted before slipping out of Kaeley's bedchamber.

Gavin looked next to the guard standing over the captive.

"Davok, seek out Commander Nervain in Rayton's quarters, inform him of the situation and have him meet us here in the outer room."

"Sire," Davok saluted, but hesitated, his gaze slipping to the unconscious man.

"Lord Protector Merikan will make sure he doesn't wake any time soon." Even as the King spoke, Merikan moved to crouch over the traitor, a soft glow haloing his hands. He gently urged the guard out of the way and towards the door, while Gavin concluded. "And the Lady Sorceress can certainly provide enough protection until you return."

Davok gave a sharp nod of his head, then followed in Tera's wake.

When they heard the click of the outer door closing and Merikan rose to rejoin them, Gavin turned to Angie with a fierce frown.

"Now, do you want to tell me what the *aentoraden* you thought you were doing, jumping on the steward like that?"

Aentoraden? Angie thought, greatly suspecting the King had just flung his own curse at her. She decided, given his obvious anger, not to point it out.

"Well, Sire," she replied, slightly perplexed. "I thought I was doing my job."

"Your job?"

"Yes. Protecting the Royal Family from harm. Unless I'm greatly mistaken, that man," she thrust out her arm to indicate the steward without turning to look, "intended you harm."

"And that's why I have guards," Gavin's tone had turned to exasperation. "Do you realise that you made their job almost impossible by getting in the way like that?"

"Getting in the way?" Angie's turn for incredulity. "Did you see what he wore? Did Tera and Davok see? Would they have taken precautions before or after he could do damage with

192

them?"

Gavin, mouth already open to offer another protest, paused. He glanced at the prone and bound man, brow creased in contemplation, searching for what Angie referred to. He closed his mouth and took a deep breath. After a brief glance to Merikan's expressionless countenance, he faced Angie again.

"What did I miss?" he asked in a more subdued tone of voice.

"His gloves," she said softly, her own voice growing gentle. "Black gloves with an emblem on each palm, designed with but one purpose; to bypass all Royal Protections." She placed a hand on his arm. "Gloves worn to kill your father."

She felt his arm tense, saw the grief and rage in his stormy eyes, noticed the fine tremor along his jaw before he clenched his teeth tight. He didn't pull away, nor did he blink, just stood staring at her.

"Gavin, I trust your guards to protect you from physical harm, but you have to trust me to protect you from what magic I can."

Angie gave a little start and pulled her hand away from him as she realised what she had just said. How could he trust her to protect him from something she barely understood and didn't know how to control? But then, hadn't she done just that? She had acted on instinct; hadn't stopped to think about what she did, simply done it. That her actions kept proving correct shocked the hell out of her, but she couldn't ignore the results.

"I do trust you," Gavin spoke quietly but with such intensity that she couldn't mistake his sincerity. Then he reached out and pulled her close in a mighty embrace. "But *ran tae nak tar* woman, you scared the life out of me, flying through the air like that."

She patted him awkwardly on the back, then a need for air had her pulling out of his embrace.

"I think you might have a few words to add to my vocabulary yourself, Gavin," she gave him a little smile. "*Ran tae nak tar?*"

Gavin reddened and Merikan covered a laugh with a fake cough. Gavin glared at the Lord Protector, but obviously saw the steward in his periphery, and grew serious again.

"Did you note his gloves?" the King asked the other man.

Merikan gave a small shake of his head.

"I trusted that Angelica knew her business." He levelled a hard stare at Angie. "Though I admit my heart may have missed several beats as she grappled with our dear steward. After all, it is *my* job to protect the Lady Sorceress." Angie bit her lip at that rebuke, though she didn't know what she might have done differently.

"Do you still have the gloves?" he asked, interrupting Angie from any further introspection.

Angie looked quickly over at the steward, then down at her empty hands, surprise and worry dancing through her stomach.

"Um" she answered unhelpfully, meeting her father's gaze with wide eyes.

"Tell me what went through your thoughts while you fought," Merikan prompted.

"I just pictured him with bare hands." She frowned, considering. "I think I saw a flash of blue before I passed out, but I don't know what happened to the gloves."

"Hrmf," Merikan grunted, his communication as helpful as Angie's.

He strode over to their captive, kneeling to examine his hands with eye and fingers. Finding nothing, Merikan gazed around the room, the golden spark tinting his eyes an indication that he searched with magic as well as sight. Again finding nothing, he returned empty-handed to Gavin and Angie.

"I'm sorry," Angie began, but Merikan stopped her with a flick of his wrist.

"No, you dealt with the threat and eliminated a dangerous weapon. Do not apologise for that."

They heard the front door open again and Commander Nervain call out.

Merikan led the way as Gavin and Angie left Kaeley's bedchamber, a traitor bound senseless and bleeding on her rug behind them.

Davok came in to Kaeley's receiving room behind Nervain, followed by Rayton and one of the boy's guards. When the small Dho'vani saw his father, his eyes lit up and he grinned.

"Papa!" He threw himself forward into Gavin's waiting arms. With an impish smile tempered with an emotion she couldn't read, Rayton smiled at Angie too. Then he pulled back to gaze at Gavin's face.

"What are we doing in Aunt Kaeley's rooms? Is she home?"

"Not yet," Gavin sighed, setting his son down. The King threw a glance to Nervain, as though questioning why the Commander had brought Rayton along, but he didn't say anything. Instead, he squatted in front of Rayton, meeting the child eye-to-eye. "But we have found someone very dangerous and I need to know that you're safe before we can bring him out."

Rayton stared with huge eyes to the closed door behind Merikan.

"Did you find the man who killed Grandfather?" Rayton whispered.

Gavin, as surprised by Rayton's astuteness as Angie, hesitated, but answered the question with a nod. Then he stood and faced Rayton's guard.

"Remy, will you please take Rayton back to his room until we can move—"

Gavin didn't get a chance to finish his request before he found himself assaulted by Remy's sword. Angie could do nothing to help, as she suddenly had her arms full of an unexpected threat in the guise of a knife held firmly in a small hand.

Chapter 22

Angie didn't remember falling to the floor, but she could feel the hard surface pressing into her back as Rayton's weight straddled her chest and kept her pinned. The boy had a surprising strength as he strained against Angie's restraining hands on his wrists, a knife poised in his fists over her face. Around her, she could hear confused shouts, the clash of steel on steel as weapons crossed, the deep bellow of Merikan as he tried to contain the situation. But Angie could spare the chaos little thought as she stared in shock at the tormented grey eyes of the child with her death in his hands pressing down on her. Eyes that teared up even as they held a hard edge hazed by ....

The faintest green nimbus swam briefly through his gaze, and Angie had a thought, but she needed time to analyze it; time neither she nor Gavin could afford. So she used a trick she had learned in her dreams; she closed her eyes and stopped time.

Their enemy had grown confident enough to send his minion after Borun's spells—though how he had known where to find them Angie would have to think on later—even after he already held two of them. But which two? Creating a clay army, and Mind Control. She remembered Merikan's words as he described the latter: *Mind Control could wreak much havoc, turning even the most loyal of comrades into bitter foes*. And Rayton's whispered question: *Did you find the man who killed Grandfather?* It seemed their enemy had found a way to understand at least one of those spells. Only after Gavin's confirmation did Remy and Rayton attack, as though triggered by this new knowledge.

Karundin did not know its enemy, but the steward did. And

perhaps the Dho'vani and his guard, under the terrifying influence of Borun's stolen spell, also knew. The enemy used the one to protect the other, those Angie and Gavin couldn't bear to kill to safeguard the real traitor. Yet that realisation only served to tighten Angie's chest in a knot of despair. She knew the problem, but what solution existed? How could she stop what a centuries-dead Sorcerer had found no answer to? She couldn't hold time forever.

A memory niggled at the edge of her awareness, and Angie grabbed at it with metaphorical hands.

The Great Hall, the coronation, six spears of golden light emanating from the crown as it touched the brow of the new King to point out his charge.

A braid of silver penetrating into Angie's very being from that same crown.

A painting of Karundin Castle used to disguise strange words of power and hidden in Angie's world. Sidvareh's voice just as Angie thought she might understand some of those words: *Now is not the time, My Lady. When you need the spell, you will find it again.*

I need that spell now, Angie thought, striving desperately to recall those elusive words. *Please, Sidvareh, help me to remember.* She put all her concentration into her need, could feel her grip on time begin to loosen.

Metal scraped in drawn out torture as someone's sword crept by microscopic increments along the tempered edge of another's weapon.

Magic-enhanced strength combined with the vile rape of a child's mind slowly pulled Rayton's shaking blade nearer to her closed eyes.

The creeping resumption of time exaggerated the depth of sound from male voices crying out in slow-motion denial.

Searing words briefly burned into Angie's brain as the sonorous tone of an unfamiliar voice boomed into her mind, helping her pronounce dangerous syllables that ripped from her suddenly raw throat and echoed throughout Kaeley's rooms.

Angie's eyes flew open and everything stopped, but not through her dream magic.

Then Remy's sword clattered to the ground and the man fell to his knees, tears wetting his cheeks as Nervain, chest heaving, held his own blade to the man's unresisting throat, Davok his silent back-up.

Rayton's knife flew violently across the room as the boy threw it hard, a gut-wrenching wail torn from his terrified and trembling form. Gavin, on his back not a foot from Remy with a bloody gash marring his tunic, turned, ashen faced, at the sound, and scrambled on hands and knees for his son. He hesitated an instant before grabbing the child off Angie and cradling him in a crushing embrace. Rayton, seeing the blood on his father, sobbed harder and tried to pull away.

"I'm sorry, I'm sorry," he kept repeating, but Gavin did not let go. Even when Merikan reached out to offer healing, the King refused to relinquish his hold on the hysterical child.

"What the *aentoraden* just happened?" Nervain demanded in a surprisingly calm, yet somehow lethal voice.

Merikan glanced to Angie as she gingerly sat up, the same question in his own expression as he no doubt recalled her words of power. Angie looked at Gavin, saw in his bleak expression that the King suspected, but did not have the strength just now to explain.

"A spell," Angie croaked, her throat feeling more abused now from the counter-spell than it had from the steward's throttling hands. "A weapon stolen by our enemy and triggered to distract us from the assassin."

"A spell?" Nervain queried, his eyebrows reaching for his hairline.

"Mind Control," she replied shortly, her gaze locked on Gavin's.

Nervain spouted off a whole strain of curses that Angie, at another time, might have found interesting. The Commander finally ran short of expletives.

"Why?" he asked, drawing Angie's attention. He waited until she met his stare. "Why go through this attack if they knew you could stop it? Did they really think they could get away with killing another king? That a boy could kill the Lady Sorceress?"

"Yes." Her answer obviously surprised him. She caressed her aching throat with a chilly hand, wondering how much she could say, trying hard to ignore a gnawing hunger quickly spreading through her belly even as exhaustion threatened to overwhelm her. She recalled Merikan explaining that every spell had a cost, and she felt like she had just used a whopper, and that on top of the price of her previous healing.

Merikan explained for her.

"The enemy does not know we have a counter to that spell."
Angie marvelled that his tone did not imply his own lack of
previous knowledge, though the curiosity staring with hungry
eyes promised many questions at a later date. "Whether Rayton
or Remy caused damage, even death, or we did, our enemy wins
by sowing discord, distrust, fear. He meant for someone to die
today, make no mistake," warned the Lord Protector.

Every eye went to the quivering child sheltered by the King,
the little hand white-knuckled as it clutched his father's tunic, the
quiet voice still hoarsely crying "I'm sorry."

Nervain swore again, his growl speaking the sentiment for
everyone in the room.

"Who would do such a thing?" Davok demanded. "Why?"

A knock sounded, announcing the arrival of Eniok and the
soldiers meant to take the captive away.

"We'll soon find out," Merikan predicted.

In that moment, Angie felt her exhaustion reach out with eager
hands to claim her and she didn't resist. She managed one final
warning to her father before sleep sucked her under to start the
necessary work of restoring the Lady Sorceress to her full
strength.

***

Rogan jerked to full wakefulness with no memory of having
fallen asleep. His eyes flashed open and he became instantly
aware of two things: he had not slept naturally, not bound hand
and foot to a chair; and he did not recognise the mostly barren
and windowless room, though he knew well the man seated in
front of him, glaring with unrestrained animosity. Rogan stared
back at his captor, keeping his expression conciliatory and
confused.

He clearly remembered following the trail of magic that the
Sorcerer had left him to the Tre'embra's chambers, taking up the
marked plate from the chest and triggering the teleport spell. At
the instant that the plate had vanished, leaving Rogan to the
mercies of those ruling in Karundin rather than teleporting
himself away as well, he had known the Sorcerer's protections
had ended. He just hoped he had managed to damage the Lady
Sorceress enough to remove her as any serious threat to the
Sorcerer in the inevitable war before Gavin's thugs had rendered

him unconscious. Rogan harboured no illusions that he himself would live to see the fruition of that battle, but he would do what he could to sow plenty of discord and discontent among those who would now kill him.

Rogan shifted in his uncomfortable, straight-backed chair, just enough to know that his restraints offered no slack at all. The stone floor and bare grey walls gave no comfort, nor did the single table beside his visitor, it's scarred surface bare of any accessories, though his mind envisioned any number of sharp objects and other implements of torture that might soon adorn its face.

His face ached abominably, his eyes squinting past the swelling of a clearly broken nose that he had trouble breathing through. Lines of fire traced his jaw and cheek, stabbed at his ribs with every breath gulped through his parted lips. He tasted blood with each swallow and spared a brief thought to how much damage he had taken already in his surprisingly physical battle with the Sorceress, and how much more he might expect to endure before they ended him with one wrong question. The spell that kept the Sorcerer's name hidden from his enemies would trigger Rogan's demise, and Karundin would continue to find itself ignorant of those who would take it apart. Small consolation, but all he dared look forward to.

In the meantime, Rogan would make any information his captors might glean a long and drawn-out process.

"What's going on?" he asked the man burning holes into him with his heated gaze.

Commander Eniok leaned forward, hands clasped in his lap as he regarded Rogan closely.

"What's the last thing you remember, steward?" Eniok asked.

Rogan blinked, intrigued by such a tactic. Could they honestly not know the depth of his duplicity? Or did the Commander merely seek to put him at ease, hoping to trick him into revealing everything? Though Eniok's tone remained cool, the fury in his eyes clearly demonstrated that this preliminary question did not offer any sort of solace. Nevertheless, Rogan decided to entertain the soldier, play up his muddled old man routine and see how long he could annoy the Commander of the castle's defences.

"I remember the King dismissing audiences for the day. I took the reports for next week's schedules and tomorrow's tax reviews with me as I left to look over in preparation for the morning briefing and I headed back to my chambers. And then ..." He allowed himself to trail off, feigning perplexity, brows furrowed as though lost in thought. "And then I woke up here," he muttered with a frown. "What's going on, Commander? Why am I restrained and injured?"

"So you're telling me you don't remember going into the Royal apartments and stealing an artifact? You have no recollection of intent to harm the King? Of strangling Lady Sorceress Angelica?"

"Stars above, no!" Eyes wide in mock alarm as he pulled back in his chair, Rogan found it difficult not to crow his satisfaction. Strangling the Lady Sorceress indeed! Had he managed to kill her? "Why would I do such a thing? What has happened? Is the King safe?" All questions a loyal servant of Karundin must ask, and information a spy needed to know.

"Ah, memory loss, then, or altered facts. Perhaps you suffered from a spell. Mind Control, mayhaps?"

Mind Control? Why would Eniok insinuate such a noxious concept? What else had happened while Rogan lay unconscious? Confusion more real this time, the steward answered the Commander.

"Would I know if I suffered from such a fate?"

"Perhaps not," Eniok allowed. "Then you only recall walking the halls toward the Royal apartments, nothing further?"

"I didn't go to the Royal apartments," Rogan argued.

"No, of course not. My mistake. So you have no idea what you stole either?"

"I didn't steal anything!"

"We have witnesses, steward. Save yourself the trouble of trying to remember your lies."

"What lies?" Rogan insisted, his voice rising on a thread of imagined panic. If Eniok didn't ask anything relevant, Rogan just might survive this encounter. Emboldened by that thought, he played up his innocent demeanour even more. "I don't know what you're talking about! I certainly don't remember doing what you think I did."

"Do you own any gloves, Steward Rogan?"

Rogan blinked hurriedly, unnerved by this new question, trying to hide it. Eniok couldn't know, could he? No one except the Sorcerer knew and he most definitely would not yield up such a potent weapon.

"Gloves? Of course I have gloves. A pair for riding, a pair for the cold months. What does that have to do with—"

"A pair for killing Royalty," Eniok broke in, his tone conversational, almost flippant. "Or perhaps more than one pair? If you have more anywhere in your quarters, my men will find them soon enough. And how many knives will they find, do you suppose?" The Commander's mien turned speculative, yet the iron in his expression, the stiff way he held his shoulders, all pointed to barely suppressed fury. "The one we took from your belt would cut far more than your evening meal. Will we find a twin to the one that took King Grayton's life, do you think?"

Rogan stared at him mutely, hoping the shock in his eyes spoke loudly enough, suspecting any words would simply go unacknowledged.

"Do you keep your poisons locked up in your rooms, assassin? Of course, with access to most of the castle, a steward could ferret any number of things in obscure places and no one the wiser." Eniok's eyes flashed, and his growl finally matched the expression.

"How long have you worked from the shadows, traitor?"

Rogan shook his head slowly, his eyes drooping in disappointment.

"I am no traitor, Commander." True enough; after all, he did not pay his allegiance to Karundin. "You're grasping at straws that do not exist." He put enough heat into that statement that Eniok actually sat back in his chair, his muscular arms crossed over his burly chest. After a moment, the soldier's gaze flicked away and Rogan felt a brief flash of elation, mixed with contempt for Eniok's weakness.

Then he recognised his own mistake. Eniok had not broken eye contact; he had glanced behind Rogan to someone standing behind the steward. Rogan silently cursed himself for his carelessness. He couldn't turn enough to see the entire room; why had he assumed that Eniok questioned him alone?

The Lord Protector of Karundin strode deliberately into Rogan's line-of-sight, his black robe barely disturbed by the motion.

"I find it interesting that you truly believe you are no traitor, Rogan," came Merikan's sonorous voice as the man made a circuit past Eniok's chair and around the table. When he turned back to face Rogan, the steward felt a cold, hard fist grasp at his heart. Not the man's magic; merely his overwhelming presence. He suddenly longed for Merikan to ask the question that would end Rogan's life.

"It suggests to me that you do not serve Karundin," Merikan continued. "Your dissembling of the Commander's other questions speaks of long ease and practice, hinting at a long history of hiding your motives. I wonder, did you ever serve Karundin, or did you come to us with deceit in your heart?"

"I don't know—"

"What I'm talking about?" Merikan interrupted. "For surely you know of what I'm capable. Anyone with as strong a connection as yours to a sorcerer ought to know that sifting lies in an unsuspecting mind does not require great effort. Strange though, that a man so acquainted with working alongside a magical accomplice did not think to ward his thoughts."

Rogan stared at the Lord Protector. Of course he knew better, yet still had failed to fully appreciate his situation in this interrogation until too late. But how had Merikan known about the Sorcerer? Did it work to Rogan's advantage now to continue his feigned ignorance, or to finally show his true colours, the slyness and cunning that had launched him on this path to Karundin's downfall?

He made his decision.

"I suppose you want to know his name?" Rogan asked, throwing off confused old man and donning confident infiltrator. If he could have managed it, he would have sat back, ankle on knee, arm draped casually over the back of the chair. As it stood, he could only provide the Lord Protector with an unconcerned gaze. He did, however, guard his thoughts, however late in the process. No need to make it any easier for Merikan now.

Merikan waved his hand in dismissal.

"We'll get to your Sorcerer later. You can clear up so many other matters first." His grim smile nearly undid Rogan, but he had a soldier's stomach, a warrior's training, and years of hiding his true feelings, so Merikan would see no outward reaction.

"I find it intriguing that you had no difficulties with the concept of altered memories, yet found the idea of Mind Control unnerving. Do you, in fact, remain ignorant of what your Sorcerer can now accomplish? Of the kind of magic you have helped him find and steal? The one has helped keep you hidden, certainly, and you have no qualms about its use. So why do you find Mind Control so much more repulsive?"

Rogan suppressed a shudder, not liking in the least that Merikan had picked up that discomfort. Rogan had barely allowed himself to acknowledge his abhorrence to the idea of Mind Control before he had turned away from the thought, buried his emotions beneath years of training and discipline.

"Changing a memory can still bring the comfort of the illusion of control," Eniok said, drawing Rogan's surprised attention as the Commander put words to Rogan's fear. "Mind Control takes even that illusion away, leaving you with no ability to determine your own actions. It makes you helpless."

"A soldier uses every tool he can," Rogan dropped into the silence after that statement, bolstering his confidence, trying to obliterate his sense of weakness.

"So long as that tool remains firmly pointed toward the enemy," Eniok countered.

"Do you see yourself as a soldier?" Merikan wanted to know. Rogan shot him a disgusted sneer, one eyebrow slightly crooked.

"Do you have any idea what you stole from that chest?" the Lord Protector went on, unmoved by Rogan's attitude.

"A plate," Rogan responded promptly. Why a plate, he had no idea, but the Sorcerer had marked it as the object of his desire, so Rogan had taken it.

"What else did you intend to take?"

"Only the plate. Nothing else was marked." Rogan bit his cheek, wondering at his ready response. He narrowed his gaze on the Sorcerer in front of him, trying to fight the influence that urged his answers, even though he couldn't confirm whether such an influence existed.

"Interesting," Merikan murmured, so softly that Rogan wondered if he had heard the word at all. "Why only that?" He focussed on Rogan again, the renewed intensity of his scrutiny speeding Rogan's pulse.

"How long have you had those special gloves?"

"Gloves again?" Rogan scoffed, keeping tight rein on his thoughts now.

"Don't even try," Merikan snarled, suddenly inches from Rogan as he thrust his face close, looming over the bound man. It startled Rogan enough that he flinched away instead of taking the opportunity to smash his head into the Lord Protector's. His nose already broken, what did a second injury matter if he could further damage Karundin's magical protections. But by the time that thought had finished forming, Merikan already stood more than arm's length away again, leaving Rogan in the cooling furnace of the man's ire.

"Let me refresh your memory, steward," Merikan said, his merely factual tone of voice somehow more ominous after the outburst. He paced slowly as he spoke, hands clasped lightly behind his back. "Black gloves with a golden sigil outlined on the palm. An inverse representation of the Royal Crest with a spell designed specifically to counter the Royal Protections." He turned dark eyes to Rogan. "Flesh to flesh," he said. "Yes, I see that means something to you."

Rogan felt the colour drain from his face and he had to remind himself to breath normally. How could he know? Rogan surreptitiously ran his thumbs along his fingers, confirming that he no longer wore those gloves, but how did Merikan know about the need for direct contact? Did he bluff? The knowing glint in his gaze suggested otherwise and that Rogan would do well to confirm the implication, but he kept his tongue. Not that it mattered, as his blanching had given him away.

"How long have you had them? What, besides King Grayton's assassination, did you seek to accomplish using them?"

Rogan clamped his jaw shut and imagined plunging a dagger into Merikan's heart, concentrating on that image to the exclusion of all else. Perhaps the Lord Protector caught an inkling of the fantasy as his lip briefly curled in wry amusement before he switched tactics again.

"Does the Lady Sorceress Angelica seem like the biggest threat to you and your master, Rogan? Is that why you took such delight in squeezing the air from her?"

The lightness forced into that remark didn't fool Rogan; he could hear the anger behind the question, see the fine tremor that passed a finger along Merikan's spine. And he laughed at the Lord Protector for it, seeing a way to cause some real damage.

"What's the matter, Merikan? You fail in your duty a second time? Not bad enough that you couldn't save the real Lady Sorceress all those years ago, now you feel bad about losing this imposter too?"

205

All motion ceased in the Sorcerer. Rogan couldn't even see him breathing. Had he not stared straight at the man, he would not have known anything but a statue confronted him now. Oh yes, he had hit a nerve.

"Why would you name the Lady Angelica an imposter?" Eniok interjected. Rogan had almost forgotten his presence, but he looked at the man now, wondering if he could form a schism here with his knowledge.

"Lady Angelica might boast some magical prowess," Rogan allowed. "But she's no Lady Sorceress to the Royal House. That line died years ago." He turned a malignant glare back to Merikan. "I made sure of that when I ripped the unborn brat out of Lady Katerina's dying womb with one thrust of my knife."

***

Rogan had certainly expected a reaction to that statement, but perhaps not the one he received.

Rather than springing into motion or shouting out some kind of denial, Lord Merikan remained utterly still, yet waves of *something* emanated from the man. An unseen force that felt like raw grief commingled with a blinding rage slammed into Rogan despite nothing physical actually touching him.

Commander Eniok stood, back to Rogan and facing the livid Sorcerer, though not blocking Merikan's line of sight. The soldier had a subduing hand on Merikan's shoulder, and although it appeared he merely cautioned the Lord Protector, the Commander's bulging biceps quivered, veins visibly straining as they corded his arm, pushing against a great force.

A light footfall drew Rogan's reluctant attention from the drama before him and he tore his gaze from the Lord Protector, both elated at having caused such strife, and terrified of the retribution he could read in Merikan's dark glare.

He nearly wet himself as he met the bi-coloured stare of Lady Angelica, looking hale and hearty when he knew he had caused her damage, but then he re-mastered his self-control.

"Ah, the imposter herself," he drawled.

The Lady canted her head just a little to the right, for all the world a bird examining the worm it intended to ingest.

"You really shouldn't bait my father like that," she said, her voice sounding raspy. Perhaps he had managed to harm her some after all. "Especially not about her."

"Your father," Rogan scoffed. "So the Lord Protector brings a bastard to court and the Royals lap it up."

"Not a bastard, no," Angelica corrected, her eyes narrowing slightly. She tilted her head the other way and her voice grew distracted as she studied him. "You may have torn up my mother and destroyed the vessel that should have housed me, but the Lady Katerina saved my spirit, as it were. Sent it somewhere safe."

She crouched on her heels in front of him, and Rogan realised that she wore some sort of trousers beneath a long tunic, making the motion seem less vulgar. He would have scoffed at this Sorceress garbing herself in the fashion of men, but something about her ease of wearing such strange clothing niggled at a memory.

"Angelica," Merikan growled. "Do not get too close to him."

If Angelica heard the admonishment, she ignored it as she locked gazes with Rogan.

"I know the feel of you," she hardly spoke above a whisper, yet the eerie timbre of her voice sent unwanted shivers crawling down Rogan's spine and he longed to hide from her almost invasive stare. "This is the real you, what you hide from the world. But you didn't have to hide it there, did you? You could show that world your true self and no one would know."

Rogan blinked uncertainly at her, beginning to question her stability. A quick glance to the men in the chamber told him nothing, as both guarded their expressions.

"How did you get there?"

Rogan swallowed a lump in his throat, the sound loud in the silence as he regarded her again.

"Get where?" he whispered, wondering what had become of his fortitude in the face of such intensity.

"To a world with strange metal beasts where you shot an arrow at a naive young woman."

He gaped at her, oblivious to Merikan's hiss of in-drawn breath. No way anyone could know about that foul place the Sorcerer had sent him, with its loud noises, cloying scents, frightening contraptions, strange clothing. Unless she could read his mind, see what he had seen? Or ...

Lady Katerina saved my spirit. Sent it somewhere safe. Angelica's words slammed into his head and he gawked like an unschooled buffoon.   Without taking her gaze from his, Angelica's hand moved to the shoulder of her tunic, then slipped the fabric aside just enough to reveal a shiny round scar. Rogan followed the motion almost against his will, seeing the healed wound where an arrow had parted sinew, yet trying not to understand.

"How—" He didn't even know what question to form first. How had she survived the pranik? How did she get here? Where was that horrible place she came from? What would she do to him? He sealed his lips instead, refusing to give her the benefit of his curiosity. His confession, if he uttered another sound.

"How did you get there?" she asked again, her hand dropping from her shoulder to rest draped over her knee. "How did you know where to find me? Why did you try to kill me?"

Rogan just shook his head, biting hard at his lip to distract himself from the urge to answer. Merikan stepped up behind Angelica, still a tightly coiled spring ready to snap, yet firmly in control of himself.

"I suggest you answer the Lady's questions, assassin," he commanded.

Rogan squeezed his eyes shut, trying to block them out, no longer confident of his ability to shield himself from one Sorcerer, let alone two. But it did no good. He could feel the Compulsion take him. He might have to answer, but he would fight every step of the way.

"You touched the knife," Rogan ground out from between clenched teeth. "We couldn't know what you had seen that night, so he examined the blade, traced it to you. I don't know how he found you, or how he sent me there; that's his domain. I just went to clear up a loose end. Badly, it would seem."

He waited for it now, the question that would kill him.

"How did *you* find me?"

Surprised, he opened his eyes, met her blue and green gaze.

"He arranged everything. Made it so that you would show up at that strange place at the right time. I just had to wait until his spell identified you, made you stand out from the rest. I fired the arrow, watched you fall, then he brought me home again."

Again he waited. And again, they refused to ask the question.

As though they knew better, he suddenly realised, a bitter taste tanging his mouth as bile rose in his throat. They wouldn't ask about the Sorcerer because they *knew* it would lose them the opportunity to get more information.

"He killed them," Angelica whispered faintly, suddenly leaning against the solid strength of her father's legs. Her eyes looked shattered, grew shiny with tears. Rogan almost smiled at her obvious pain, even if he didn't understand its source. "Somehow, he caused my parents' accident, sent this *scum* to wait until I blundered along and—"

With a suddenly feral scream, Angelica lunged forward, her hands like claws as they dug into his shoulders.

"How the *hell* did you get there, you *son of a bitch*?"

"Angelica!" Merikan cried out, reaching out to grab her as the chair started to topple, Rogan and Angelica caught in its momentum. As soon as Merikan made contact, the world went grey and the room disappeared.

Chapter 23

The Royal carriage glided along the road through the forest, less than a water-cup away from the castle now. The young Dho'vani slept peacefully in his mother's arms after a busy day as the King and his entourage returned from celebrating Gavin's first birthday at the estate of Grayton's aunt in the country. King Grayton himself rode beside the carriage, his face relaxed, content, as he escorted his family home. A family that would soon grow, or so the queen had recently informed him.

And not the only growing family, Merikan thought as he rode beside his King. His gaze drank in the sight of the woman he could see sitting across from the queen though the windows of the carriage. Katerina's sapphire and emerald gaze met his, her love and joy reflecting from the depths of her fiery soul as her hands rested lightly on the swell of her abdomen. Gavin stretched, stirring briefly, his little hand brushing against Kat's stomach before the small Prince settled back to sleep. Both women smiled at the child as the progression continued smoothly along.

Angie watched the scene play out in the unsettling role of both spectator and participant. She saw everything that happened, yet also felt what Merikan felt on that fateful day, sometimes witnessing through his eyes, sometimes as though from above. Not understanding why she experienced this moment now, she knew that she needed to keep track of the events she knew would follow.

Without warning, Kat jolted straight up, her jewelled eyes wide.

"Stop the carriage!" Merikan called, worried at his wife's urgency. Had the child chosen to arrive already? But no, as her

210

stare met his, now glazed with the gold of her power, Merikan knew danger lurked nearby.

"'Ware danger," Kat confirmed as she slipped down from the carriage, her condition slowing her not at all. "Sire," she looked up at Grayton, "Get under cover in the carriage."

Merikan wove a protective shield around the conveyance as Grayton responded to the tension in Kat's voice, dismounting and climbing into the carriage with his wife and son. Kat closed the door and banged the heel of her hand twice on the side of the vehicle.

"Ride like the wind," she called up to the driver. "Get them to safety."

A snap of reins had the whinnying horses leaping forward, drawing the Royal Family away in haste, surrounded by the bristling barrier of swords and pikes wielded by the King's Guard as their mounts thundered alongside.

Four soldiers remained with the Lady Sorceress and the Lord Protector. Reaching up to Grayton's horse, Kat set her foot in the stirrup and hauled her weight over the gelding's back, a sweep of her hand making the saddle comfortable enough for her condition as she settled her skirts in place.

"What comes?" Merikan asked, gaze sweeping the area as he stretched out his senses.

"Ill intent, malice, conviction," Kat also searched her surroundings, features pinched tight as she tried to determine the exact nature of the danger, to put into words what she felt. "An ambush."

Merikan stared in the direction the carriage had taken, though only a trace of road dust lingered to mark its passage.

"We have to draw their attention," Kat said, turning the horse to retrace their steps. Merikan knew she headed just a small distance back to a side trail, more rough than the main road yet still accessible to a cart, if one didn't mind the less-than-even grooving of the rutted path. With their small guard in tow, the two Sorcerers raced back to create a diversion.

Not a hundred paces along the side path, Kat pulled up and stared in consternation back the way they had come, then around at the trees flanking them. The frustrated frown gave him pause, but not so much as the way Kat suddenly wrapped her arms protectively around her midsection and met his anxious stare with dawning horror.

"They're not after the Royals," she whispered, aghast.

Merikan swallowed his fear and wrapped his wife and child in layer upon layer of protection, adding to Kat's already impressive defences.

A shout from one of the guards drew their attention as the man reached a quavering hand to an arrow jutting from his shoulder, his features twisting in pain, then dread as the colour leeched from his face.

"Poison," he gasped, already urging his horse in the direction of the attack, trying to draw his sword, even as the life slipped from him and he crashed to the road, his body convulsing briefly before stilling forever. The other three guards already charged into the trees, each nimbused by shields.

"They won't last," Kat breathed, eyes anguished with the knowledge. "There's some kind of magic aligned with the attack."

"Go," Merikan commanded, holding her gaze, drinking in the sight of her, the vibrancy, intensity, beauty. Her love. "Get somewhere safe. Protect yourself, protect her; protect them all." He smiled gently, his heart breaking as she shook her head, not wanting to abandon him. "Go, my love. Let me do my duty."

Kat blinked back tears, threw a glittering barrier of gold around him, then turned and raced away into the woods, taking the most precious things in the world with her.

Merikan steeled himself, dismounted, and prepared to meet his fate.

Angie couldn't begin to describe the torrent of raw power that ran through the Lord Protector as he threw spell after spell into the woods in search of those who would harm his family, save that it felt as though her blood burned, her very essence ripped and tore into a thousand shards of glory and agony. The world shuddered and thundered in her ears, her hair floated in an electric current, her skin tried to crawl off her bones. She wondered if Merikan felt like this every time he used his magic, shuddering at the possibility.

"I don't, you know," he said in her mind, the present-day Lord Protector somehow watching alongside Angie as his past played out before them. "I tapped into more power on this day than ever before or since. It nearly burned me out. And didn't matter." The last thought came through as bitter as nettles.

The hard impacts of projectile weapons had bounced

harmlessly off his shields as the afternoon wore on, but then, as a startling flash of angry red fluctuated around his protection, Merikan felt something unexpected.

The first shaft struck him in the back of his left calf and he stumbled, turning to meet this new threat. Another arrow found a gap in the shield as so much raw power seeped the strength from him, dribbling away with the spill of blood. The third impact came from a flung dagger, the hilt sunk to the flesh in his right shoulder. He could feel the spread of poison, though his magic fought to slow it.

By the time Merikan found himself staring up through a narrowing tunnel of speckled grey at a darkening sky, half a dozen arrows and two knives had pierced him, and the leaf-strewn floor of the woods cushioned him as his mind struggled to rise and fight on even though his body had given up.

"I woke much later in the castle, drained of magic, barely alive, and far too late to save Kat," Merikan admitted heavily. "And I never knew who—"

He broke off as the scene shifted. Angie could somehow feel the disembodied presence of her father at her side as they watched through the eyes of another as the truth of Lady Katerina's last minutes finally came clear.

Rogan waited from the boughs of a sturdy maple, attention focussed on the path he could just see several paces away. His benefactor, concealed at the base of a tree not far off, earth-toned cowl pulled up to help keep him camouflaged against the rough bark, stood utterly motionless. Rogan could achieve a certain stillness—enough that the insects traipsing across his exposed arm paid him no heed, nor did the squirrel perched a dozen limbs higher chatter at him—but the Sorcerer *blended* into the world around him, for all intents *one* with the tree, rather than merely posing next to it. Rogan didn't know what the Sorcerer's studies had revealed that led him here today, to this grisly task, but he understood enough to know that, should they succeed, the man would have no more need to simply blend; he would change the world.

In the distance, Rogan heard shouts, felt shuddering impacts to the air that had leaves and needles and other woodsy detritus jittering in a macabre dance on the forest floor as someone tossed out powerful spells. He imagined he could see flashes of angry light reflecting here, shimmering there, burning all around, though he knew the chances of him actually *seeing* magic remained remote. His skills lay elsewhere.

A horse and rider came into sight, just as the Sorcerer had predicted. Rogan even knew her, had occasionally spoken with her as scribe to the steward at the castle. He had expected a terrified mother-to-be, ignorant of her true danger, fleeing from enemies; perhaps tears streaming down her face, eyes wide and unfocussed, panic making her reckless and an easy target. Instead, he watched a composed and imposing woman expertly guiding the King's horse along the path, her eyes flashing with a contained fury, her back straight despite the bulge of her stomach.

Rogan didn't hesitate. On an exhalation of breath, he released the nocked arrow, his aim true. In a strange slowing of time, he watched as first the shaft and then the fletching cleared the bow, heard the whoosh of air as his missile flew, the slap of string hitting his arm guard. He measured the trajectory and distance in his mind as the enspelled arrow soared, knew exactly where it would penetrate Lady Katerina's shields and slam into her shoulder. As a precaution, as instructed, he had already taken up his second arrow, drawn back the string to nock it, when the first quarrel reached its target.

She didn't even bother to glance in his direction as she snatched the arrow from the air a whisper away from her flesh and burned it with barely a thought, continuing on her way.

Rogan realised in that moment that he had never truly seen the Lady Sorceress in full fury and in complete control of her power. It didn't stop him from releasing the second bolt, but it did make him reassess this adversary.

The arrow took the horse in its left fetlock and the beast stumbled as Rogan leapt down from his concealment. The Sorcerer stepped out from cover, hand held up as though pleading that the Sorceress stop, though Rogan knew he worked some form of magic intended to pull the woman from her perch.

Katerina kicked free from the stirrups and threw herself over the side, tucking to roll with the motion. Her condition hindered the movement, turning the jump into more of a sprawl, but she didn't let it stop her as she used her momentum to scramble into the underbrush at the side of the road, remarkably fast for a pregnant woman encumbered by skirts. Rogan and the Sorcerer followed her thrashing.

It took Rogan about a hundred paces following in the wake of the Sorcerer, racing after the fleeing form of the Sorceress, to recognise what seemed off about this pursuit. Although handicapped by the babe in her womb, the woman moved surprisingly well and still managed to keep just out of reach. Too well actually, weaving around obstacles with alacrity and grace and a certain nimbleness that the men following could not match. Rogan halted, skidding in the leaf mould, and looked back over his shoulder, scanning the dappled shadows, his mind racing. The Sorcerer continued on, the snap of deadfall under his booted feet growing fainter as he hurried further away.

Rogan strained to hear anything amiss. He discerned the moment the Sorcerer also paused, imagined the curse before the crunch of feet retracing their steps back through the underbrush approached, stopping just shy of Rogan. Blind to magic, he could only assume that the Sorcerer had tried to net his fleeing foe only to discover what Rogan had already suspected; that they chased shadows while the real Sorceress sought to escape.

"Where?" the Sorcerer growled, voice low.

Rogan, bow and arrow nocked loosely in hands ready to draw the weapon taut, thrust out his chin in the direction he would have taken from where Katerina had flung herself from the horse. With more care than their initial pursuit, Rogan brought them back closer to the road, scanning the ground as he moved. Though not an expert tracker, he knew enough of what to watch for that he found her trail after a moment's search. More mindful of their quarry and her strengths, the two men followed the new path.

"There," the Sorcerer pushed ahead of Rogan. Rogan stopped at the edge of the tiny clearing, his arrow drawn and aimed, while the Sorcerer dashed in. The Sorceress knelt in a small space devoid of vegetation, sweat drenching her, chest heaving in hungry pants as she gulped for air, hands spasming as they clutched protectively at her mid-section. He couldn't see her face, nor make out the meaning of the words he could just barely hear her reciting. He narrowed his focus to the target of her shoulder, ready should the Sorcerer demand he let his missile fly, though he doubted its efficacy given how little regard she had shown his first arrow. Still, he stood ready while the Sorcerer advanced. Strangely, it seemed to Rogan that time slowed and he blinked quickly, trying to dispel that notion.

The scene shifted, panning around until Angie could see Katerina's face. The sensation made Angie dizzy. She watched as the Sorceress closed her eyes and time did slow, much as Angie had stopped time as she searched for an answer to the threat from Rayton and Remy. It seemed Katerina had a similar ability to affect time and Angie almost smiled at the comparison, but the smile tasted bitter.

"By the power of the bond forged in times past, I call upon you now to fulfill my request." A violet-green halo spun out of Katerina's words, a distortion rippling the air. With a painful pop, a door between realms wrenched open and a figure no larger than a hand span stepped through the mist. Iridescent double wings held the golden-green body clad in a diaphanous bark-brown dress aloft. Crooked teardrop eyes of sparkling emeralds regarded Katerina a moment before the Faery Sidvareh bowed, her coppery-gold hair trailing over her bare shoulders.

"How may I serve?" came the familiar peal of Sidvareh's chime-like voice.

"She must survive," Katerina stated, hand held to her stomach. Angie could see a stain of red spreading around the kneeling Sorceress, knew she had suffered damage in her scramble to escape, could see in the menace of the two men pushing against time to reach this woman that they did not intend to let her escape again.

The Faery glanced at the protective hand, then back up into Katerina's eyes.

"How may I serve?" she asked again.

"The bridge," Katerina gasped. "You must find a vacuum, a vessel. Span the bridge, take her spirit to safety. We must protect the Royal House. Can you do this?"

Sidvareh glanced behind, to the glacially approaching Sorcerer, now slowly drawing a dagger, as though gauging how long Katerina could hold off the inevitable.

"I can, but My Lady, it will divert your strength. You will have little left for defence."

"I fear he wants what he must not have. I am damaged already. This is Karundin's only hope."

"Then ready yourself, dear heart," Sidvareh sighed.

Time resumed, thrusting Angie's awareness back into the assassin standing in readiness behind the Sorcerer.

Rogan concentrated on his target, on keeping the cowled form of the Sorcerer out of his line of fire as the other man drew his blade and laid the sharp edge against the pale skin of the Sorceress's neck.

"Long have I searched," the Sorcerer spoke just loud enough to carry to Rogan. "I know now that what I seek lies in this realm, and you, Lady Sorceress Katerina, will lead me to it."

Katerina laughed in his face.

Even blind to the glow of magic, Rogan had no problems feeling the heat that washed off the two combatants. The hair on his arms and head crackled in a fierce static storm as elemental powers vied in the strangely silent and motionless tableau. Had Rogan not known the awesome forces arrayed against each other right in front of him, he might mistake the stationary pair as waiting for the other to make a move, when in truth, each fought with what he simply couldn't see. The results, as blood flew, sweat oozed, heat flared, and each breathed faster and harsher yes, but the physical use of magic remained an invisible weapon to his watching eyes.

"You've wasted your efforts, Sorcerer," Katerina gasped out from between clenched teeth. Had Rogan known she fought on two fronts—both struggling to keep the Sorcerer at bay and while her greater power trickled away aiding Sidvareh in sending Angie across worlds—his respect, already heightened by this display, would have magnified beyond measure. He almost wished the Sorcerer would spare her when he learned what he wanted.

"You *will* tell me where our ancestor hid those spells," the Sorcerer compelled.

Again, Katerina laughed, more harsh this time, blood filling her mouth, dribbling from her nose.

"She will destroy you for this," the Sorceress whispered, hands flat against the bulge in her stomach. Where, Rogan finally noticed with a strange sense of trepidation, she had held them since the Sorcerer first kissed her flesh with his dagger.

"Give me Borun's spells!" Spittle from that shout landed on Katerina's pale cheek.

"I don't have them," she replied. "I never did." Then she smiled, an oddly beatific expression passing across her face just as the Sorcerer pulled back, his blade drawing a red line across her throat.

"Oh Spirits have mercy, no," Merikan moaned from his *disembodied state next to Angie.*

"You don't have to watch," Angie argued.

"Yes, I do."

For the briefest moment, Katerina knelt alone, her smile radiant as the light of day faded. Then the mark lining her neck parted, blood spreading in a gruesome necklace, painting uneven lines of crimson down her front. With a last exhalation, she slumped to her side, her life hemorrhaging to feed the thirsty ground.

Rogan stared, his muscles aching from strain as he finally lowered his bow and arrow, slackening the tension.

"Did you have to?" he asked softly as the Sorcerer moved to stand next to him.

Rogan felt the heat of the man's regard though the shadows of twilight kept his cowl in deep darkness.

"She guards those with the power I seek, not the power itself." The Sorcerer's covered features turned back to witness the last breath of the Sorceress. "Without her to stop me, I will fill the void her end will create."

Finally, the Sorcerer spun away, began to retrace his steps to where their horses waited in a hidden copse of trees.

"Make sure of the babe," he tossed back over his shoulder.

Rogan stumbled mid-stride, hating the Sorcerer in that moment. But he turned, knelt on the far side of the Sorceress, away from the puddle of her blood. With a gentle hand, he grasped her shoulder, rolled the unresisting, cooling body onto its back to expose the swell of her belly. Without the mother, surely the child could not survive. Yet he remembered Katerina's words, understood the Sorcerer's need for thoroughness. So he pulled a knife from his boot, carefully unsheathing it, releasing the sour stink of pranik. With a twist of his wrist, he laid the blade tip against the swollen stomach, then carefully shored up his thoughts. Staring at the slack features of the woman, he pushed down, divorcing his mind from the actions of his hand. The honed edges slid in with little resistance until the hilt met flesh. He pulled the dagger free, carefully wiped the blade and resheathed it, sliding it back into his boot. Holding tight to a shell which no emotions could pierce, Rogan rose and followed the Sorcerer, as he had before, as he would again.

As he walked into the darkness, the memory shattered ...

... and the chair continued its fall, Angie's fingers tangled in Rogan's tunic, Merikan's restraining hand on her shoulder. All three toppled to the floor under the startled eyes of Eniok, the shared memories leaving them shaking and disoriented.

Angie stared at the assassin lying inches from her, met his astonished gaze.

"She was right," Angie whispered for Rogan's ears alone. "I will destroy him."

Chapter 24

"Why that memory?" Merikan wondered. "Why now?"

He and Angie stood outside the secured room holding Rogan, Commander Eniok still within, keeping an eye on the unnerved steward. Although *stood* implied a lack of motion. In truth, Merikan leaned heavily against the wall as though it alone kept him upright, his clasped hands mottled with the strain of keeping them from shaking, while Angie paced in agitation. She ceased the motion with an abrupt jerk as Nervain rounded the corner at the end of the hall, Gavin and his two guards behind him. The King looked haggard, and Angie knew he had just left Rayton.

The sun had just risen when Merikan had checked in on Angie, surprised to find her awake after the drain of power and energy from the previous evening. Angie had insisted on accompanying him to question Rogan when Merikan had made his intentions to do so known.

After a hearty meal to help replenish her strength.

From the moment of the attack, Gavin had cloistered himself with Rayton, soothing the boy's fears and misery, tending to his son as best he could under the circumstances. That Rayton had suffered such a trauma devastated Gavin, but not as much as knowing that the cause of his torment came as a result of one of Borun's spells, the very thing that Gavin had held in trust and failed to protect. The Royal Protectors had left the King sleeping fitfully next to his child, giving them time to heal.

But now, by the grim set of his features, Angie knew Gavin wanted answers and would brook no arguments.

"What memory?" Nervain asked, letting Angie know the obvious keenness of the man's hearing.

With an effort, Merikan pushed himself off the wall and straightened to his full height.

"Lady Katerina's death," he said, meeting Gavin's wounded stare. "Caused by our mysterious Sorcerer as he searched for the location of what you guard."

Gavin frowned, trying to digest that thought.

"But," Nervain, face set in consternation and growing dismay, worked it through. "That means this Sorcerer has worked against Karundin for at least twenty-eight double-seasons. Do we truly have an enemy who has remained unknown for so long? How can no one have suspected?"

"No one suspected Rogan of such treachery," Angie countered. "Yet he worked at the court even then, knew the woman whose child he thought he had killed."

"He—"

"Scribe to the steward then," Angie cut off Gavin's remark before the King could dwell overlong on the implications. "Risen now to steward, a rank of high accord and privy to a great deal of information. Also easily overlooked by the nobles as someone beneath their notice, yet granted a certain respect and privacy by the servants. The perfect position for a spy."

"Or an assassin," Nervain snarled.

"Exactly," Angie agreed. "An assassin who has crossed worlds."

"He—" Gavin's stare bored into the door separating him from his father's killer. "He's responsible for shooting you?"

"In a way, he's also responsible for bringing me here," Angie said, not liking the wild gleam threatening to overwhelm the King's gaze. When he turned that hard stare on her, Angie tried to sooth his temper. "Without that arrow, I wouldn't have known to come home." Without the Sorcerer somehow causing that accident on Earth that sent her parents to the hospital, Angie wouldn't have shown up where Rogan waited; without the dream calling her to King Grayton's side, the Sorcerer wouldn't have known to look for her. Hell, without the Sorcerer's avarice to gain what should never have existed, he wouldn't have challenged Katerina, who then wouldn't have sent Angie away ....

And Karundin's history, Angie's own existence, would have turned out very different.

Ironic that the Sorcerer's own actions had both saved Angie's life as a babe, and then brought her back to Karundin twenty-

221

eight years later to thwart his plans.

"And he told you this?" asked Nervain.

"Not exactly," Angie met Merikan's glance. "But he's been to Earth, to my world. I recognised the feel of him from when he shot me." She absently rubbed at her shoulder. "That sensation that made me turn, look for him."

"You said it was the real him, the person he didn't have to hide," Merikan confirmed, following her line of thought as they searched for an answer to the Lord Protector's initial question. "And you asked how he got to your world."

"But he didn't know," Angie argued, trying to piece it together. "So why that memory?"

Merikan nodded.

"He brought up Kat's death, my failure to save her, in order to hurt me, so my emotions may have influenced where the magic took us."

"What magic?" Gavin asked, voice soft so as not to disturb the flow he sensed between father and daughter.

"I think," Merikan let the word stretch. "Angelica's magic helped recreate that day, showed us what I had seen and endured, and then what Rogan experienced. The missing details regarding Kat's death." He shook his head, still not liking the shape of this puzzle. "But why? We still don't know enough."

"No," Angie felt it click into place, her eyes aglow with understanding. "Rogan doesn't know how to bridge worlds, but Katerina did. Don't you see? Your memory, Rogan's, they blended, painted the whole picture. They showed us *why* she sent me to Earth. More, they showed us *how*."

"They showed us how *Kat* did it," Merikan countered. "I don't think we could recreate that power."

"But we know someone who can," Angie insisted, knowing Sidvareh's name hung between them, though it remained unspoken. "We know there's a way back to Earth that I can use."

"You want to leave? To go back there?"

Gavin's question, barely above a whisper, held an anguish that tore at Angie's heart.

"I have to."

His expression, already bleak and forlorn, shattered, and Angie took a hasty step toward him, grasping his shoulders, keeping him upright.

"I have to get the painting," she qualified, searching his eyes for comprehension.

"Why?" his voice trembled.

"What's hidden in that painting?" Merikan asked.

Angie glanced briefly at Nervain, again wondering how much, if anything, the man knew about Gavin's charge.

"I think it's a spell to counter Borun's folly," she said.

That sharpened Gavin's gaze, gave him something to grasp onto. She felt him steady beneath her hands.

"But—" Merikan looked dumbfounded. "How can such a thing exist?"

"I don't know," Angie admitted. "But it's how I saved Rayton and Remy."

She blinked, hesitated, chased down a thought, then stared in astonishment at her father.

"I think it's the bridge!"

"What?" he exploded, taking a startled step toward her.

"Katerina must have known about it, used it as a link between worlds."

Merikan stumbled back and sank against the wall, a hand held to his head.

"I don't know how many more of these revelations I can take today," he muttered.

Angie suddenly recognised Merikan's exhaustion. While she and Gavin had managed some sleep and restoration of their energies, she suspected that Merikan had allowed no such luxury, had probably not slept for a couple of days. With a concerned mien, she made to go to his side, but he waved her off with a weary smile.

"Don't worry about me, Angel; it's just a lot to take in. I will adjust momentarily."

Ever protecting the Lady Sorceress, she thought, touched by his term of endearment, wondering if he had even noticed its use.

"You said you used this spell to save Rayton," Gavin gently regained her attention, taking her hands from his shoulders and holding them lightly in his own. At her nod, he continued. "How, if you need the painting from your world? Did you ... somehow go there? And if you've already used the spell, why do you need the painting at all? Can you not simply recall the words, recreate their effect?"

Shaking her head in negation, Angie explained.

223

"During the coronation, I saw a glimpse of the painting, of the words beneath. Before I could understand, the image faded. I remembered it again yesterday and begged for help. Something else spoke through me, using my voice, my connection, to utter the counter to Mind Control."

"Something else?" Merikan spluttered.

"A voice," Angie qualified, hating to burden him with yet more unexpected information, but understanding that he had to know. "Or perhaps the memory of a voice. Somehow connected to the painting, knowing how to pronounce words in a language I don't comprehend."

"And you listened to this voice?" Nervain demanded. "Not knowing its source or the implications of following its directives?"

"To save the King?" Angie retorted. "To reclaim the sanity of the Dho'vani? Yes, I did. But understand, Commander, though I could not fathom the origin of the voice, didn't know the language, don't recall the words now, I *did* know, in that instant, that they would break the control the Sorcerer had over Rayton and Remy."

"The power felt almost elemental," Merikan murmured. "I can't recall the words either, but they clearly require raw magic. A spell only in the sense that it used words, but an ability more akin to your own than mine, I believe."

"I don't understand," admitted Angie. "Though that shouldn't come as any surprise."

Merikan's lip twitched in acknowledgement of her quip.

"It nearly stripped you of your strength. For a single utterance of magic to bring about such a result strongly suggests it requires will, focus, not ceremony. Your desire to achieve your goal, your conviction that it would work, your desperation to find an answer, all combined, and your magic drew desire into fact."

Angie stared at him, nodding absently, not entirely sure she followed him.

"I'm going to just take your word on that," she said finally. "It hurt like *hell* but it worked. And I woke up this morning, so, *bonus*."

"*Bonus*?" Gavin repeated with a frown.

"Um," she tried to think of the Karundin equivalent, wondering how she kept managing to throw in English words without realising she did so. "It's a good thing."

"*Bonus*," she heard him repeat under his breath, testing out the word. *Better than shit,* she thought.

"Anyway," Angie tried to bring them back on topic. "We know this Sorcerer has three of Borun's spells, and that a counter exists to at least one of them. I need the painting here, in this world, to protect us from—"

Her voice trailed off. She remembered her nightmare of the future; the golems risen from the clay, the vacant expressions of tortured souls, the eager strength of those who could not see their enslavement, all arrayed against the waning strength of trees. Three missing spells; three branches of a dark army.

"What spell did Rogan steal?" quavered Angie's voice, wondering how she could possibly have known, yet certain she did.

Jaw held firm, Gavin glanced at Nervain.

"You'll know soon enough, Commander," said the King, ready to take his ally into his confidence. "They all will," he admitted in a whisper before facing Angie again. "He took Adoration."

"As the Lady predicted," Merikan confirmed, his thoughts obviously aligning with Angie's.

"I need to get that painting."

"We need to know who has orchestrated all this," Gavin retorted. "If we can stop the Sorcerer before he can use the spells, we may not need the counter."

"Then what are we waiting for?" Nervain demanded, his gaze on the door separating him from Rogan.

"A way to get answers that won't kill our source of information," Angie replied.

"What do you mean?" Nervain's head jerked in Angie's direction, but Merikan answered.

"Angelica cautioned me not to ask him about the Sorcerer. After contemplating her bizarre admonishment, I felt it a reasonable precaution. In fact," he paused, eyes narrowed in thought.

"I wonder, Commander, if you have any memory of the time after Katerina's death?"

"Only a boy's memory," Nervain said. "I remember you had nearly died and no one seemed to know who was responsible. The only brigand captured died before he was questioned."

"Not quite," Merikan shook his head. "He died after one question."

"Let me guess," Nervain scowled.

"I had recovered enough that King Grayton allowed me to accompany him. He had me put a Compulsion on the survivor to ensure truth. In the full sight of the court, Grayton said three words: *Who sent you?* The man opened his mouth to answer, but started choking instead, his air supply cut off. Rumours abounded about what had happened. Had he taken something to end his life? Had someone used magic to silence him? Had he simply succumbed to his injuries? I know now that he had a previous spell woven into him, one that prevented him from betraying his accomplice. Given the memory we shared with Rogan, I would surmise that the steward suffers the same affliction, only now I see it also shares the same source."

"So Rogan can't give us the Sorcerer," Gavin concluded, stopping when Angie's hand tightened on his. He inclined his head to her, waiting to hear what she had to say.

"He's not the only one who knows the Sorcerer. He's just the only one willingly obeying him."

"No," Gavin tried to pull his hands away, failed.

"Rayton knows who he is. So does Remy."

"And if this same spell prevents them from speaking the name?" Gavin ground out, grey eyes flashing dangerously.

"Gavin," she said, holding his gaze. "You *know* I can't hurt Rayton. Please, trust me to keep him safe."

Gavin shook his head over and over, a father's fears overwhelming a king's duty.

"We can ask Remy," he finally agreed. "But I won't risk Rayton."

"I understand. We'll speak with Remy first."

She could see he wanted to argue, insist they spoke with *only* Remy, but she spoke as Lady Sorceress Angelica, and she would find a way to keep *all* the Royals safe, even if she had to go against the wishes of the King to do so.

***

Rayton woke stiff, shaken, and alone. He whimpered briefly before taking hold of himself. The indentation next to him, where Papa had lain all night, still held the faintest hint of heat, so he had not lain there all alone for very long.

Trying to keep the horrible feeling of betrayal from consuming him, the memory of what he had almost done—his body moving

226

on its own even though his mind kept screaming at it to stop—Rayton sprang from the bed and tossed on some clothes, not caring whether they matched or not. He needed to talk to someone, somebody who would understand the clinging fear and not look at him with pity. He needed to find Remy.

Oni and the other guards waiting outside his rooms didn't want to take him to where they held Remy, but Rayton insisted. In truth, he had railed, cried, implored, wheedled he had heard Nurse call it once, and finally given a Royal command. Oni spoke quietly with the others, then they took Rayton to a guarded cell with no windows where Remy stretched out on a cot behind some bars.

Rayton tried to hold back his sobs at the sight. Not fair that Rayton had slept in comfort next to his father when Remy had to suffer this place. They both hadn't wanted to do what Shanor made them do, but Remy ending up here while Rayton sat in his own room struck the boy as just wrong.

"I'm sorry Remy," he whispered, slipping to the floor outside the cell. Remy moved quickly to sit opposite him.

"No, Dho'vani, don't take the blame for this. Don't let him win."

"But it's not fair, you in there."

"I attacked the King," Remy said.

"You didn't want to," Rayton objected.

"Does that matter?"

"Yes!" Rayton jumped to his feet. "Of course it matters! *You* don't let him win, Remy. It's my fault we went there instead of to see Papa like I should have."

"It's *not* your fault, Dho'vani. Neither of us could stop it."

Rayton crumpled to the ground again, biting back his tears, determined to find the same strength Remy had.

After a few minutes, Remy backed away, head bowed low.

"Remy?" Rayton cried out. Then flinched so hard he nearly smashed into the bars separating him from his friend as a hand tried to take his shoulder. He spun, rising to his knees, then stopped in trepidation. Papa knelt behind him, face pale and eyes tight. Merikan and Angie hovered behind and only Oni remained of the guards, standing on one side of the door while Nervain stood on the other. Rayton wanted to fling himself into the comfort of Papa's embrace, but fear and shame kept him from doing so. *What must Papa think?*

Then he firmed his trembling lip and clenched his fists to keep them from shaking.

"Why is Remy in there and I'm out here?" he demanded, pretending to ignore the sniffle in his demand. "I attacked Angie, just like Remy attacked Papa, and neither of us meant it."

"Oh Rayton," Papa tried to console, but Rayton pulled away.

"No, you can't treat us different just 'cause I'm Dho'vani and he's my guard. We both done something wrong; we should both receive the same punishment."

"He's not there as punishment, Dho'vani," Merikan said, crouching beside Papa, who looked as ready to shatter as Rayton himself.

Rayton frowned up into the dark eyes, but couldn't see a lie.

"He's not?"

"He's there for protection, to keep him safe."

Rayton looked through the bars at Remy then back at the Lord Protector, and finally to Papa.

"Truly?" his voice trembled.

"We don't know if the Sorcerer put any other orders into Remy's mind, Rayton." Papa sounded almost scared, and that frightened Rayton. Nothing scared Papa. "He's there so he can't harm anyone against his will again, not even himself."

"But, you must have thought the same of me," he whimpered. "And I slept in my own room."

Papa's eyes filled with tears and spilled down his cheeks, mirroring Rayton's own. The Dho'vani tried to blink his away, thinking hard.

"But I didn't sleep alone, did I Papa?" he whispered. "You stayed all night, to keep me safe too."

Papa nodded, his chin trembling as he bit his lip. Rayton threw himself into his father's arms and held on tight.

He felt a gentle hand on his back and turned his head to rest it on Papa's shoulder, seeing who else touched him.

"Rayton," Angie said, so close he could almost see his reflection in her pretty eyes. "We have to ask Remy some questions."

Rayton nodded, still not moving from Papa's warm embrace.

"I can be quiet," he said. "You won't even know I'm here."

Something passed across her face, something like worry, he thought. He straightened up off Papa's shoulder and stared at her.

"You don't want me here," he accused Angie.

She studied him, weighed him. And then she told him the truth.

"We don't know what these questions will do to him. We can't ask the steward because we know it will ... hurt him."

"So you'll hurt Remy instead?" he demanded, not wanting to believe Angie would do such a thing.

"No, Rayton, we're going to be very careful. But if something goes wrong, if something unexpected happens—"

"I'm not going." He pulled away from Papa entirely and wrapped his arms around the bars of Remy's cage.

"Rayton," Papa started.

"He did this to both of us, Papa. I won't let Remy suffer this alone."

"Dho'vani," Remy spoke from his prison. "Let me guard you from this."

But Rayton shook his head, tears forgotten. He drew a cloak of confidence around himself.

"You did try to guard me, Remy. I'm the one who followed him to the pantry, who went to see him instead of Papa." He turned to look at Papa, holding tight to his resolve when he admitted the next. "I think I'm the one who helped him see the spells, though he made me forget." Papa's eyes closed and Rayton sought refuge in Angie's gaze instead. "He made Remy and Oni forget too, but Oni didn't come in the room with us. It gets kind of fuzzy, but if I think about it real hard, try to hold it in my head, I can almost remember everything."

Angie pulled her legs under her and sat down, right there on the ground in front of Rayton. She gently pushed Papa behind her even though he didn't want to move. Then she took Rayton's hand, looked him in the eye, and smiled.

"Tell us everything you remember, Rayton. If something doesn't feel right, if it feels like you shouldn't tell us a memory, or a name, then don't."

"Angie," Papa shook his head, but she shushed him with a calm pat on the arm.

"Trust me now, Gavin."

With a huge sigh that hitched his breath, Papa finally nodded. He tried to smile encouragingly, but Rayton could see his fear. *For me,* he realised. Angie gave his hand a little squeeze. When he looked back at her, he knew Papa had nothing to fear. Not with Angie watching out for them.

So he told them everything, from the compulsion to study in the library where he saw Sorcerer Shanor, right through to going to Shanor's rooms after seeing the Sorcerer in the pantry.

"I remember waiting until his valet left," Rayton concluded. "And I asked why he'd gone to the pantry. He got a really strange look on his face, then leaned forward in his chair and said something that made us both freeze. I don't know the words he used, or what happened after, only that we all ended up back in my room, and none of us remembered why."

"He escorted you both out," Oni said quietly from his post by the door, drawing everyone's attention. He frowned. "I didn't even remember that until now. But the Sorcerer seemed, I don't know, drawn? Exhausted? He saw me and ... I had my hand on my sword and he ... waved a hand in front of my face. He almost fell over with the effort of it. And then bid us all a pleasant afternoon and we walked away like nothing had happened."

"He took our memories and he made us do things we didn't want," Rayton said, gaze steady on Angie's. "Did he do what I think he did, Angie? Did he use—" Rayton leaned forward and whispered in her ear "—Mind Control?" He pulled back, staring at her. "Did he use that spell?"

Angie nodded slowly, and Rayton swallowed hard, feeling it all the way to his stomach.

"So he can still make us do anything he wants?"

"No," Angie replied, her eyes dancing with silver. "He can't use either of you that way again." She turned to look at Papa. "You can let Remy out now."

"You're sure?" Merikan asked.

"The counterspell protects them, protects all of us in that room. It broke not just this one order, but any influence that spell might have had in the future."

"Counterspell?" Rayton wanted to know. "I didn't think it had any."

"None of us did," Papa admitted. "But Angie, as we keep seeing, is full of surprises."

Rayton stared at her, hope filling him and chasing away the fear and shame.

"Then Shanor can't hurt us anymore?" he wondered.

She bit her lip.

"Not using that spell, he can't. Beyond that ..."

Rayton's eyes flew to Papa.

"He's gone with Uncle Alvin and Aunt Maraenda, and little Maraedeth—" he blurted.

"I know," Papa's voice had gone eerily flat, and Rayton knew he never wanted to hear that tone aimed at him. He grinned then. Shanor had a world of trouble coming after him now that Papa knew. He and Angie and Merikan would make the Sorcerer pay.

Chapter 25

White and grey stone paths meandered through small grassy patches and large swaths of incredible gardens in a profusion of brilliant autumnal colours. Asters and phlox, coneflowers and black-eyed Susans, shrubs of varying hues of greens, yellows, and purples, all carefully tended yet somehow maintaining an air of wilderness. A small pond, cradling flashes of orange and white fish darting from beneath water plants to sun-dappled clarity to the shelter of scattered duckweed, sat in a semi-circle of reeds next to a gazebo.

Angie sat on a bench adjacent to the gazebo, gazing at the fish pond while the afternoon sun warmed her face. According to Merikan, Katerina had often used this courtyard garden as a refuge, and Angie could understand why. It exuded such a sense of peace, begged to help one relax, to revitalise. She didn't have much of a green thumb herself, but she very much appreciated the genius of others who could tend to such beauty.

A small red and brown bird flitted among the branches of a slender tree overhead, accompanied by the trill of a goldfinch perched in the reeds, inspecting the buzzing insects busy collecting pollen, both avians welcoming the Sorceress to their garden. Butterflies swooped and soared in a lazy dance, and she could hear the thrum of a hummingbird searching for sweet nectar somewhere nearby.

Angie closed her eyes with a sigh, leaning her back against the gazebo wall, just wanting to sit and take in the ambience. But she had searched out this place for a reason, although the location probably didn't matter. Still, if Angie intended to call upon a Faery, it seemed only fair to ask her to come somewhere a creature of pure magic might also find peaceful.

Angie took a deep breath and tried to let her thoughts settle. She pictured Sidvareh in her mind, the dragonfly wings, the green-gold skin, copper-gold hair, emerald eyes; an exotic creature composed in hues of precious metals and gems, like bits of the earth itself all fused together by elemental forces. Angie's eyes popped open at the comparison. She had always thought of Faeries as creatures of the air—if she had ever thought of them before Karundin, she revised with a sardonic little smile—not as somehow associated with the earth.

"Not the time for a philosophical debate with myself about the nature of magical beings," she scolded with a shake of her head, and closed her eyes again.

She remembered Sidvareh's last instructions, let herself hear the words in the Faery's tinkling voice:

If you have need of me, you have but to call.

"I need you, Sidvareh," Angie breathed. "Please, if you wish, come and speak with me."

A gentle breeze fanned her cheeks and Angie slowly cracked open her eyes. To see Sidvareh standing on a piece of air in front of Angie's face, her iridescent wings creating tiny whorls out of the remains of a violet mist. The tiny woman smiled, her joy brightening an already radiant day. Angie found her own cheeks stretching happily in return.

"Hello, dear child," Sidvareh's bell-like voice rang warmly.

"Sidvareh, it's so good to see you," Angie grinned, but she tempered her joy with the harsh knowledge of why she had to call upon this wondrous woman. "I wish we could just sit and talk, as friends of old."

"Ah, but such pleasures would not require a summoning, would they My Lady."

Angie's felt her face fall.

"Is that what I've done? A summoning?"

"What did you think?"

"A request," Angie replied. "Certainly not a demand. I'm so sorry if—"

Sidvareh cut her off with a chiming laugh.

"Do not fear, Angelica. Had I not wished to respond, I would not have come." She smiled. "You have come a long way in the mastering of your strengths, Angie, but in some things you remain but a novice. I find that refreshing." Sidvareh scanned their surroundings. "Your Lady Mother used to sit in this very spot, especially when something troubled her." Large green eyes regarded the Sorceress. "What has brought you here today?"

Angie bit her lower lip, then just blurted it out.

"I need the painting, Sidvareh. The bridge to Earth. I need it here, in this world."

"Why?"

"Because Shanor has stolen something that will lead to war, and the words beneath that painting will counter the horrors he will bring to Karundin."

"You have no doubts about that?"

The wary tone made Angie pause, think through everything that had led to her certainty that she needed the painting.

"I have seen the future," she whispered, and briefly recounted her dream. "The counterspells beneath the painting offered the only ray of hope. I know they work because it broke the Mind Control on Rayton. But the use of a counterspell on just two people wiped me out for most of the day. What cost its use on a larger scale? I can't be the only one to learn the spells, and I can't seem to recall them beyond the moment, so I need them, here, before Shanor unleashes something we cannot counter."

Sidvareh's wings had stopped fluttering, her face expressionless.

"How could you use a spell you did not have?" she asked slowly.

Angie described her memory of the coronation and Sidvareh's own admonition about waiting for the right time, and then the mysterious voice grating in her head and using her vocal chords to free Rayton and Remy.

Sidvareh sat, the air cradling her in an invisible chair.

"The voice of the spell's progenitor," Sidvareh murmured, her eyes clouded now. "If she spoke through you, then the time may have indeed come to return her last work to Karundin."

Angie hardly dared breath, but she had to ask.

"The spell's progenitor?"

Sidvareh blinked and met Angie's gaze, face growing sad.

"Lady Sorceress Daneka had managed to halt Amaekar long enough for victory in the war, but her counter could not hold forever. Borun strove hard in the years following Amaekar's betrayal to perfect Daneka's stop-gap, and he and Sorceress

Daneka finally achieved the near impossible, or so they hoped; their last great work. They designed the antidote to Borun's folly, but could never test the full efficacy nor the cost of its implementation. How could they, without employing that which Borun swore never to use again?

"And so they linked the counterspells to the Lady Sorceress as they linked the original spells to the Royal Family."

"So why doesn't anyone know about them?" demanded Angie. "Why hide them away on Earth, even more removed than the spells? In fact, why not hide everything on Earth, where no one would have found them?"

"Perhaps they felt the sacrifice too great," Sidvareh suggested.

Foreboding filled Angie.

"What sacrifice?"

Sidvareh sighed, her face taking on a far-away cast.

"We can cross from our world to this with little effort, as can many beings of magic. Each realm connected, accessed in some way, by means of power. Daneka searched long and hard for a place lacking such easy access. She finally found your Earth, a world that did not support its own system of magic, though it clearly retains some memory of a time when such abilities flourished.

"In order to push the spell through and keep it intact, she needed to create a bridge with the spark of magic upon it. We Faeries helped. My own mother opened the door to your world, held it wide while Daneka prepared to transfer the first spell through."

Sidvareh paused to draw in a steadying breath.

"I believe the Protectors intended to convey all the spells through the gate, but something went wrong. Perhaps your world could not support such an influx of power, or mayhap the gate to such a barren land could never stabilise or accept something so paradoxical to its nature. I don't know, but the gate began to collapse as soon as the counterspell became a fact on Earth, trapping it there. Like you cannot remember the words from the painting, nor could Daneka or Borun once it left Karundin.

"A moment of joy as they thought they had found a solution to Borun's folly, for if they could erase the memory of his vile spells in this manner, simply toss them through to Earth where they could do no damage—"

With a shake of her head and a tightening around her eyes, the Faery woman visibly steeled herself for the next part of her tale.

"Alas, that they could not employ this solution, for we of Faery alerted Daneka to a rapidly growing instability in not only the gate, but in the world we had connected to; a disharmony that would reflect back through the gate to this world, possibly to every world. Daneka tried to retrieve the spell, mend the breach, but the gate had grown too small, and it claimed her hand. In a desperate attempt to stabilise the bridge, one Faery slipped through and managed to stop the collapse. No one could ever confirm how she did it, but she anchored the gate, fixed the bridge to the painting; and remained forever bound to a world without magic.

"Because of her sacrifice, Karundin has a link to Earth, one in which thoughts and dreams can pass, an essence, a spirit, even a being for a short time. But to send through Borun's spells would have risked a further destabilization, negating the sacrifice."

"And to bring that one spell back?" Angie whispered. "To retrieve the bridge?"

"It would close the breach, seal off your Earth once again."

Angie thought of that a moment. To never return home, to her life on Earth. Never to see Irving or Jerry or any of her friends again—a certainty, not just an abstract. Would she miss it? Certainly, but she had a life here in Karundin, a place, friends, family. A purpose. Already, Karundin felt more real than her time on Earth. *Home,* as Sidvareh had indicated.

To save this world, would she give up her claim on Earth? Definitely. Yet something in the way Sidvareh held herself told Angie she had more to consider than simply closing off her access to Earth.

"What else would it do, closing the breach?" she asked.

"The life of a Faery maintains the bridge," Sidvareh said. "To retrieve what she bound to your world, one would need to reopen the gate to its full extent and pull the bridge through. In doing so, you would destabilise the gate. The only way to anchor the gate long enough to remove the bridge is to have something on the other end, able to hold the gate until the link vanishes."

"And the gate would collapse, leaving the anchor trapped on Earth."

"Correct."

"What would act as such an anchor?" Angie asked, dreading the answer.

"In all likelihood, the life of a Faery."

Angie closed her eyes in defeat.

"Then we have no way of bringing that painting here."

"Of course you do," Sidvareh countered, the matter-of-fact comment snapping Angie's eyes open.

"I will not sacrifice your life, or the life of any being, without—"

"Without what, Angie? Without the threat of war? The imminent annihilation of life in Karundin?"

Tears blurred her vision.

"We can stop him before it comes to that. We must."

"And if you cannot?" Sidvareh asked, voice soft as rose petals drifting in the wind. "If the only way to save the world comes from sacrificing a friend, what will you choose?"

Angie swallowed a hard lump, felt its painful course slide down her throat and lodge with a heavy weight in the pit of her stomach.

"I pray that it never comes to that," she answered, voice thick, tears etching harsh lines down her cheeks. "But if it does, then I pray I have the strength to choose life."

Sidvareh nodded, a sad smile playing at her mouth.

"So too did my mother." She stood on her piece of air, opened a swirling portal of purple mist, and met Angie's uneasy regard. "When you need to choose, call me."

She stepped through, back into Faery, leaving Angie alone on a bench next to a little pond in the garden, thoughts sombre. With a shudder, Angie leaned back against the gazebo, closing her eyes to the remains of the afternoon's light, fighting off her rising despair.

***

"I'm sorry, we're closed for the day," a voice tinged with consternation said. Angie's eyes flew open and she stared up in surprise from her chair to see Jerry just closing up the workshop space, his face lit by the setting sun streaming through the front window and the eerie half-light of a dream. "Did you have an appointment?" he asked, frowning as he swept his gaze around the waiting area, as though wondering whether she had slipped in past the closed front door, or if he simply hadn't thrown the lock yet.

Resisting the impulse to greet him as an old friend—it almost seemed he had difficulties focussing on her, and certainly no spark of recognition illuminated his features—Angie made herself nod, pulling a business-like mien about herself as she stood to meet him eye-to-eye.

"I'm here to see Irving."

Jerry's face cleared.

"Of course," he said. "I think I remember him mentioning one last meeting today, Ms ...."

Angie found herself at a loss for a reply. Jerry didn't remember her. Irving had said no one remembered her. So, did she give her real name, or make something up? And what if Irving's real appointment arrived? *And what the hell am I doing here?* she asked herself. Sidvareh had just told her the cost of retrieving the painting, yet now she sat back at the office, hopefully within reach of that very painting? What did that portend?

"Ange?" Irving's incredulous call as he stepped from the hall leading to his office saved her from having to answer Jerry. He wore his beige trench coat, his hat askew as though he had just jammed it on his head. And he had turned out the light behind him, clearly on par with Jerry's closing up shop for the day, not at all someone waiting for a last appointment.

"Um," Jerry grew uncertain, stumbling for words. "I thought ... you had a meeting?"

Irving scrunched his eyes in confusion at his assistant, then opened them wide as he stared back and forth between Jerry and Angie, suddenly understanding the situation.

"Yes, I did," Irving confirmed. "Though I didn't know if you'd make it in today." His gaze invited Angie to supply an excuse.

"My apologies Mr. Wallman," she said. "My travel plans don't always coincide with my desires. I didn't know I would arrive until the last minute. Sorry if it came as a bit of a surprise."

Irving quickly snorted back a laugh. He turned to Jerry.

"This is Ms. Angelica Karundin," he introduced, and Angie forced herself not to gape at the name. "And she's here about her painting."

The hint of malaise and mistrust swept clear off Jerry's face.

"Of course, it's lovely to meet you." Angie shook his proffered hand and made the appropriate noises in response. Then Jerry turned back to Irving.

"I'll leave you to it, then, boss. See you in the morning." With a polite nod and a "ma'am" tossed her direction, Jerry swung out the front door and headed home, the whole encounter gradually slipping from his mind.

Angie stood staring at the door until Irving gently pushed past her to set the lock. He spun to face her, back leaning against the closed door.

"Christ, Mermaid, if he'd had even a shred of recognition for you, I'd truly believe you stood there."

Surprised, Angie looked down at herself.

"I don't?" she asked, studying her hands, pinching her arms. She pulled her gaze up to meet Irving's. "It feels real, Irving."

His brow furrowed and he pushed off from the door. Two hesitant steps brought him toe to toe with her and he reached a hand out to her shoulder, as though testing its solidity.

"But how?" he whispered. "Have you come back?" He sounded hopeful.

Angie shook her head and his expression fell. She studied their surroundings again, took note of the half-light.

"Irving—" She didn't know quite how to ask. "Do you see anything strange about the light in here?"

His hand dropped from her shoulder, fingers rubbing together absently as he looked around. Frowned.

"Now that you mention it, it seems almost ..." He paused, faced her again. "Dream-like."

"I don't know how I'm here, Irving. Or if I'm here."

"But you know why you're here." She quirked a questioning eyebrow, amazed at his calm acceptance of a situation she did not understand. He gestured to the door Jerry had locked up. "It's here."

"The painting?" she sputtered as her head whipped around to follow his arm, remembering that Irving had mentioned it to Jerry. She met Irving's gaze. "Angelica Karundin?" she enquired.

He nodded and gave her a little shove toward the workroom.

"I've discovered some interesting things, Mermaid."

They had set aside a corner of the workroom so that nothing encroached on the single object housed there; the now-familiar painting set upon its easel. Only, the picture stood intact, no part of the image removed.

"I did have it set up in the middle of the room when I obtained it, like in your dream," Irving told her. "But it rather took up space that I couldn't justify without explaining what didn't make sense to Jerry."

"I can hardly believe it still makes sense to you."

"Well," he hedged. "I had some help in that department."

When Angie glanced at him in invitation to explain, he slid an envelope from his inner coat pocket and handed it to her in silence. She pulled a piece of paper from the blank envelope, unfolded it, and read the note written in an elegant hand addressed to the museum curator.

On behalf of the Lady Angelica Karundin, her agent, Mr. Irving Wallman, has permission to relocate the painting known as Castle of Dreams *to his restoration workshop, Wallman Restorations, where Lady Angelica will make further arrangements.*

Documentation providing proof of ownership accompanied the letter.

Angie stared at Irving in mute appeal.

"I found that the morning after we spoke in your dream," he explained. "No idea where it came from, but everything's there, right down to the record of acquisition number and proper catalogue information. I simply went in and spoke with the museum's curator and he directed me to the lead cataloguer, who tracked down the painting in their storerooms. Went through the whole reacquisition process, always somehow having the proper documentation whenever they needed it. Signed off for their files, then, with all due diligence, had the painting brought here."

"You're saying the painting was on loan?" she asked.

"And, according to provenance, you're the owner."

"What?"

"Assuming you are, as I surmised, the Lady Angelica Karundin?"

"Lady Sorceress Angelica of Karundin, if you want to get technical," Angie replied, dumbfounded. "From what I can determine, no one much uses surnames there."

"Then who's Daneka Borun, or Katerina Merikan?"

Angie's jaw dropped and she stood gaping at Irving. Who merely nodded and smiled, producing a sheaf of papers from a nearby table.

"Provenance for your *Castle of Dreams*."

Angie took the sheets carefully, scanning the names, the signatures, the dates. The original owner, Daneka Borun, also listed as the artist, had produced the artwork c. 1463. The list of owners spanned the centuries, always a woman's name with a different surname, until the museum received it on loan twenty-eight years ago by Katerina Merikan, whereupon ownership had also transferred to Angelica Karundin. Angie suspected she could now name every Lady Sorceress and Lord Protector in Karundin's history. But the how of it baffled her. As did the final signature, for it matched Angie's handwriting exactly, and she *knew* she had never penned it.

"What the hell, Irving? How does any of this exist?"

"How do I remember the last five years differently than anyone else, Mermaid?" he countered. She stared at him in consternation. He took an agitated breath, the first sign she had seen that any of this troubled him.

"I told you before that I could sort of remember you if I concentrated. Well, since that dream, I remember it all. But every memory of you has this strange overlay, like two worlds colliding in my mind; the one with you in it, and the one without. Both existing at the same time, but only for me. I can speak about you abstractly, but I can't name you or anything you've done, except in my head. I wonder sometimes if Jerry thinks I'm losing my wits. Hell, there are days when I wonder the same thing." He took a calming breath. "The point is, this *does* all exist. I can't explain it, but I sure as hell can't deny it either. So I just go with it, let events unfold as they will.

"So here we are, with that painting standing in front of us. You said it had words beneath?"

Angie nodded, lost in thought, then glanced sharply at Irving. He just raised an eyebrow. She turned to the painting, leaned in close. No flaws marked the surface.

"Before, when you brought it in—"

"I remember," he interrupted. "The flaw the museum wanted you to uncover, you starting to work on it. Yet now," he flung his hands up in exasperation. "Perfect condition." He met her gaze. "So what's under it?"

"A spell."

"A spell," Irving repeated. "And you can cast it? You really are

241

some kind of sorceress?"

"Yes."

He thought a moment.

"What does it do?"

"It can reverse what a very bad man plans to do, which is basically start a war."

He stared at the image for a time.

"Then I guess you'd better take it back with you."

"I can't, Irving," she moaned.

"Why not?"

She groaned out her frustration.

"How do you measure a life?" she wondered. "It's like this painting is some sort of paradox. It's here because a Sorceress sent it here to protect it, but it can't go back without ripping things apart. She sent it to a world without magic, and that nearly destroyed both worlds. Someone gave their life to stabilise it here. To send it back needs another sacrifice." She cast wide eyes his direction. "How can I ask anyone for that kind of sacrifice, Irving? When does one life become less important than another? What gives me the right to make that choice?"

"You don't have that right," he agreed. "You can only choose for yourself."

"Exactly," she cried.

"But that doesn't mean that you can overrule someone else's decision."

She frowned at him, waiting for him to explain.

"If somebody else deems it necessary to make that kind of sacrifice, you'd have to abide by their wishes, wouldn't you?"

She nodded uncertainly.

"Then you wouldn't be asking for anyone's death; you'd just have to accept their decision, freely given, if they chose to make that sacrifice."

"Shit, Irving, that's a morbid thought," she grimaced. "But one I guess I'd better keep in mind."

The light flickered, startling them both.

"Um, Ange?" said Irving. "Does this mean this weird-ass dream that's not a dream is about to end?"

Angie laughed, the sound tasting bitter in her mouth.

"No idea, Irving," she admitted. "I usually just show up in my dreams. They start and end on their own."

"Well then," he said, a tremulous smile forming on his face. "I guess I'll just keep your artwork for a while longer while you try to save your world. You'll know where it is if you need it."

Angie threw her arms around her old friend.

"Thank you, Irving," she whispered.

He patted her on the back and squeezed tight.

"Take care of the Lady Sorceress Angelica for me," he said.

Angie laughed. And woke to the first stars gracing the clear night sky above a fragrant garden in Karundin.

Chapter 26

How could he not have seen it? All these years, first Grayton, and then Gavin himself, had sheltered traitors. Trusted men standing so close to the Royals, men who plotted from the shadows how to topple the family into the abyss, taking all Karundin with them, and no one had discovered their duplicity, nor even suspected such existed. How had they not foreseen something so troubling after Lady Sorceress Katerina's death?

Two vipers nestled in the bosom of Karundin's rulers; one now in custody, one beyond their grasp, safely ensconced in his homeland, and in possession of hostages.

But how far did this conspiracy stretch? All the way to King Dorn of Sahkarae and his sons? Or did it stop at the feet of Sorcerer Shanor? How many other snakes smiled at him in the light of day, yet plan to destroy him by night? Whom could he trust? Whom dare he trust?

Angie, of course, even now searching for a way to counter Shanor's stolen powers. Merikan, devoted to Karundin, but more, to Angie. Nervain. His family—

But no, Gavin shook his head with a snarl. Shanor had Alvin in his grasp. That the Sorcerer had perverted Rayton's mind infuriated him—terrified, shocked, disgusted, disturbed him, near brought him to his knees at his own helplessness in that moment—but if he looked at the incident as King and not as a father, he had to acknowledge that Rayton could only have caused limited damage. He and Remy might have injured Gavin and Angie, but chances of them killing either power remained small. Even Rayton's death—Gavin's chest constricted at the mere thought—would only have incapacitated the King, not those who would defend Karundin's borders should it truly come to war.

But with Alvin, Gavin's chief tactician, held in thrall, Shanor could cause so much more turmoil. Alvin knew Karundin's defences, her generals, troop training, garrison locations and strengths. He had a brilliant mind for strategy, one now most likely devoted to an enemy, for Gavin held no illusions about Shanor casting Mind Control, or worse, Adoration, upon Alvin and those travelling with him.

Karundin now had the best military mind set against her, paired with an unscrupulous Sorcerer who could raise armies of clay immune to pain, hunger, fatigue. A man who had the stolen knowledge to enslave hundreds, thousands of men to supplement that unnatural army, turn brother against brother, father against son.

Gavin had an unprepared populous at the outset of harvest that he must rally, gather into a defending force to counter an enemy who could move at any time, or wait until Karundin's people chafed at being pulled from their fields with no army in sight. Shanor could strike at any time without the need to secure a supply line. Gavin had to consider mouths to feed, families left behind to support, travel time to ensure troops did not arrive too weary to do battle.

If Angie could gain the counterspell to Borun's folly, they stood a chance, though the likely cost frightened him. Merikan had said the raw power to remove Mind Control from Rayton and Remy had nearly stripped Angie of her strength, and Angie herself admitted how much it had hurt her. To have to use the counterspell on a wider scale would only increase the pain, the exhaustion. To have to use such power to quell an army of clay soldiers? A mob whose captured minds lay at Shanor's feet? Gavin could only imagine the cost.

He had one weapon at his disposal to help her, but he shuddered at the thought of her having to use it. His ancestors had hidden away Borun's spells for a reason; the thought of having to unleash them now did not sit easy, but he didn't know a better way to protect his people and his land. If using Borun's spell of Immeasurable Power to widen the influence of the counterspells would defend Karundin, save her people from torment and slavery, did they not have an obligation to employ it? How could he measure the terrible cost against the probable gain?

He needed more magic users to protect his fighting force, which brought him back to whom he could trust. He also needed soldiers to fill in that force, men he would have to take away from the upcoming harvest, and a way to shield them from the interference of Mind Control or Adoration.

Gavin shook his head again, his thoughts chasing each other in endless circles.

First things first; put into action the elements he could control.

He handed off his orders to gather the levies from his nobles to the under-steward who, under the watchful eye of Commander Eniok, would take those orders to the aviary. A flurry of messenger birds would soon litter the skies of Karundin, sending out the call to prepare for war. An extra bird would find its way to Kaeley, bringing his sister home. Gavin couldn't protect Alvin, but by all the powers, he would keep his sister safe. He hoped.

He had the two spells retrieved from Kaeley's room, their camouflage removed, now under his direct care in a pouch secured to his belt by Merikan's magic. Now to retrieve the third, an inconceivable spell to augment untried counterspells in an impending war. Gavin rather wished they stood in one of Angie's dreams, that they could all wake up and find none of this had happened.

As well wish for the stars to fall from the heavens, bringing with them fanciful delights to amaze and inspire. He sighed, his heart heavy, then headed off to make arrangements for an early morning departure to the hunting lodge where that spell still lay hidden. One step at a time, he instructed himself. First secure the spells, then, if they didn't find a way to stop Shanor, figure out how best to employ a power none of them should ever have had to wield.

***

Dawn had introduced a gloomy countenance, leaden clouds hanging low and ominous, yet the heavy scent of rain did not materialise into the promised downpour until they had nearly reached their destination.

Gavin had found her last night as she returned from the garden. When Angie had explained her reticence about retrieving the painting from Earth now that she knew the consequences, the King's expression had turned grim.

"Do you think you can recall at least the counter to Mind Control without it?" he had asked.

"Maybe in dire circumstances, but I wouldn't want to rely on that," she had replied.

With a grimace, Gavin had then explained his intention to ride out in the morning to the Royal Hunting Lodge to recover the last of Borun's spells, his hand unconsciously hovering protectively over the pouch that held the other two at his waist.

Leaving Merikan behind to safeguard Rayton and the castle, Angie and Gavin had set out before sunrise—though the dark clouds obscured any view of the sun when it did rise—with Nervain, Tera, and Davok flanking them. They had ridden steadily, but with far less recklessness than their flight to the city near a week ago. Upon reaching a side trail Gavin had informed her led to the Lodge, the skies opened, relinquishing their hold on a cold torrent of lashing rain.

Now the five rode hunched over their mounts' necks, cloaks and hoods pulled tight, as they raced through fat, cold drops, toward the promise of shelter. The path turned to mud, churned up by pounding hooves, and the horses' exhalations began to mist the air as the temperature dropped.

Praetorian, Gavin's mount, let out a sharp *whuf* as he marked the familiar building ahead, and the beast put on an extra spurt of speed. The other mounts caught his excitement and bore their riders quickly to the shelter of the stables next to the Lodge.

Angie gingerly patted her mare's neck in appreciation, then slid from the saddle. She glanced at the others and couldn't suppress a tiny giggle at their appearance, knowing she must look equally bedraggled. Hair plastered to faces, sodden clothing clinging in awkward wrinkles, mud splattered up their legs, they looked like they had just run a tough mudder. *Or maybe mud wrestling?* The thought of either didn't help her control her mirth, and the incredulous frowns thrown her way just added to her laughter.

She pressed her forehead into her horse's heaving side to block out the sight, her shoulders shaking with her giggles, and tried very hard not to let those snorts turn into tears. She hadn't slept well and her frustration and despairing thoughts left her far too open to hysterics. *Better it come out as laughter,* she thought, trying to hold on to the humour. She pulled back from the horse, wiping tears and mud and horse sweat from her face, not sure she succeeded at holding the anxiety of making painful decisions at bay.

Gavin stood at her side, tilting her chin so that their eyes met. Without taking those compassionate grey orbs off her, he spoke over his shoulder.

"See the horses groomed and fed, please. I'll take Lady Angelica over to the Lodge, see if we can't get her cleaned up."

Angie pulled away in embarrassment and Gavin quirked his lips in a cheeky grin. She flicked a slap at his shoulder, but couldn't hold her scowl in light of his attempt to cheer her up.

He offered his arm with an elegant flourish.

"If my mud-streaked Lady will allow?" he said with mock seriousness.

Swallowing her turbulent emotions, she accepted his arm with as gracious and dignified a gesture as she could manage. She lightly touched her fingers to his wrist as she had seen the court ladies do, trying to look aloof, knowing the shimmer in her eyes gave her away.

"Lead on, my sodden King," she intoned.

They made it as far as the stable door before both dissolved into laughter, and Angie linked her arm firmly in his. Together, they ran into the storm toward the Hunting Lodge. Nervain shook his head at their antics, though he well understood this outlet to their concerns.

"Let's give them some time, lads," he instructed as the three soldiers saw to the horses.

***

Throwing his shoulder against the slight swell of rain-dampened wood, Gavin shoved the door to the lodge open, Angie hard on his heels as a gust of wind harried them. Together, they pushed the door shut, gasping in exhilaration and the chill of the rain. Staring at the man beside her, Angie, suddenly quite aware of his allure, caught her breath and swallowed hard, laughter forgotten. With an effort, she tore her gaze from his, felt her cheeks heat, hoped he'd mistake the flush as weather-caused.

She hurried away from the door, fingers clawing at the tie at her throat that kept the cloak in place, wanting to rid herself of the dripping garment. Hands gently lifted it from her shoulders, icy fingers caressing her neck to send shivers down her spine that she couldn't entirely convince herself came only from the cold. She almost turned to look at him again, feared what she'd see, what he'd see. Instead, she retreated to the barren hearth, concentrated on laying a suitable base for a fire, suspecting they would wait out the storm, and desperately needing something productive to do with her hands that did not involve any lustful thoughts toward the King.

After a moment, she heard Gavin moving around behind her. Glancing out the corner of her eye, she saw he had hung up their cloaks, shucked out of his boots, pulled off the leather baldric with his sword and hung it over the back of a chair. She tore her gaze away as he reached to pull the drenched tunic over his head, heard the plash of water as he wrung out the cloth. She stared blankly at the pile of wood in the grate before her, wondering how to light a fire without matches or a lantern. Maybe the intense heat from her face would help.

The sounds of rummaging behind her, fabric rustling, distracted her further and she closed her eyes, trying to marshal her thoughts, her self-control. It didn't matter that an incredibly gorgeous man walked around half-naked behind her; nothing could ever come of it. They had far more pressing issues than her wobbling libido.

"You should get out of that wet clothing," he said from right beside her. With a squeak, Angie leapt to her feet, eyes wide as she stared down at the man crouching next to her wrapped in a blanket, a second one for her cradled in his lap.

With a breathy laugh, Angie pressed her palms over her eyes, willed her breathing to slow, then brought her hands down, reaching for the blanket.

Expression unreadable, Gavin merely relinquished the warm material and rose to take a container from the mantel. He pulled out a striker for the fire. Angie moved to the table and chairs in the corner, sank into a seat to pull at her boots while Gavin coaxed the fire to life.

By the time he had a good blaze going, Angie had managed to temper her emotions. Dressed only in her thin under-tunic, blanket securely around her, she laid out the rest of her muddy wet clothing on a drying rack already holding Gavin's finery. She wondered how often the rack dried cloth and how often it held hides from a hunt, decided she'd rather not know, and turned toward the fire.

And nearly bumped into Gavin standing at her back. He steadied her with one hand, the other tightly holding the folds of the blanket around him. She stared at him in mute appeal, then pulled away and moved to stand next to the fire, letting it warm her already overheated skin.

Wordlessly, he stood beside her. She imagined she could feel his gaze, but refused to acknowledge it. She finally took a breath, tried to keep her mind on the real situation.

"Where is the spell?" she asked.

"With my sword," he replied in a low voice.

She glanced back, saw a stuffed hare perched on the chair. Eyes wide in incredulity, she met his shrug.

"Huh," she managed, staring back at the unfortunate creature. "Guess Queen Teraenda had a bit of a morbid sense of humour."

He grinned, nearly undoing her resolve.

"It's the mounting plate beneath, not the critter," he said. She smiled back, then faced the fire again. A splat of water tickled her bare foot and she traced it back to her hair. She ran a hand over her wet locks, bunched the ends into a ball and squeezed, wringing out what she could, then ran her fingers through the tangles. Or tried to. Rather, she caught her fingers up in the knots. With a snarl, she concentrated on pulling free, her hand so close to her face it filled her vision.

A second hand joined it and she froze. Gavin tugged gently at the strands, loosened the knots holding her captive. Her hand fell limply. His did not, instead combing through the honey-dark strands, made darker by the damp. She stared at him, so close, knowing she should pull away again, but somehow her body refused to heed her brain.

"What are you doing?" she asked breathily, unable to force out more sound.

"Something I've wanted to do for a long time," he murmured, mesmerized by his fingers in her hair. Did his eyes smoulder, or did she just see shadows from the fire?

She swallowed.

"I think the cold and rain have affected your brain, Sire," she tried for amusement, maybe even derision, but she only heard a husky desire, and cursed herself for her lack of control.

"The only thing affecting my brain is you, and the fear that I might lose you before I—"

No longer limp, her hand flew up, fingers pressing against his lips, holding in his words.

"We can't do this, Gavin," she whispered, blinking back tears. "You're the King, and I'm supposed to protect you."

His hand fell from her hair to wrap gently around her wrist. He lightly kissed her fingers before pulling them off his lips, wrapping them in his own fingers. She followed the motion with suddenly frightened eyes, each sensation sending tingles quivering through her body.

"Can you protect me from my own heart, Angie?" he sighed, stepping back, giving them both a bit of room to breathe, but not releasing her hand, her gaze. "From the moment I saw you in the woods, before you even opened those incredible eyes of yours—"

"Stop, don't," she interrupted. She tried to step back too, managed a minute shuffle. "Love at first sight is *bullshit*, Gavin."

"What is *bullshit*?"

Angie choked off a moan.

"*Baloney, hokum*, make-believe, a fairy tale."

"A dream?" Gavin suggested as he retook that small step, gazing deep into her eyes, trailing a hand down her damp hair. Their fingers still entwined in his other hand, she spared a thought to how his blanket still clung to his shoulders.

She closed her eyes in defence, but couldn't stop a sigh.

"I think I started falling in love the moment you burst through the door when I got here," she finally admitted, voice so soft he had to lean in to hear.

"When we found you in the woods," he replied, something in his tone forcing her to open her eyes, meet his close scrutiny, "the thought of doing you any harm should you prove an enemy nearly took my breath away, it hurt so much."

"Oh Gavin," she huffed. "What are we going to do?"

"This," he replied, pressing his lips against hers. She lost herself to the moment.

Chapter 27

Shanor remembered when he had first discovered the old manuscript that hinted at the existence of Borun's spells, of their potential, and above all, of their likely location. He had brought his findings and suppositions to King Dorn, who had adopted the concept of reclaiming Karundin with alacrity. For all that three decades had passed, the man had lost none of his ambition.

When their entourage had arrived at Sahkarae's court, Shanor had already ensnared the will of Alvin and his guards through Mind Control, using the Tre'vani to unmask his latest prize. And what a prize! Dorn had practically swooned at the possibilities presented by the trio of power Shanor now offered him. How could they fail to reclaim their ancient heritage with these weapons in hand? An inexhaustible army, flanked by obedient troops—willing or not, no need to fear loyalty from Adoring or Controlled minds—Sahkarae all but had Karundin in hand, the land and peoples enfolded back into a united whole. What Borun's spells had unravelled under the misguided hand of Amaekar, they would now rebuild through the efforts of King Dorn and Shanor.

Somehow, Shanor doubted Gavin or his sorcerous protectors would bow so easily to the logic of Shanor's solution.

Unfortunately, some of Sahkarae's own nobles had also failed to see the benefits of reclamation and reunification with their northern neighbour. Rather than deterring Dorn, their reticence had incited the King to some bold measures.

"We could spend seasons without end trying to change their minds," Dorn had mused. "I've put out feelers through the years since you first embarked on this mission, and still too many barons and dukes balk, content to allow Karundin to wallow under an inferior bloodline." He had shaken his head in sadness, and a bit of frustration. "The time to strike is now, before Gavin can truly marshal any decent forces. The longer he has to plan, the more unnecessary blood we all will shed. If only the nobles would understand the potency of the weapons in our hand; that we cannot lose if we act quickly."

Shanor, following the line of the King's thinking, knew what Dorn wished, what he couldn't actually propose or officially sanction. Ever the faithful servant to Sahkarae, Shanor had merely nodded.

And then proceeded to further test the powers of Borun's spells. He had met with the recalcitrant nobles, explained the brilliance of the King's plan and the extent of his newest arsenal, and experimented with Mind Control and Adoration on those who still adamantly refused to support Dorn's initiative.

Shanor had learned some important lessons during that time. For instance, he could project the recipient of Adoration onto a second person rather than the spell-caster. It looked as though Duke Melner and Baron Brak, the first two nobles he had spun his magical web upon, would follow Shanor around like puppies for the rest of their days, but Duke Ahren and Viscount Trega stood smitten by the King. Easier to order one under Mind Control to obey another than trust one enspelled by Adoration to follow someone not intended at the outset of the spell. Now Sahkarae's nobles presented a unique blend of voices; some Adoringly added their praise to the initiative, some contributed Controlled input, and others, already convinced of the righteousness of their cause, continued their support for Dorn.

But most importantly in his research, Shanor had learned a certain limitation to the spells; the sheer energy required to cast them. He had thought his exhaustion after bespelling Rayton and Remy an effect of employing a new and unfamiliar spell, done with no preparation. Now he understood that Borun's spells simply required an immense output from the sorcerer. He could only envision the cost of bringing an army of clay to life. Dorn had allayed Shanor's fear with a simple solution.

"Seek help," he had said.

Sahkarae had other sorcerers and sorceresses available. Shanor chose two of the strongest and made them his allies; his Adoring compatriots, but how else to entrust such power to a rival? With Sorceress Jaen and Sorcerer Flornum at his side, Shanor now had greater strength to draw upon when Dorn needed his inexhaustible army.

Weeks of discussions, preparations and planning had ensued. Dorn and his advisors worked on strategies and timing, utilizing Alvin's knowledge of Karundin to their advantage.

However, Shanor had discovered a startling limitation to Mind Control, at least where it concerned Alvin. The Karundin Prince fought Shanor's control whenever he could, following commands easily enough, but only fulfilling the exact order, and no more. When he had first used the spell on the Tre'vani, made Alvin unmask the third spell, Shanor had instructed the man to forget that he had done so until they reached Sahkarae. As soon as they crossed the border, Shanor just happened to turn in time to see Alvin's eyes widen, then search with scorching intensity for the Sorcerer who had betrayed him, mouth open to call a warning. Shanor had met Alvin's stare with a finger hurriedly thrust against his own lips, urging the man to silence. Alvin's lips had pressed together in a painfully thin line and he spoke not another word that day, no matter who tried to engage him.

That evening, Shanor had rectified the situation by ordering the Prince not to speak of Shanor's duplicity, nor of his own magically induced situation. He had followed up the order with instructions that Alvin would not raise a hand against Shanor or King Dorn or any in authority within Sahkarae.

Later that night, he had quickly amended the order to specify that Alvin cause no harm in any way to those mentioned previously, the Sorcerer just managing to hold off the knife at his throat as the Prince knelt over him in bed. Shanor had determined that by using the word *hand* instead of *weapon*, he had left Alvin an opening; following the words used, not the intent behind them. If Alvin could find a loophole in Shanor's instructions, he would exploit it.

Now, whenever a military mind from Sahkarae demanded Alvin's thoughts, he had to frame the question carefully to gain a useful answer.

"How will the King deploy his forces along the border?" General Shantz wanted to know.

"I don't know," Alvin replied, countenance set in stone. "I am not the King."

Shantz, a large man whose many muscles strained against his

uniform, leaned back, arms folded imposingly across his chest, eyes narrowed in menace.

"How would *you* set up his forces?" Dorn clarified.

Alvin's mouth tried to snarl as he fought to keep from answering, but Shanor had instructed the Tre'vani that he must answer the questions of these men.

"In ranks," he finally grated out.

Shantz sighed deeply, head bowed for a moment. When he raised his eyes to meet the angry glare of the Prince, he spoke very carefully.

"Tell us, in exact detail, how you, Tre'vani Alvin, would deploy all the troops Karundin could possibly muster—including numbers and abilities—at the border between Karundin and Sahkarae, and at which part of the border you would so deploy them."

And so they had learned how to squeeze details from Karundin's recalcitrant Prince. Or so they hoped. Shanor had to admire how hard Alvin fought within the confines of the spell. If Shanor could have overlaid Adoration on Alvin, he would have done so, making the Prince only too eager to share his insights, but it seemed the two spells would not work in unison. At least, not upon Karundin Royalty. Shanor wondered how much the Royal Protections worked to try to help Alvin, and how much simply came down to the Tre'vani's incredible will. He didn't think he wanted to spare the energy required to find out.

Now, with reports of the first snowfall of the season in their northerly neighbour, Sahkarae stood ready to stretch forth her hand and gather up her lost peoples. With Borun's spells in hand, all but eliminating the objections to winter warfare from troops that would not, or could not, complain, Shanor set out for the border once more, Sahkarae's King and Karundin's chief tactician at his side. How long this unnecessary war would last would depend upon Gavin. Somehow, Shanor suspected Karundin's King would drag it on longer than necessary. Karundin had become far too used to standing apart from Sahkarae and would resist any overtures of reunification. Patting the secure and shielded pouch at his belt that held his reclaimed prizes, Shanor would just have to convince Gavin of the folly of resistance.

A wolf's grin stretched across his face in anticipation of the forthcoming lesson.

255

***

"How did I let you talk me into this?" Nervain grumbled yet again. Angie had lost count of how many times he had asked, how long since they had started to ignore the complaint. By now, Angie suspected he used it as a personal mantra, something to take his mind off their situation; where they waited, with whom, and why. Anything to distract himself from the danger to the King.

In all honesty, Angie half-wished for a mantra of her own. Maybe, *don't let anyone die?*

In all her dreams, she had never envisioned herself involved in reconnaissance for an army, let alone the head honcho for the spy network. Unfortunately, with a war brewing in which the enemy held such potent weapons as Shanor had, Karundin needed all the information they could get, and that required scouting.

When Angie had come up with a plan utilizing their own portion of Borun's spells, Gavin had put her in charge with Nervain as her second; she overseeing the magic, he the might. It had seemed simple enough; use the spell of Transformation, send a team into Sahkarae to learn Shanor's plans, and return to report, rather like how Merikan had first explained the potential uses of the spell. However, the implementation raised some questions that required experimentation.

The first such question being: how did Transformation affect the subject? Could they turn back into themselves after, either on their own, or with the spell-caster's help? Did it hurt? How often could one person undergo such a spell?

Eniok had come up with a way to find out.

"We have a traitor locked up. Does he have more use providing dubious information, or acting as a guinea pig?"

He hadn't used the example of a guinea pig, but Angie didn't recognise the critter he named, so she substituted something more familiar in her mind.

After that kiss at the cabin that Nervain had eventually interrupted, Gavin had found many excuses to touch Angie—a brush of the arm, a passing caress of her hair, a companionable shoulder to lean on. So when Gavin had relinquished the Spell of Transformation into her keeping, she had thought, at first, that his hand lingered on hers in a gesture of affection. Only when he didn't move away did she meet his gaze, and saw a glitter of gold-green dancing in his grey eyes.

"To reveal the words as truth, a Royal hand must give proof," he recited, an odd reverberation to his voice as he invoked his own magic, the first time Angie had seen the King use it. She felt a warm tingling pass from his hand to hers and beyond, to the spell itself. It drew her attention to the page they held, and she watched as a metallic green sheen bathed the strange letters, reforming them into Borun's spell. The magic faded from Gavin's vision and he slowly withdrew his hand, leaving Angie with the translated spell.

"Shanor would have had to work much harder for that, but he obviously found a way," he said, tone no longer other-worldly as he studied her, locked her stare with the determination of his expression. "Make him regret his efforts."

So Angie and Merikan had proceeded to test the limits of Transformation on their 'guinea pig'.

Eniok's men had taken Rogan to a cell in the dungeon, the windowless stone room all the more dismal with its metal bars separating the room into two sections. The one area lacked any necessities beyond a bucket and pallet of straw for the prisoner, and the other had space enough for those interrogating said prisoner with a single wooden stool nestled in the far corner. A musty odour that itched at the back of Angie's throat overlaid the stark chamber.

"Ah, come to play with the prisoner?" Rogan sneered, not bothering to rise from his recline on the straw, nor take his gaze off the ceiling.

"How do you want to start?" Merikan asked, ignoring the steward.

"Something small," Angie mused. "Alter a feature or two, colour maybe, shape. See how much effort little changes make. Then we'll work our way up."

Rogan had glanced over at them, frowning.

"What are you babbling about?" he demanded. The two sorcerers just stared back. Then Angie formed an image in her mind and recited the spell.

A patina of silver swept over the supine man, almost like watching the waver of a mirage.

"What are you doing?" Rogan croaked, jackknifing to a sitting

257

position, glaring at them. He frowned, noting something amiss, then glanced down and with growing alarm began frantically patting at himself.

Angie nodded in satisfaction at his altered state. Merikan tried to keep a straight face as he watched a middle-aged woman with dusky skin and long dark locks groping with true distress at slight bulges and folds of skin on arms, legs and abdomen, and most of all, large plump breasts that pulled him off balance.

"What did you do?" shrieked the prisoner, even his panicked voice sounding huskier, higher-pitched from the changed larynx.

"What did you feel?" Angie countered.

"Put me back!" Rogan screamed, launching himself at the bars, enlarged chest mashed painfully against the unyielding barrier. "I'll kill you, bitch; put me back!"

"Now, now, do you really want to upset the woman who can restore your manhood?" Merikan admonished with a chiding cluck of his tongue.

Rogan frantically grabbed between his legs, his eyes enormous as he discovered the extent of the Transformation, squeaking his outrage and distress. Angie had a hard time not laughing at the absurdity of his reaction.

"I thought you said you'd start small," Merikan said in an aside.

Angie shrugged.

"Curiosity got the better of me," she admitted. Merikan snorted, then looked back at the prisoner.

"The Lady asked you a question," he continued, power sliding into his words as he Compelled Rogan. "What did you feel? Answer her truthfully."

The captive finally did so, and father and daughter began learning about Transformation. Small changes did draw less power, and the recipient only noticed little discomforts, akin to stretching seldom used muscles. The more altered the end result from the original person, the more energy it took from the spell-caster, and an increase in pain to the subject with each Transformation.

Merikan found he could also use the spell with like results, and after a few transmutations, studying the thresholds on all parties, the two called a break. While Angie and Merikan could feel the drain of their magic, Rogan suffered a drain on his stamina, leaving him ravenous yet exhausted. They left him in his own form to sleep off the trials of the day.

And started exploring further the next morning.

By the time Nervain had gathered a scouting party to head south, Angie and Merikan had learned a great deal about Borun's seemingly least impressive spell. For one, its sheer versatility had incredible and frightening potential, far more impressive than just changing the appearance of someone. They could make Rogan *believe* he had become someone else, right down to their quirks and memories, at least those known or suspected by the one casting the spell.

Something had put Angie in mind of a high school friend, one who had liked to pull pranks. She thought Dylan would have found this experimenting amusing, and without thinking it through, Angie had Transformed Rogan into him. And 'Dylan' had proceeded to regale Merikan with exploits he and Angie and a group of them had experienced one summer, everything as Angie had remembered, though she hadn't intentionally relayed the knowledge to Rogan, who literally did not remember *not* being Dylan.

Merikan had expanded on that unintended discovery by Transforming Rogan into one of the castle servants, but with a trigger phrase—much like what he learned through hypnotising Angie—that would recall Rogan to himself while in the other's body. They found that they could hide instructions within a Transformation, a notion that had Angie shuddering with the implications, especially given Rogan's abilities as an assassin. Imagine having the ability to send someone to a target in disguise, trigger a command to kill, then Transform them back to another form that had no memory of the deed. Shanor's ability to cloud and alter memories combined with the ability to actually change the person committing the action ... it chilled her just thinking about it.

As for giving the person Transformed the ability to reclaim his own appearance, a change in inflection in Borun's spell allowed that, so long as the original spell-caster willed that intent into the words. Similarly, if they turned Rogan into something lacking human speech—Angie's favourite being when she made him a collie and called him Lassie—if they willed an ability to communicate into the spell, Rogan could make his comments known. Often uncomplimentary and offensive sentiments, nevertheless, he reported all he experienced with brutal honesty thanks to Merikan's Compulsion.

Now, with a good working knowledge of how to use Transformation against those who hoped to ensnare Karundin, Angie and Nervain, along with their new-formed spy network, prepared to head out.

"Still don't know how far we can trust them," the Commander had admitted to Angie on the eve of their departure. "If we have to Compel every soldier and farmer who marches with us to swear they're loyal, we'll spend more time sowing dissent than battling the real enemy."

Angie had nodded thoughtfully, having given the matter some thought. She didn't much like the implications of her solution, but suspected it would satisfy Nervain.

"Come with me," she'd said, and led him down to the cell for one last experiment.

"Oh, for *aentoraden*—" Rogan had grumbled, slowly uncurling from his straw pallet as Angie and Nervain stepped into his adjoining room. The steward looked wan and dishevelled, evidence of the hard pace Angie and Merikan had put him through. Still, he managed a disgusted grimace. "What now? A dancing bear? A giant cockroach you can smash under your heel? What?"

Angie stared at him, made herself acknowledge the vileness of what she intended. Sully herself more to lay to rest their quandary? If this worked, she would have to live with the fact that she had killed a man. Would it matter that his death might save others?

"Commander, do we have a compelling reason to keep this man alive?" she asked softly, making herself hold Rogan's narrowed stare. "Can he tell us anything more of use?"

Nervain stared at her, the weight of his regard pressing down on her. She sensed more than saw his shrug out of the corner of her eye.

"If his death answers my question," Nervain finally replied in a measured cadence, "it will help us more than any information we can gather through other means."

"You don't know what I know," Rogan scoffed. "Can't possibly understand—"

"Steward Rogan," Angie interrupted, gathering her resolve. "I only have one question for you."

Rogan's mouth snapped shut with a painful-sounding click and he glared at her. She thought, though, that she detected a hint of resignation, even relief, as though he knew what she intended. She feared she might have imagined it to soothe her conscience.

But then he laughed, the sound a harsh grating on her nerves as he pushed off the bars and retreated to the pallet, sitting with his back to the wall and a defiant grin stretching across his face.

"Go on, then," he mocked. "I waited a long time for this question. Ironic that you ask now, even though you know the answer."

"Tell me true, Rogan," she intoned, forcing her voice to Compel an answer. "Who do you work for? Name the Sorcerer."

The grin never left his lips as he struggled to breath through a suddenly constricted throat. He even managed a wheezing giggle before he toppled to his side, convulsing as Shanor's spell fought Angie's command. Face purpling as he asphyxiated, Rogan slid into unconsciousness, lack of air shutting down his body. Finally, his shudders eased and he lay unmoving, unbreathing, killed by a Sorceress's foreknowledge of a Sorcerer's precautions against revealing his true nature.

For a long moment, Angie and Nervain had stood in silence, staring at a dead man. Nervain broke the silence with a grunt.

"Guess we have a question to ask before we set out tomorrow."

Angie blinked back a tear that Nervain pretended not to see.

Five days later, the two waited in the concealment of scrub and boulders for their Transformed Wolfpack to report their findings across the border, the beginning of the swath of dead land that demarked the boundary between countries just over two hours (or rather water glasses, Angie corrected herself) run distant. They knew, for both had run it in wolf form that morning, as they saw off a party of their spy network.

When Kaeley had returned from the aborted Progress circuit while Angie and Merikan had worked with Rogan, an unexpected group had accompanied her. Many of the people from Chasta Village, led by their miller and joined by various others from the surrounding countryside, had learned of Gavin's need and had determined to lend what services they could. To that end, they had appointed themselves part of Gavin's and Angie's guard, no matter what anyone said. They had set off for the capital, encountered Kaeley on her own return, and joined in the Tre'embra's retinue as she hastened back to the castle.

Nervain had taken some of these folks and incorporated them

into the spy network, now doubly confirmed loyal to Karundin thanks to a single question. They had proudly taken on the guise of wolves to scout into Sahkarae and learn what they could of Shanor's plans; had even taken to naming themselves the Wolfpack.

Their involvement did not bother Nervain, nor the mission parameters he had helped Angie set out. No, what irritated the man, what had him reiterating his mantra and fretting about the unexpected inclusion, sat to Angie's right, waiting alongside them for whatever the scouts might relay.

"Really," Nervain groused under his breath. "How did I let you talk me into this?"

"I'm not leaving Nervain," Gavin finally snapped. "So deal with it."

Chapter 28

The sun had not yet crested the horizon to proclaim the arrival of dawn when Nervain had had their party assemble to depart five days ago. Merikan had reluctantly agreed to remain behind to provide the mantle of magic to protect the Royals, while two Sorcerers he had vetted would journey with Angie, add their strength to hers if she should need them. Yamar and Tograth between them could cast formidable shields and illusions to keep the scouting party hidden and, although neither boasted overwhelming stamina, Merikan felt they could aid with a Transformation or two if required.

Besides the Sorcerers, their party consisted of ten additional members; one woman and five men of Chasta Village, including their miller, Darbison, and four soldiers from the castle's barracks who most often served as scouts. The party had mounted, ready to head for the bridge that would take them from the castle, when three more riders had emerged from the stables. Nervain pulled up with a curse, calling a halt to the proceedings. When Angie had seen Praetorian in the centre of the trio, she understood the Commander's quandary.

"Planning on accompanying us to the city limits, Your Majesty?" Nervain enquired, a hint of sarcasm lacing his question. He knew as well as Angie what Gavin likely planned.

Gavin bestowed a thin smile on him, acknowledging his disapproval but not about to bow to it.

"To the city limits and beyond, Commander," Gavin confirmed. Angie recognised Tera and Davok as the guards flanking the King, their stoic expressions revealing nothing of their thoughts regarding Gavin's actions.

"Sire," Nervain had let out a heavy sigh, bringing his horse alongside Praetorian, with only Angie and the two guards close enough to hear the exchange. "As Dho'vani, you could get away with sneaking around like this. Those days have passed."

"You forget your place, Commander," Gavin warned in a low voice.

"As do you, Sire. The King cannot go traipsing off on a reconnaissance mission; he waits until he has all the information he can get, then, maybe, gets to join the fray."

Angie shook her head, pretty sure of Gavin's reaction to that.

"Actually, Nervain, I can cite many instances where the King did just that." Gavin, his tone perfectly level, pulled on his riding gloves as he spoke, eyes focussed on the action. "Or I could point out my skills as both tracker and scout. That no one can anticipate Alvin's actions better than I. That my two chief protectors are already on this mission. That Merikan and I already discussed this, as he will remain to safeguard Kaeley while she assists Rayton, and the Lord Protector himself agreed my presence at the border can only speed up the information gathering, seeing as you wouldn't have so far to report. However, instead of making any of these points," and now he met Nervain's stony stare with implacable resolve, hands folding placidly across Praetorian's pommel. "I will simply inform you that your King has made the decision to join this mission."

Nervain scowled, but couldn't come up a suitable reply, at least not one Gavin would heed. Gavin tossed a crooked smile his way.

"Don't worry, though, Commander. You still have lead of this expedition, you and Angie."

Gavin had gotten his way and Nervain had grumbled about it. All day.

In an effort to act as peacekeeper, Angie had come up with a plan to keep them otherwise occupied on the ride by the time they set up camp that first evening, the air having turning bitterly cold as winter stretched forth its frigid fingers.

Nervain sat muttering into his stew bowl, Gavin scowling across the campfire, his smug mien having evaporated some time mid-afternoon. Angie had stood, hands on hips, studying the pair.

"Worse than a couple of children," her breath plumed the air at her grousing, drawing their startled attention. She jabbed a finger at a spot between the two. "Come here, both of you." Each opened his mouth as if to protest. Angie snapped her fingers, pointing at Gavin. "I'm ordering you as Lady Sorceress. And you," she rounded on Nervain, cutting short his triumphant smirk. "You, I'm ordering in my capacity as the person in charge of this expedition. So both of you, come here, now."

Gavin shot a rueful glance to Nervain, but at least he had stood and moved next to Angie, Nervain following suit.

"Good. Now, we're going to work on a little project, we three." So saying, she sat down on the chilled ground, waited for the men to do likewise, then scooted around to face them, forming a triangle. She leaned in, drawing them in too, before whispering furiously.

"Are you trying to lower morale? Make these brave people who we've drawn in our wake question whether we're actually fit to lead them into war? You two sniping at each other, bickering like kids, does not inspire confidence. So, here's what we're going to do. I'm going to teach you English, and if you still want to gripe at each other, you'll do it in a different language so that others don't know what you're saying, and might mistake you for a couple of grown-ups with some level of maturity." She paused, thought for a second, then shrugged. "Or that you're trading secrets. Either way, hopefully you won't scare these people any more than you already have."

Both men hung their heads, chagrined. Then Gavin peeked up through his hair, and Angie bit her tongue hard not to gasp at the gorgeous and alluring picture that presented.

"English?" he asked quietly.

"My 'secret language' that you wanted to know."

His grin matched Nervain's in anticipation of the challenge ahead.

They had learned so well and so quickly that Angie wondered if she had subconsciously tweaked their lessons with her magic, her desire for them to learn translating into the ability to absorb English at unbelievable speeds. However they had learned, Angie felt her lips twitching in an effort not to break out laughing as Gavin told Nervain, in English, to 'deal with it' rather than retreating to the safety of their camp further from the border where they now waited for the Wolfpack. They had learned their idioms well.

Angie and Nervain had accompanied six of their group—Miller

Darbison, Handras and Carsien of Chasta Village, and the garrison scouts Untath and Farin, along with Sorcerer Tograth—to the border early that morning in the guise of wolves. Each would fan out in a slightly different direction once they reached the end of the 'dead zone,' as Angie had taken to calling it, on the Sahkaraean side in order to cover more ground. They would keep in touch with the rest of the pack, but not overlap the search pattern, looking for any sign of danger.

In this first foray, they didn't expect to find anything amiss, but it would give the scouts a good feel for the lay of the land, doubly useful if it snowed again. Yesterday had warmed enough to melt what had fallen the previous night, but Angie held no illusions. Soon the temperature would stay below freezing and whatever snow fell would remain on the ground to mark anyone's passage. The more the scouts knew now about how best to mask their tracks, the less chance of footprints giving them away. They would have enough other problems waging a winter war against immune opponents without leaving an obvious trail for others to follow. Assuming Shanor made his move in the winter.

Angie and Nervain had turned back after seeing the group off, and found Gavin waiting at their appointed rendezvous spot in the brush rather than sheltered at the camp below with the rest of the team. At least he had kept Tera and Davok with him until the two 'wolves' had returned.

Nervain had practically exploded out of the large grey wolf back into his own form at the sight of the King. Angie took a moment to breathe a silent note of thanks that she and Merikan had learned how to ensure clothing survived a Transformation, even if one part of the metamorphosis did not include garments. Stripping every time they made a change would cause delays, and clothes on wolves would rather stand out. No clothes on an angry Nervain did not bear thinking about.

Angie had more calmly shed the skin of her honey-dark wolf, placed herself between the two men, and shoved them both down to sit amongst the rocks and wait.

And complain, and snipe, but at least in English, and only her to hear it all.

"We're here on a mission, guys," she said, gaze cast to the south, refusing to give either the satisfaction of actually looking at them. "If you keep going over old ground, we might miss a report."

They subsided and settled in to wait, not for a verbal communique, but a mental one. Sorcerer Tograth had suggested the idea of speaking mind-to-mind, if Angie could conquer the spell. He had explained how he could engineer a spell to work between magic users, but didn't know how to implement it on those without training. Angie had considered, then suggested telepathy. He didn't know the word, but could grasp the concept, and they had figured out how to Transform the Wolfpack into telepaths. Each had a trigger to turn the skill on and off, and keyed only to others in the group in an effort to minimize chances of outsiders hearing reports. Without the trigger, they had found thoughts spreading on the wind that no one had meant to share yet all had heard, causing no end of embarrassment and headaches.

This allowed the scouts to keep in touch with each other without having to maintain line of sight, and it made reporting back faster and simpler, as they did not have to return to share information. However, they did not know the range of their telepathy, how much distance played a role.

Just another part of the exercise for this first investigation, along with the exercise of patience.

About a water glass after their return, with the sun already past its zenith and heading in a hurry toward the western horizon, gathering a thickening bank of clouds in its wake, they received their first report.

'Sorceress Angelica, Commander Nervain, can you hear me?' A soft-spoken man at the best of times, Sorcerer Tograth's mind-voice surprised Angie with its intensity and she fell back with a startled expletive, a hand to her temple as though to hold the thoughts in.

'Tograth, you're a little overbearing,' she admitted, trying to keep her own 'voice' as normal as possible. *'Don't shout your thoughts.'*

'Sorry, didn't know if they'd carry,' he responded, 'voice' at a more reasonable level. *"our* telepathy,' he pronounced the word carefully, *'obviously works well thus far. All's quiet here, no unusual activity. Some decent places to set up a lookout should they send an army this way. Darbison and Untath suggest we continue scouting, go as far in as possible before nightfall looking for other, perhaps better, early warning sanctuaries, then return in the morning. What do you instruct?'*

Angie glanced at Nervain, then filled Gavin in. The Wolfpack hadn't expected the King to wait alongside Angie and Nervain, so had not known to include him in the report.

"Secondary access route or not, we have no guarantee that Shanor will use the road. He must know our suspicions, so might choose a different path," Gavin mused.

"Or believe the spells he has will give him such advantage that he won't care if we anticipate his location," Nervain countered, and Gavin agreed.

"We don't know when he'll move, or even *if* he'll move," Angie added. "He might come at us tomorrow, or next week or next year. Or he might sit and let us stew. The border has enough accessible entry points that we'll have to guard that we'll spread ourselves thin watching them all. We need to know what Shanor plans and when he plans it. That means we need access to Shanor."

"Which means sending someone to the capital," Nervain said. "Do you suggest we send these first scouts?"

"Not yet," Gavin answered. "Have them continue for the day, make sure they can still contact us come nightfall. For any of them to journey all the way to the capital will mean more supplies than they have at present, and then constant reports to find out if the telepathy will extend that far. If we still have reliable contact this evening, we can prep another unit to leave in the morning with full supplies and instructions to head to the capital while these scouts return. Agreed?"

"Agreed," Angie said, and let Nervain relay the instructions.

'Will talk again about two water glasses past dusk,' Tograth answered. *'These wolf forms move fast. Don't think we outrun the sun, but don't want any worries if we don't report as soon as the light fades.'*

Angie smiled as they broke off communication. She rose, stretching stiff muscles.

"Back to camp, then?" she asked. "No need to stay up on this rise in the cold, now that we know the telepathy easily reaches this far."

"I could use some real food," Nervain agreed as he and Gavin stood to join her, the three heading back toward the rest of their party. "Always best to eat and sleep when you can on a campaign. Never know when something will steal away the time to enjoy such basic necessities."

Chapter 29

Darbison Miller remembered his fear and anger when he had first encountered King Gavin, that day when fire nearly consumed the future of Chasta Village. He remembered his fury at the stranger taking his shoulder, turning him away from the sight of the greedy flames devouring the inn—his daughter one of many trapped within—to show him the bucket line. How he had wanted to strike out at the temerity of the haughty man, point out the ferocity of the blaze that had already defeated any attempts to enter the inn to rescue their treasured babes. But something about his manner had helped dampen Darbison's terror, unlocked his paralyzed limbs to follow in the stranger's wake.

He could still hear the pounding rain, the hissing frenzy of fire swirled to greater life by the howling wind, the tiny plashes as each bucket tried to bathe the unrelenting conflagration with their small loads of water. The stench of scorching smoke as it hungered for thatch and timber, the incredible heat radiating from the angry red and orange inferno, all etched in excruciating detail in Darbison's mind. Could even recall the damp roughness of the wooden buckets passed hand to hand along the line.

But what haunted his dreams, what most readily claimed his memory of that day, came after the strangely dressed woman had pulled the stranger aside, started leading him toward the inn. Darbison could not say what had made him follow, but the woman and man had both welcomed him despite grim expressions as all three plunged into the flames, somehow made tolerable with the woman's words, *The fire will not touch you.* Such certainty had shocked him, but he didn't question it. And her words had proven true. They reached the children, fought through the burning supports trapping them, pulled every wee one to safety.

Whereupon Darbison and his fellow villagers learned the true nature of their mysterious benefactors. The King himself and the Lady Sorceress.

Even now, Darbison found himself shaking his head in surprise and admiration that the King had faced the prospect of death to save those he didn't know. He had given orders and expected others to obey, yes, but then he had put himself in harm's way to carry out those instructions alongside the meanest villager, rather than stepping back with a refusal to get his hands dirty.

They had always toiled under the knowledge that some distant King claimed lordship over them, but on that day, Darbison and every villager from Chasta had found cause to praise that King. They had encountered true nobility in the face of a man who did not look down on them, who stood shoulder to shoulder with a miller to pass a bucket hoping to quench a fire, who threw himself into danger to rescue the children of peasants.

"A King is nothing without his people," King Gavin had said, and won an entire village to his heart.

That he had shared of his own supplies for the wedding, left some of his own people behind with provisions to help rebuild, only added to the villagers' ardour. They would do anything for this King.

So when Carsien had returned from the market in the next village with the news that King Gavin had called up his levies, Darbison didn't hesitate. Nor had anyone from Chasta Village. Their saviour needed able-bodies to defend Karundin. The women and children insisted they would see to the harvest alongside the older men and whoever else remained—even had new buildings to house their supplies, thanks to the King and those Baron Hestian had sent to help—while Darbison and about half the men would set out immediately for Karundin Castle. Three women, too; Aebigail with her impressive archery skills, and the sisters Jaeneth and Jaerina, both deadly accurate with a sling. All told, nigh on thirty of them set out for the capital.

Darbison had served a couple of double-seasons in Lady Fairlae's militia in his youth, mostly helping to keep the roadways clear, settle minor disputes, keep any bandits at bay. No great battles or feats of daring-do, but he had learned how to swing a blade. Carsien and Handras knew how to wield pikes, a few of the others had some experience with weapons. But for the most part, farmers, miners, and shepherds headed off to lend support to King and country, no less stout of heart for their lack of any formal weapons training.

Others from the nearby villages and the surrounding countryside joined them as they travelled, folks who had heard of King Gavin's selflessness at Chasta and his need now, so that when Tre'embra Kaeley and her entourage had encountered the group, Darbison's party had numbered fifty strong. The Tre'embra had matched their pace, bringing them to the castle and the attention of Commander Nervain, and thus the King, upon their arrival.

Darbison had tried hard not to ogle his surroundings at the castle, didn't know how well he succeeded, but something had gone exceedingly well when Commander Nervain selected the miller and several of his companions to act as scouts and infiltrators. He swelled with pride as he became one of the select few to travel with the Lady Sorceress Angelica to the border, joined surprisingly by King Gavin on the morn of their departure. The King may have thought no thanks necessary for his bravery in that fire, but Darbison intended to pay that debt in every way possible.

Thus, when the six members of the Wolfpack scouting Sahkarae finally stopped for the night, Darbison quickly curled up to sleep, knowing he would need to rest before he set out again. Sorcerer Tograth informed them they must begin the return to Karundin come first light. If Darbison rose two water glasses early, he could use one to continue to scout ahead and still return in time to fulfill the Sorcerer's requirements.

A hand shook him awake only moments before his body would have done so naturally. Stars glittered overhead in a black sky, the moon low to the horizon. Darbison squinted to make out the features of Carsien.

"I'm guessin' yer of a like mind," his neighbour whispered.

"Long's we're back afore sunrise," Darbison agreed, rising on silent feet. A third shadow rose and joined them at the edge of their little camp. Handras merely nodded, content with the absence of sound.

The three villagers moved off a few paces before murmuring the word to trigger their Transformation, just as Lady Angelica

271

had taught them. And three wolves sped south on fleet and silent feet, their vision exceptional despite the lack of light.

They had covered a goodly distance by the time their allotted water glass had ended. Darbison didn't know much about real wolves, but these forms the Lady Sorceress had given them had incredible endurance. He deemed they had run about 400 furlongs, certainly faster than any horse, and without need for pause. Still, as they finally slowed in preparation for their return, and then halted, their sides bellowed as they panted. Not precisely out of breath, but it would do them well to pace themselves for a bit.

When they turned to retrace their steps, Darbison stopped, sniffed the air, cocked his furry ears. A myriad of scents assailed his nostrils, but one smell that didn't fit their surroundings caught his attention, teasingly snatched away by an errant breeze before he could pinpoint it.

'Did you catch that?' he thought at his companions.

'It almost smells familiar,' Carsien replied as he too scented the breeze. *'Don't know what, though.'*

'Men,' Handras said shortly, the word clipped as though his wolf's teeth had bitten it off. *'And old smoke.'*

'Horses?' Darbison enquired, drawing in a deep breath.

'A merchant caravan?' Carsien wondered. *'Peddlers? Bandits?'*

Darbison shook his muzzled head in amusement as Carsien's suppositions grew more creative.

'We'll take a peek, then head back.'

They crept forward, keeping to what cover they could find, the fall of each foot pad soundless.

A small gust of wind ruffled their fur and Darbison heard the gentle nicker of a horse somewhere ahead. He froze. He had helped enough with the sheep back home not to know the signs of agitated animal.

'The beasts will smell wolves,' he realised. *'We'll spook them if we creep up with the wind at our backs.'*

So they circled around until the sporadic wind washed over their faces. Then continued forward far enough to see what they had only smelled and heard.

A group of about fifteen men lay in slumber around the remains of a couple of campfires. The silhouettes of two others presented themselves to keen wolf senses; one sitting a short distance from the sleepers, facing away from his companions, staring into the dark; the second just returning from checking on the dozen horses.

Darbison didn't know anything about Sahkaraean livery, but he suspected he looked at it now. Too orderly and uniform for any bandits; no wagons or goods to suggest merchants or peddlers; too well-armed for farmers. That left soldiers. But why here? A routine patrol? Men out training? Recruiting? Deserters? Scouts?

'We should get back,' he said, suddenly very wary. Whatever these soldiers represented, it all just became far too real to the miller. He could watch, scout, report, but could he honestly stand against seasoned fighters and hope to come out unscathed?

The others seemed to share the sentiment, and all three turned tail and fled as fast as their four legs would take them. For all of a minute, when they encountered another wolf in their path.

Darbison skidded to a halt, lips pulled back to expose sharp teeth, a growl threading up his throat, the menace and fear echoed by his companions.

'Oh, please,' the wolf tossed at them disgustedly in a familiar voice before flowing into the form of Untath the scout. Darbison snapped his jaw shut, chagrined that he hadn't recognised the man/wolf immediately, but his appearance had surprised him. He spoke the word to Transform back into his human body, and four men stepped into deep cover to converse.

"How did you find us?" Carsien asked quietly.

"You think you're the only ones who can run in the dark?" Untath replied. "The only ones eager to explore all we can before heading back? I followed you, of course. Wise of you to approach from downwind."

"You saw them, then?" Darbison asked.

Untath nodded, expression sober.

"I'd like to say they're a standard patrol," the scout began. "But I wouldn't rule out scouts, outriders, an advance team."

"In advance of what?" Carsien asked, foreboding in his tone.

"An army."

Darbison shuddered.

"What do we do?" he asked.

"Get back to the others, report the sighting, get out of Sahkarae," Untath answered promptly. "I'll keep an eye on them, see what direction they take, maybe overhear something. Chances are, I'll be on your heels shortly. If they're an advance team, the King has less time than he'd hoped, but more than if we hadn't all trooped out here without permission. If they're just a routine patrol, well then, at least we'll have learned something."

He flowed back into wolf form.

'Now get,' he said, padding carefully back toward the soldiers.

Darbison, Carsien, and Handras exchanged worried looks, then, dropping to all fours, followed orders, three wolves pounding back to their camp, sincerely hoping they didn't carry the fate of Karundin with them, terrified that they did.

***

"Untath confirms it, Sire. It's an advance team," Nervain informed him, and Gavin's heart sank. "The others have regrouped, but Untath requests permission to circle around the scouts, continue further into Sahkarae, see just how far behind their army follows."

Gavin watched Angie's face pale, her eyes dull with worry despite the crisp clearness of the rising sun in a cold blue sky bathing her features.

"Bring them back," she pleaded. "They're not soldiers."

"Untath is," Nervain disagreed, and Gavin nodded his agreement.

"Untath and Farin, yes, but not the others." Gavin pondered his options. To have someone behind enemy lines, able to report on Shanor's movements, would certainly benefit them, but Untath had no additional supplies. As a scout and tracker, he could live on the land, though winter drew in in Sahkarae as well. How far could he journey, though, until his mind communication grew too distant?

"Send Untath in. Have Farin hold his current position, act as relay for Untath's findings. I don't want them out of range. Bring the others back. They're stalwart men, but farmers and millers, not trained scouts. We'll have more use of them here."

As Nervain passed along those instructions, Gavin stared south, toward a border too far away to see, too close to ignore. He had chosen this location for the initial foray into Sahkaraean lands for two reasons; first because it saw less travel, being a minor route between the two countries, and so should have provided ample time and space to test the abilities of Angie's Transformed Wolfpack. Second, Gavin knew how Alvin thought, and feared his brother, under Shanor's influence, would seek a less observed entrance into Karundin. Which, unless the Sahkaraeans travelled cross country through some less hospitable terrain, would have them either invading here, or several furlongs further west. It seemed Gavin's initial instinct had proven true, though far sooner than he would have hoped.

He turned and called over Sorcerer Yamar and the remaining two soldiers Eniok had sent from the castle, Banor and Pendarak.

"I want you, Banor and Pendarak to head west," he informed the Sorcerer. "You will stop at the garrison guarding the Highway along the main road, find some volunteers willing to both undergo Transformation and cross the border. Gather what supplies you need. Then Banor and Pendarak will continue on to the Western Trade Route, one to wait near the border, the other to scout into Sahkarae, just as Untath and Farin will do here. Make sure Shanor doesn't have other troops trying to sneak in along either of those routes too. I'm hoping Alvin will convince him to keep his army together, but we cannot afford to trust that will happen. Make haste, gentlemen."

The three gave him solemn salutes, then hurried to pack up their gear, readying themselves to Transform into wolves and test their endurance.

Could he afford to wait for those reports? Or did he make a huge assumption, send for Karundin's defenders to gather here, pray Shanor did not divide his efforts? The Sorcerer must know Gavin had warned his nobles of an impending war, that Karundin knew to prepare for battle, but could he know that Gavin already had fighters heading south?

Be ready for anything so that none can surprise you. So his father, King Grayton had taught him, and Gavin planned to take that warning to heart.

"Commander," Gavin pivoted to face Nervain. "We need to get word north to Baroness Vordaeth. Have her send riders to all units in the east, every nobles' forces on the move between here and the Highway. Have her birds sent to those keeps and castles further north who can still divert troops in this direction. We need all able bodies willing to fight here as soon as possible." Though likely not soon enough, unless Sahkarae's

275

army followed far behind her advance team. But an army backed by the three spells Shanor had stolen would have little need to reserve strength, to move slowly, making their movements unpredictable. Gavin had to assume they did not travel far from their scouts.

"And our forces west of the Highway?" Nervain asked.

"Keep them between the Highway and the Western Trade Route. If Shanor *does* plan to attack on two or more fronts, we'll need them able to respond quickly."

Nervain nodded and moved to confer with the remainder of their group; Aebigail and her two companions from Chasta Village, Tera and Davok. Soon, Aebigail and Davok, instructions written and sealed into messenger tubes and slung across shoulders, started running north, their strides turning to loping gaits as they flowed into wolves. Though they all had ridden fast mounts to get here, they found the power and endurance of their Transformed wolves outdistanced even the energetic Praetorian. Angie had at one point expressed a worry that too long in any altered state might have unexpected consequences, but so far, none had reported any strange behaviours, and all agreed that speed outweighed uncharted dangers. Gavin desperately hoped none came to regret that decision, and knew Angie did too.

Finally, just he and Angie stood, staring toward Sahkarae, and Gavin knew he couldn't put it off any longer. He had to ask the woman he loved to commit an act that might tear her soul apart.

"Angie," he began, swivelling to look at her, but she already faced him, tears glistening in her magnificent, bejewelled eyes though they did not fall.

"I know," she sighed.

"If I could do this in your place—"

She hushed him with a finger laid gently on his lips.

"This is my task," she said.

He ran his hand up her arm, lightly grasped the wrist captivating his speech, and drew her hand into his own. He didn't fully understand the sacrifice she said they needed to retrieve the counterspells from her Earth, but she had assured him it did not affect anyone in Karundin. He shuddered to think who it did affect, though she said he could not make the choice. It pained his heart to see how this hurt her, even though both knew the importance of what she must do. One sacrifice to save thousands. If he could take away her agony, he would.

"Maybe we won't need it," he began, but she shook her head.

"You know we will," she reprimanded softly. "We're protected, you and I. Everyone in that room when I removed the spell from Rayton and Remy, safe from Mind Control." Or so they hoped. "But no one else is immune. We cannot defeat deathless armies with strength of arms alone, nor constantly block our ears to the call of Adoration. Even the first Sorceress and Borun couldn't prevail without those counterspells. I have to go, Gavin. We will close the rift between my world and yours when I get that painting, and that will need—"

"I know," he sighed. "A sacrifice. Angie," he hesitated, holding both her hands now, losing himself in her gaze. "Will this harm you?"

"Only in my heart." Her voice trembled before she swallowed her doubts. "But I will not fail."

He marvelled at how she could wrap such strength and determination around herself like a cloak, blocking out the chill of impending loss. He smiled, stroked her cheek.

"Hurry back," he whispered in English before kissing her with a fierce determination, and she melted into his embrace.

"Oh, you bet," she sighed on a shaky breath when he finally released her, and he grinned.

She moved a few unsteady paces away and stared into the near distance.

"Sidvareh, I need you," he heard her call softly, her voice heavy with regret. "Please, take me to Earth."

A violet mist swirled, grew into a whirling vortex devoid of wind that expanded to encompass her, and then the Lady Sorceress of Karundin, beloved of the King, disappeared.

Gavin stared after her, trying to mask the pain threatening to leak from his eyes. He knew a little of the Hidden Peoples, mostly gleaned through conversations with Merikan, and he suspected Angie had just asked for help from one of them. Would this sacrifice doom a creature from another realm, then? *No one of Karundin,* Angie had said, and now a tear did escape to scar his cheek. He feared the ambitions of mortals would claim the life of an immortal, a truly noble sacrifice in a battle that should not have affected the one who might choose the lives of petty mortals over their own. And he wept for the loss.

Chapter 30

Angie blinked, trying to make out her surroundings. Purple haze engulfed her, but she could see nothing else, feel nothing beyond a comfortable warmth, hear nothing at all. She wondered what she stood on, if anything.

"Sidvareh?" she called tentatively.

"My dear Lady Angie," came a tinkling reply.

"Where are you? Where are we?"

"In the realm between worlds." A slight pressure on her shoulder had her turning her head to meet twinkling teardrop eyes of emerald. Sidvareh's wings gently fanned Angie's cheek, played with her hair. Angie smiled, though she could feel the sadness that pinched the edges of her lips, her eyes.

"Oh, Sidvareh, I'm so sorry."

"Don't be, Angie." The Faery wiped a stray tear from the Sorceress's cheek. "I chose to answer your plea, to escort you across worlds. You have great need; I have the ability, nay the desire, to assist."

"Why?" Angie whispered. Sidvareh only smiled.

The purple suddenly parted like a curtain, and Angie looked upon a sight she knew well. She stepped out of a dream and returned to Earth right across the street from Wallman Restorations.

A quick glance around showed that no one remarked on her sudden appearance, though it looked like rush hour hadn't quite relinquished its grip on groggy commuters. Untath's report had come in maybe an hour after dawn in Karundin; judging by traffic and the sun's position, Angie guessed the clock here on Earth had barely rung out nine in the morning. She wondered if anyone had come in to work yet or if hours of operation would delay her retrieval of the painting.

She took a steadying breath, about to cross the street, when she realised that Sidvareh still sat upon her shoulder.

"Sidvareh," she spoke low. "How can you ... are you safe here, in this world?" Angie well remembered the Faery describing Earth as a place that did not support a system of magic. "What if someone notices you?"

"The bridge still exists and so can sustain me," Sidvareh assured her. "And no one else can see me."

Angie blinked and glanced surreptitiously around at others with her on the sidewalk, hoping they hadn't just watched her talking to herself. No one paid her any heed, concentrating on their own daily grind, cognizant of others only insofar as to avoid bumping into them. If you don't acknowledge anyone, you don't have to interact with them. How long since Angie had immersed herself in that same oblivious world?

"All right then," said Angie. "Let's see if anyone answers the door."

She waited for a break in traffic, then strode over to the front door of Wallman Restorations. She saw a shadow within despite the lack of illumination. Someone had made it in to work even if he hadn't turned on the reception lights yet. Angie tapped on the frame of the glass door. The shadow hesitated and Angie could imagine the thought processes: *We're not open yet; do I see who it is, or hope they go away?*

Luckily for her, curiosity won out and the shadow resolved itself into her dear friend. Irving's eyes widened when he saw her and he hurried to unbolt the entrance, swinging the door wide to grant her admittance.

"Mermaid!" he gave her a quick hug before re-locking the door. When he turned back, he stopped and stared long enough to make Angie nervous.

"Irving? What's wrong?"

"Um," he frowned, licked his lips, his blinking eyes flicking all around her. "Two things pop to mind," he finally squeaked out.

"What is it Irving?" Heart in her throat, she had a horrible thought. "Is it the painting?"

"No, no," he waved that worry away. "It's not that. It's—Angie, you're really here, aren't you? I mean, you didn't just appear out of nowhere, you look fully solid, and there's no weird dream-light

279

haloing you."

"Well, I popped out of nowhere across the street, but the rest I'll grant you." She smiled. "That is, I crossed through a kind of gate from Karundin to get here, so yes, I'm really here."

"So you've come to terms with your dilemma."

Angie felt her shoulders slump and forced herself to straighten her back, refusing to release any more tears at the moment.

"What's the second thing, Irving?"

"Did you know—" again he paused, swallowing hard, his attention caught by something. She thought he would comment on her Earth-influenced Karundin attire, given the direction of his gaze, but his next words shocked the hell out of her as they came out in a rush. "Did you know you have a little winged woman sitting on your shoulder?"

Angie's head snapped around to stare at Sidvareh and the Faery stared back, her eyes so large in their surprise that they nearly engulfed her delicate face. Sidvareh shot to her feet atop the perch of Angie's shoulder, her attention redirected to the human standing uncertainly in his own offices.

In a high-pitched buzz of agitated wings, Sidvareh launched herself to hover inches from Irving's nose. Angie might have laughed at how his eyes almost crossed trying to concentrate on the being examining him from such close proximity had Sidvareh's intense scrutiny not disturbed her so. What did it mean? Sidvareh had seemed so certain that no one would see her, yet here Irving stood, gamely returning her study. His initial shock had quickly faded into curiosity and awe.

"Is she—" he stopped, his gaze lighting on Angie for an instant before he moved it back. "My pardon." He addressed Sidvareh directly, barely a hitch in his voice. "Forgive my impertinence, but are you a fairy?"

Sidvareh fluttered back, hanging midway between the two mortals, a deeply speculative mien to her features.

"A Faery, if you will," Sidvareh corrected, a heavy tolling of bells. "And you, human, present a greater surprise than I expected."

"Ah, thank you?" he offered, unsure whether the statement praised or doomed him.

Sidvareh inclined her head—nod or salute, Angie didn't know—and lighted on a piece of air as though she had found solid ground, her wings barely moving, like the tail of a contented cat about to nap. After a moment, Irving nodded back, one firm dip of his head. He looked at Angie, his eyes serious in their contemplation.

"You've come for the painting, then."

Without waiting for her reply, he headed into the back work area, Angie following behind. There it stood, *Castle of Dreams* resting on its easel, waiting for Angie to take it home, back to Karundin. The means to take away Shanor's greatest advantage, if it didn't destroy two worlds before it made the final passage through a rent between realms. She could keep the horrors of her dream-prophecy from coming to pass with the words of power hidden beneath the paint.

A sudden foreboding had Angie clasping a hand to her mouth in an effort to keep a moan of dismay from escaping. With leaden steps, she neared the artwork, taking in every detail, noting her most obvious obstruction, the facet she had somehow managed to overlook every time she envisioned this moment. The image showed Karundin Castle in exquisite, lifelike detail, but it currently revealed nothing of the symbols behind the colour, the words she needed to stop Shanor.

"I can't take this yet," she bemoaned. "Not as a painting of the castle. We have to peel away the picture, unmask the spell beneath."

And that would take time, a commodity Angie feared they had little to spare.

"Maybe not," Irving said. He drew her attention to the nearby table, flipping up a laptop screen. "On a hunch, I took the painting back to the museum and had them do a couple of tests. Of course, the letter of permission and funds to do so that I found when I presented the artwork to their experts helped, both with facilitating the process and backing up my conjecture."

He called up a file on the computer, and Angie marvelled at what Irving had to show her.

"Is this an X-radiograph?" she asked, studying the grey tones on the screen. A method sometimes used to discover previous compositional changes an artist had made to a piece using the short wavelengths of an x-ray, x-radiography could help reveal the hidden work beneath. Or in this case, it gave a tantalising depiction of the characters shrouded by the paint. "My God, Irving, you can almost make out the symbols!" said Angie, her excitement growing.

"Combine it with this," he brought up another file, "and the picture's even more clear."

"Holy shit, Irving, is this IRR?"

Irving grinned at her squeal of enthusiasm and nodded.

Infrared Reflectography, or IRR, made the castle seem transparent while bringing the lettering out at the same time, giving a sort of double image; castle overlaying spell. The method, similar to x-radiography, used longer wavelengths to penetrate paint layers. Together, the two methods basically revealed what Angie needed.

"I can't believe this!" she exclaimed. "You just happened to have the right paperwork?"

"Just like in obtaining the original," Irving confirmed.

"Where are these papers coming from?" Angie demanded incredulously.

Sidvareh answered, startling Angie, as she had nearly forgotten the Faery's presence in this world where magic came from science transcribed onto a computer screen.

"When Sorceress Daneka sent the original spell through, she keyed it to every future Lady Sorceress. When your need arises, so too does the aid you require." Sidvareh made it sound so simple.

"That's ... that's one hell of a spell," Angie could barely even begin to encompass the complexity behind the concept, let alone untangle any ramifications.

"It might—" Sidvareh added hesitantly. "It might also draw upon the Faery who stabilised the bridge. It's possible some essence of her still remains to engender these papers."

The way hope tinged Sidvareh's conjecture confirmed a theory in Angie's mind.

"This brave Faery who saved worlds, she was your mother, wasn't she, Sidvareh?"

"She was," the small woman confirmed, her tear-drop eyes glittering with sorrow and pride. "And it would honour us both should I dare to match such bravery."

"We can print these up," Irving said quietly into the silence after Sidvareh's statement. "Recreate the symbols so that you can read them, or use them, or do whatever you need to activate them back in Karundin. That way, you won't even need to take the painting away, risk ripping things apart."

"Oh!" Angie felt the ache in her cheeks as her smile near

cracked her jaw. "Sidvareh, we could—" she bit off her joyous outburst as the Faery shook her head in negation.

"It is not so simple, My Lady Sorceress," she advised. "You can see the writing, yes, but you cannot decipher it. That requires holding the original, unmarred spell, in your hand, disentangling the concealing shield from the parchment, much as King Gavin allowed for the Spell of Transformation." Angie recalled the magical sheen reforming the strange letters into Borun's spell as Gavin touched her hand, wondered how Sidvareh had known of it, and her spirits plummeted.

"Then I *do* have to take the painting back to Karundin, figure out how to reveal what Daneka masked."

"No, dear one," Sidvareh said. "You have to take the *spell* back, not the painting."

Angie frowned her consternation.

"You mean, she has to restore it here?" Irving asked. "Remove the layers making up *Castle of Dreams*, leaving just the words underneath?"

"I do," confirmed the Faery.

"But, that takes time," Angie sputtered. "Time I don't know that Gavin has."

"Regardless, the bridge must return as it arrived, unmarred by elements of Earth."

"Whoa, wait," Angie stared at the painting. "Sorceress Daneka didn't paint this? Someone here did?"

"The hand of the artist belonged to Earth," Sidvareh said. "But the mind directing it belonged to the Sorceress. Much as you visited Karundin in your dreams, so Daneka spent time in the mind of another here, creating something worthy of preservation, and devising the tools necessary to maintain that preservation. The provenance, as you call it."

"So she used Earth methods, not magic. Meaning Earth methods have to uncover it."

"At least you won't have to worry about other projects intruding on your time," Irving consoled. "And you'll have every resource at your disposal, Mermaid. As long as it takes, this space is yours. We'll find you somewhere to stay until it's finished."

She glanced at Irving with tears in her eyes. So close and yet so far from her goal. How long did Gavin and Karundin truly have? Well, sooner started, sooner finished. She had the x-radiograph and the IRR to help her, and dear Irving's blessing.

Now to get to work.

"You have any spare overalls I can borrow?" she asked, rolling up the sleeves of her tunic. "And maybe some tea?"

Work always went best with tea.

***

Angie had worked into the early evening in the well-lit corner Irving had sequestered for her. Jerry had glanced askance at her presence at first when he came in, but upon seeing her professionalism and obvious skill, had left her to her own devises. Every now and then, as he went about his own work, Jerry would pause, give a little start at seeing her in the corner as though he had forgotten her existence, then just shrug it off and carry on with the day.

Now, with the first layers of paint carefully scraped away, Angie's aching back and arms, not to mention her straining eyes, demanded she call it quits for the day and pack up, start fresh in the morning. Jerry had left at closing time, leaving only Angie and Irving in the building. And Sidvareh, though she didn't always make her presence known. Angie debated whether she slipped between worlds or back to her own when she wandered off, if she went exploring, or if she simply made herself scarce out of boredom. Or maybe hid herself in Angie's mind like her early days physically in Karundin. With a shudder, Angie pushed such speculation aside, not sure she really wanted to know after all.

Midway through a stretch, hands reaching for her toes as her back waffled between protest and relief, Irving entered the workroom, his coat draped over his arm while he juggled his hat and his briefcase. He walked over to her, examining the canvas.

"Great progress," he commented. He swivelled to face her as she rose from the stretch. "Ready to call it a night, Mermaid?"

"More than," she replied, trying and failing to suppress a yawn.

"Let's go then. We'll grab a pizza on the way."

In his generosity and amazing understanding and ability to go with the flow, Irving had insisted Angie crash on his couch for the duration of her stay. She couldn't very well go to her old place—someone else lived there, and remembered having done so for some time, no doubt—and she had no funds to draw upon, ruling out any possibility of a hotel. That Irving had solved her housing predicament without batting an eyelash touched her deeply, and she had no idea how to repay him.

So she regaled him with stories of Karundin; not only her recent time there, but her memories of growing up in two worlds. She had never told anyone about her dreaming adventures, but it felt right to share them with Irving now. Occasionally, Sidvareh would chime in, add a detail or two, either something Angie had forgotten, or something that had affected Karundin that Angie had not known. Angie wondered at the Faery's knowledge from both sides of each event, but, not wanting to spoil the mood, did not delve for deeper details or explanations.

Eventually, voice straining from overuse, belly satiated with pizza and wine, eyes barely open from exhaustion, they called it a night, and Angie drifted off to sleep cuddled under a fuzzy blanket on Irving's astonishingly comfortable sofa.

And opened her eyes to the half-light of Karundin.

She stood at the entrance to a field tent and her gaze latched eagerly onto the man pouring over a map in the glow of a lantern.

"Gavin," she greeted with a smile.

His head snapped up, grave eyes wide, and he sprang from his seat to enfold her in a powerful embrace.

"Spirits have mercy, you're safe," he breathed into her hair, a tremor in his words.

"Of course," she rubbed his back briefly, surprised at such ardency, then pushed him back to study his face. "Gavin, what's wrong?"

"I thought I'd lost you." He pressed his forehead to hers, drinking deep of her eyes.

"What do you mean?" she asked, confused. "I had hoped to return sooner, but it's going to take a little time to unmask the counterspells, another few days at least, and it seems I can only do it on Earth. But then I'm coming home. How could you think I wouldn't?"

"Angie," a hitch in his voice as he ran his hands down her arms, entwining their fingers. "You disappeared a week ago."

Her brow furrowed and she stared at him in concern, wondering if he had come down with a fever or something. Amnesia? Yet a horrible wrench in her gut suggested something far more worrying.

"I've only been gone a day," she whispered.

His frown matched her own now.

"Not here," he said after a moment. "We've set up fortifications here ahead of Sahkarae's army. Shanor and King Dorn stand poised to cross into Karundin, delayed only because Shanor and his sorcerers can only raise so many clay soldiers a day. But they're ready to push through soon. Angie, we need that counterspell. We've managed to counter their ability to bespell our forces with Mind Control or Adoration by blocking our ears to their call, but we cannot stop those clay soldiers."

"But how can—" she shook her head, tears of frustration and despair tracking down her face. "No, it doesn't matter how time has slipped, just that I use what's left quickly." She stared at him, studied the drawn face, the hope that barely clung past the helplessness. She freed her fingers, cupped his face, and kissed him deeply.

"Just hang on for a little longer," she whispered when she had her breath back. "Send for Merikan, if you haven't already. He can at least help to slow them down. Trust in me, dearest; I will bring back the counterspell as fast as I'm able."

Before she could step back, awaken herself from this dream—nightmare?—he pulled her in for a final kiss.

"I love you, Angie," he murmured. "We'll hold out as long as we can."

"I love you too," she answered.

And woke as dawn gilded the sky outside Irving's window.

She threw off her blanket and leapt to her feet.

"Sidvareh?" she called softly as she hurried to the bathroom.

The Faery appeared, keeping pace as she flew beside Angie, expression grave though she didn't speak.

"What's happened, Sidvareh? I thought time ran congruent between Karundin and Earth. How can a whole week have passed there and only a day here?"

"I am sorry I did not foresee this possibility, Lady Angelica," Sidvareh said, a dolorous weight to her words. That she used Angie's title rather than the familiar form of address worried Angie, for it spoke to the Faery's agitation. "When I brought you to Karundin, the buffer between the two worlds began to fray. It seems your presence here linked the worlds as much as the bridge. While you resided on Earth, you held time in synchronization, but once you left, it began to revert, each world spinning to its own desires."

"Will it get worse?" Angie asked in dread.

"I don't know," Sidvareh admitted. "Time flows differently in many realms. I had not visited this one until your mother sent you across, so I cannot say how great the discrepancy will grow. But I would suggest as much haste as possible."

Angie sniffed back a sob, fear flipping her stomach with nauseous spasms. She wondered if Irving had a sleeping bag she could take to the workshop, for she didn't think she could waste any more time commuting. Didn't even know if she could afford to sleep.

Whether he heard her stumbling about or sensed her urgency, Irving appeared at the door to his bedroom.

"Irving, I've got to get back to work. Time's running out."

Bless his heart, he didn't even argue.

***

Angie worked steadily, methodically. She longed to just rush through, rip off the layers concealing Daneka's counterspell, but knew that would spell disaster. Sure, she had the x-radiograph and the IRR to guide her, give her an idea of the result she strove for, but if she grew too zealous in her efforts, if she marred even one of the original symbols, the ramifications included far more than just a botched job; it would signal Karundin's defeat and enslavement at the hands of Shanor and his King. So she strove for precision, exactitude, quality, and while she certainly didn't dawdle, she forced herself to check her impatience, her desire to hurry, with practicality. She remembered her little mantra while she waited with Nervain for the report of the Wolfpack: *don't let anyone die*, and she reiterated it in her mind any time her fear and impatience threatened to swamp her.

Don't let anyone die, she thought, taking up a small sponge and dipping it into her diluted solvent. *Don't let* ... gentle swab across the right corner ... *anyone* ... watch for drips and over-saturation ... *die* ... wipe off excess material. Repeat. *Don't let anyone die.*

She took comfort in the monotony of her task, let it draw her into a sort of trance where only the work mattered, leaving no room for anxiety.

Kaeley and Rayton stood listening as Merikan gave their guards final instructions.

"None to approach the Royals without full knowledge of their intentions. Remember, 'who do you work for?' Protect them at all costs."

"To the death, Lord Protector," Remy replied.

Merikan gave a solemn nod, turned one final time to Kaeley and Rayton. He placed a hand on each head, a swath of golden light extending to cloak the pair.

"For what good such a shield might do," he murmured.

Kaeley took his hand.

"Go, Lord Protector," she said, sombre overtones weighing in her expression, her posture, but she smiled with as much good cheer as she could. "Look after my brother. Watch over Karundin until Angie can return."

Merikan nodded and without another word, strode away, two towheaded women in his wake, the sisters Jaerina and Jaeneth from Chasta Village, intent on lending what aid they could. As they reached the castle's gate, their forms flowed into that of a great black wolf and two blonde wolves, quickly disappearing in a flurry of furred feet.

Rayton turned to look directly at her as she watched the scene from afar.

"Hurry Angie."

Angie blinked, startled to find herself sitting before Daneka's painting. *What the hell?* She scrubbed at her eyes with her sleeve, careful not to rub her gloved fingers anywhere near her face. Obviously she hadn't managed to banish her trepidation about Karundin entirely while she worked.

She gave herself a fierce shake, head and shoulders. Then bent back to work.

It took a few moments to get herself back into a calm rhythm, but she finally managed to find that sense of peace again.

"Here they come," Nervain said, staring unflinching across the field at a lumbering collection of about a hundred creatures as they advanced. Gavin stood at his side, sword drawn, tension singing along his lightly armoured limbs and torso.

A line of people fanned out from the pair, soldiers in blue with the golden tree of the Royal house mingling with those wearing the device of a salmon on a charcoal background, the crest of Baroness Vordaeth. A smattering of farmers and other villagers, brave men and women from the countryside determined to aid the King. Nobles and peasants mingled, infantry, archers, even

288

some cavalry, all equal today as they sought to hold back Shanor's unnatural force in this, the initial foray.

Angie could see Aebigail with her bow next to Darbison and Carsien and the rest of the Wolfpack near Gavin, and with that observation, realised she watched events currently occurring in Karundin even as she sat at a workbench on Earth. She wondered where the humans of this invading army lurked.

"Fire," Nervain called, unleashing a volley of flaming arrows into the clay soldiers. The creatures didn't even bother to brush the fiery brands away before the arrows sputtered out in their earthen lodging; the clay men simply continued their advance.

"Horsemen," Nervain swept his arm forward, and a group of cavalry, double mounted, charged in. The lead riders rode through with vicious sword strokes, but any severed limbs simply regrew, a knitting together of roots and soil. Their passengers, equipped with sloshing buckets, tossed streams of water over their adversaries. The liquid spilled down the bodies, deforming many as it rearranged the frames, yet the momentum barely slowed, mud-streaked monstrosities now adapting to altered gaits that left bands of slime in their wake. Any truly slowed by their deformity stopped just long enough to regrow more serviceable parts, then started moving again.

"Well shit," Nervain muttered in English. Gavin nodded his agreement, lips drawn tight and bloodless.

Angie found herself standing next to Sorcerer Tograth and another man, the salmon sigil embossed on the shoulder of his charcoal robe naming him Vordaeth's Sorcerer. She knew she still sat on Earth, could feel the repetitive motions of her hands and fingers as she worked on revealing the counterspell, yet she also stood on the front lines of Karundin's forces, the hint of the half-light of her dreams suggesting she might influence events here. She couldn't yet undo Borun's Army spell, but could she use a different one?

She stepped forward, not realising the spectral aspect clothed in overalls and latex gloves she presented, but aware of the attention she instantly garnered. Staring at the nearest clay soldier, she uttered the Spell of Transformation, rendering it inert. Tograth and Vordaeth's Sorcerer quickly moved forward to bracket her.

"Take away their life," she said. "Transform them into something harmless, or back to immobile clay."

They set to with alacrity. But each could only focus on one being at a time, while the rest of the army steadily gained ground.

"Make them into a wall, a blockade," Gavin called.

"And keep sending in water," Nervain added. "It at least slows them down."

Karundin's forces scurried into motion, mounted men and giant wolves harrying the enemy, seeking to slow the advance any way they could, give the Sorcerers time.

And Angie blinked, the half-light replaced by the strong glow of the lights in the workroom.

"You okay Mermaid?" Irving asked at her shoulder. She stared at him, eyes refocussing on her surroundings. "You didn't respond, and I began to worry."

"I—" she suddenly swayed and Irving reached to steady her. "The war's begun. I saw it, Irving. I was just there."

Before he could point out that she hadn't left her chair, a slight but insistent voice interrupted.

"You must eat something, My Lady," Sidvareh lightly touched Angie's face, her eyes wide with concern. "If you continue to share worlds like this, you will require sustenance. Already you've used enough magic to drain your strength."

As though to confirm the Faery's statement, Angie's stomach growled. Angie stripped off a glove and rose from her seat, reaching for her tea on the nearby table. She nearly stumbled as a wave of exhaustion draped a heavy mantle over her, but managed to snag her mug as the table top took her weight. She grimaced as the cold drink slid down her throat, but drained the cup anyway. Irving appeared at her side with a glass of water, and she only now noticed that he had briefly left.

"What's going on?" Jerry asked as he left off his own project to explore the commotion in the corner.

"Just need a little food to bolster strength," Irving replied as Angie gulped water. "Run next door and grab us something?"

Jerry looked a bit put upon in his puzzlement, but he shrugged gamely, waved off the money Irving offered, and headed out.

"Here's something to tide you over until he gets back," said Irving as he handed her a granola bar. Angie took it gratefully, peeling off the wrapper and biting into the chewy mass in bliss.

"So what's going on?" he asked when she swallowed.

Angie explained as best she could.

"Events are moving rapidly there," she concluded miserably. "I don't know how much time has elapsed, but I do know they can't stand long against another force like that. I fear Shanor will have already sent fighters affected by the other spells before I can help." She turned back to her corner. "I have to hurry."

Then she stopped, staring without comprehension at her progress. Irving stepped to her side.

"That's kinda what I wanted you to see, Mermaid," he said softly. "Ask if you even knew you'd done it."

Angie shook her head, mute.

"How long did I work?"

"It's about one now, so nearly six hours."

In her peaceful trance, Angie had managed to reveal half of Daneka's counterspell.

"If you hadn't told me it doesn't work here," confided Irving, "I'd suspect you used magic."

"Does tenacity count as magic?" Angie tried to joke.

"Maybe desperation," Irving allowed, bringing a small smile to Angie's lips. Then he turned more serious. "Promise me you'll eat as soon as Jerry returns," he insisted. "The afternoon is yours undisturbed after that, but you won't do anyone any good, here or there, if you don't have enough fuel."

"Agreed. Let me know when he gets back." She returned to the canvas, sliding on her glove and reaching for her brush. Until lunch arrived, she could always start on the next section.

Chapter 31

Things had gone according to plan, and yet also horribly wrong, depending on which moment Shanor chose to focus upon. King Dorn had gathered a decent sized fighting force and they had marched north. Towns and farmsteads along the way had supplied food and shelter, continued to send support, whether by royal order or spell-induced influence. They had confirmed Tre'vani Alvin's grudging advice that the lesser used route into Karundin didn't usually see any traffic in winter and so would prove the stealthiest way for an unexpected army to sweep into the land.

They had hit the first snag at the border. Scouts had hurried back across the ravaged swath of land separating the two countries, riding hard into camp to announce the presence of an opposing force awaiting their arrival just beyond the sea of desolation.

"How is that possible?" Dorn's eldest, Prince Marnor, heir to the Sahkaraean throne, demanded.

"Indeed, you assured us no one uses this route throughout the winter," General Shantz snarled, turning on Alvin.

The Tre'vani stared back mildly.

"You yourself confirmed that fact," Alvin rebuked. "Do you seek to blame me for the truth?"

"What truth?" Shanor demanded, glaring with undisguised animosity at Karundin's Prince, wondering just how the Tre'vani had managed to find yet another loophole to his orders to provide accurate and current information, to assist King Dorn's initiative to the best of his abilities. "How did Gavin know to bring his forces here? Did you send him a message?"

"I did not," Alvin bit off the words, forced to answer Shanor's questions. The Sorcerer waited, but Alvin provided no further information, indeed seemed to ignore Shanor's first query. General Shantz also noticed the oversight.

"We agreed that this route provided the best access, somewhere Gavin would least expect. So, why would Gavin think to guard this entryway?" the burly soldier asked. "Your honest opinion, your best guess, Tre'vani."

Alvin met his stare with heated intensity.

"This unmaintained road *does* provide the best access to an unexpected army. Gavin knows that as well as I do."

Once it became clear that Alvin intended to offer nothing else, General Shantz slapped him across the face, hard.

"That does not answer my question."

Then King Dorn began to laugh.

"Yes it does, General," Dorn said. He shook his head, studying Alvin with grudging respect. "Gavin knew we would come. Somehow he has discerned our intent, and so we do not lead an *unexpected* army into Karundin. We all used that same phrase, over and over." Dorn's voice trilled mockingly, "*Gavin can't possibly know we're coming, so he won't expect us.*" He spat, disgusted at their overconfidence. "How, Alvin, did your brother know we would come with an army?"

Alvin shoved a hand at Shanor, the unexpected force causing the Sorcerer to stumble.

"Gavin knows what you stole," Alvin hissed, oblivious to or ignoring the weapons suddenly drawn upon him. "Exactly what you took, and what it does. He has obviously figured out that *you* orchestrated the thefts, Sorcerer, and that you would seek to use me in this way. Of course he knew to guard the most likely incursion point, knowing I'd have to tell you exactly what you wanted to hear. I just applaud how quickly he marshalled his forces."

"Then let us test what we have *reclaimed*," Dorn said, looking directly at Shanor. "Gavin may know what we have, but can he defend against it? I think it's time to use this dead land to our advantage. Raise me a clay army, Shanor. We'll see if we can't force Gavin to rethink opposing our reunification."

Shanor and his sorcerous companions then proceeded to test the limits of Borun's spell to create a deathless army. As Shanor had suspected, the effort left them weak and exhausted at the end of each day, but Dorn merely encouraged them, using the time to fortify their position, much as Gavin had done across the border. By the time they had raised nigh on two hundred soldiers, Dorn had them pause.

"Send in half of them at a normal walking pace. I want to see how Gavin reacts."

"Do you want them shielded in any way, My Lord?" Sorceress Jaen enquired.

"No. Treat them as any soldiers; no advantages beyond the fact that they don't breathe and won't stop. Let's see if we can't capture ourselves a King."

They sent the unit across the dead expanse of their birthplace, watching from afar to see Karundin's reaction.

"Fire arrows and water," Shantz commented, peering through his farseeing lens. "Descent enough thoughts, I guess, but—"

"What's that?" Dorn interrupted, gazing through his own lens, as did Shanor, who could only stare in consternation as first one, then a handful of the clay soldiers stopped, rooted in place by an unseen force. Shanor swept his enhanced gaze across Karundin's lines until he spotted the strangely garbed figure of Sorceress Angelica.

"How did she do that?" Shanor demanded, but then had his question answered as the soldiers began to fuse together into something different, and Gavin's men leapt into the fray, changing into giant beasts before reaching their opponents.

"Shanor?" Dorn asked, noting the curses of the Sorcerer.

"She's using the Spell of Transformation."

Alvin laughed.

"Imagine that," the Tre'vani commented. "Using the spells you failed to steal to block your efforts."

Shanor glared at him, but Dorn waved it away.

"No matter. Now we know some of their resources, and with little expenditure on our part." Dorn turned away from the battle, seemingly unconcerned with the final result. "We'll give Gavin a day or two, then invite him to a parlay, see if we can't convince him to give up this paltry defence. Shanor, you and Jaen and Flornum continue to create clay soldiers. Best to have the numbers to crush my counterpart, should he prove resistant to our overtures."

The second morning after that first foray, Dorn invited Shanor to his tent. Shanor grabbed a steaming bowl of porridge on the way, needing extra sustenance to complement the rest he'd managed after working late to bolster Dorn's unnatural troops. Dorn, noting how quickly the Sorcerer plowed through his meal, asked,

"You have enough strength for a different spell?"

"Such as?" Shanor put aside his empty bowl.

"I plan to invite Gavin for a little talk. You've Controlled his brother; can you Control the King and anyone he brings with him?"

"Easily," Shanor replied, his mind already supplying images of Gavin and his protectors under Control, especially that blasted Sorceress. Without her strength to employ the spells Shanor should rightfully hold, Karundin's defences would fail. In fact, he would force her to hand over the remaining spells, even make her use them herself on those she once thought to protect. The prospect pleased him. "When do you need me?"

"I think we'll send the Tre'vani to hurry Gavin along, so I expect the meeting to happen before the sun even reaches its zenith."

"Tread carefully, Majesty," Shanor warned. "We've seen how Alvin pushes at his bonds."

Dorn merely smiled and called for General Shantz. Obviously awaiting the summons, the General entered, Alvin walking stiffly at his side.

"I'm sending you to visit your brother, Tre'vani. Just a quick trip to let him know I'd like some friendly words with him." Shanor saw a calculating spark light Alvin's eyes as Dorn spoke, though his face remained passive. "You and General Shantz will cross the border under a white flag, going no farther than the dead ground reaches. Once there, you will speak with Gavin, and only Gavin. You will say these words, and only these words. 'King Dorn requests an audience with King Gavin to discuss terms of peace.' You will not pass on any other information to anyone there, whether through speech or action. You will await submissively while Shantz provides the details of this purposed meeting, and then you will return here without fuss in the company of General Shantz. Do you understand?"

Alvin nodded briefly, face mottled in suppressed ire as he strove for some way to contravene Dorn's explicit instructions. Shanor had to admit that the King had thought it through well, but then Alvin had sorely surprised them before. Best prepare for some calamity to ensue, though Shanor couldn't imagine what.

Indeed, if all went as Dorn hoped, they might achieve their goals by nightfall. If Alvin did as instructed and Gavin acquiesced. Shanor planned to make sure Jaen and Flornum continued to strengthen their army's numbers while he accompanied the King, just in case.

***

Dorn had actually brought along a travel table and two chairs, had them set up under a canopy midway between the demarcation of dead land that separated Sahkarae and Karundin. He had placed a small white flag at the top of the pavilion. Shanor applauded his temerity. The King sat with Shanor standing behind to his right, and Marnor to his left. Shantz had taken up position just beyond the cover of the canopy on the Sahkaraen side. None of them bore any weapons.

The four waited, watching, as Gavin strode confidently toward them, Commander Nervain and Lord Protector Merikan flanking their King, a guard Shanor remembered often standing with the King a pace behind. Shanor didn't see Lady Sorceress Angelica anywhere, which immediately sparked his suspicion.

"She's not with him," he murmured. Dorn leaned back slightly in his chair, head barely angled to catch Shanor's words, though he never took his attention off the approaching quartet. "Sire, I don't trust this. Gavin hasn't gone anywhere without her since she appeared after the coronation."

"Maybe one of your clay soldiers ate her," Marnor offered lightly, but his considering frown as he scanned the bare field beyond Karundin's King suggested the Prince, too, distrusted the Sorceress' absence.

"Well, in case it didn't," Dorn put in, his lips making almost no motion, "keep your wits about you. That woman has a way of spoiling our plans."

Gavin reached them, spun the chair around, and straddled it, crossing his wrists on the seat back.

"Greetings, gentlemen," said Karundin's King. "I understand you wish to explore peace terms."

"Indeed—" Dorn began, but Gavin interrupted, a hard cast to his face and an unrelenting edge to his voice.

"Good. Then you will have your Sorcerer there return what he stole, relinquish control of the Tre'vani, and not set foot on Karundin soil. I'd prefer you send your troops home too, but over there's your land. Your land, your people; just keep them away from me and mine."

The Sahkaraeans stared at him in mute disbelief. Surely Gavin jested. Shanor glanced at Nervain, then Merikan, but both men stood stoic, their gazes unwavering.

"You cannot be serious," Marnor broke the silence. "You stand outmanned, outmagicked. You have no bargaining power."

Gavin never took his eyes off Dorn, so completely ignoring the Prince that he might as well not exist. Marnor did not enjoy the slight, but he had enough brains to swallow his pride when Dorn flicked a finger at him, warning him to keep silent.

"Perhaps you do not fully understand the gravity of the situation," Dorn said.

"Because you think you have us outmanned, outmagicked?" Gavin taunted. "Because you think you have some right to invade our land, take what doesn't belong to you?"

"But it does belong to us," countered Dorn. "The book, the land, as much ours as yours. We were stronger together, more prosperous. Two lands under one Over King. Amaekar and Borun sundered it, but we can make it right."

Gavin stared expressionless at his fellow monarch, though his jaw clenched tight enough for a vein to throb at his temple.

"You want to reunite our lands?" Shanor heard the quiet incredulity behind the question, understood that fury backed it, but Dorn seemed to only hear a dawning understanding.

"Yes!" the Sahkaraean King nodded, face animated.

"By using the very spells that destroyed that unity? By enslaving us? Forcing us to your will? Kill us, if needs be?"

Dorn's eyes narrowed.

"Only if you force us to take those steps. Don't be a fool, Gavin. Think of what we could achieve."

"And those you've already slain in your mad bid for dominance?" Gavin's glare landed on Shanor and the Sorcerer could feel the heat of rage and hatred. "Lady Sorceress Katerina and her child?" The glare swung back to Dorn. "King Grayton? Are we to forget their deaths in the grand unity you propose? And who would sit as Over King, Dorn? You?" Gavin's chin jerked toward the Prince. "Marnor? Maybe the Tre'vani's babe, as a sign of equality between the nations. And if any object, you

297

have Shanor steal their minds, is that it?"

Dorn sighed, his shoulders slumping marginally.

"Then you refuse peace?"

"I've given you our terms," Gavin replied, pushing up from the chair. "Do you accept them?"

Dorn snorted his disgust.

"I'd hoped you would think about your people, Gavin. Do you wish them to suffer the same fate as your son?"

Gavin's eyes narrowed.

"Given that Rayton sits well protected in the loving arms of his aunt, freed from the shackles your treacherous Sorcerer there tried to enslave him with, then yes; I do hope my people fare as well."

Dorn's turn for contemplation. Shanor didn't know whether to believe Gavin or not. Yes, he had used the Mind Control spell on Rayton when newly deciphered, but surely it had worked better than Gavin let on. A bluff, then. Bravado to mask his pain. Shanor almost smiled.

"Spare yourselves from unnecessary bloodshed," Dorn cajoled, changing his tactics. "You must understand that you cannot prevail against the kind of armies we can raise."

"We will not bow to your threats."

"Then you leave us little choice." Dorn leaned back in his chair and flicked his hand dismissively, as though brushing away a noisome insect. In truth, Shanor had waited for this very signal, and he uttered the words to Borun's spell of Mind Control, his main focus on Gavin, though he knew the effects would spread somewhat to the others. But once they had the King, his people would fall.

Only, nothing happened. The four men from Karundin gazed at him with near identical expressions, a sort of polite disinterest.

Dorn leapt to his feet sputtering, shoving back Marnor in his surprise; Shantz groped for his missing sword; and Shanor stood gaping. Not possible! Borun's spells had no counter. Perhaps he had misspoken? Then he spun in a tight circle. Or maybe that Sorceress had deflected it. But they stood alone beneath that canopy, the Lady Angelica nowhere in sight. So what had gone wrong?

Shanor curled his lip in a snarl. He would *not* give up the Sahkaraean dream so easily. He prepared another spell just as a sphere of gold enveloped Gavin and his companions. Shanor

298

sneered; not even the mighty Merikan's magic could hold back what Shanor unleashed. The spell tore from his lips, his voice raw as he screamed it out. Let's see how Karundin's King handled becoming Shanor's thrall.

Merikan's shield tumbled, and Shanor crowed his triumph as the light of Adoration suffused their faces. Jaws slack, eyes wide, waiting to hear and obey the whim of the Sorcerer from Sahkarae, Gavin, Merikan and Nervain stared at Shanor with fervour. Strangely, Gavin's guard did not. Before he could puzzle out the discrepancy, Shanor heard something that made his blood run cold.

A sonorous voice, resonant with power, spoke behind him, though he couldn't discern the words. He whirled, and there she stood, the Lady Sorceress Angelica. She looked almost insubstantial, a trick of the sun over her shoulder, but Shanor had no difficulties recognising her, strange garb and all. An eerie silence descended.

"You're too late," Shanor forced his triumphant words into that quietude. "They belong to me."

"They're mine," she retorted, and vanished. Shanor couldn't help it; he gasped, his consternation echoed by Dorn.

"The Lady sounds *pissed*," Shanor heard Nervain comment, and Gavin's guard laughed. Shanor didn't know the word, but could guess its meaning. He turned back to his captives. Only, none of them bore the glow of Adoration now. With a sinking feeling, Shanor perceived that she had done it again. Somehow, the Lady Sorceress had thwarted his scheme.

"And under a flag of peace, no less," Gavin spat, stormy eyes on Dorn. "You still refuse our terms?"

"You might belong to that harlot, Gavin, but Karundin belongs to me." Dorn no longer masked his loathing for his counterpart. "One way or another, I will take what belongs to me."

Dorn turned his back and strode away, fury in every motion. Shanor and the others hurried to follow.

The four from Karundin also made their retreat. The guard tossed aside the cloth that had blocked his hearing, having removed it after Shanor had unleashed the Spell of Adoration. Nervain glanced at him.

"That was an awful risk. How could you know that would work?"

"I told you," the guard said. "I trusted Angie to protect me."

Then he spoke the word Merikan had taught him, and Transformed himself back into Gavin. A similar word from each companion, and Merikan shook off Gavin's features while Davok ceased acting as Lord Protector. Only Nervain had entered that parlay as himself.

"It was still a hell of a risk," Nervain muttered in English.

"That's why I deafened myself to that snake's tongue," Gavin murmured back, and Nervain realised that, although the King trusted Angie, he had feared his precautions might not work. He had heard relief in Gavin's voice.

"It worked for us," Merikan, who had arrived only the day before, cautioned as they made their way back to camp. "But until Angelica returns with the full counterspell, our people remain vulnerable. Best hope Shanor doesn't figure that out."

The others could only agree with Merikan's sentiment.

**

Angie had managed another couple of hours of work after lunch, had hoped to finish before morning. But then she felt her consciousness ripped away from Earth, summoned forcibly to Karundin. She dropped into what looked like a peace negotiation with such a sense of vertigo that she knew something there had required her immediate attention, and when she saw the vacant yet smitten gazes of her friends trained on Sorcerer Shanor, she understood their dire situation. With her physical hand on Daneka's counterspell providing a tactile connection betwixt realms, Angie had called upon her need to protect Karundin's leaders, and, like when she had freed Rayton and Remy, she felt the power build. The words came to her mind, tore up her throat in the voices of the long dead, and birthed balming protection over Angie's charges. She felt the immediate drain of her resources as magic spanned from one world to another, and she only managed enough strength to claim those men as her own, stealing them away from Shanor's vile clutches, before reality snatched her back to Earth, and she had slumped from her chair, nearly burned out.

She had only the vaguest notion of someone carrying her, snugging her into the warm comfort of a sleeping bag. She thought perhaps she had a little liquid poured down her abused throat, maybe heard the tinkling of bells formed into incoherent words as Sidvareh spoke to someone, but she could only concentrate on her pressing need for restorative slumber.

Too bad her dreams decided to infringe upon her desire for blissful oblivion.

Shanor fumed, an anger almost overshadowed by fear. Instead of succumbing to that dread, he took it, reshaped it, fed it into his wrath. They stood at the brink of success, indeed should have achieved it at that parlay, but instead, that cursed Sorceress had snatched it away with some unfathomable trickery.

"They're mine," he mimicked, forcing his voice into a falsetto before dropping back into his usual cadence. "You can't protect them all, Sorceress." He paced, working out how best to foil her and still achieve everything he had toiled so hard for, for Sahkarae, for his King, for himself. He slowed, a plan formulating in his mind, something to vex her while creating a more flawless transition once Dorn and his heirs resumed rule over all. "Smoother transition without the confusion of multiple bloodlines anyway," Shanor murmured, a malicious smile tugging at his cheeks.

In her dream, Angie shuddered at the deliberate cruelty behind that expression.

"I've a way to ensure that your line succeeds while Gavin's fails," Shanor explained to Dorn, the two conferring privately in the spacious confines of Dorn's command tent. The Sahkaraean King listened avidly, agreed with both plan and implementation.

"Maraenda must never know the details," Dorn cautioned.

"Of course not, Sire."

Then Shanor called for Alvin.

Every word they said sickened Angie. She longed to step in, to halt this evil action before it began, but if she revealed herself now, the Sorcerer would undoubtedly concoct something equally dire that Angie did not know about. Better to wait until they sent Alvin on his gristly task.

"Tre'vani Alvin," Shanor began once the guard who had escorted Alvin into the tent had left, pulling the canvas of the door shut, blocking out the light of the day as surely as the Sorcerer planned to shutter the light within Alvin. "We have a final assignment for you to perform. You will take the most expedient route to Karundin Castle, using the swiftest means available. Make sure to circumvent Gavin's army and allies first,

301

keep out of their sight. Avoid detection and confrontations when possible, but do not deviate from your course."

"You will ensure you arrive healthy," Dorn added. "Not exhausted, not starving." He met Shanor's inquisitive glance, spoke quietly to his compatriot. "If we don't specify such basic necessities, he might attempt to thwart us by arriving too weak to fulfill our desires."

Shanor nodded his appreciation of the King's astuteness.

"You will find a way to enter the castle without raising suspicions. Convince them you are well, uncompromised, free from any outside influence."

Shanor's grin at the falsity of what Alvin must report turned Angie's stomach, and Alvin's, judging from the Prince's agonised expression, the bleak despair filling his eyes, twisting his features.

"Once there, you will gather your family to you; your sister, your nephew." Shanor's eyes turned hard, cold, his voice an implacable shard of steel. "Gather them to your heart, and kill them."

Alvin trembled, the Prince trying desperately to throw off the chains of Mind Control, but Shanor held his manacles in a firm grip.

"If any try to stop you, kill them. If your brother or his vile Sorceress appear, kill them too. The Lord Protector, the house guards, the lowliest servant, should any impede your way to the Dho'vani and the Tre'embra, eliminate them."

"And when you have destroyed your blood kin within Karundin," Dorn concluded, his expression equally as uncompromising as his Sorcerer's, "you will complete the job of eradicating the line of the Royal House of Karundin. Once Kaeley and Rayton lie mortally wounded, you will take your own life."

"Alert no one of your orders, your purpose," Shanor warned. "Do you understand?"

Given leave to speak, Alvin unleashed his fury.

"I will kill you," he said, staring with such intensity at Shanor, his whole body vibrating with the desire to span the gap between them, to take the Sorcerer's throat in his hands and squeeze the life from him. But Borun's spell held him in check, and Shanor chuckled.

"No you won't," Shanor avowed with a dismissive wave of his

hand. "Now, do you understand your instructions?"

Though Alvin's lip twisted in a snarl, the Tre'vani finally hissed out a "yes."

"Then go, Tre'vani. Go with all haste to secure the fate of your family."

With an inarticulate scream of rage, Alvin swept from the tent, Shanor and Dorn following slowly behind. Without hesitation, Alvin strode to the nearest picket line, selecting a horse seemingly at random. Dorn waved off the protesting guard, sent him for a bedroll and rations for the Tre'vani, and issued orders for his army to allow Alvin safe passage once he had the mount saddled and provisioned. Dorn watched with a certain lightheartedness as this powerful weapon that Shanor had fashioned arrowed north, sights set on his targets.

"Now to make sure we keep Gavin occupied," Dorn said, clapping Shanor heartily on the back. "I want as many soldiers as possible ready to move by tomorrow. Real or clay, willing or coerced, our troops push into Karundin with the rising sun. Get to work Shanor."

"Right away, Your Majesty." The Sorcerer afforded the King a half-bow.

Angie paid them little heed, staring off after Alvin. She closed her eyes, imagined herself standing in Alvin's path, then opened her eyes again to see his horse pounding toward her, free at last of Sahkarae's forces if not her stinging claws. Knowing his orders, she dare not hesitate, wait for him to acknowledge her, and possibly put a knife in her gut.

She dredged up her need, her ability to span worlds, her connection to the counterspell that would free the Tre'vani from his torment. But when she opened her mouth to shout out the words, only silence greeted her. The spell would not come forth.

"No," Angie cried, her grasp on the dream wavering, then snapping as she woke.

The sleeping bag trapped her in its sweaty confines, the material twisting around her frantic movements as she fought to disentangle herself.

"My Lady," a gentle voice sought to soothe her, Sidvareh suddenly fluttering in front of her face. "Easy, Lady Angie. Calm your mind enough to make your body obey."

"I have to stop him," Angie sobbed, still struggling.

"And you will, but only if you quiet your thrashing."

Angie forced herself to stop moving, to put her mind to the task of extricating her body rather than further ensnaring it. She pushed the sodden sleeping bag down off her overheated torso, slid her legs free, and swung around to put her feet on the floor, discovering she perched on the leatherette love seat in Irving's office.

Pulling in a shuddering breath, Angie took stock of her situation. Gritty eyes from not enough sleep, arms and back aching from constantly bending over her work, stomach growling in an effort to gain her attention, point out its hollowness, its need for sustenance.

Her certainty that the next few hours would shatter her heart.

"Sidvareh," the name hitched as Angie tried to speak. She cleared her throat. "I have no time left," she whispered.

"I know," the Faery responded, her face holding such compassion. "It is time to return home."

Angie stood unsteadily.

"I have to finish unmasking that painting," she said, hating the time still needed to accomplish that, equally despising what would follow once completed.

"It is done," Sidvareh said, stopping Angie in her tracks.

"What?" she demanded, certain she had misheard.

"Your Irving finished the job while you recovered."

"But," Angie spluttered. "But that means ...." She drifted off, her emotions in turmoil.

"It is time to remove the bridge," Sidvareh said. "To choose, once and for all, which world you will claim as your own."

"I have a choice?" Angie whispered, bewildered, never having thought such a decision hers to make.

"You always have a choice." The Faery brushed a tear from Angie's cheek.

"But if I stay, what happens in Karundin?"

"In all likelihood, Shanor and his King will win both lands, at least for a time. Shanor will gain all of Borun's spells to do with as he pleases. The Royal line will revert to those of Sahkaraean blood, but the land and the peoples will endure."

"And Gavin?" Angie asked. "Those who fight with him? Kaeley and Rayton and poor Alvin? They will all die."

"And for you, it will all be as a dream," Sidvareh said. "Karundin as you remember it from your youth. You can resume your life here, recall the past months as nothing more than fancy, an especially vivid dream."

"Then I'd be living a lie," Angie shook her head in disgust. "My family here, still dead, and my family there, forsaken, left to die horribly by an unthinking act of selfishness. No, Sidvareh, that is not a choice I'd make."

"Then it is time to bid farewell to this world," Sidvareh said, a beauteous smile blossoming on her face.

Angie felt her own face fall as the full implications began to sink in.

"To return with Daneka's spell and save those I love, I only have to sacrifice the most generous, patient, best friend I have," she sniffed. But Sidvareh swooped close, her little hand pressed against Angie's lips.

"My choice," she said. "Do not take that burden upon yourself, Angie. We both choose to follow our hearts."

Lower lip quivering as she checked her tears, Angie managed a nod of acceptance.

Then, resolve blooming in her chest, Angie wrapped her fingers around the doorknob, opening the way to the future.

Chapter 32

"We have to pull back farther," Gavin called to Nervain. "Retreat, give Angie more time." *Please, Angie,* he thought silently, where no one could hear his desperate pleas, *come back to me. Hurry.*

Gavin maintained an outward calm, tried to exude it to those he led—he didn't think he'd fooled Tera or Davok, but Miller Darbison and his companions from Chasta Village, who had formed their own protective detail around the King, seemed to take heart from Gavin's supposed composure. Nervain and Merikan also managed an exceptional likeness of unflustered competence, but Gavin didn't know how much longer they could all hold their fears at bay. Four days had already crawled by as they retreated north, ever pursued by deathless or enthralled soldiers pushed ahead of Sahkarae's main force.

Reluctantly aided by the sparing use of Borun's cursed Spell of Immeasurable Power, Merikan and Tograth, together with the three other minor sorcerers Gavin's call for aid had brought to his side, had Transformed countless clay creatures into barriers, or forms more benign than a mindless horde bent on destruction. But the Power spell took its own toll, draining others of their vitality, and only Merikan and Tograth had enough finesse to wield its energy. Merikan had aimed at the enspelled mob, hoping to steal their strength to help Karundin, weaken the bodies of those who had no control over their own minds and actions, but Borun's spell proved more capricious, chafing at direction, preferring to take from those nearest the spell-caster. They dared not overuse that spell for fear that it would simply drain all and sundry, incapacitating those the Sorcerers sought to defend as well as those they retreated from.

Gavin had sent scores of people ahead of their retreat—those volunteers with the least military experience but enough fervour to fuel large-scale projects—to build fortifications, dig trenches and traps to slow the advance of Dorn's army. Every undead soldier who fell into a hole and had to struggle to climb out again gave the Karundin army time to escape.

Nervain came up with the idea to disguise the holes and fill them with water, while the Sorcerers bent their skills on causing the water to freeze, trapping all who fell in. While the clay soldiers had mostly taken the lead, their bodies turning sluggish, and finally ceasing all movement once frozen, not all those so encased in ice lacked life.

"We'll be no less dead from the weapon of one enslaved than from the crushing blow of clay," Merikan had implacably explained when a sorcerer had hesitated, allowing a group of howling souls with the light of Adoration blinding them to escape and advance on the left flank. Nervain led a handful of soldiers to cut them down, losing one of their own before eliminating the threat. "Do not hesitate at the cries of the enemy, for these people will not even hear yours."

Gavin had seen the pain in the Lord Protector's eyes at having to deliver such harsh revelations, felt it himself with every thrust of his sword, every order to advance or retreat, but neither could allow that heartache to dictate their actions in this brutal and petty war. They could only do their best to limit bloodshed while they desperately awaited Angie's return, hopefully with a workable solution to the senseless slaughter.

"Sire," Nervain caught Gavin's attention before the King could order the next retreat. Nervain nodded to the side and Gavin followed the direction of the Commander's gaze, seeing a large wolf approaching from the west. One of the scouts he had sent out with Sorcerer Yamar to muster troops and gather intelligence on the extent of Sahkarae's incursion. No foreign forces had appeared near the Western Trade Route nor the major Highway connecting Sahkarae to Karundin; it seemed Dorn and Shanor had committed the entirety of their efforts here, where Gavin fought to maintain some sort of impasse, sacrificing land rather than people. Gavin hoped to bring the allies guarding those passages to his aid, swing them in behind Sahkarae's army, funnel them onto land Gavin and his people hastened to make ready for ambush and entrapment. Delaying tactics, but anything to buy Angie the time she needed.

Hurry, my love, he thought again, before giving the scout his undivided attention.

The wolf, its salt-and-pepper fur bristling with drops of moisture as it shook off snow flurries trying to settle on its shoulders, padded to a halt, awaiting the King's acknowledgement. After a confirming nod from Merikan, who scanned the wolf to ensure his identity, Gavin beckoned the scout near. The wolf approached, shook his muzzle, then sat, tail wrapping around his clawed toes for warmth, and regarded Gavin from amber eyes. He did not retake his natural shape, and Gavin worried that he may have spent too much time in this Transformed state, found the animal form more comfortable, more preferable, than his own skin. But Gavin could not force the man into any form. They all suspected the risks; if the scout chose to hold to his wolf shape for a while longer, none would gainsay him.

'Sire,' the wolf spoke, his 'voice' confirming him as Pendarak. *'Your forces to the west stand at the crossroads. Do you want them to circle north to bolster your might, or swing in behind the enemy, push them in the direction of your choosing?'*

Angie had ingeniously structured her Wolfpack so that they could either send thoughts telepathically within their own numbers, or communicate to an individual or group using a strange kind of speech, their growls and barks somehow translating into words understandable to the human ear. Odd to hear words overlaying a wolf's howl, but effective.

"I'm inclined to follow the original plan," Gavin said, his gaze seeking out both Nervain's and Merikan's council. "Have them drive Sahkarae's troops from behind, harass them, send them in the direction we want. Dorn still outnumbers us, especially given the clay soldiers, but that will force them to divide their efforts."

"Agreed," said Nervain. "Surprise will aid us, and when surprise loses its effectiveness, direct the withdrawal toward our traps." He held Pendarak's piercing scrutiny. "Draw them in after you. *Send* to us when you're ready to retreat and we push from our side."

"It may lose effectiveness on those clay men," Merikan warned, not a new caution. "The regular soldiers will likely try to engage the reinforcements, but we cannot rely on the mindless men of mud turning from harassing the front lines."

"True," Gavin said. "If you suspect that driving or leading their army isn't working Pendarak, instruct our forces to flee north, circle around to join our western flank. Take reasonable risks, but no foolish ones."

"Keep us informed of your progress," Merikan added.

With no further instructions to impart or receive, Pendarak rose to all fours, bow-stretched to the King, then turned and loped back towards Gavin's secondary army.

"Let's get moving," Gavin instructed, clay soldiers already lumbering into view. Nervain signalled the next retreat, a blare of horns calling out the orders.

About to mount Praetorian, Gavin noticed another wolf, this one auburn, hastening toward them, evading the enemy lines. He frowned.

"Commander," he caught Nervain's attention. "Who else do we have scouting the south?"

Nervain swung around, his intent stare focussed on the approaching beast.

"None that I know of," he replied ominously, sword already pulling from his scabbard, confirming the unease Gavin felt gnawing at his stomach.

"I think it's Aebigail," Jaeneth spoke up diffidently from behind Merikan. Jaerina's wide eyes also tracked the wolf, her sling dangling from mottled fingers. The two sisters had shadowed the Lord Protector from Karundin Castle and had appointed themselves his guards.

"Aebigail?" Gavin glanced around, startled. How had he not noticed her absence among his unique protective detail? For that matter, he belatedly noticed one other missing body. "And where is Handras?" Easy enough to overlook the quiet and taciturn man as they constantly retreated and regrouped, yet his continued absence sent a thrill of dread dancing along Gavin's spine.

"Do you think they succeeded?" he heard Carsien murmur worriedly. Gavin turned to look at the man, saw Miller Darbison shake his head, a fine tremble playing along his jawline.

"Told them not to go," Darbison hissed. "No good to come of it."

"Come of what?" Nervain demanded. "What do you think they did?"

Darbison looked around, but none of his fellow villagers met

309

his eyes. With a heavy sigh and slumped shoulders, he faced the King.

"They wanted to sneak past their sentries, see if they could kill that Sorcerer," he admitted. "Thought we'd talked them out of it, but—"

"*Shit!*" Nervain exclaimed with heated eloquence, his weapon leaving its confines with a scraping *whoof* as he sprang forward.

The wolf didn't slow, just gathered her muscles taut and leapt high, impressively soaring over them all. Gavin found himself crouching low, an unconscious reaction mirrored by those around him. He spun to follow her trajectory, saw the woman land as she emerged from the wolf, an arrow already nocked to her bow, aimed at Gavin's heart.

She released and time seemed to slow as Gavin recorded every detail.

Nervain's frantic grab at his shoulder.

Merikan shouting out a spell.

The whir of a sling and the solid thunk as it found its mark against his assailant's temple.

Miller Darbison smashing into his body and riding it to the ground, his eyes enormous in fear and pain as he stared at Gavin through the flicker of the King's Royal shield.

An instant of blackness that swallowed time, then spit it back out at normal speed.

Gavin stared up at an overcast sky, flakes of fluffy snow drifting down to tickle his exposed flesh with cold, wet kisses. A much warmer spill of liquid heated his chest, originating from the man laying protectively over him. Hands pulled the miller off of him, searched the King for injury, but Gavin pushed them aside. He sat, staring at Darbison, who stared back from a pallid face, an arrow lodged near his heart, his breaths coming in panting gasps. Aebigail lay in a crumpled heap, blood leaking from a ruinous gash on her head, her eyes fixed sightlessly though Jaerina stood over her, clutching the sling that had slain the archer.

Gavin crawled the few paces to kneel at Darbison's side, taking the miller's cold hand in his own. Nervain crouched to take the other hand.

"You fool," Nervain whispered, intent on Darbison's face. "Why would you throw yourself in the way like that?" Far from a harsh criticism, the Commander spoke with genuine regret.

"Woulda done the same for me," Darbison managed between swift intakes of air, his hands convulsively spasming.

"He probably would," Nervain allowed, a hand laid gently on the miller's brow in an oddly protective gesture as he half-heartedly chastised the man. "But he'd be wearing armour."

Darbison managed a shaky laugh.

"Thank you," Gavin said, drawing a brilliant smile of pride from Darbison. A smile that never left his face as the man hitched a last desperate breath, then lay silent, the life fleeing his body.

"Gavin," Merikan spoke softly, kneeling beside the King, his grip on Gavin's shoulder insistent though not painful. Gavin blinked and looked at the Lord Protector. "We have to go."

Gavin wanted to argue, take a moment to honour the sacrifice just made for him, but a quick study across the field showed the advance of Shanor's soldiers, the near-silent footfalls of clay men not more than a stone's throw away. He nodded, extricating his hand from the embrace of death.

"Let's go," he said shortly, taking Praetorian's reins in a tight fist.

They hurried away, leaving behind two brave souls, both trying to honour their pledge to aid Karundin in order to fulfill a debt they did not owe, each destroyed by their decisions. Gavin prayed the others didn't follow him to similar deaths.

Oh Angie, I could really use your strength about now.

***

The violet mist turned violent. Angie tried to orient herself, but with only the turbulence of strobing mist thrashing at her with invisible fists, she had nothing tangible to grasp onto save the rolled parchment cradled fiercely in her embrace. It felt like sharp shards of stone spinning within a whirlwind scored every inch of her, from exposed hands and face to clothed arms and legs, yet no breath of true wind tugged at her tunic, combed through her hair. Flashing patterns painted in impossible shades of purple distorted her vision, burned her eyes, left crazy after-images on her retinas. She ran through a maze of nothingness, sprinting on a surface that did not exist, abraded by forces seen and felt and scented yet only existent to her ephemeral self, given life by her imagination. She tasted the bitter truth of her actions, heard the wail of accusation, endured the wild assault on her senses, as she fought to complete her frantic journey across realms.

"Remember," Sidvareh had said as the Faery opened the gate between Earth and Karundin. "Daneka's spell must leave this realm last. Once you remove the bridge and sever its connection to Earth, you will have the space of mere heartbeats to reach the other side."

Irving had put on a brave face, kissed her forehead in farewell much as her father had done in the past.

"I'll see you in your dreams, Mermaid," he had said with a crooked smile. Angie had hugged him hard, biting her lip to hold in her tears.

Then she had taken up Daneka's spell, freed now from both concealing paint and canvas. She rolled it loosely and turned so as to put her back to the gate. The violet mist had swirled gently around her shoulders as she stepped back, balanced on the threshold. Holding the scroll out horizontally in front of her, Angie watched Sidvareh light upon the far end facing the Sorceress. Holding Angie's unwavering gaze, Sidvareh walked backwards until she perched on the very edge of the spell. She had nodded once, confident, brave, composed. Angie took another step back, the mist of the gate enveloping her with gentle, reassuring arms. She continued to retreat until only the hand firmly clasping the scroll remained untouched by mist; and then she took another step.

As the spell touched the threshold, began to slip into the gate with Angie, those gentle arms turned hard, reassurance replaced by a strange tension that built around Angie. Static crawled up her spine, crackled all around. She didn't dare hesitate now. She backed up more until only an inch of the scroll remained in Earth, grasped in the small, fragile hand of a Faery.

"Now, My Lady Angie," Sidvareh called, the chime of her voice discordant, coming as though from far away. "Run!"

The bridge snapped, swallowing the agonized shriek of the wide-eyed Faery as the gate collapsed, slamming closed the pathway linking two worlds.

Angie fled through the violence, desperately trying to find the other end, the slit in space that would tumble her back to Karundin. She tried to block out the trembling colours, the blazing smells staining her tongue, the screaming sensations abrading her every step. Finally, as her lungs burned in the constriction of the dissolving gate, she squeezed her eyes shut, tried to ignore the unnatural input flaying her awareness.

Karundin, she thought desperately. *Take me to Karundin.* And then, picturing him with every ounce of clarity she could summon, she sent out a final plea. *Gavin, please, hear me. Help me get home.*

She stretched out her unburdened arm, imagined her hand in his, then exploded into the agony of real sensation, falling forcibly through the tattered edges of a collapsed gate.

***

Merikan and the Sorcerers had set up a series of three shield walls between them and the Sahkaraean army. The first they had erected about fifty furlongs back, an invisible wall intended not to stop the advance, but to slow it. The clay army, certainly effective in close quarters—and, frankly, as a force of intimidation—nevertheless required direction. It would take a conscious mind to instruct the golems to find a way around the invisible barrier, each end stretching a goodly distance before curling back on itself, forcing the enemy to cover more ground than the Karundin forces had, even pull back south a small way before they would discover the wall fading into oblivion. This would allow a brief respite for the retreating forces.

The second shield lay around twenty-five furlongs distant, this one designed in a wedge shape. It should funnel the golems to a U-shape at the bottom of a gully, currently encased in a shroud of snow. Gavin's army had left their trail highly visible to draw in the Sahkaraeans; Merikan's wall would trap them until they could define and circumvent the edges, retracing their steps.

The third and final shield lay only a dozen furlongs out. This one Merikan had laced with a trigger spell, so that the first creature lacking a pulse to test its limits would ignite a wave of lightning strikes aimed south. Intended to warn Gavin's people when to make ready to rise, it would also, hopefully, disable any of the living within Shanor's front ranks. Gavin desperately hoped Shanor had not placed Alvin with those lead troops.

This last wall also stretched across the most defensible ravine in the area. It wouldn't require great skill to scale the walls, but it would take time, and the foreknowledge to evade the two teams Gavin had lying in wait above. The first, a handful of archers with instructions to fire at anything alive and to cover their companions; the second with levers and a pile of snow-capped boulders. When enough of the enemy army stood hindered by the wall, this team would pry loose the boulders, triggering an avalanche and with luck, bury clay with rock and ice.

Unless Shanor found a way to unmake the walls.

While they waited, Gavin's forces rested, taking small comfort in sheltered fires, warm food, and a collection of tents to keep the elements at bay. They dare not set up a full encampment, but Gavin had pitched his command tent, along with a handful of the larger structures, heated coals piled in buckets taking the worst chill from the air, for those who could find the ease to sleep within.

Too restless and anxious to make proper use of those comforts, Gavin, with Tera and Davok his close companions, roamed from group to group in the night, trying to bolster confidence, maintain morale, find some shred of hope to share.

He found Jaerina standing a little distance away from the other villagers from Chasta, arms clutching a rabbit-fur lined cloak as she wrapped her arms around herself, staring into a night pin-pricked with a dazzling display of stars, the quarter moon gently sliding below the horizon. Jaeneth stood with Carsien and the others, but her forlorn gaze tracked her sister. Gavin hesitated, then altered course so that he stood beside the solitary sister. One look at her anguished eyes told Gavin all he needed to know. He stood silently beside her, gloved hands clasped lightly behind his back as he stared across the night-enshrouded landscape, saying nothing, waiting to see if Jaerina would choose to speak. Their breath fogged from cold noses before drifting into the darkness, puffs of life floating away while they recalled death.

"I grew up with her, you know," Jaerina 's voice drifted to him. "We all did." A vague wave of her arm behind her before snatching at her cloak again.

"I'm sorry you had to kill a friend," Gavin offered quietly when she said no more.

"I didn't." She gave a firm head shake. "Aebigail died as soon as she stepped foot behind enemy lines. Handras too. Foolish of them to think they could pull off the assassination of a man who hid his dark intent for many double-seasons. Such a man takes precautions, and how could a potter and a farmer hope to overcome seasons of such caution?" She smiled briefly, though the expression looked brittle. "But then they always thought they could beat the odds. The schemes those two would concoct, the mischief, the pranks." She shook her head in fond remembrance. "But ever in fun, never causing humiliation or hurt."

They stood in silence for a time. Jaerina finally turned to regard him, boldly meeting his gaze.

"Darbison didn't deserve to die," she stated. Gavin wanted to flinch, but strangely, he did not hear reproach or blame; just a statement of fact. "But he died to protect something bigger than himself. When you came to our village, saved our children, you sealed our fate."

Gavin wanted to deny that responsibility, but Jaerina hadn't finished.

"I know you think we came to discharge that debt, pay you back for your selfless actions. We didn't. We came to defend what you represent. We've seen it again and again, whether we fight or run, and each time we see it, it just strengthens our resolve, our need to protect that precious gift."

"What gift?" Gavin asked, frowning, trying to understand what she needed to express. "What do you see?"

"Compassion. A leader willing to put himself in front of others, not as a tyrant to rule over us, but to spare us, take away our pain. You see our suffering, and instead of turning a blind eye, you give of yourself to help ease our burden. That was my cousin's wedding you saved from disaster. Not only did you rescue our children, you also made sure that her wedding became a day for all to remember and cherish. You fed us, celebrated with us, even danced with us; not because you had to, but because you felt it the right thing to do. We see your anguish when you have to send people to fight, knowing you might have sent them to their deaths. We notice your relief when those same people return. And we all watched you give Darbison the gift of respect and gratitude in his final moments. He went to the next world feeling pride and joy for his sacrifice, when you could so easily have left him alone in his pain."

"I couldn't do that," Gavin said, and Jaerina smiled.

"And that is why we came to your aid. A monarch who sees his people as people, not just subjects.

"Darbison didn't deserve to die," she repeated. "But none of

315

us will ever blame you, King Gavin. I could blame Aebigail for her pigheadedness, but mostly, I choose to blame the monster who stole Aebigail's mind, forced her to betray all she held dear. I'm mightily sorry her and Handras's scheme to get rid of that Sorcerer didn't work, and I will forever bear the weight of wielding the weapon that ended her misery. But I will not allow their deaths to diminish the ideal we fight for. We fight for the compassionate Karundin you would have us live in, and against the hatred and fear that killed Aebigail, that pushes even now against our fragile barriers. I don't know how we can win, but know we will not stop fighting at your side."

Gavin stared mutely at this woman, a villager chanced upon because Angie had insisted they turn aside to avert disaster. They owed their gratitude to Angie, not him, yet he didn't know how to correct her, if he even could.

A prickling sensation suddenly assaulted Gavin, ripping his attention away from Jaerina, though he noticed peripherally that she too fixed her stare on the empty space in front of them.

"Your Majesty," he heard Merikan rush to his side, summoned by the call of magic. The Lord Protector pulled up abruptly, power-enhanced gaze intent on the shimmer of air that warped the world mere steps away. He summoned a sphere of pale light on his palm and waited.

Help me get home, Gavin heard, the desperate plea echoing in his mind. Already he reached out a hand, thought he felt slim fingers slip into his as green light nimbused him, streaks of silver flashing though the halo, magics mingling. A small part of the world imploded as elements beyond his ken tore asunder and discharged Angie into his waiting arms.

Exhausted and sweat-soaked, tears bathing her face and falling from her chin, breath gasping through clenched teeth, eyes squeezed shut, Gavin thought her the most extraordinary, exquisite woman he had ever seen. Her whole body quaked, tremors dancing along her limbs, rattling her teeth, and not from the cold, though he suspected that would assail her soon enough as sweat froze in the wintry air. She clutched at him as at a lifeline, but she also grasped something else, kept it sheltered between their bodies.

Some sort of rolled parchment.

A rabbit lined cloak draped over Angie's shoulders, Jaerina parting with her warmth to see to the comfort of the Lady

Sorceress.

"Get her to the tents," Merikan instructed, ushering them along, sending his light sphere ahead to guide the way. The Wolfpack closed in all around, an honour guard beside Tera and Davok. Jaeneth, however, ran ahead.

"Angie," Gavin said softly, one arm around her shivering shoulders, the other holding the cloak tight over her body and the scroll held close to her breast. Her feet shuffled in wooden obedience to his lead, but she hadn't opened her eyes yet. Until he spoke her name. Then those gems of sapphire and emerald flew wide on a swift intake of air and she stared at him in anguished relief from a breath away.

"Gavin?" She touched his face as they moved, a smile blossoming on her face and catching her glistening tears. "Am I really here? Did I make it?"

A quick glance to their surroundings, those marching alongside them, seemed to quell some of her trembling and she managed a more active role in her steps, her stride evening out, matching Gavin's. But rather than pulling away to walk on her own, she leaned into him and Gavin nearly stumbled with the euphoria that intimacy evoked. She dropped her hand from his face and laid it over his hand on the cloak, curling her fingers around his.

"You're here, my love," he murmured, content at last despite their dire circumstances.

"I did it," she said, heartache warring with elation in her voice. "I have the counterspell."

"At last," Merikan breathed a sigh of relief.

Her sharp glance, first to Merikan then to Gavin, reminded the King of the perceptiveness of his dear Sorceress. She could read the worry, the barely veiled desperation that had marked their recent actions, that haunted their party. She acknowledged it all with a single nod before fixing her gaze on the looming tents ahead.

Jaeneth met them at the shelter, her arms full of warm clothing and a steaming bowl. Angie's teeth chattered from the aching cold, but she pulled out of Gavin's embrace, removed the borrowed cloak and slipped it back over Jaerina's shoulders with a warm smile of thanks. Jaeneth quickly wrapped the Sorceress in a quilted garment before pressing the bowl into shivering fingers and gently pushing her into the tent. The Wolfpack then stationed themselves near the entrance, awed by the regard

317

shown them by King and Sorceress alike.

Gavin leaned close to Davok.

"Find Nervain and have him meet us within." The guard saluted and hurried off. To Tera, he said, "Wait for them to return, then join us." Tera nodded and took up his post.

Gavin and Merikan followed after Angie.

Chapter 33

Angie found a corner free of slumbering bodies and sank to the canvas floor, huddled selfishly around a bucket of hot coals she had pulled close as she devoured her stew. For a fleeting instant, she feared she dreamed, that she still sat somewhere on Earth. But no half-light sharpened her vision—in fact, the only illumination came from Merikan's globe of magic that hovered over her shoulder—and she didn't feel the separation between body and mind that had subtly marked her recent excursions into Karundin. She felt real, solid, wholly present for the first time since she had called on Sidvareh to aid her on her journey.

The memory of the beautiful little Faery, of her last anguished shriek as the gate slammed shut, put a hitch in Angie's breath, a sharp pain in her heart. She closed her eyes and sent her silent gratitude for all Sidvareh had shared; her aid, patience, occasional wry humour, love, support, and above all, her ultimate sacrifice and trust. Angie vowed to live up to that trust, even if Sidvareh would never see what her life had bought so dearly.

When she opened eyes filled with determination, she saw that Gavin and Merikan had joined her. She pushed the warming bucket aside and brought forth Daneka's spell, unrolling it to lie flat in the space between King, Lord Protector and Lady Sorceress. The three stared at it a moment, Merikan's light hovering above, before the Sorcerer whispered in consternation.

"Can you read it?"

Angie stared at the foreign writing, her hopes that the words would resolve themselves into something legible upon her return fading. Nor did they become any clearer with scrutiny as they had in her visions.

319

"We only deciphered Borun's spells through Gavin's magic," she contemplated softly. "This might work the same way."

Gavin immediately extended his hand to her and she took it gladly. But when he recounted the words that had unmasked Borun's spells to her use, nothing happened. Together, they frowned, studying the scroll, willing it to relinquish its secrets. It stubbornly remained an old piece of parchment riddled with strange markings.

"Hm," Merikan mused as Nervain and Gavin's guards entered the tent, wove their way through sleeping soldiers. Although, as Angie watched their progress, she noticed that not all those forms lay in slumber. An increasing number of open eyes reflected Merikan's light as they silently watched their leaders form a circle in their midst. She could feel the renewed hope radiating from them.

Oh please, let us find a way.

With Gavin pressed close at one side and Merikan sitting at the other, Nervain directly across from her and bookended by Tera and Davok, Angie thought furiously, tried to remember what the spell had looked like, sounded like, in her dreams. What she had glimpsed on the day of Gavin's coronation, what had formed in her mind and issued from her throat when she freed Rayton, released these men at the parlay ... she needed that now, only not as second-hand information. She needed to figure out how Daneka and Borun had hidden these words.

Daneka and Borun, she thought. *Daneka Borun.* An image of the pages providing provenance for *Castle of Dreams* that Irving had uncovered appeared in Angie's mind, the list ending with *Katerina Merikan* and *Angelica Karundin*.

"Merikan," she addressed her father, following a hunch. "Do you know the names Theraese Gormain, and Onyka Skylaran?"

The Lord Protector blinked at her in surprise.

"Theraese was Kat's mother, Gormain her Lord Protector. And Onyka and Skylaran the Lady Sorceress and Lord Protector before them. How do you know their names?"

"A list I saw on Earth," she said, excitement building. "Of all who supposedly owned this through the years." Her hand rested lightly on the edge of the scroll as she met Merikan's gaze. "All the way back to Daneka and Borun."

"Daneka?" Gavin asked.

"The Sorceress who found a way to stop Amaekar. The first

Lady Sorceress."

"I never knew her name," Merikan said, stunned. "No one did."

"Does her name help?" Nervain demanded. "Do any of those names help?"

"Yes," Angie said, grabbing for Merikan's hand. "The painting belongs to the Lady Sorceress and the Lord Protector, whoever fills those roles. The Royal hand might reveal Borun's spells, but it's the joint hands of the Lady Sorceress and the Lord Protector that will reveal Daneka's counter."

With a jubilant grin and her hand nestled in Merikan's, she stared at the encoded spell and waited. And waited.

"Um," Nervain eventually ventured as Angie's grin soured, then dissolved. "I hope you can read it now, 'cause we sure can't."

Tera and Davok shook their heads in unison as though to confirm Nervain's remark.

"*Damn it,*" Angie snarled, unclenching her hand from Merikan's. Thought about adding a few more expletives to vent her frustration, but refrained, knowing it would do no good.

"Wait," Merikan intoned, brow furrowed in speculation as his eyes shimmered with gold. "Do you remember the day we found Angelica in the woods, Gavin? How our magics combined to save her life?"

"Hers unexpectedly rose to join yours," Gavin recalled. "And before you could pull away, I pressed your hand back to her wound. Something tugged at my power with the contact and I let it roam free to mingle, stop the poison, speed the healing."

"Lord Protector guards the Lady Sorceress so that she might protect the Royal line," Angie murmured, dream-like, her gaze flashing with silver highlights as Merikan took her hand again. She reached for Gavin's hand, the connection imbuing rich green streaks to his stormy grey eyes.

Both men reached forward with their free hand to touch an edge of Daneka's spell. Angie gasped as they completed the circuit.

Reveal your counterspell, Daneka, she thought, her hands convulsing between Merikan and Gavin. *Please, we must stop Borun's folly.*

A thick braid of silver fountained from her chest to strike the scroll, and the lettering writhed in gold-green flames etched in silver. Nervain, Tera and Davok fell back with startled oaths, engendering a wave of motion as everyone else in the tent fell into defensive postures. But the trio linked by love and power sat mesmerized, magic dancing in their eyes as they eagerly drank in the sight of the counterspell morphing into its original form, the words devised and refined ages ago to stop the madness of war suddenly becoming clear.

The power slowly faded, thrusting the tent into darkness, Merikan's sphere of light snuffed as other magics took precedence. Harsh breathing rasped in the darkness before someone finally struck flint to a lantern, birthing a small flame of light. Angie joined the others in leaning toward that spark before Merikan gently pulled his hand free to cup a freshly glowing globe of illumination that he sent soaring to the peak of the tent. Angie's gaze tracked its progress.

"We've done it," Gavin whispered, drawing her attention back down. He stared at the paper unfurled before them, then to her. He brought their still joined hands to his lips and kissed her knuckles. Angie could feel the heat of her blush suffuse her face and a giddy grin spread across her lips, and could stop neither. Didn't even care to try. She laughed her relief, the sound spreading to release all present from the tension that had held sway moments before.

Jaerina pushed into the tent, her grim expression shattering the levity.

"Lightnings to the south," she announced, her worried gaze latching on to the three in the corner. "They've reached the last wall."

And just like that, Angie felt the weight of responsibility try to crush her. They had the counterspell; now she had to figure out how to use it.

***

The rumble of the avalanche soared and echoed from ahead, jouncing boulders tumbling over each other in their race to the ravine floor. Tree limbs cracked and snapped, snow and ice thundered as they cascaded to cover clay forms. The shockwave expanded outward, vibrations making the horses shy. They quickly dismounted, ran ahead of the nervous beasts. The ground still trembled up hurrying feet to jar knees and arms, straining backs and necks, stealing away any surety in footing, but better to stumble drunkenly under one's own power than risk the weight of a horse crushing a body because of a bad turn.

Angie skidded to a halt, Gavin and Merikan beside her, a handful of others steps behind. A plume of powder smoked ahead, clouds of rebounding snow and ice puffing against the barrier Merikan had constructed, the dirty white somehow starkly visible by starlight, dawn as yet only a thought in the east.

"How long until the weight of the snow weakens the shield?" Sorcerer Tograth asked.

"We folded it back on itself across the ravine's mouth," Merikan replied, though he sounded far from certain. "It will have provided some extra strength, but I'm not willing to risk our lives that this new constant pressure won't puncture it sooner than we'd like. I don't know that we took into account an accurate estimate of just how much weight that avalanche would add."

"Looks bigger than I had expected," Gavin said as they edged slowly closer. "I didn't think it would engender that much debris."

"Any movement?" Nervain asked, scanning the area.

"There." The sharp-eyed scout Untath pointed out shadows descending on the near side of the shield, those Karundineans who had initiated the avalanche.

"Get them headed back," Nervain ordered. "Rearguard as our forces push on to the rendezvous. With luck, this shield holds long enough that they won't see any fighting this morning."

An ominous crack and boom as the tumbled ice and rocks shifted, settled against the barrier made visible by the presence of the piled snow. Angie felt the ground beneath her feet tremble lightly, imagined how much less stable the rock wall must have become, and hoped their climbers maintained a firm grip as they scrambled down.

Nervain sent the Wolfpack to assist and lead the brave soldiers back to some semblance of safety. Angie left them to it, trusting their skills. She studied the shield, watched its edges, looking for movement on the opposite side. Nothing stirred save final drifts of snow coming to rest atop the confined mess.

Until the first hand crested the top as it climbed the mound, hauling a hairless head, an unclothed body behind it. A second figure pulled itself up from the snow, then a third. Clay soldiers continued to amass at the barrier, slowly pushing along it, seeking its end. For a moment, Angie flashed on her dream, the nightmare that had warned of this incursion.

From the dust rose clay figures, human in form yet lacking any features or personality. Hundreds, then thousands, adding up to uncounted hordes of deathless soldiers, each aimed unerringly at the trees. They reached the demarcation between vitality and enervation and pressed against an invisible wall. The shield held for a time, but numbers told, and the wall bent inward, then fell.

She remembered desperately wishing for some way to stop the approaching horror, being led to the painting that camouflaged the counterspell. The revealed scroll that she now held in her hands as clay warriors pressed against an invisible wall, inexorably aimed at the people of Karundin.

Time to find out if Daneka's promised salvation warranted the sacrifices.

"Father," she called softly, gaining Merikan's attention. The Lord Protector moved closer to her side, watched as she unfurled the rolled scroll in the light of a small sphere of illumination he conjured to assist them. "Help me with the words, make sure we pronounce everything exactly so."

They studied the words, written in neither Karundin nor English, yet somehow still understandable to the pair. However, they couldn't know the precise emphasis of the sounds—some more drawn out and complex than others—until they enacted the spell against what Borun's folly had wrought, truly tested the efficacy of Daneka's solution.

"I think we should move closer," she suggested.

"And if that shield wall fails?" Gavin asked from her other side, his warm presence both balm and distraction.

"We can erect a small barrier to divert the run-off," one of the two Sorcerers who stood with Tograth offered. Angie didn't know their names, had only seen them in glimpses of her dreams while she had toiled away on Earth. She did not demand an introduction now.

"It can funnel any secondary avalanche away from the Lord Protector and the Lady Sorceress," Tograth added. "Hold long enough for them to escape."

Gavin stared at the other sorcerers a moment, then sought Angie's gaze.

"You don't think it will work from here?" he asked.

"I believe his spells work both audibly and in proximity. If you can hear one, it will affect you, and the closer to the spell-caster, the stronger the spell's hold. If the counterspell works the same way, the closer we get to those clay soldiers, the more we can disable."

She glanced to Merikan for confirmation.

"From what we've observed, I'd have to agree. Not that I relish moving any closer," Merikan admitted, "but I also believe that will give us the greatest hope of success."

"Then let's go," Gavin said, starting forward. Angie grabbed his arm, pulled him to a stop.

"Not you, Sire," she said.

"She's right," Nervain hastily agreed, planting himself bodily in front of Gavin before the King could offer any protest. "We're nothing more than observers here. Leave this to Angie and the Sorcerers. This is their forte."

Angie read the anguish in Gavin's face, forced herself to turn from that uncertainty. Instead, she looked to his guards, Tera and Davok.

"Take the King to safety," she instructed.

"But—" His guards cut short Gavin's objection, forcibly holding him back. Angie relented just enough to plant a quick kiss on his lips.

"Go," she whispered, letting her eyes plead her need for his safety. He finally nodded and allowed his men to lead him away.

She and Merikan moved closer to the barrier, now aswarm with clay figures. The other three sorcerers followed close behind.

"Whatever happens here," she spoke quietly to her father as they walked, "we need to get someone back to the castle as quickly as possible. With the counter to Mind Control."

"What's happened?" Merikan kept his voice equally low.

"Shanor sent Alvin to kill Kaeley and Rayton, Gavin if he can find him, and then himself."

Merikan stumbled with a curse, hurried to catch up.

"When?" the word choked out.

"Just after the parlay," she replied. "He seemed somewhat upset that his plan failed. They both did."

"Both?" he squeaked. Angie thought his face might have gained a greenish tinge.

"King Dorn approved the action. Even helped in wording the order."

Merikan expanded Angie's knowledge of Karundin curses.

"I think we're close enough," she interrupted, voice raised to its usual level. She met Merikan's worried gaze. "You needed to know, but one crisis at a time," she counselled.

He took a steadying breath, then nodded his understanding.

They had angled their approach so that they stood near the edge of the ravine, the towering wall of encased snow rising to their right. Angie scrambled up a rise afforded by a cluster of large boulders, Merikan hauling himself up beside her. Tograth and the others measured out a suitable location for their new shield, then worked together, the colours of magic shimmering in their eyes as they combined their powers and called up a barrier around the Royal Protectors.

"We've left a path back the way we came," Tograth told them once they completed their work. "It weakens the farther back it stretches, but it should afford you an escape if the first wall fails."

"Good," Merikan acknowledged. "Now get yourselves back, guard the King, shelter the people. We'll join you once we've found the key to this spell."

The Sorcerers bowed and retreated, their faith bolstered by Merikan's air of confidence, though Angie suspected the same doubts and uncertainties that haunted her also troubled him. She admired his ability to push ahead in the face of such apprehension, tried to emulate the same strength.

Her gaze travelled up the caged snowdrift to the golems milling some eight or so metres above. As though attracted by a magnet, they pressed closer and closer to Angie's and Merikan's location, their eyeless faces seeming to stare back at her. She shuddered, again flashing on an image from her dream.

Every eye trained upon her. Sound rushed in, as frightening in its volume as the silence that had preceded it. The golems turned to swarm toward her, faces stretched in unnatural hunger and feet drumming in terrible unison as they ran.

She blinked away the picture that painted in her mind, the paralyzing terror it tried to engender in her cold limbs, frigid fingers.

"You've got this, child," Merikan murmured, drawing her startled attention. He smiled, though it looked forced. "Trust your instincts. After all, she left this for you."

He means the counterspell, Angie realised. Whether Daneka truly had created these words specifically for Angie's lips to speak, or had simply put to paper what had stopped Amaekar, Angie couldn't begin to guess, but she fully intended to employ the first Lady Sorceress' best efforts at putting an end to war.

"Can you amplify my voice?" she asked Merikan. "Make sure it spreads a far as possible?"

His eyes glowed golden as he moved behind her, placed his palms to either side of her throat.

"Ready," he said, magic shading the word.

One final check of the scroll, and she lifted her gaze, stared at the clay soldiers. She felt power build within her, a warm tingling spreading from her core, and she uttered the words burning in her brain. Her voice vibrated through the ravine, trembled against the waiting golems. And fell flat.

"Oh, *fuck*," she hissed with feeling. Not only did the clay soldiers still shift and shove above, now they pressed against the shield enough that she saw it start to bow outward.

She glanced at the scroll again, searched its words, determined a different inflection. She flung the words out again, changing the cadence, staring hard at the creatures who stared back, unharmed.

A fissure formed in the shield near the cliff wall, a puff of snow belching forth from it. Clay fingers pressed against a spider-webbing flash of silver as the barrier lost its invisibility, the entire wall turning into a frosty translucent shell.

"It's going to fall," Merikan warned. "We have to get away."

Angie shook her head violently. Then screamed. That scream turned into a torrent of words, Daneka's spell tumbling from her parted lips, amplified by Merikan's magic. The counterspell streamed forth, wrapped around every clay soldier it could find beyond the barrier, and tore away the animating forces, unbinding the unnatural forms. Clay melted into formless sludge, coating the debris momentarily held back by magic.

But then the wall snapped, releasing the pent-up avalanche. For the space of a breath as Angie leaned heavily against Merikan, her strength drained, silence reigned. And then the snow found its voice as it roared free of its confines.

"Run," Merikan yelled, pushing Angie before him, dropping to all fours as he ground out the word to Transform into a wolf. Angie managed the same, and two wolves, one black, one honey-dark, raced a furious funnel of churning snow, ice, and clay.

***

327

Angie huddled under a blanket, her back cushioned against Gavin's chest, his arms bracing her as he held Praetorian's reins lightly before them, the horse pushing gently north with the Karundin forces. The sky had lightened with dawn, but lay heavy with leaden clouds promising snow. Angie soaked in the warmth where her legs straddled Praetorian's flanks, her back snugged against Gavin, tried to ignore the chill where neither blanket nor body touched.

Her shoulder burned where Merikan's teeth had grazed her as he hauled her out of a stumble after a chunk of icy rock missed her by a scant breath in their wild flight. Another unwitting weapon of the snowslide had gouged Merikan's hind leg, and Angie returned the favour of dragging him from harm. The two had tumbled clear of the last vestiges of the avalanche, their fur wet from snow and blood, sides heaving as starved lungs greedily gulped in air, and threw themselves down long enough to recover from their mad dash.

Sooner than she had wanted, Merikan's cold nose prodded her to her feet and they followed the tracks of the army. It didn't take long for the rearguard to find them. They reverted to human form, had their hurts quickly tended to, and Angie soon found herself scooped up into the King's embrace, water and travel rations thrust into her hands to help combat the toll of Daneka's spell.

She might have dozed as they travelled near the rear of the army, content to find herself in Gavin's arms, but the reality of their situation crept up on her, demanding that she put her mind to finding a more permanent solution to their troubles. She wanted to tell Gavin to ride as hard as he could for the castle, pray they arrived before Alvin, but she couldn't, not yet. As long as Shanor had the ability to summon more undead soldiers, he wouldn't stop until Karundin lay crushed under Sahkarae's heel. They had to take away the Sorcerer's ability to harness the horrors of Borun's spells.

Angie had an idea how they might achieve that, but knew Gavin wouldn't like it, might even try to forbid her attempt. Didn't see that they had many other options, and they certainly didn't have any time to waste. That included, to Angie's mind, taking any time to stop and strategize. So she triggered her Transformed telepathy, sent her thoughts to include Gavin,

Merikan, and Nervain, and braced herself for a flurry of arguments and objections.

'We can destroy all the clay soldiers Shanor throws at us, but he'll just make more unless we stop him.'

There, fairly safe way to begin.

'I agree,' said Nervain. Merikan simply nodded, and Gavin's nod tickled her neck as his stubbled chin caught on her hair. *'So how do we stop him?'*

'By taking away the spells he stole.'

'And how do you propose we do this?' Merikan asked. Angie felt Gavin tense even before she could put forth her plan.

'You can't just walk in and demand he return them,' said the King. *'Aebigail and Handras already tried to get to him.'*

'They didn't have our protections,' Angie said. *'Nor the necessary stealth. I don't plan on presenting a visible target.'*

'He'll sense an illusion,' warned Merikan. *'And he'll have protections in place.'*

'Nothing that will stand against me,' replied the Lady Sorceress. *'We don't have time for subtle.'* Merikan met her gaze, glanced at the King, then looked away with a reluctant nod.

'Why not?' Nervain demanded warily, studying father and daughter. *'What don't we know?'*

Angie shook her head, pushed past his question.

'I propose we use our half of Borun's spells to strip Shanor of his.'

'Again, how?' Nervain's eyes flashed dangerously at Angie's evasion.

'Merikan and I will go in unseen, get as close to King Dorn and Shanor as we can. Then we use the Spell of Immeasurable Power. Recited in unison, it shouldn't affect either of us, and that close to their command structure, it will only take strength from our enemy.' She shivered involuntarily, recalling the devastating effects of that spell, even if she had only experienced it vicariously through dreams. *'With that filth coating us, we cast Daneka's counterspells, negating the effects of Mind Control and Adoration, break Shanor's hold over the Sahkaraeans here against their will. Then we have a few words with Shanor.'*

'And what's to stop them from killing you where you stand before you can even utter the first syllable?' Gavin's mind-voice, choked with emotion, nearly scalded Angie's mind.

'Before we go,' she said, laying a calming hand on his rigid

329

arm, *'we use the Spell of Instantaneous Healing. Whatever they think to throw at us cannot cause lasting damage.'*

She felt Merikan alter his telepathy so that it reached only her.

'Do you understand the power drain that spell will cost you? You haven't recovered from destroying the clay army; to add the price of another major spell—two, for it will take strength to cast the Power spell—will likely incapacitate you before you finish uttering the words.'

'I understand that we've run out of time and options,' she sent back. *'I will make it work.'*

'Even if it kills you?'

She smiled at his sarcasm. She had to make it work, could afford no other outcome. If she went in fully committed to this plan succeeding, no matter the cost, then how could she fail? Swallowing bile that chased panic up her throat, she forced herself to entertain no doubts. Or at least to push them kicking and screaming, along with a good portion of her sanity, into a room in the back of her mind, slamming the door and tossing away the key. What else could she do?

She switched back to group telepathy in time to hear Gavin's next objection, the one she had most dreaded.

'If Dorn has kept Alvin near him, you will steal his energy too when you throw around that Power spell.'

'Alvin's not here.'

'What?' Gavin jerked, as though looking around, searching for his brother. *'Where is he then?'*

Angie slid her hands down to his, took the reins from his loose grip.

'He's on his way to the castle.'

'The castle?' Gavin parroted.

Angie met Merikan's stare, acknowledged his brief nod. Saw dawning comprehension as her gaze tracked to Nervain.

'Oh shiiiit,' he drawled.

'Shanor and Dorn instructed him to kill the Royal Family,' Merikan confirmed. *'All of them.'*

'We have to stop Shanor before we can stop Alvin,' Angie said.

'We have to stop Alvin now!' Gavin exploded, his thighs squeezing to order Praetorian into action. Angie's control of the reins and a gentling hand on the horse's neck stayed the command, though Praetorian danced nervously under the conflicting desires. *'Ride out and use that counterspell to free*

330

him.'

'Alvin will delay as long as possible,' Angie said. 'He fights the Mind Control, has since Shanor unleashed it. You said yourself that he's a brilliant tactician. I'm telling you that he's using every bit of that brilliant mind to utilise every loophole. He can't not obey, but he can evade completing Sahkarae's objectives with delaying tactics, draw it out, find ways to slow his passage.'

'It won't work forever,' Nervain warned. 'He will reach the castle eventually.'

'Damn it, this is my family,' Gavin roared. 'My son! My sister! Slain by my brother's hand!'

'We will stop it!' Angie averred, digging her fingers into Gavin's rock-hard arms. She twisted to capture his eyes, held his tormented stare. 'We will save them. But we have to save Karundin first. Do you hear me, Gavin? Once we get those spells away from Shanor, even the playing field, then we can deal with Alvin.'

'And if you do get the spells?' Gavin asked sourly. 'Their army won't just turn around and go away, not without orders. Even free from Shanor's influence, the army will follow Dorn's orders, leaving a rather large obstacle to us leaving the field. Unless you plan to kill the King?'

'Follow the initial plan,' Nervain spoke up. 'Without a clay army and ensorcelled soldiers, it's mortal against mortal. The rules of winter warfare come back into play. They will need rest, supplies, none of which they will receive with our forces ready to harass them into our traps. Keep as we're going and we can win. The loss of discipline and morale by Angie's attack can only aid us. That plan, Sire,' he gave Gavin a hard stare to enforce his point, 'does not require your presence, nor Angie's. She takes away their greatest weapons, then you see to your family.'

Gavin didn't like it, but he agreed.

'When do we do this?' Merikan asked.

Angie pulled Praetorian to a stop, then pressed the reins back into Gavin's hand.

"We go now," she said aloud, and slid unsteadily out of the saddle.

"My Lady, are you sure?" Nervain wanted to know as he and Merikan halted their own mounts. Angie gave him a reassuring smile. Still holding his eye, she sent him a private message.

'Do not let Gavin out of your sight. He can't go after Alvin on *his own.'* At Nervain's questioning frown, she added, *'Alvin has instructions to kill him too, if he can.'*

Resolve hardened Nervain's posture and he bent his head curtly in promise.

"Have Tograth and the others assist with the Healing spell," Gavin said as he alighted next to Angie. The rearguard had stopped with them, but Gavin motioned for them to remain mounted, ready to continue the retreat. "Save your own strength for when you need it most."

"Sire," Merikan said. "I don't know if they have the stamina to pull it off and still have anything left to protect you."

"We'll make do," Gavin's tone left no room for argument. Merikan simply nodded and called the other sorcerers over. As he briefly explained the situation, Gavin grabbed Angie in a fierce embrace, burying his face in her hair. She clasped him with equal fervour. They needed no words.

Finally, they separated. Gavin, stormy eyes tight in anguish, whispered, "Don't get yourself killed."

"You neither," she begged.

She leaned in and kissed him, savouring his taste, his scent, the warmth they shared. Then she pulled away to stand next to Merikan.

"Once more unto the breach," she muttered under her breath, steeling herself for the daunting task she had set. She wrapped resolve around herself like the blanket she handed to one of the sorcerers. They had to get this right the first time. No walls holding her enemies in place while she fumbled for pronunciation, no do-overs. Get in, incapacitate Shanor's most potent weapons, and preferably the Sorcerer himself, then get out.

Easy peasy.

Chapter 34

In the end, Merikan cast Borun's Healing spell on Angie, and then Tograth cast it on Merikan. The other sorcerers caught Tograth as he crumpled to the ground, utterly spent. Angie, though, felt pretty damn good.

As the sorcerers bundled up Tograth, Gavin and Nervain remounted and finally turned to continue with the army. Angie and Merikan began walking back the way they had come, toward the Sahkaraean forces.

"Who do we disguise ourselves as?" Merikan asked.

"We don't."

He glanced at her sharply.

"You told Gavin we would use all the spells we have. Do you plan to rush in as wolves, then?"

"We're not using Transformation on ourselves this time," Angie hedged. What she planned did not sit well with her, but it somehow felt the right thing to do. "I'm hoping you can conceal us to get us close, like when we followed the steward Rogan. And then a shield, like I saw in the memory of the day mother died; the protections around Grayton's carriage. That should hold long enough for us to invoke the counter to Shanor's Mind Control and Adoration on those closest to him."

"I suppose," allowed Merikan, though his pointed stare demanded more information.

"I propose we start casting the Immeasurable Power spell as soon as we cross their line, speak it as we make our way to Shanor's side."

"They likely travel closer to the front than the rear, but do you think starting so soon will render those surrounding King and

Sorcerer vulnerable? It seems to me it will only weaken the vanguard."

"I plan on us moving fast enough to accomplish both," Angie said. "They won't know what's coming for them, and by the time they figure out our target, we'll have already arrived."

"And how do you plan on making that work?" he asked.

Angie stared ahead, but she didn't precisely see their path; she saw the man at the end of it, still several furlongs distant. Her vision narrowed so that Shanor filled it, the man riding next to King Dorn and Prince Marnor. The Sorcerer's features bore a fierce scowl overlaid by a hint of perplexity, no doubt trying to determine just what had happened to the clay soldiers at the front of his army. Angie could feel a slight tug, a thread that connected her to Shanor. She knew that once she took hold of that bond, grasped the end and pulled, it would propel her to this final destination, the confrontation she both longed for and dreaded.

"Have you ever had a dream where you knew where you had to go and then suddenly arrived; you just stop being here and find yourself there?" she asked. Merikan tilted his head in consideration.

"I suppose I might have," he answered.

"I can see our goal," she told him. "And I can get us there."

"Very well." He accepted it as fact, and Angie hoped her intuition proved accurate. She wondered if magic danced in her eyes as it did now in Merikan's as he wove a concealment spell around them. Couldn't know that she, in fact, fairly radiated with power, her blue and green eyes spitting silver sparks that wreathed her in a nimbus of energy. Wouldn't know the depth of Merikan's anxiety that she would expend her strength before they reached the enemy, before any more of Borun's words left her lips. He kept his concern battened behind a mask of complete confidence.

A bird called hesitantly from a stand of trees off to the side of the trail, the bare limbs drifted with a layer of fluffy white snow. From farther back, a second bird sent its song into the snow-scented sky, and the two feathered companions began a duet. Angie fancied they sang encouragement; daren't muse that they might offer a dirge.

"Assuming all goes to plan," Merikan said, "that we cast the counterspells, cause confusion, and actually manage to have

words with Shanor before someone tries to kill us, then what?"
He pulled Angie to a stop, forced her to meet his gaze. "How do
we force Shanor to give up the spells?"

"By Transforming him."

The answer had clearly surprised him. Angie could see him
trying to work it out, discover what form would force compliance.
A raised brow and crinkled nose suggested he hadn't discerned
what could accomplish that.

"Into what?" he finally asked.

"Do you remember explaining the spells to me when you and
Gavin told me of the Royal charge? That one could use
Transformation as an aid to spying, to surmount inhospitable
terrain, to infiltrate an enemy, but the concept seems that, of
Borun's six spells, it holds the least respect, causes the least
amount of fear. Would you agree?"

"It's a powerful and useful spell, but when you compare it to
the damage the other spells can cause—as Shanor has amply
demonstrated—then yes, I would agree it holds a lesser degree
of fear."

"That's because, as far as we know, no one has truly
employed it to its fullest extent. I would argue that Transformation is, in fact, Borun's most dangerous spell."

"Why?" he asked, not in doubt, as Angie had expected, but
with curiosity and an open mind, and no little trepidation.

"Because it can do everything the other five spells do, and
more."

He blinked, drew in a quick breath.

"Transformation is only limited by the imagination," Angie went
on. "The farther from the original being, the greater the energy
required to make a Transformation, but for minor changes, we
use less magic. Imagine Transforming a cripple into a whole
person, a diseased body into a healthy one. A minor sorcerer
Transformed into a mighty mage. A blood and flesh soldier
Transformed into an indestructible warrior, even one that doesn't
require sustenance. We've Transformed into other creatures;
how much less power did it take to make telepaths?

"How easy to turn Shanor into an Adoring slave, his mind
incapable of going against my wishes?"

Now Merikan paled, looking as sick as Angie felt. She nodded
slowly, holding her wide-eyed gaze on her father's face.

"Transformation is the most heinous and terrifying of Borun's spells," Angie concluded, her voice trembling as her lower lip quivered. "And I propose we use it to destroy a man."

She turned away, facing the unseen army, again seeing her target leap into focus. She held out her hand and Merikan took it, his grip steady. He wove a protective shield around them.

"When I signal," she squeezed his hand to demonstrate, "we unleash the Power spell. Ready?"

With a grim nod, Merikan braced himself. Angie took off, drawn like an arrow to a target, shooting down a tunnel of time that blurred the landscape at the edges, hauling them into the heart of the invading force.

***

Shanor waved a hand in front of his face, brushing off the sensation of eyes tracking his every move. He had enough to worry about without some imaginary watcher stalking him. Like, what exactly had happened to his clay soldiers?

The army had encountered the vestiges of tumbled rock, snow and ice that had crushed their lead troops, evidence of some kind of avalanche. Enough of a demarcation remained to show where Karundin's sorcerers had erected a third wall in order to bury his golems as they searched for a weak point. After the first barrier, Shanor, along with Sorceress Jaen and Sorcerer Flornum, had had to instruct those charged with leading the clay soldiers on how to turn the golems from a single-minded entity aimed straight at Karundin into a more cohesive unit capable of solving very minor problems. Such as where a magical wall ended.

Seeing the clay soldiers all trying to walk in a straight line while that first invisible wall held them back, none of them with enough consciousness or intelligence to turn aside until they found a more accessible route, infuriated Shanor. Prince Marnor had found the sight of golems piling upon each other, uncaring of a barrier they couldn't detect, vastly amusing. Even the King had chuckled at the embarrassing spectacle of deathless creatures gouging ruts into the ground as they walked the same track over and over, but not Shanor, nor the other sorcerers. To them, that wall represented Merikan and that vile Sorceress Angelica issuing a challenge, a slap across the face. Did they honestly expect Shanor to stop because of a mere wall?

He had directed his ire at the precise point where the majority of the clay men churned the snowy ground to a muddy sludge in their mindless drive forward. The shield, showing the first signs of buckling under the relentless weight of the soldiers—how long had they wasted, pushing at the same spot over and over—shattered as his magic hit it, toppling the clay army through the breach. Those that had fallen picked themselves up to rejoin their brethren as they continued their relentless march, oblivious to the delay they had suffered, slowly outdistancing the human army.

Shanor and the King had caught up to the golems at the second barrier, the night-enshrouded landscape crawling with dark forms stretching back across the path in a U-shaped arc as the soldiers searched for the end of the shield. Shanor snarled at this new delay, suffered the indignity of Marnor's snort of derision and Dorn's less amused expression. But before he threw yet more power at the obstacles in their path, General Shantz pointed out beyond the barrier.

"Unless I'm mistaken," the large man had said, arms bulging across his chest as he calmly sat astride his horse, waiting, "not all those forms are on our side."

Shanor looked harder, gestured beside him to Jaen. The Sorceress sang a brief word, and a globe of light suddenly bloomed in her hand. She tossed it up and forward where it expanded to illuminate the milling soldiers. Indeed, some had reached the wall's edge, had begun to circumvent the barrier. Lines of golems flowed to either side, followed the curve of the shield far enough that Shanor couldn't actually see where it faded, and then, apparently traced it back to its base before turning once again in the direction Gavin had taken. It didn't take long before the near side of the barrier lay empty of golems, the creatures following ant-like in the wake of the front-runners.

Rather than waste yet more time following the rerouted trail of the clay soldiers, Shanor, Jaen, and Flornum sent concentrated bursts of magic at the shield. As the golems had not weakened this shield like they had the first, it took all three to bring the barrier down, further enraging Shanor. He considered sending Jaen or Flornum ahead with the last of the clay army to begin to weaken any other shields Merikan and Angelica pestered them with, but decided against it. The golems didn't need light to traverse the night, but a sorcerer would, giving away his location.

Better to conserve their strength for when they might need it.

But that third barrier, the ravine littered with the remains of both landslide and smears of clay, baffled him. Obviously the wall had fallen (*did any golems get through?* a small voice nagged at the back of his mind, *or did she bury them all?*), yet they had found no trace of their further advance. Stranger still, nothing stirred beneath the snow. Even buried, the clay soldiers should have struggled for freedom, tried to continue their mission, but only stillness had greeted the dawn as the Sahkaraean army arrived.

So what had happened to his creations?

Still struggling with this question furlongs later, convinced the Sorceress Angelica had something to do with it, Shanor finally roused from his musings as he sensed something strange, an unusual disturbance emanating from the north. The front ranks began to wilt under the affect of an odd bubble of energy heading straight for his position.

"Beware another attack," Shanor warned as he wove protective shields around those in command: Dorn, Marnor, Shantz, himself. Jaen and Flornum strengthened his efforts. They all remembered the two wolves who had sprung upon them, beasts who had turned into humans intent on bloodshed. Marnor had dispatched the man easily enough, but the woman had unleashed an arrow that took Flornum in the gut. Jaen had managed to heal her fellow sorcerer enough that he hadn't died, but Flornum had not appreciated the wisdom of keeping that archer alive. He would never go against Shanor, not while he functioned under Shanor's Adoration, but he would rather someone had killed the intruder. Instead, Shanor had stolen her mind and sent her back to Gavin with the gift of another arrow. He doubted she had succeeded, but he felt confident she had caused damage, even if only to Karundin's spirits.

Perhaps they sought retaliation now? Well, they wouldn't find Sahkarae's defenders unprepared this time.

Except wolves did not step from the sphere of energy; Lady Angelica and Lord Merikan did, a pair of avenging spirits wreathed in undulating whirls of power. Shanor heard the last chord of a spell he couldn't fathom, but he saw, and felt, the results as weakness washed over him.

Dorn also swooned, but it didn't deter him in the slightest.

"Kill them!" the King shouted, and flagging soldiers rallied to his command, blades and arrows springing into wavering hands. Not one reached the invading duo, a green-gold shield flashing and absorbing every strike. Shanor knew it wouldn't last forever, and gathered his strength for when it inevitably fell, determined to bring down the meddlesome Sorceress who so foolishly exposed herself.

She met his gaze, her blue and green eyes filled with wild elation, and Shanor suddenly understood the weakness that swept up the army. The Sorceress and her compatriot had invoked Borun's spell of Immeasurable Power. Shanor's grin stretched wide as he realised that ultimate spell lay within his grasp. But Angelica's answering grin gave him pause, a malicious glint shading her expression, sending a shiver of foreboding coursing through Shanor.

She and Merikan spoke, voices resonating with tendrils of power. Shanor couldn't discern the words, only that they seemed to recite different spells though they spoke in concert. With the last syllables reverberating and spreading in a visible ripple of magic, the attacks on their now failing shield faltered until Marnor and Shantz found themselves the sole oppressors. At first, Shanor didn't understand.

"What's wrong with you?" Marnor screamed as he slashed his sword against the barrier wavering around the Karundinean Sorcerers. "We're almost through; keep at 'em."

The Prince looked angrily at the soldiers nearest, saw what Shanor saw; blank incomprehension, bewilderment sliding into resentment. *What just happened?* he wondered, turning to Sorceress Jaen and Sorcerer Flornum to demand their opinions. What he saw, especially on Jaen's face, turned his blood cold. No longer did Adoring subjects regard their master, but clear-headed Sorcerers with dawning hatred glared at the captor.

Impossible! Nausea rose as he realised he had seen that loss of Adoration before, at the parlay. He had thought the Lady Sorceress had somehow interfered with the spell as he tried to claim Gavin and his people, and that intervention had garnered his ire. But he had held these people in his thrall for weeks, and somehow, she had broken those chains. Worse, it had affected not only those under Adoration, but the soldiers and nobles under Mind Control as well. Every soul within hearing distance of these cursed trespassing obstacles—all those who had followed him and Dorn under magic's influence—now stared with contempt at those who had manipulated them into waging this war.

With a growl of fury, Shanor spun back to the intense stare of the Lady Sorceress, his fists aglow with destructive magics. As Marnor landed one more blow to the shield, Shanor thrust his arms forward, launching a spear of death through the crack the Prince had created. The bolt, red and orange flames licking its edges and sizzling with the weight of Shanor's rage, slid through the breach and straight into the Lady Angelica.

Her grimace of pain elated him, and Shanor waited with barely restrained glee—a heady feeling on the heels of so much anger—for her to collapse and put an end to her interference.

That didn't happen.

To Shanor's horrified disbelief, she just looked down at the smoking hole in her chest—or rather, in her tunic—and shook her head.

"I liked this shirt," she said, tone unbelievably conversational. Then she glanced at Merikan.

"Father, if we could have less of an audience—" at which point, Marnor slashed his sword through the jagged remains of the shield, fully shattering the barrier. The blade sliced across Merikan's arm, but the blood that welled into the gash stopped flowing immediately.

"Oh, stop that," Lady Angelica scolded, as though admonishing a child, but Marnor dropped his weapon and hastily stepped back. "Why don't you take a nap, leave the negotiations to the grown ups."

To Shanor's utter surprise, and Dorn's as well, given the King's slack jaw and enormous eyes, Marnor simply lay down in the snowy road and curled up, eyes closed, already breathing in deep slumber.

"Now, where were we?" the Sorceress mused, though her unwavering expression clearly showed she had forgotten nothing. "Ah yes, removing some of these unnecessary bystanders. Father?"

"Certainly, daughter," Merikan replied, and with a curt gesture, sent the majority of the army on its way, seemingly oblivious to the drama unfolding around them. Only Dorn, Shantz, Jaen, Flornum, and Shanor—and the gently snoring lump of Marnor—remained to confront the pair.

Father? Daughter? Shanor thought, studying the pair in a new light.

"It's not possible," he whispered, not even aware he had spoken aloud until Merikan focussed on him. Shanor had feared Sorceress Angelica, an unknown factor in his schemes, but he had never truly found reason to fear the Lord Protector, until now. That flat, unwavering glare of baleful animosity turned Shanor's knees weak, his insides liquid.

"Why not, Sorcerer?" Merikan's deep timbre overlaid with venomous sarcasm forced Shanor to clench his jaw so as not to betray his trepidation by jabbering like an idiot. "Because you killed Katerina, or because you had Rogan rip the child from her womb?"

"Mother sent me across worlds to protect me from your villainy." Angelica studied the hole in her tunic briefly, as though discussing something as trivial as the weather, but when she raised her sharp gaze, Shanor found he couldn't look away from the force of her bi-coloured stare. "Ironic that, when you sent Rogan to that world to try to kill me, you ended up giving me reason to come home."

Sent Rogan to—

Shanor felt the blood drain from his face, leaving him pale and shaken, and faintly dizzy. He had sent Rogan to kill the potential witness to Grayton's death; he had never, not even in his wildest dreams, considered that that witness—the child of Karundin's most powerful couple—could bring about his downfall.

"So let us end this," Angelica said, the embodiment of sorceress composure. She held out a delicate hand. "Give me Borun's spells, Sorcerer."

Shanor couldn't help it; he let out an incredulous guffaw, regaining his composure as the sound washed over his countrymen, bolstering them as it did him. Dorn shook his head with a smirk smearing his face, trusting Shanor to regain the upper hand. Shantz had pulled back from the adversarial pair when the Sorceress had put Marnor to sleep, but the General still had his sword bared, ready to strike should Dorn or Shanor order it. Sorceress Jaen and Sorcerer Flornum looked, well, not pleased—animosity might prove too gentle a term for the fury in Jaen's features—but ready to defend their country should Shanor demand their aid. He had best keep a cautious eye on them until he could reverse the damage the vile woman in front of him had caused.

341

He met Angelica's stare now and gave her his answer.

"No."

Obviously she could have expected no other reply, yet she set her jaw, preparing for some disdainful task. Shanor took a step toward her, drawing himself up to his full stature. As unobtrusively as possible, he also slipped a knife from his belt. Though she and Merikan had evidently employed the spell of Instantaneous Healing—how else to explain her surviving his assault, Merikan's wound closing almost as soon as Marnor had inflicted it—Shanor wanted to test a theory. Could she survive the loss of a limb? Perhaps her head? He had but to draw near enough for a swift blow. If nothing else, it would hurt.

"I'll give you this one last chance, Shanor, though I don't know why I bother," Angelica said, biting off her words. "Return those spells of your own volition."

He waited for her ultimatum, but she said no more.

"Or what?" Dorn asked for him, amusement and disdainful impatience crinkling his eyes. "You'll talk him to death? We grow weary of this."

"King Dorn," Merikan boomed, overriding Dorn's condescension. "You stand uninvited on Karundin soil, an army at your back and treachery in your heart. You lost any right to speak when you betrayed my King under a flag of truce. Your Sorcerer alone holds the key to your survival here. If you must make noise, then I strongly suggest you order him to follow the Lady Sorceress' dictates. Otherwise, hold your tongue and you may yet live."

"What say you?" Angelica asked, taking a step closer to Shanor. She made it so easy. Shanor lunged, knife aimed at her throat. She spoke a flurry of words, their meaning lost beneath Shanor's growl of effort.

The Sorcerer stopped, staring mutely at the blade in his hand, the weapon held to the throat of ...

"Mistress, forgive me!" he cried, dropping the knife and falling abjectly to his knees. How could he have raised a hand against this most wondrous of women? Tears flowed down his cheeks as he wept his contrition. He saw Dorn gaping at him, couldn't fathom the King's dumbstruck look of disbelief, didn't care so long as the Lady bestowed him with a glance. She did now, looking down at him with those bejewelled eyes full of ... sorrow? Pain? What had caused his mistress such distress?

"Please, mistress," Shanor begged. "How may I serve you?"

"Give me the spells you stole," she replied, voice thick with disfavour.

"Of course!" He ripped off the pouch at his belt, horrified that his odious behaviour had caused her such grief. "Please, Lady, forgive me," he whispered, offering up the spells with all the reverence due the Lady Sorceress Angelica. Around him, Shanor sensed Merikan erecting shield walls to keep Dorn, Shantz, Jaen and Flornum from interfering, holding them in place long enough for the Lady to relieve Shanor of his shameful burden. He bowed in delight as she tucked the pouch away safely.

"You will never utter the words of any of those spells again." Shanor shook his head vigorously, fervently agreeing with her command. "Nor will you allow any others to whom you taught those spells to do so. Do you understand?"

"Yes, mistress. None will cast them, I promise."

"Now go home," she said.

Then she and Merikan pivoted, turned themselves into giant, beautiful, powerful wolves, and loped away. Shanor gazed after them longingly.

He felt Merikan's chains snap from his companions, freeing them. Even Prince Marnor roused from his blissful slumber. Yet to his utter dismay, Dorn didn't praise Shanor for obeying his mistress. Rather, the King exploded in red-faced fury.

"How could you do that?" he screamed, jerking Shanor's attention away from the vanished Sorceress. "You just let them escape? Gave that aentoraden whore the spells and let her walk away?"

Shanor's eyes narrowed.

"Be careful how you speak of the Lady," he warned.

"What's going on?" Marnor demanded, regaining his feet.

"This foul snake," Dorn gestured rudely at Shanor, "just gave away our most potent weapons to that base wench from Karundin while he drooled all over her. What's wrong with you? For months, you've complained about that vile wretch, wanted nothing more than to rip her head off." Shanor's gut clenched at the vitriol spewing from Dorn's mouth. He grabbed his knife as he stood, confronting the King.

"Did you turn coward when she absorbed your strike with nary a glance?" Spittle flew as the King raged. "You should have killed the bitch! Now we have to track her down, take her head before she can use those spells against us."

Such a simple thing with Dorn standing chest to chest with Shanor; an easy and elegant way to make sure the King never laid a hand on his beloved mistress. It even took a moment for Dorn to notice the blade of Shanor's knife shoved into his middle, his royal blood flowing as freely as any common man's. The scald of red liquid quickly coated Shanor's hand as he twisted the blade, dragged the handle up and then out, drops of crimson flying to decorate the snowy landscape.

"No one will harm my mistress," Shanor hissed to the incredulous King as he slammed to his knees.

In the brief silence that ensued, Shanor turned and flung the knife at Flornum, taking his fellow sorcerer in the heart. Sorceress Jaen wove a hasty shield that Shanor swatted away contemptuously. She had strength, but no finesse, and Shanor had studied her in every way possible on their march from Sahkarae. He tossed a ball of compressed air her way, but she threw herself aside at the last moment, avoiding the full brunt of the force.

With a cry of outrage, both Marnor and Shantz recovered from their shock and lunged at the renegade Sorcerer. Shanor pulled his attention away from Jaen and smashed his fist into Marnor's face. The Prince crumpled next to his father. Shantz, however, did not miss his mark, and Shanor shrieked his agony as the General sheared the Sorcerer's left hand from his arm. He could see murder in Shantz's eye. He didn't fear his own death, but the pain that searing glare promised his dear mistress set Shanor's blood boiling.

"You will never hurt her again!" Shanor yelled, and uttered a spell he had never thought he'd have to use, though, like many sorcerers, he had prepared it long ago.

"No!" Jaen screamed, pulling herself painfully to her feet and leaping onto Shanor's back, her own knife in hand. But the blade across Shanor's throat came an instant too late, Shantz's sword through his chest only providing a kind of lightning rod to fuel the fire. Shanor's death spell ignited in a blaze of glory, expanding to engulf everyone within a ten foot radius.

When the smoke cleared, only charred bodies remained to mark the passage of Sorcerer and King, Prince and General, and the Sahkaraean army, oblivious to the machinations that had led to this final confrontation, milled in confusion, unsure who to follow, the nobles not knowing where they should lead. Without Shanor's and Dorn's influence, Karundin no longer seemed a wise place to invade, especially given the burned out crater in the midst of where their monarchs and sorcerers once stood, and no reliable witnesses to explain the phenomenon.

When Gavin's reinforcements arrived, ready to harry the Sahkaraeans into the jaws of Gavin's traps, they found instead an army ready to surrender, sick of bloodshed and fear. Gavin's intermediaries arranged for safe passage back to Sahkarae for those who had not already deserted in the confusion. Pockets of resistance still sprang up along the way, those too far from Angie and Merikan when they had unleashed the counterspells, and so still under the influence of Mind Control or Adoration, but Gavin's people hunted them down and dealt with them, and Shanor's long-awaited war came to an end.

Chapter 35

He had delayed as much as possible each step of the way. When a horse tired, he had rested it rather than push the pace. He sought places along the way to trade horseflesh for fresher beasts, forcing horse and rider to accustom to each other's quirks more than once. Those brief moments of acquaintance with every new horse didn't last long given his extensive experience, but every minute stolen from his task helped.

One gelding had turned up lame as he cut across country, and he had left it in a farmer's field, continuing on foot until he reached the next town. He had tried to avoid the stables, but his orders did not allow that luxury. *Using the swiftest means available* unfortunately meant searching out another mount no matter how he wanted to turn away.

Stopping each evening with time enough to hunt up and cook supper, and also to construct crude sleeping shelters, worked in light of the demand to arrive neither exhausted nor starving. Yet while he had attempted to halt earlier each night, the order to move quickly forbade abusing the daylight thusly, and he found himself pushing further on succeeding nights if he tried to circumvent his instructions too far.

He had tried to justify bypassing villages under the pretext of obeying the command to *avoid detection and confrontations when possible,* but his logical mind had insisted that in his current state of unshaven face and travel stained clothing (he had only what he wore on his back and, even forced to stop and wash often enough to fulfill the stricture to *arrive healthy,* he knew he presented an unkempt and somewhat pungent appearance), no one would recognise him, especially so far out from the capital. The closer he drew to his home, the more he could override that logical little voice, but still not enough for his liking. He had only managed to add a handful of days to his journey. Now the castle loomed before him and he could put off the inevitable no longer.

Not far out from the city's gates, he had encountered a familiar face. The woodcutter who supplied the castle stood off to the side of the road unhitching a mule from his full cart. He led the limping animal a few paces away, then, with a weary sigh and a shake of his head, tied the beast's reins to a nearby bush, bare for the winter yet sporting sturdy limbs. When the woodcutter turned and saw him, no recognition lit his face, though he had expected no different; the man had had little direct contact with him. He offered to assist the woodcutter if he wished to haul his load into the city.

"Why, that's mighty kind of ye," the woodcutter smiled, appreciating not only the offer, but the horse his new helper led. "My dear Molly slipped on a bit o' ice there and slid herself into a strain. Think maybe we can improvise a bit of her harness to fit that lovely beast of yours, and mayhap I won't run too far behind schedule." He paused, taking in his companion's sword and physique, noting the cut of his clothing, the colours visible beneath the cloak despite the grime of travel. "Be ye on yer way to the castle?"

"I am," he nodded.

The woodcutter gave an affable grunt as they worked on adjusting the harness.

"Seen the occasional messenger come through with tidings of the goings on in the south," he said. "Ye've come with news of the war?"

He made a noncommittal noise in reply.

"Ye sure ye can spare the time with me?" the woodcutter wanted to know as he cinched the straps in place. "If'n ye've tidings for the regents, I'll just slow ye down."

"Not at all, my good man," he replied, desperately trying to ignore the small voice that suggested he listen to the advice. "We're both heading to the same place. My task will get done as surely as yours."

And to his inner voice, he insisted that he would find no better way to *enter without raising suspicions*. He longed to wrap his hands around that traitorous Sahkaraean Sorcerer's throat and make him remove the obscene orders trying to usurp his thoughts. Lacking that option, he settled for placating the irksome voice that pushed him on by pointing out that the woodcutter's misfortune became his aid. The gate guards waved them though once the woodcutter explained how the helpful messenger solved his predicament with the loan of his horse, thereby gaining the would-be Royal assassin access to the castle. He wanted to rail at them for their easy acceptance—had Gavin not warned them of the need for vigilance? Even, or especially, against him? How could they not realise that danger walked past?—yet he could do nothing to warn them of his intentions.

Shanor's voice rang in his mind: *Alert no one of your orders, your purpose.* His heart bled knowing he would kill his sister and his nephew with dry eyes and a stoic facade, no matter how loudly he screamed his anguish from within. He had nothing but tears left in his breast, yet couldn't even weep at the injustice of it all. Each step closer brought him more pain while stealing any emotion from his face.

He prayed never to see his kin again, knowing the futility of that even as they crossed into the shadow of the castle walls, heading toward the kitchen courtyards to make their delivery. And then he saw them in the main courtyard. Against his volition, his feet changed course, abandoning the woodcutter and his load, and he strode forward, hand on his sword though he fought with all his strength to release the grip.

Gather your family to you, he thought desperately of Shanor's words, and his hand relaxed its tension, fell from the pommel. A small victory.

He saw Kaeley's joy and wanted to look away. Then he saw Rayton's terror, his little hand gripping his aunt's arm to stop her from running to her brother, and a swell of pride briefly rose to fill the emptiness in his chest. *Run child,* he wanted to cry, and though his lips remained tightly shut, Rayton reacted.

Alvin smiled as his sword cleared its scabbard.

***

Rayton felt restless. Had felt restless all day, maybe longer. He had sat in the morning audience sessions with Aunt Kaeley and the advisors Papa had left to help run the kingdom, but he hadn't really concentrated on anything, his mind constantly wandering. Mostly about Papa and Angie and the nasty war Sorcerer Shanor had started, but also about Uncle Alvin. Rayton supposed he worried about them all, but didn't know how daydreaming when he should listen would help. Not that he always understood (or cared to hear) all the little details people wanted to talk about, but he always tried to make an effort not to show his boredom.

But today (yesterday too, if you agreed with Aunt Kaeley), Rayton just couldn't keep still. He wanted to get out, move around. No, he admitted to himself, he wanted to run; he just didn't know from what. It felt a little like the compulsions he had felt before he went looking for Sorcerer Shanor—before they all knew he'd turned bad. But it felt different, too, and it frustrated Rayton that he couldn't explain his discomfort.

"Can't you feel it?" he asked Aunt Kaeley as they wriggled out of the formal robes they wore over their clothes for today's meetings. Commander Eniok had ended the audiences in time for lunch. Rayton wondered if his restlessness and lack of attention had prompted the early release. He didn't remember if anyone else had stood waiting to speak to the regents or if the last petitioner had already said his piece. That inattention should bother the young Dho'vani, but his unease overrode almost everything, even hunger.

"Feel what?" Aunt Kaeley asked, hanging her robe neatly on a hook on the wall.

"I don't know," Rayton admitted in frustration. "Just something wrong. It's like when I had to talk to Sorcerer Shanor; this weird tingling in the back of my head. Almost like a warning or something."

Rayton loved Aunt Kaeley for so many reasons, not just because he had to, but most especially right now because she didn't discount his strange fears. She regarded him with a very serious expression, her face scrunched up in thought.

"Do you think it's Lady Angie trying to talk to you?" she asked. "Or maybe your Papa?"

Rayton felt his nose crinkle as he frowned in thought, trying to make any sense of the worry churning in his belly. But it didn't feel like Angie or Papa or even Lord Merikan. He shook his head. Aunt Kaeley bit her lip before asking her next question.

"Might it be *him* trying to use Mind Control on you again?"

Aunt Kaeley never said Sorcerer Shanor's name, almost like she thought if she didn't name him, he might go away. Rayton wished that would work.

"No, Angie fixed that," Rayton stated, but a little lurch in his chest, as though his heart had missed a beat and then tried to run away scared, left him shaking just a bit. Sorcerer Shanor couldn't make him do stuff anymore, but what if *he* didn't know that? His aunt suddenly stepped closer and crouched, pulling him into a fierce hug. Rayton hugged her back just as tight, and felt a little better.

"Why don't we get out of the castle for a little bit," she suggested. "Go for a short ride, see if we can't pin-point this feeling you have. If nothing else, we can at least clear our heads."

Rayton agreed, a sudden urgency coming over him. Maybe he *could* outrun the restlessness. He grabbed Aunt Kaeley's hand as she stood up again and practically dragged her toward the courtyard. Remy and Oni joined them as the two Royals emerged from the little room that housed their court robes, as did Aunt Kaeley's guards and her maid Dorthaea. Aunt Kaeley sent Dorthaea to her rooms for warm riding cloaks and gloves.

"We'll meet you in the courtyard," she told her maid, then followed easily at Rayton's side. Rayton kept his pace to hers even though his feet wanted to hurry. He glanced at their guards, then up to his aunt.

"Maybe we can send someone to the stables, let them know we're coming?"

A slight quirk of her eyebrow betrayed her surprise, but Aunt Kaeley gave him a smile.

"In a hurry little one?" she asked. Rayton just nodded, but couldn't find a return smile. Aunt Kaeley's face smoothed, no more emotion showing except a shadow in her eyes. Rayton didn't want her to worry—he worried enough for both of them—but he didn't want to lie to her either. So he just kept going, his hand tight in hers. She flicked her other hand to one of her guards.

"Perhaps you could run ahead and have someone ready our horses for a short ride," she said. He bobbed his head in a bow before trotting ahead of them to hurry around the corner.

By the time they all reached the doors to the main courtyard, Dorthaea had returned with outdoor wear for both the Tre'embra and the Dho'vani. Rayton barely paused to throw his cloak over his shoulders. Aunt Kaeley tugged on her gloves as a guard opened the right side door for them, and their little company swept through. Aunt Kaeley's guard stood just outside, a nod indicating that the stable master knew to prepare their horses.

Not far away, the woodcutter who helped keep heat in the castle lead his full cart toward the kitchens. Strangely, a horse pulled the cart—Rayton had watched the man work often enough, sometimes even helped him and Molly the mule make their delivery, that the different animal registered in the Dho'vani's mind—but the woodcutter's assistant stole his attention, sending stark terror coursing through his blood.

A muddy nimbus of sickly brown rimmed the bearded man, an aura of magic, and Rayton didn't stop to wonder how he could see it. Somehow, he recognised it, remembered that same dark cloud swallowing his mind, drowning him in desires not his own.

That man turned toward them now, abandoning the woodcutter, his hand on his sword. Rayton stopped dead, pulled Aunt Kaeley to a halt beside him. She glanced at him, noted the direction of his stare, and looked up.

To his horror, she smiled wide enough that her teeth glowed in the sunlight.

"Alvin!" she breathed, her joy at seeing her brother briefly pushing aside the knowledge that he shouldn't be here. Rayton grabbed her arm, trying to pull her away, his mind screaming even though his voice had frozen in his throat.

He thought he heard someone telling him to run, maybe even his own mind. He met his uncle's unflinching gaze, read his intentions, and nearly wet himself. Then he jumped in front of Aunt Kaeley, physically pushing her back now, regaining her full attention.

"Run!" he whispered urgently.

"Rayton, what—"

He didn't give her a chance to finished the question. He turned his head to stare up at Remy.

"He's like us, Remy!" he called, his voice rising. "He's under Mind Control!" He screamed the last, not caring that his voice broke into a terrified squeak.

That got through to everyone, along with the sound of a sword clearing its scabbard.

"Go," Oniak ordered, drawing his own blade as he eyed the

Tre'vani. "Keep them safe."

Remy seized Rayton around the middle and took off running back into the castle. Rayton held on tight, wrapping arms and legs around the guard, trying not to slow his mad dash. Aunt Kaeley ran at their side, her skirt clenched high in a white-knuckled grip so she didn't trip on it. She yanked off her cloak and tossed it to Dorthaea, shoving the maid aside.

"He's not after you," she called as the maid peeled off down another hall. Only one of Aunt Kaeley's guards ran with them, the other having remained behind with Oni.

"Oh, Oni," Rayton cried, terribly afraid for his guard. No one fought better than Uncle Alvin, not even Papa. Even with the help of Aunt Kaeley's guard, Rayton didn't think they stood a chance.

"Rouse the House guard," Aunt Kaeley panted, focussing on her remaining guard. "Find Commander Eniok. Tell him Tre'vani Alvin fights under a spell. Try to disarm him, but know he'll fight. Go."

The man spun away in the direction of the barracks, leaving Rayton and Aunt Kaeley with Remy as their only protection until someone found help. Rayton couldn't help the sob that broke free.

Papa! he wanted to cry. *Angie!*

He imagined the Lady Sorceress heard him and flung out a desperate plea, just like he had when Lord Merikan had left.

Hurry, Angie! Uncle Alvin's here to kill us and we can't run forever.

***

Angie crouched low over her mount's withers, her fists dug deep into the fur. When she and Merikan had returned from the Sahkaraean camp with the spells Shanor had stolen, Gavin gave them no opportunity to rest. Not that Angie would have agreed to a rest anyway. He had simply stated that they would leave for Karundin Castle immediately. Angie had tried her trick of arrowing in like she had with Shanor, but whatever had connected them, whatever had allowed her to slip through time and appear where she needed to go, no longer worked. She couldn't get a bead on Alvin, or anyone else from Karundin Castle, couldn't replicate her dream ability. It frustrated her beyond belief and she wanted to scream her outrage at the world. Why could she get to Shanor, but not find a way to reach Rayton and Kaeley before Alvin did?

Gavin had gripped her shoulder in sympathy and shared irritation, then turned his mind to finding another way.

They narrowed the party that would race to the castle down to nine, leaving the rest of the army to carry out their campaign under the direction of Baroness Vordaeth.

Angie and Merikan rode north with the King, along with Commander Nervain, the guards Tera and Davok, the scout Untath, and the sisters Jaeneth and Jaerina. Gavin had proposed they run in wolf form despite his fear that such a long run might leave them thinking more wolf than human.

"We have to stop Alvin," Gavin had said, voice and features barely under control against his overriding fear for his family. "And the wolf forms run faster than horses. The benefit is worth the risk to me, but I won't order anyone to follow."

"May I suggest something, Your Majesty?" Jaeneth had asked deferentially. "If human into wolf moves faster than horses, might not horses turned into wolves run even more swiftly?"

Merikan had stared at her for all of two seconds before he quickly gestured her off her horse and spoke the words of Transformation over the beast. It flowed into the form of a wolf but of the same size as the horses around it, who shied and snorted their unease at the sudden appearance of the enormous predator. The wolf shook it muzzle, then leaned its head into Jaeneth's shoulder.

Angie and Merikan had then Transformed the other needed mounts, and the group sped away, each loping stride eating the distance in a blur of motion. Still riding on the heady effects of Borun's Immeasurable Power spell, Angie had cast Transformation with ease. Everything she and Merikan had done since uttering that Power spell left her feeling euphoric and she found herself wanting to recite the words over and over, borrow a little energy here and there, see what she could do with a magic that worked at her command rather than her instinct.

Except Borun's spell didn't borrow; it stole. It took the life essence of another to bolster her own. She shuddered at her longing, glanced aside to Merikan to see her father regarding her with a very serious expression.

'The price of Borun's spell,' he spoke in her mind, clearly

reading her plight. *'A seduction we have to overcome.'*

Angie nodded, swallowing a lump in her throat. She suspected what she struggled against bore frightening similarities to an addict jonesing for her next fix. Becoming addicted to such an immoral spell sent shivers of dread up her spine, even as a delicious memory of intense euphoria swept through her. She wondered how long the effects would last, prayed she would never have to use that spell again, even as she longed to send the words caressing across her tongue.

Had struggled against the gradually fading urge all along the harrowing three day ride until the castle appeared as a tiny speck in the distance and a new fear suddenly gripped her heart.

Hurry, Angie! Uncle Alvin's here to kill us and we can't run forever.

"Oh my God," she breathed. A brief sense of vertigo as she felt what Rayton did as his guard ran through the castle corridors, his young charge wrapped around him.

"Faster," she urged her valiant steed, pressing herself as tight against his neck as she could. Even at this ground-eating pace though, she feared the worst.

***

They had simply run at first, Remy trying to get them as far away as he could before they found somewhere to hide, or some place they could defend. *A defence against Uncle Alvin?* Rayton swallowed the tears that so desperately wanted to run from his eyes. He was Dho'vani, and the Royals of Karundin protected their people. He had to find some way to protect Aunt Kaeley and Remy. Uncle Alvin, too; protect him from himself. Only, Rayton remembered the influence of Mind Control; seeing and hearing everything, experiencing every little bit, but not having any ability to stop his programmed actions. He could try to talk to Uncle all he wanted, but Shanor's orders (who else could have sent him with death ruling his hands?) would make him unable to respond in any way beyond the silence of his mind.

Rayton's hands began to shake as he held in his terrified screams, and he fisted his fingers to keep the motion from betraying their location. Remy had pushed into a storage room near the kitchens, unwrapped Rayton from his embrace, and hurried the young Prince into a corner, pulling a gasping Aunt

Kaeley beside him. Now Remy stood with his back to the wall beside the closed door, his sword in one hand and a dagger in the other. Sweat shone on his face and his chest heaved as he slowed his breathing, all in silence. He had his head tilted toward the door, straining to hear anything from the hallway beyond, every muscle tense. It would take time to gather other guards, longer for them to locate the Royals and to subdue Uncle Alvin. Rayton feared Uncle would find them first, even though Remy had outrun him. Uncle knew how to think tricky and he also knew the best places to hide from pursuit. If only they could hide long enough for Angie and Papa to come home.

"Secure the castle," they heard from somewhere out in the corridor. "Find the Dho'vani and the Tre'embra; get them to some place secure."

"That's Commander Eniok," Rayton whispered.

"Shh." Aunt Kaeley held a finger to his lips, luckily not from the hand clutching the dagger she had retrieved from her belt. She craned her neck forward as though that might help her hear better. Remy glanced at them briefly and shook his head. Rayton understood. If no one knew where they hid, then no one could lead Uncle Alvin to them.

"Sir," a second voice called out. "We have the Tre'vani secured."

"Take him to a cell. Make sure he can't escape," they heard Eniok respond.

Then a moment of silence. Remy met Rayton's eyes, sent a questioning look to Aunt Kaeley. Rayton also stared at his aunt, wondering what to do. She chewed nervously at her lip, eyes scared and sad.

"If they really have him—" Rayton began softly.

"He could still get away," Aunt Kaeley said.

"He could have an accomplice," Remy barely spoke loud enough for Rayton to hear, but he shivered at how serious Remy sounded.

"We dare not give away our position," Aunt Kaeley finally said with a firm nod.

"Too late," Eniok's voice came through the door, followed immediately by a heavy weight smashing against the wood. Remy flew back to stand as a shield between the Royals and the intruder, weapons held ready. Only, Commander Eniok didn't shoulder his way into the storage room; Uncle Alvin did, with no

355

other soldiers in sight.

"He disguised his voice," Aunt Kaeley cried out, grabbing Rayton and shoving him even further into the corner. He stumbled and fell in a heap, his mind reeling as he remembered listening to Uncle tell stories after many suppers, speaking in a different voice for every character. Rayton hadn't known he could mimic Commander Eniok too, but it shouldn't have surprised him.

Uncle seemed even more frightening than he had in the courtyard. His sword dripped splashes of blood, and the knife in his left fist looked attached to his hand by a swath of red. A cut over his left brow leaked blood into his flat grey eyes. Another had torn his right sleeve away, leaving streaks of crimson painting fiery lines down his arm, and the broken shaft of an arrow pierced the flesh on the back of his right calf. Rayton saw anguish in Uncle's eyes, but no tears, and again, he recalled the horrible cloak that locked emotions away behind the unstoppable need to obey Mind Controlled commands.

He screamed, high and loud, as Uncle engaged Remy in a flurry of sword strokes that his friend couldn't hope to keep at bay forever.

***

Angie screamed as they gained the outer walls of the castle, but she didn't see those walls. She watched through the terrified eyes of a child as Alvin deflected Remy's sword thrust with the crossguard of his own sword, tangling the two weapons. Alvin released the hilt and struck the guard across the face, sinking the blade of the knife in his other hand into Remy's chest at the same instant. Without slowing, Alvin leapt the falling body, crashing into Kaeley, twisting her wrist mercilessly as he disarmed her, riding her to the ground. As they slammed to the floor, Alvin's weight trapping Kaeley, a flash of golden light enveloped the pair, streaming out from Kaeley. Angie remembered Merikan shielding Rayton and Kaeley before he left, felt a spark of hope as that shield flared to life now, adding to Kaeley's own inborn protections. Alvin flipped the captured dagger and caught the hilt so that it pointed down, right over her heart, and he leaned his weight against the straining shield.

Angie growled in the courtyard, already sliding off her lathered mount and tearing toward the castle, Gavin and Merikan in her wake, alerted to the seriousness of the situation by her cry and the gleam of magic spitting from her eyes. The others barely kept pace. How she didn't crash into a wall she didn't know because she saw nothing of her surroundings; only the storage room where Alvin tried to kill his sister. Angie didn't stop to think, just reached out to grab that blade as it dimpled through the Lord Protector's protections, whispered against the cloth of Kaeley's tunic. And to her surprise, felt something solid beneath her desperate hand. She wrenched it aside.

***

Uncle's blade didn't stab Aunt Kaeley. Rayton saw a shadowy outline, someone reaching out to pull the knife away as the golden shield hissed under the strain. And he knew Angie had arrived. If he could only give her time to find them.

His scream turned into a rallying cry. He pulled himself up and jumped onto Uncle's back, straddling him like a horse. He pummelled him and kicked him, yanked at his hair. Aunt Kaeley wriggled under their combined weight and squirmed free when Uncle reared back, trying to buck off his unexpected rider. But Rayton didn't let go.

Uncle Alvin pushed to his knees, then to his feet, his strong hands wrapping painfully around Rayton's wrists as he struggled. Rayton suddenly understood that, much as his actions might hinder Uncle, Uncle now held him captive, and completely at his mercy. Uncle spun, bracing himself as he smashed against the back wall, crushing Rayton between the hard-muscled man and the unyielding stone surface. A golden shield rose to protect Rayton too, tiny snakes of blue trying to keep it woven together under the pressure of Uncle's attack. Uncle just struck again and again, bursting the bubble of protection.

For a moment, Rayton could feel nothing as Uncle pressed him against the wall, couldn't even breath. Then everything felt on fire and he managed to suck in enough air to shriek in unbearable agony, the sound deafening in the little room. He hadn't imagined so much torment could fit in his little body, and only stopped screeching when Uncle flipped him over his shoulder, slamming him against the floor and stealing away his ability to breathe. Rayton shattered into a thousand pieces as

357

Uncle's weight followed him to the ground, his hurt blinding him to reality. How else could he explain a giant charcoal coloured wolf clamping its jaws around Uncle and flinging him with bone-crushing force through the door?

Rayton surrendered to peaceful oblivion.

***

Gavin hadn't thought he could run any faster, but when he heard Rayton's shrill cry, he flowed without thought into the form of a wolf and cleared the length of the corridor in two strides. What he saw in the storage room turned his blood to ice.

Remy lay next to the door in a pool of blood, one of Kaeley's hands pressed tightly against the gaping wound in his chest. Her other hand flew forward, releasing the glint of a blade stained red as it arced through the air, sending the weapon to bite into Alvin's shoulder, just as his brother tried to throw Rayton through the floor, cutting off his son's painful wail. The blade pulled Alvin's head up to meet the new attack, and Gavin could see nothing but murderous intent on his brother's face. He snapped him up in powerful jaws and flung him out the door for others to deal with, then turned back to the frighteningly still form of his son.

Gavin threw off the wolf form to kneel as a stricken father over his child. With great care, he gathered the crumpled and bloody body into his arms, pressing his face to his child's neck.

And wept.

***

Angie knelt next to Alvin. By the looks of it, Gavin had broken his brother's back, though the splintered arrow and quivering knife couldn't have done him any good either. Still, the man looked ready to try to stand again anyway. After the briefest glance in the bloody room, Nervain stepped up beside Angie, his sword held ready over Alvin's throat, his eyes burning with angry tears. Angie pushed the blade away, her hand bloody from pulling Alvin's dagger away from Kaeley. *That's twice now, a dream knife cutting me,* she thought.

"He's killed enough," Nervain snarled.

"Shanor wielded the weapon," Angie said. "Alvin couldn't help it."

"That doesn't make them less dead!"

"No, but if you kill him in retaliation, you'll have done Shanor's work for him."

Before he could argue further, Angie spoke the words she couldn't before, and freed Alvin from the clutches of Mind Control. Tears immediately scalded his face.

"Let him kill me," Alvin begged, his broken spirit cracking his voice. "After what I've done—"

"Shh," Angie laid a hand over his mouth, spoke a second spell. Instantaneous Healing swept over the Tre'vani, leaving him weak, but free from injury.

Angie met Nervain's heated glare.

"Don't kill him."

She stood, gently moving aside the small crowd that had gathered in front of the storage room. Castle guards reluctantly made way, their judging eyes swinging between her and the Tre'vani, seeing their Prince wracked with shuddering sobs, assessing the resolve of the Lady Sorceress. Tera and Davok, perhaps recalling how Shanor had tried to use another Royal in the net of his Mind Control, gave her firm nods, standing now to either side of Alvin. Untath and the sisters Jaerina and Jaeneth simply stood aside, lending their silent support. Angie moved past them all, drawn by the mournful moans of a despairing father.

Just inside the door, Merikan crouched next to Remy, the Lord Protector's hands blood-smeared as he wiped away the last traces of a Healed wound. Kaeley clutched at Merikan's arm, but had eyes only for the pair across the room. Remy slowly sat up, assisted by Merikan's unencumbered hand and watched, face pale, eyes red, as Angie sat next to the King.

She laid a hand across Gavin's shoulder, squeezed until he turned blind eyes to her. Then she reached for the hands cradling Rayton. Gavin tried to curl himself around his child.

"Let me help," spoke Angie in a gentle voice.

"My son," Gavin sobbed. "He took my son."

Angie shook her head.

"Let me help," she said again, more firmly.

Gavin blinked at her, tears finally clearing just enough that he could really focus on her face. She gave him all the confidence she could muster. He nodded jerkily, his eyes seeking Rayton again, the tears flowing anew.

Angie took his hands once more, and Gavin let her. She placed his right hand over Rayton's heart, his left tracing the curve of Rayton's cheek. She placed her own hands so that her fingers feathered the boy's temples.

Merikan knelt next to her before she could do anything else. Kaeley stood right behind him.

"Angel," he said. "The Power spell has faded. Do you have enough left in you for this?"

Angie smiled and whispered back,

"I could always borrow a little from Alvin."

Merikan blinked, startled, and shook his head gravely.

"I hope you know what you're doing," he muttered.

She shrugged, trying not to reveal the depth of her uncertainty, her fear.

"I could use a little help, if you're willing?"

"How?" he asked immediately.

"Share the spell," she answered. "You Heal from without, I Heal from within."

In reply, Merikan shifted so that he knelt at Rayton's head. Kaeley sat across from the King, completing the circle around Rayton, her stare daring Angie to chastise her. Instead, Angie took Kaeley's hand, cupped it around Rayton's other cheek, held the young woman's steady gaze. Then Angie touched Rayton's temples again, looked down at his pain-lined face. Merikan folded his hands over hers, forming an outer and an inner circle for the magic. Gavin shuddered once, then held still.

Angie met Merikan's eyes and gave a firm nod. As one, the Lady Sorceress and the Lord Protector recited Borun's spell of Instantaneous Healing, weaving the words together to share the cost.

Rayton, Angie called, trying to send her thoughts into the boy's mind, closing her eyes to better concentrate. She let Borun's scripted spell work at rebuilding Rayton's bleeding innards and shattered bones, knitting him back together as Merikan smoothed out the abused flesh. Her own magic instinctively searched for more.

Can you hear me, Rayton?

Angie? she heard as though from a great distance and felt her heart jolt.

Can you see me? she asked.

It's so dark, his little voice seemed to recede. *And peaceful.*

Nothing hurts here.

Please, no.

We miss you, Rayton, she said. *Your Papa misses you something fierce.*

Take care of Papa. He needs you.

He needs you too, love, Angie called. *Please, won't you come home?*

Hurts. The word scraped against Angie's skull and she fought a flinch.

It's all better now, she crooned. She had a thought. *Rayton, do you remember waking me from a bad dream?*

A moment of silence, and Angie feared she had lost him.

Tabitha got mad, Rayton said.

But I didn't, she said, her relief nearly overwhelming. *Do you know why?*

No.

Because you saved me, she told him, letting him hear the horror he had averted when he pulled her from her dream of an Earth where no one knew her. *You led me home.*

I did? Did the voice sound just a little stronger? She clung to that thought.

Let me lead you home, Rayton. Let me save you, too. Bring you back from this dream.

And you'll be there? he asked, a lost little boy looking for hope. *You and Papa both?*

Always, she promised.

And opened her eyes when a breath hitched in Rayton's chest. He stared at her, a small smile tickling his lips.

"I knew you'd come," Rayton said, then looked up, saw who held him so tenderly. "Papa!" he cried as Gavin held him close to his heart.

Before she could move, Angie found herself included in that hug, Gavin's arm pulling her close on one side, Kaeley sandwiching her on the other, Rayton folded in the middle. Even Merikan had not escaped the embrace.

But then little hands pushed them all aside, and Rayton adamantly squirmed free and gained his feet. Near the door, Remy knelt on one knee and Rayton hugged him hard. But the Dho'vani sought another face.

Despite every protest, Rayton forced his way to Alvin's side. Alvin turned his head away, covered his face with his hands as he shook. Rayton stared down at his uncle for a moment, then collapsed into Alvin's lap. The move startled the Tre'vani enough that his hands shot out to instinctively support this new weight. Rayton snatched those hands and refused to let go. He made sure Alvin didn't look away

"I know it hurts," Rayton said quietly. "What he did to you. What he made you do."

Alvin's lower lip quivered and fresh tears ran down his face as a seven-year-old tried to share his pain, to give him comfort.

"And what everyone told me after?" Rayton went on. "It's true."

"What's true?" Alvin managed to ask, his throat raw.

"That none of this is your fault."

Alvin shook his head.

"Would that I could remove all blame, child, but I can't." Alvin tried to pull away, but Rayton wouldn't let him. "I killed people, Rayton. Your guard, Kaeley's. Would have killed you too. Wanted to, even." His voice broke and he couldn't continue.

"Sorcerer Shanor wanted you to, not you, Uncle. You told me to run."

"I—what?" Alvin stared with wide eyes.

"I heard you. Shanor wanted you to hurt us, not you. *Don't let him win.* That's what they told me, and they're right."

"I had to kill my friend because that man did to her what he did to you," Jaerina said, pushing through to stand over Rayton's shoulder, glaring down at the Tre'vani, heedless of his station. "I chose to blame the person who took away her will, forged her into a weapon to do what he could not; destroy Karundin and all it stands for. Do you have that kind of courage?" she challenged.

Alvin stared up at her, frowning.

"Who are you?" he finally asked.

"A brave woman from a village filled with truly amazing people," Gavin told him. He lowered himself to sit beside his brother.

Alvin hung his head.

"It doesn't change what I did," he murmured. "I tried to fight, used every bit of leeway their instructions gave me to delay, to find some way out. But it didn't work."

"Yes it did," Angie said, drawing everyone's attention as she stumbled wearily into the hall. "You gave us the time we needed, Alvin. The time to stop Shanor and Sahkarae, Dorn's foolish war of ambition. If you hadn't fought, that victory wouldn't have mattered." She knelt, putting herself on a level with Alvin. Leaning forward, she told him quietly, "I heard their instructions, *everything* they ordered you to do." He met her gaze. "I couldn't stop it," she admitted. "Though I tried. Will you blame me for that failure?"

"Of course not!"

"Then why blame yourself?" she asked. "I could have gotten here sooner, but that would have left Shanor still in possession of the spells. I chose to believe that you would find a way to stall, give us enough time to stop Shanor *and* you. You did that, Tre'vani Alvin."

"And it got people killed."

"So feel remorse, but not blame. Can you do that?"

"I—don't know," he admitted. He stared into the solemn eyes of his nephew.

"I'll help, Uncle. Me and Remy, we know what it's like. That feeling of betrayal. But Shanor did the betraying, not you. So don't let him win."

Not even the most hard-bitten guard left that hallway with a dry eye. If the Dho'vani could forgive the uncle sent against his will to kill him, the King forgive the brother, the Lady Sorceress forgive the weapon unleashed against those she protected, could they do any less?

Epilogue

"Do you really think this will work?" Gavin asked, resting his chin on Angie's shoulder as he stood behind her, his arms loosely draped around her like a necklace.

"Only one way to find out," she replied, eyeing the sheets laid out before them in the morning sun. After all, she had already achieved the improbable shortly after their arrival at the castle by slipping into the dreams of those still affected by Shanor's use of Borun's spells, whispering the counterspells and freeing captives—most notably those ruling in Sahkarae: the queen, Dorn's youngest son Bareth, Maraenda—why not aim for the impossible too.

Spring had opened her arms wide, bringing the promise of rebirth and renewal. Alvin had returned to the Sahkaraean court to oversee the transferal of power from Dorn to Bareth, make sure the son did not harbour the same thirst for reunification at any cost as the father. Also to await the birth of his second child. Angie suspected he had jumped at the role of envoy as a means to escape the eyes that haunted him, though the eyes staring back from his own mirror likely held the greatest judgement. He needed time to come to terms with being a victim, and having to see the faces of those he might have killed every day did not sit well with the Tre'vani. His family had forgiven him, but he had yet to forgive himself. Hopefully, time away with his wife and child—children—would help heal his heart.

The people of both Sahkarae and Karundin, soldiers, nobles, and peasants alike, had come through the winter amid confusion and fear. Gavin had ridden through his kingdom on a second Progress to reassure everyone that the war had ended, trying to

364

explain to those who did not understand why the land had seen war in the first place. It would take time to heal those wounds too, but Angie felt optimistic of the end result.

Which brought them to this day. Under the light of the sun in the secluded courtyard of Angie's old suite, a select group of people gathered: Gavin and Angie, Merikan, Rayton and Kaeley, Nervain, Remy, Tera and Davok. They formed a semi-circle around the six spells that had caused them so much grief, and the counterspell that had saved them all. Today, Angie planned to take Borun's folly and erase it forever.

She looked back over the last span of months, everything that had happened to her in this land she once thought of as only a figment of her imagination. She took every experience, every thought and emotion, every episode of that fantastic experience, and she imagined having written it all down in one of her dream journals. Then she closed her eyes and reached out her hands. With no one touching them, the spells floated together into a pile, the counterspell folding around them like the cover of a book. Angie spoke the words to the Transformation spell, adding her desire that no one ever remember those words, or any other spell connected to Borun's Spells of Supremacy, nor Daneka's clever counter. Those pages would reveal a different story now, one fraught with strange and amazing magics, but written on completely unmagical paper, pages susceptible to destruction. In a surprising, but pleasing, lack of fanfare, the spells Transformed, and when Angie opened her eyes, a spiral notebook remained in their place.

"Did it work?" Merikan asked. Angie picked up the book, opened it to the first page, smiled as she recognised the writing.

The dull pain from just below my collarbone drew a sharp gasp and my eyes flew completely open.
This wasn't my room. Moreover, it wasn't even my apartment. A canopy spread overhead, lit by a single candle on a small bedside table. I sat up, trying to ignore the twinge in my shoulder that drew a hissed breath through my teeth. A strange sight greeted my vision.

Her first real day in Karundin.
"It did," she confirmed.
"What do we do with it now?" Rayton wanted to know.

Angie put it back down on the bench, gave it a little spin with the flick of a finger.

"Send it away," she said as she shoved it off the end of the bench. Only, it didn't land anywhere they could see, disappeared completely.

She looked at Gavin now, her smile lighting her face far more than the sun ever could. He grinned back and extended his arm.

"I believe we have an appointment, My Lady," he said, leading the procession out of the courtyard, through chambers Angie wouldn't need anymore, and toward the Great Hall where so many of Karundin's people, noble and base born together, awaited their arrival with barely suppressed jubilation.

"Indeed, My Lord," replied Angie. "We don't want to be late."

Rayton skipped ahead of them, his excitement palpable. After all, a Royal Wedding didn't happen every day.

***

"Way to go, Mermaid," Irving sighed happily as he closed the book, filling in the details of Angie's and Gavin's wedding in his mind, imaging the life they would live together. He wondered if he would ever dream of her again.

"You've a unique mind for one born wholly of Earth," the tiny woman at his shoulder said. He held up a hand, and Sidvareh stepped onto his palm.

He remembered his last sight of Angie as a swirling world of purple mist took her away. The gate had slammed and Sidvareh had screamed, dropping like a stone. Irving had reacted immediately, cupping his hands as he jumped forward, catching the Faery before she hit the ground. At the contact, a new voice had whispered instructions in his head on how to revive Sidvareh before the last of her life force followed Angie through the portal. Having already thought himself crazy once before Angie explained some of her tale, Irving had thought nothing of listening to a disembodied voice instructing him on the care of a Faery who had just had her wings sheered off.

"Which is why I brought you and Angelica together in the first place," a second Faery said, as Sidvareh's mother materialized next to her daughter. "A mind open to the possibility of something fantastic can make its own bridge between worlds. Can even sustain the life of a Faery bound to hidden scroll."

366

Mother and daughter exchanged meaningful looks, and Irving knew what came next.

"And now that I know the full story," he said, tapping Angie's journal against his leg—a journal transported from a courtyard in Karundin to his kitchen counter as it followed the map of his mind—as he sat in a secluded corner of a vacant park. "There's only one thing left to do."

He tossed the book, along with all the other journals that had appeared with Angie's disappearance, all depicting her early dream years in Karundin, into a large metal bowl he had bought special for the occasion. Then he struck a match, and tossed it in. The pages caught despite a gust of wind that breezed past, and a piece of non-magical magic went up in flames.

They watched until nothing but ash remained, and then Sidvareh and her mother rose into the air, Sidvareh supported by her mother. Irving watched them with a question in his eyes.

"Our tale has finally come to its end," Sidvareh said. "And we thank you for your part in it. But this is not our world."

He frowned in concern.

"Can you return to yours?" he asked.

"Only if we can find a bridge to walk," replied the senior Faery. "A bridge that may or may not remember the story once we leave its path."

Irving smiled and sat on grass warmed by the late afternoon sun.

"Please, ladies, take that bridge. Find your way home."

Hand in hand, the Faeries moved closer to Irving until their tear drop eyes filled his vision, and then they disappeared in a swirl of violet mist, following the bridge of his open mind.

"Thank you," he thought he heard, then nothing as the sun dipped behind the canopy of trees.

He sat there until dark, wondering what, if anything, he would remember come morning. After all, wonders filled the world every day; you just had to know where to find them.

He gathered up his bowl and left the park.

"See you in my dreams," he whispered.

ABOUT THE AUTHOR

Author of two previous fantasy novels (*Druid's Daughter*, and *Spirit of the Stone*), Kelly has loved writing since the third grade. She has an Honours Bachelor degree in English with a Minor in Classics, and finds ancient history enthralling. She also enjoys playing her flute and sailing with her husband. Kelly currently lives in Ontario, Canada.

Manufactured by Amazon.ca
Bolton, ON